The Head Hunters

Elmer Carrington, former Captain of the Texas Rangers, is the victim of a horrendous crime committed by the Mexican bandit, Mateo.

Accompanied by Daniel Ramos, another victim of Mateo, he sets off in pursuit of the man they hate. With the trail leading them deep into Mexico, through dangerous mountains and blistering desert, they encounter terrifying hazards and unforeseen enemies. But nothing has prepared them for the treachery and torture that awaits them when Carrington is given a hideous task. Failure to carry it out threatens death for both him and Daniel Ramos. . . .

The Head Hunters

Mark Bannerman

A Black Horse Western

ROBERT HALE · LONDON

@ Mark Bannerman 2012
First published in Great Britain 2012

ISBN 978-0-7090-9996-3

Robert Hale Limited
Clerkenwell House
Clerkenwell Green
London EC1R 0HT

www.halebooks.com

Typeset by
Derek Doyle & Associates, Shaw Heath
Printed and bound in Great Britain by
CPI Antony Rowe, Chippenham and Eastbourne

CHAPTER ONE

Elmer was in his corral, forking wild hay for his horse. Before he saw the boy, he heard his heaving breath – the sawing and panting of somebody running so fast that they were almost stumbling ahead of themselves. Elmer looked up and for the first time set eyes on the youngster who was rushing down the hill towards the smallholding. Elmer cast aside his rake and stepped outside the corral, closing the gate. He sensed that something unusual was happening.

He was standing by the water pump when the boy came charging in and pulled up, gasping air into his lungs, too tuckered to form words. But his eyes were pleading with Elmer, pleading for help.

Elmer said, 'Steady on, son. Ain't nothin' to fear here.'

At that moment, his wife Lauren came out from the cabin, wearing her apron and shading her eyes against the Texas sun. She called, 'What is it, Elmer?'

He could not answer because he didn't know. He

judged the boy was about fifteen, rail-thin, and Mexican. He had never seen him before. He was bare-footed and his feet were bleeding from the running. His shirt and pants were ragged and dirt-smeared. He had a tangled mop of black hair and his hollow-cheeked face was dusky. At last he found his tongue: 'Help me, sir . . . please.'

Elmer put his arm around the boy's shoulder. 'Come inside,' he said.

The youngster cast a worried glance back. 'They're after me,' he gasped.

Lauren had joined them. 'Who's after you?' she asked.

The boy tried to explain, but his breath caught audibly in his throat. Eventually he said, 'Them!'

'What's your name, son?' Elmer inquired.

The boy looked at him, as if he was deciding whether it was safe to reveal his identity. 'Daniel Ramos,' he finally said.

The three of them went back to the cabin and stepped into the cooler interior. Lauren pressed Daniel onto a chair and fetched him a cup of water, which he gulped down.

'Tell us who you're runnin' from,' Elmer repeated.

The boy's eyes widened. He gazed at the open doorway, as though expecting his pursuers to burst in at any moment, then his lips formed the name as if it pained him: '*Mateo*.'

Elmer felt a sudden chill twist his insides. He muttered, 'Jesus Christ!' and Lauren looked at him disapprovingly for taking the Lord's name in vain.

6

He walked to the doorway and gazed up the hill. All he saw was the green slope and the naked ridge, which were devoid of visible life. The sky was a searing blue and on the high thermals a buzzard was cruising.

Daniel noticed the picture of Elmer hanging on the wall and asked, 'You are a lawman, sir?'

'I was captain in the Texas Rangers,' Elmer said, 'but I'm retired now.'

'You know Mateo?' the boy pressed him.

Elmer frowned. 'Sure I know him. An *hombre malo*. I hunted him for five years. He played cat and mouse with me, and I never caught him. I thought he and his gang had gone south into Mexico.'

'No, sir. They are chasing me. They kidnapped me from home. Last night they were pretty drunk. I wriggled free of my ropes and ran off while they slept, but I know they will have missed me now.' He shuddered. 'They will be after me.'

Since Elmer's retirement, Mateo had haunted his dreams. Now, it seemed, his worst nightmare was being fulfilled. Mateo was a Mexican *bandido*, said to have both Mexican and Mescalero Apache blood in his veins. He and his band had left behind them a trail of havoc – murder, plundered banks and trains, cattle rustling, horse theft, rape and kidnapping. Elmer knew that white children could be traded to the Apaches, either as slaves or for ransom, usually south of the border. The worst thing about Mateo was his incredible delight in torture. It made no difference whether his victims were men, women or children.

Elmer picked up his .44 Henry Repeater. It was said that it was a weapon you could load on a Sunday and fire all week. He slid shells in to the chamber.

'What are you gonna do?' Lauren asked in an agitated voice.

'I'll just take a look around,' he responded and went outside. A few minutes later he was climbing the hill.

Elmer Carrington was fifty years old, his face weather-seamed from years spent in the open, but he was still handsome. His eyes were pale blue. He was a big man, powerfully muscled. Three years ago, he had retired from the Rangers after a career of chasing Comanches, Apaches – and Mateo. He'd hung up his six-shooters and he and Lauren had moved out from Calico Springs to establish their own smallholding here on the Hildago River.

He'd built their cabin with the help of friends from Calico Springs, and hauled a big, black cookstove from town on his wagon. He had planted out a field of corn, imported a milk-cow, hogs and chickens, and he'd provided a plentiful supply of food with his gun – antelope, wild turkey and venison.

Lauren had chosen furniture for the rooms. She'd made colourful curtains for the windows, and provided her 'woman's touch' in abundance. She was a happy woman, pretty too. Ten years younger than him, she had never been one to nag or find fault, but was a hard worker who was quick to laugh and have fun. They had never had children of their own, although Lauren had miscarried twice.

In other respects, life had been kind to them, flowing peacefully, like the river behind them. However, he had never forgotten Mateo, though he had taken solace from the rumour that he had left the territory and gone south. Now, it seemed, he was back.

Elmer was sweating when he reached the crest of the hill. Before him stretched a huge swathe of grassland, beyond which the rugged line of mountains showed.

Some way out across the plain were ten riders, spread wide, moving in a line at a steady pace, looking like approaching black beetles. Mateo. Elmer swallowed hard, backing down below the skyline. He cursed himself for ever coming to this place to set up home, but he'd got on well with the Indians and offered hospitality to travellers and all had seemed idyllic. Now he was struck by the premonition that everything would change.

He debated what he should do. The intruders should cross the ridge in about twenty minutes. That would give him ample time to get back to the cabin and fort up. Lauren could use a rifle if need be . . . but it would be two guns against ten if it came to a fight. Maybe the boy could do the re-loading.

Elmer knew that if Mateo recognized him, his black soul would be fired with bitterness. Old hatreds would spring up like rekindled fire. Elmer feared not only for himself, but mostly for Lauren.

He broke into a run, descending the hill in giant strides. He passed by the hog pen and the chicken coop and Lauren was waiting for him as he entered the cabin. He glanced around.

'Where's the boy?' he asked.

She shook her head, perplexed. 'He ran out,' she explained. 'He said they would catch him if he stayed here. Last I saw of him, he was runnin' towards the river.'

'Mebbe it's for the best,' Elmer said. 'Mateo's comin' with a bunch of riders. I seen him out on the plain. We must be ready for him. Lauren . . . load up the old Winchester an' take the window, but for God's sake, keep down. I'll take the doorway.'

She nodded and hastened to comply.

Elmer wondered if Mateo knew that he was approaching the home of his old adversary. If he didn't, it might be possible to bluff him. Failing that it would be a gunfight.

Elmer remembered Mateo as a swarthy, crab-like man, bandy, thick-set and muscular in stature. His droopy moustache covered most of his lower face and his eyes had a predatory quality that was fearful.

Time slipped by in an all-pervasive silence. Looking through the doorway, Elmer's eyes ached with his constant surveillance of the hill's summit.

At last they appeared, and his heartbeat quickened.

They rode over the crest; ten horsemen starting the descent towards the cabin. As they drew closer, he saw that they were all wearing sombreros. He even distinguished Mateo. He again cautioned Lauren to keep well down, out of sight. The intruders reached the flat, and for a moment they were hidden by the barn.

It was then that Mateo's voiced called: 'Captain Carrington. We come for the boy. Send him out to us and he will come to no harm.'

Elmer's hopes of being able to bluff the Mexican vanished.

Lauren listened anxiously as her husband cupped his hands to his mouth and shouted his response. 'The boy is not here, Mateo.'

'I think you lie,' came the response. 'We followed his tracks. You must pay the penalty. It will be like the old days, eh? But this time you will die!' and with that a rifle cracked out and the bullet struck the cabin's logs close to the doorjamb.

Elmer ducked back under cover, wondering what form their attack would take.

The answer came quickly – a fusillade of further shots crashing like giant hailstones against the walls of the homestead. After the sudden burst, their ears were singing. In the ensuing lull Elmer risked a quick glance through the doorway. He could see nothing of his adversaries. They had taken cover behind the barn.

His gaze swung to the milk-cow in the corral. Simultaneously, a single shot cracked out and the beast bellowed, crumpled down onto its side and lay unmoving. Elmer cursed but didn't waste his ammunition in retaliation.

After a moment, the beat of hoofs sounded and he saw three horsemen move out from behind the barn, then ride away until they were well out of range of his rifle. They circled to the left and dread grew in him as he realized their intention: to get between the cabin and the river and attack from the rear.

He looked at the pale face of Lauren. 'What can we do, honey?' she gasped.

'When we can see somethin' to fire at, we'll try to down them,' he replied. 'If we can reduce their numbers, mebbe we'll scare them off.' His voice did not carry much conviction but it was the best he could manage. 'Keep an eye on the front,' he instructed. 'I'll take a look out the back.'

He rushed through the cabin into the back room. It had a window giving a view of the land sloping off to the cottonwoods that lined the river. He grunted with displeasure as he saw that the horsemen had made it to the trees, but a moment later his displeasure turned to horror as he saw the flicker of flame and realized the intent of his enemies. They were going to burn them out!

CHAPTER TWO

Somewhat earlier, Daniel Ramos had fled from the cabin, terrified that Mateo would recapture him if he remained with the ex-Ranger and his wife. Running madly he passed through the cottonwoods, reached the river and without hesitation plunged in and swam across. On the far bank he glanced back but his view of the cabin was obscured by trees. Taking a deep breath, he ran on, ignoring the pain from his lacerated feet. He had no doubt that Mateo would have followed his tracks and wondered if he would pause at the homestead or would continue in pursuit.

As he ran, thankful of the miles he was putting between himself and his kidnappers, he knew that Calico Springs was some distance ahead of him. He was glad he had learned to race as a youngster.

Ten years ago, Daniel and his Mexican father, mother and two young sisters, had been travelling in a canopied wagon across the prairie when a band of marauding Comanches had appeared as if from

nowhere. In a savage attack, the Indians had massa-
cred the entire family apart from five-year-old Daniel.
He had been hiding in the wagon when a troop of
US cavalry had charged onto the scene and driven
the attackers off. The major in charge of the troop
was a Texan called John Garfield and he had rescued
the boy.

In the subsequent years, John Garfield had left the
army and established his own ranch. This had flourished beyond his wildest dreams and he had become
a rich man. He had taken Daniel into his family and
brought him up with his own children. The boy had
grown to his teens in a happy household.

Everything had gone well until one day when he
was out riding on his stepfather's range. He had been
seized by Mateo and his men. He had been beaten
into submission, robbed of his boots and carried off,
trussed up like a chicken. If any communication was
subsequently made with his stepfather regarding a
ransom, he did not know. For days he had been
dragged along at a rope's end and shown no mercy.
But then had come the night when Mateo and his
thugs had indulged in their drunken carousal and,
while they snored, he had wriggled free of his ropes
and got away.

But now, when he glanced over his shoulder, he
groaned with dismay; he saw two riders following him
and instinct warned him that they were Mexicans. He
felt that his energy was flagging. He was pretty sure
they had not seen him, nor were they tracking him
because the thick, wiry grass over which he had come

would reveal nothing of his progress.

Desperately glancing around, he spotted a gully to his left. Maybe he could hide. He ran to it, seeing that it was bone dry; he slumped behind rocky cover. He waited for what seemed a long time, and then he heard the pounding of hoofs growing closer. He shrank down, not daring to breathe. He imagined that the ground beneath him was trembling with the thud of hoofs. He pressed his hands over his ears, curled himself into a tight ball.

He expected that at any moment the riders would descend into the gully and his freedom would be doomed. But presently he removed his hands from his ears and listened. He heard nothing. Taking a risk, he raised himself to glance around. He was relieved to see that the riders had passed him by. They were no longer in sight, though he could see a distant cloud of dust. They had obviously pushed on towards Calico Springs, perhaps expecting to find him there.

He pondered on what he should do. He still thought it best to get to the town where he might be able to gain help, but he knew he would have to be very careful not to encounter the Mexicans. Perhaps it would be best to stay where he was and wait for nightfall. He stretched out on the ground. He felt exhausted, mentally and physically, and decided to take a doze. Within seconds of closing his eyes, he was asleep.

When he awoke, stars were sprinkled across the velvety blanket of the sky; there was a thin sliver of moon and a coolness chilled the air. He rose to his feet, climbed up the side of the gully and gazed about. He could see no movement in the surrounding terrain, but the lights of Calico Springs glowed in the distance.

Climbing from the gully, he felt stiff and his feet pained him but, gritting his teeth, he set out towards the lights of the town. Now he was obliged to stop frequently for rest. Thirst nagged at him. He remembered the cup of water he'd had at the cabin and wondered what had become of the couple who had befriended him. Perhaps they'd had nothing to fear from Mateo.

As the distance fell behind him, and the glow of lights got closer, he heard sounds coming from the town – the tinkling of pianos and the burble of voices. He knew that his first objective must be the marshal's office. He also hoped he would be able to make clear his predicament and that he could get help. But he had only been to Calico Springs twice before and he had no idea where the law office was located.

He passed outlying cabins from which lamps shone and shortly he reached the main thoroughfare of town – Eagle Street. This had lights illuminating some of the canopied sidewalks and was lined with assorted buildings and stores. There were also two saloons from which raucous sounds and light spilled.

He started along the sidewalk, passing boarded-up windows, anxiously seeking some friendly person who might direct him to the marshal's office. He kept to the shadows as much as possible. At first, everywhere seemed deserted, but then he saw somebody standing in the shadow ahead of him. The man struck a match to light his cigarette – and Daniel glimpsed the outline of a sombrero.

He stemmed back a surge of panic, started to backtrack. Suddenly a voice called out in Spanish: 'There he is!' and boots pounded on the planking.

His heart pounding, Daniel fled down a dark side alley, aware that two men were pursuing him. He had no idea where the second man had come from, but he could hear the jingling of their spurs and the heaving of their breath.

He ran with all the speed his legs could muster, terror giving him renewed strength, ducking along another alley that led off – but then he tripped on a block of wood and went sprawling, grazing his knees and hands. Glancing to the side he saw an overhang in the planking that fronted a cabin and scrambled across to it, seeing a dark hole. He forced himself into it, realizing that he was amid smelly garbage.

With bated breath, he watched as his two pursuers, cursing in Spanish, rushed by and shortly disappeared into the darkness.

He lay still until his heartbeat steadied. He worried in case there were snakes sharing his hiding place. He balanced that possibility with his fear of the Mexicans and decided to remain where he was for the time being.

A dog came along, sniffed at him and moved on.

He waited for what seemed a long time. He had no

way of telling the time. He was aware of something nudging his bare foot and guessed it was a rat. With no sign of the Mexicans returning, he reckoned he was ready to make a move. He still harboured a hope of finding the marshal's office, which had to be somewhere in the main street.

Pushing himself out from his hiding place, he took a furtive glance around. All appeared quiet. Moving stealthily, keeping to the darkest places, he retraced his way towards Eagle Street.

When he reached the main thoroughfare, everything appeared quiet – even the saloons – and he guessed the hour was late. He shivered, for the night was cool.

He was about to move off again, when a hand clapped him on the shoulder. Panic tightened his belly in a cold, sick grip. Somebody was standing behind him.

'Where you goin', skulkin' round this time o' night!' The voice was deep. He turned and saw a big man towering over him. He also saw something else: the glint of a badge pinned to the man's vest.

'You the marshal?' he gasped.

'Sure I am,' came the response. 'Who're you?'

'My name is Daniel Ramos. I was kidnapped by Mateo. I escaped and came here. Mateo's men are chasing me.'

'Mateo.' The marshal sighed deeply. 'Back in these parts, eh? I figured he'd departed long ago. I guess you better come with me, son.'

The marshal, whose name was Tom Henson, led

Daniel along the sidewalk and they eventually came to an office from which a light glowed. They went inside. Two men, obviously deputies, were standing by a stove, drinking coffee. Daniel could see that a jail led off the main office but there was nobody in it.

The marshal made Daniel sit down and fetched him a cup of coffee. 'Now tell me your story,' he said.

The other men stopped talking and stood listening. As best as he could, Daniel related his grim experiences. When he explained how the ex-Ranger and his wife had helped him, Henson interrupted.

'That must be Elmer Carrington. Better let McAfee know straight away.' He turned to one of his deputies, Ben Prebble, and said, 'Go round an' tell McAfee that Elmer may be in trouble.'

'Go an' tell him now?' Prebble exclaimed. 'He'll be asleep.'

'Go right now an' wake him up. He'll wanna make sure Elmer's OK.'

'Yessir!' The deputy rammed on his hat and departed.

'Who's McAfee?' Daniel inquired.

'Captain of the Rangers,' Henson replied. 'An old friend of Elmer Carrington. Took over from him as captain, in fact. He'll wanna check things out. He won't be none pleased about Mateo bein' back in these parts.' He rose and gestured towards the empty cell. 'You better bed down in there, Daniel. Don't worry, we won't lock you in.'

CHAPTER THREE

Captain Paddy McAfee was as Irish as they come, his voice touched by the Blarney Stone. He was forty years old and slightly overweight. He had been captain of the Rangers for three years and before that he'd been a corporal, serving under Elmer Carrington. He was not very pleased when an insistent hammering on the door of his house roused him from a pleasant dream. He disentangled himself from the arms of his wife and climbed out of bed. He lit a lamp and checked his stem-winder. It was 4 a.m. He stumbled down the stairs to his front door and opened up. Straight away Deputy Prebble imparted the bad news.

At the mention of Carrington, McAfee cursed and said, 'Elmer may be in trouble. I hope to God we're not too late. Tell the marshal I'll rouse my men an' get out there just as soon as I can.'

Prebble nodded and departed.

Within the hour, in the tentative light of dawn, McAfee was leading his troop of six Rangers out of town and heading for the homestead on Hildago River.

As they progressed, the sun rose before them. McAfee turned to his corporal, Bob Justin, and said, 'You smell somethin'?'

'Sure I do – smoke.'

The captain gave a grim nod, alarm gnawing at him. Sure enough, they soon saw how the sky ahead of them was darkened with a spiralling haze of smoke. He urged his men to greater speed. By the time they crossed the river the air was thick with smuts, and after they had passed through the cottonwoods lining the water, they saw all that remained of the homestead – a smouldering ruin.

With heavy hearts, they reined in their horses, feeling the heat that emanated from the blackened timbers. With supports and walls burned through, the roof had caved in. Crackling flames and sparks still plumed upwards and the final wall collapsed as they watched.

Cursing over and over, McAfee spurred around the ruin, his eyes probing for sight of blackened skeletons, but he saw none. He noticed the milk-cow and hogs, all lying dead in their enclosures and coated with flies.

There was nothing he could do here – and a harrowing suspicion was forming in his mind: *his good friends Elmer and Lauren Carrington had been carried off by Mateo.*

The beginnings of tears stung his eyes, caused partly by the acrid smoke but mainly by the grief gripping his soul. By the time he re-joined his men, his grief had changed to a raging hatred for the devils who had perpetrated this evil crime. Fused with a blistering craving for retribution, he ordered the column forward. Seeking tracks in the ground, they spurred their animals up the hill and away from what had so recently been a happy home and haven of hospitality.

Elmer became aware of searing pain throbbing through his head. He groaned. Suddenly the vision of Lauren's haunted face came to him – and her screams; they sounded each time she was penetrated. The full horror overwhelmed him and his groan changed to snarling anguish.

'You will watch,' Mateo had told him, 'and you will see her suffer, or mebbe she will enjoy it, and you will remember how you dogged my trail for five years so that I could never rest. When we have had our way with your woman, we will kill her. And afterwards, we will kill you … slowly.'

Right then, Elmer had broken free of the man who had held him, hurled himself at Mateo. After that, he remembered nothing. He had not seen the rifle butt descending with brute force upon his skull.

But now, the pain in his head was the lesser evil as memories of the traumatic events flooded back to him.

He could recall how he and Lauren had fled from the burning cabin, having no alternative. There had been no fight. Laughing, the Mexicans had closed in about them, barring further flight with their horses and guns, Mateo foremost. They could have been gunned down there and then, but Mateo had other plans for them. Their hands had been bound with rope, their boots removed, and they had been dragged away, cruelly forced to stagger onwards until the day had darkened and they had come to a canyon. Its sides rose gradually, pitted with deep overhangs and strewn with boulders and rocks, all commanding a view, had there been moonshine, of the canyon floor. It was beneath a particularly deep overhang that Mateo made camp. They were obviously familiar with this place.

Night had deepened, and a fire was alight, around which the bandits sat drinking whiskey. Elmer was sprawled in the shadowy spot where he'd been felled. As he emitted his cry of torment, Mateo rose and stepped away from his companions and stood over his prisoner, his teeth showing white in a mocking grin.

'It was a shame,' he said, 'the boy got away. It was more of a shame that you did not see all the fun we had with your woman. She put up quite a fight until we held her down. She was mebbe too old to be frisky.' He laughed.

'What have you done with her?' Elmer gasped.

'When she was worn out, I, myself, strangled her. She will not trouble us any more with her screams.'

Black hate consumed Elmer, and with it a rage that shook his body with uncontrollable fierceness; it chattered his teeth and jerked his head. He struggled to rise, to reach for Mateo's throat, but could not; he was bound hand and foot. 'You bastard!' he cried out. 'Bastard, bastard, bastard!'

'Your turn will come soon, *amigo*!' Mateo struck him across the face with the back of his ring-encrusted hand.

Elmer, tied with his hands behind his back, was unable to defend himself. He gritted his teeth against the pain, feeling blood dripping down his cheek. The knowledge that his beloved Lauren was dead choked him. Let them do what they liked with him; he didn't care any longer.

Mateo turned away, checked that the poker he had thrust into the fire was glowing red and grunted with satisfaction. He always carried the poker for opportunities such as this. His motley crew rose to their feet expressing the excitement of anticipation. Having lifted the poker from the embers, Mateo had returned to Elmer, when suddenly there was a disturbance.

A man who had been posted as guard lower down the canyon wall came rushing into the main camp, hissing in Spanish, 'They are coming. I see them entering the canyon. Rangers!'

Mateo cursed angrily and slung the poker to the ground. In a hushed voice he ordered his men to take up position. Quickly, dirt was thrown onto the fire and the flames stamped out. The bandits grabbed their guns and hurried off to pre-arranged vantage points, disappearing into the darkness. Mateo drew his pistol. He appeared to lose interest in Elmer. He, too, moved stealthily away and was swallowed up by the night.

Now there was a deathly silence. The moon was obscured by cloud and everywhere was cloaked in gloom except for one thing – the still-glowing poker. A wild desperation filled Elmer. Hoping that attention had been diverted elsewhere, a plan formed in his mind. He levered himself across to the poker and turning his back, manoeuvred the linking strands binding his wrists across its hot extremity. He grunted with satisfaction as the smell of burning rope came to his nostrils. It seemed to take an age for the strands to weaken and finally burn through; his wrists were singed, but he ignored the pain and suddenly his hands were free. The redness of the poker was diminishing, but he placed the rope linking his ankles across it and to his relief, after what seemed an eternity, he felt the rope give.

He crouched, working his painfully stiff limbs, his heart pumping. A tiny spark of hope came to him. Had Mateo been lying when he claimed he had killed Lauren? He glanced around and saw the shadowy form beyond the doused fire. He staggered across and found her; his worst fears were confirmed. She was lying with her eyes open, her body already stiffening. He knelt and cradled her in his arms. He'd loved her, always had done, and now she was gone. Angry tears coursed down his cheeks. He should bury her in some secluded place, but there was no time. He gently rested her down, praying that she would understand what he must do.

He rose and all at once heard the clip-clop of

approaching hoofs from the canyon below. *Rangers*! He expected at any second to hear the blast of Mexican gunfire.

He realized what he must do. Cupping his hands to his mouth he bawled out with every ounce of strength he could muster: '*Ambush*! . . *Ambush*!' And then he staggered out through the overhang opening and up the incline, away from the direction he believed the Mexicans had taken. He cursed, stumbling twice with the stiffness in his legs. He wondered if they would come after him, but he heard no sound of pursuit. He progressed between shadowy boulders and rocks, bruising and grazing himself, expecting at any moment to be shot at. As he went, the roar of gunfire crackled out from behind, but it was not directed at him. He realized that a battle was ensuing. He hoped that his shout had given the Rangers a few seconds to prepare for attack. He also hoped that he would somehow be able to exact vengeance against the evil monster who had murdered his precious wife.

CHAPTER FOUR

Captain Paddy McAfee responded immediately to the shouted warning. It had come from the right-hand side of the canyon and he snapped out an immediate command for his men to dismount and take cover on the left. There was no time to secure the horses and they galloped off further into the canyon. Even as the Rangers scampered to crouch behind the scattered boulders, the crash of gunfire thundered and lead whined amongst them, ricocheting off the rock faces. One man cried out, but he had only been struck in the back by a sliver of rock and soon recovered. The Rangers had all snatched their rifles from their saddle-scabbards as they dismounted and now were quick to take action, aiming their fire at the night-shrouded slope on the other side of the canyon.

The actual place of attack had not been entirely ideal for the Mexicans, as, in response to the shouted warning, the Rangers had taken refuge short of reaching the intended point of ambush; they were thus afforded better cover. Nonetheless the initial exchange of bullets was fierce, the orange spurts from gunbarrels piercing the darkness, the smell of gunsmoke tainting the air.

Presently, the guns quieted. Targets could not be seen and McAfee considered it a waste of ammunition to proceed. The Mexicans must have reached the same conclusion. It seemed that the Rangers were pinned down, because any movement within the canyon would no doubt be spotted by their assailants and McAfee was loath to expose his men. Minutes lengthened into hours as the night dragged away. A cool breeze had the Rangers shivering and, with no water available, thirst plagued them.

McAfee had been in tight fixes before and now he tried to put the present events into perspective. What would Elmer Carrington have done in such circumstances?

The captain pondered on the shouted warning. It had probably saved them from wholesale massacre. It had come from the Mexicans' side of the canyon, and now the conclusion dawned on him. It must have been Elmer. But what retribution had his captors since inflicted upon him?

McAfee tried to form a plan.

It occurred to him that there might be a means of escape behind them. There, the canyon rose more steeply than the other side, but it might be scalable. And whilst it was still dark, such movement might go undetected. He put the idea to his men, and it was agreed that they would attempt it, one at a time.

Corporal Bob Justin was the first to volunteer and he set off with the best-of-luck wishes of his companions. With his rifle strapped across his shoulders, he ascended slowly, taking infinite care to avoid dislodging any rocks. As he disappeared into the darkness, the remaining men waited with bated breath. After some ten minutes, the second man followed Justin.

It took the best part of an hour for the remaining Rangers, apart from McAfee, to complete the climb, but the last man inadvertently sent a pebble rattling down when he had almost reached the top and the captain feared that their movement must have been detected by the Mexicans. Also, the approaching dawn was making the sky lighter which would increase the hazard.

But McAfee was determined to make the climb. He would have to use every scrap of cover. He set out, making good progress to start with. He was halfway up, and could see the cliff top outlined against the pale sky, when a single shot cracked out from the far side of the canyon. He felt a heavy thud in his back just below the shoulder blade and knew he had been badly hit. His fought for his breath, but blood welled up into his throat. He staggered and collapsed. He rolled downward until he was stopped by a large ridge, where he remained wedged.

Above him, his men crouched, alarmed by events. Eventually, with the light growing stronger, they were able to see their captain's sprawled body.

Ranger Josh Simpson suggested that he could go down and attempt to bring McAfee up. Corporal Bob

Justin, now in command, reluctantly agreed and ordered the remaining men to train their rifles on the far side of the canyon and to fire at the slightest movement.

Accordingly, Simpson undertook the descent. He was a brave man. He knew that at any moment a bullet might fell him, but he went calmly, sending lizards skittering across the rocks before him. He reached McAfee unscathed.

The captain was lying face down, and Simpson could see the great hole where the bullet had entered his back. Dark blood was caked over his shirt.

'Captain,' he whispered hoarsely, 'can you hear me?' There was no response. He peered closely at the body, then tried to turn it over. McAfee had his mouth sagged open, his wide eyes staring at nothing. A nightmarish certainty struck Simpson: McAfee was dead.

Grunting with exertion, Simpson hoisted his captain's body across his shoulders and commenced the ascent.

Elmer Carrington had watched the sun rise, painting the eastern ridges with gold. He had paused high on the canyon rim, weary from his desperate flight. His naked feet had been cut and battered by the sharp rocks over which he'd come, but he'd been anxious to put space between himself and the Mexican camp. All along he'd had the daunting sensation of being followed, although he could not be sure. Perhaps, even now, he was being watched. He wondered what Mateo's action had been at finding him gone. Then he thought of Lauren, lying unburied, and he shuddered.

Earlier, he had heard the roar of gunfire from behind him, but that had eventually faded away – after that, nothing.

Suddenly a slight movement, below him and down to his right, caught his eye. At first he was puzzled, but then he realized what it was. A number of horses were grazing on the sparse vegetation of the canyon floor. A surge of interest went through him. He rose, glanced around for sign of his enemies, but saw none.

He hastened along the canyon rim until he was level with the horses, then he began to descend, scrambling from one ridge to the next. Several times he slipped but arrested his falls by grasping outcrops of rock. Halfway down the steep gradient, he stopped to rest. He gazed again at the horses. He counted seven and saw that they were saddled. He recognized them as the mounts of Texas Rangers.

Fifteen minutes later, he reached the canyon floor and, casting caution to the wind, made his way towards the animals. They raised their heads at his approach, whickering nervously. He paused, standing still as they grew used to his presence and resumed grazing. Then he walked up to the nearest, murmured calming words and reached out to gently smooth its withers. He grasped the reins, was about to haul himself into the saddle when the shot came.

31

He felt a sharp slam of pain just below his knee and his leg gave out. As he collapsed, he was aware that the horses had stampeded off, scared by the crack of the gun. His pain seemed to increase in throbbing waves. And then he heard oncoming footsteps and the gurgle of laughter.

'Mateo said, "Bring him back alive",' a Mexican voice pronounced, 'So I just shoot you in the leg so you can't run away again. You are lucky, eh? For the moment. Maybe I shoot you in the other leg too! That would be good, *amigo*.'

Elmer raised his eyes, realized the man was standing over him – a scrawny greaser with a leer on his face. His pistol was levelled unwaveringly. He appeared to be alone. He must have been coming up the canyon floor and had spotted Elmer as he approached the horses. Elmer grimaced with pain, conscious that blood was pumping out from his wound.

'Get up, or I plug the other leg!' the Mexican said.

Elmer cursed his luck. If only he'd stayed on the canyon's rim. He pushed himself into a sitting position, and attempted to rise. He couldn't make it and collapsed. That was when another shot boomed off, coming from behind him.

The Mexican was thrown back; the bullet had struck him in the chest bringing forth a great spurt of blood. He lay on his back, a single shudder going through him. His breath came in a hoarse rasp, then it weakened and stopped altogether.

He was dead.

Elmer glanced over his shoulder and gasped with relief. Two Rangers, Corporal Bob Justin and Ranger Clay Forrester, were hurrying towards him, their rifles held in readiness. They had both been serving when Elmer commanded the troop and he knew them well. They had come to round up their horses; their arrival had certainly been opportune. Seconds later they were with him, expressing surprise at finding him.

Elmer uttered his profound gratitude at being rescued.

While Forrester kept watch, Justin unfastened his bandanna and tied it tightly around Elmer's leg to form a tourniquet above the knee. 'You need a doctor, Captain, as soon as we can get you back to town. Let's hope he can save your leg.'

'Where's Mateo?' Elmer asked.

'I guess them bandits pulled out during the night,' Justin explained. 'We had a shoot-out with them, but after a while things went quiet. We took a scout-see this mornin', found their camp and they'd all gone.'

'Gone?' Elmer queried.

'Sure,' Justin nodded. 'Pulled out while it was still dark, I guess. We also found the cave where they'd left their hosses.'

Elmer's next words came with obvious grief. 'When you went to where they'd camped, did you find . . . did you find my wife's body?'

Justin frowned. 'Why no. We didn't know she was . . . dead.' He reached out and gave Elmer's shoulder a sympathetic pat. 'I'm downright sorry, Captain.'

33

Elmer said, 'Mateo raped her then strangled her.'

For a moment the two Rangers were wordless with disgust.

While they were helping Elmer across to the shelter of boulders at the foot of the far canyon wall, they told him that Captain McAfee had also died and Elmer shook his head in dismay and experienced renewed sorrow. His wife and now his friend – dead.

Mateo had much to answer for.

They left Elmer seated in shadowy cover with a gun in his hand, then went to round up the horses. Gritting his teeth against his pain, Elmer kept a wary eye open, but he saw no movement apart from the turkey vultures that had descended to rip out the entrails of the Mexican; in time they and other scavengers would reduce the corpse to a skeleton.

Somewhere in the background a woodpecker was hammering on an elm.

He guessed that when Mateo had pulled out, he had left the one man to hunt him down, but that man had been thwarted, thank God.

When the two Rangers returned, driving the herd before them, they assisted Elmer into the saddle; this was difficult at first because he couldn't put the foot of his injured leg into the stirrup. Forrester recovered the pistol from the dead Mexican so Forrester could determine the calibre of bullet that had hit Elmer. Now, with all three men astride their mounts, and herding the recovered animals, they set off to re-join the other Rangers.

It took three hours for the dejected troop, bearing

the body of their captain, to reach Calico Springs. They'd travelled with the depressing knowledge that Mateo had eluded them and was still at large to vent havoc wherever he chose, and the cost had been high. For Elmer, every jog over the ground brought fresh waves of torture to his wounded limb, causing pain to seep up through his thigh into every cranny of his body, and his head still throbbed from the blow it had received. Added to which he felt a fever taking hold of him. Even so, right then, the greatest pain he suffered was in his heart.

CHAPTER FIVE

Doctor Silas Hathaway was a portly man of sixty-five, wearing wire-rimmed spectacles. His hair had already turned white and his rosy-cheeked face showed an excess of flesh. He had served as a surgeon-physician in the Confederate States Army and was no stranger to amputations.

Yesterday when Elmer had first been brought to his small infirmary at Calico Springs, he'd removed the blood-soaked tourniquet and dosed his patient with laudanum. He'd then washed out the wound and the sucked-in clothing. Afterwards, he'd applied a bandage, having noted the .35 calibre bullet had buried itself in the leg, fracturing the tibia, tearing muscle and tissue and leaving a large entry hole.

Today he'd removed the bandage and examined the limb again. He frowned.

Elmer, clad in a nightshirt, was resting back on the surgery couch. He didn't miss Hathaway's grim expression.

'I won't lose the leg, will I?'

'It would only be from below the knee,' the doctor said, half to himself.

Elmer felt woozy with fever and laudanum.

The medical man leaned close to the wound. He sniffed, wrinkling his nose. 'Sure doesn't smell so good, Captain.'

Elmer, too, had noticed the sweetish, fetid odour and his stomach churned. He risked a downward look, catching a glimpse of greenish flesh.

'Putrid,' Hathaway announced.

Elmer groaned. 'It ain't gonna kill me, is it, Doc?'

'Not if you receive the right medical treatment straight away.'

Once Mateo had lost the element of surprise, he had tired of the engagement with the Rangers and had slipped away into the night. Before he had quit the canyon campsite, he had had a hole dug; the body of the woman was dropped into it and covered over. He had left the grave as indistinguishable as possible. If anybody chose to search for it, they would have a difficult task.

He was still furious at losing both the boy and Carrington. He had vented his rage by bullying his six men. The reason they stuck with him was greed, for he offered the prospect of ill-gotten fortune. Gradually, Mateo lost hope that the *hombre* he had despatched to recapture the *gringo* captain would bring him back.

But now he set his mind on new business, business involving *mucho dinero*.

37

He enforced a stiff pace as the gang rode south, crossing tortile mountains and arid desert where the heat was nigh suffocating. They were a ragged, unshaven bunch, disinclined to wash even when water was available, and dangerous as rattlesnakes. Heavy pistols sagged in holsters from their waists, also long knives. The only sign of civilization they encountered came from defunct ghost towns, relics of long-gone mining communities, in which the sole movement was the wind-blown tumbleweed, rolling down forsaken streets.

Three weeks later found them camped in a canyon in the foothills of the Sabine Mountains, close to where the Smith & Atchison Railroad went into a sharp curve. The Red Rock Express passed along this track every night. Mateo had long cherished a dream of hitting the train when it was loaded with miners' pay, reputedly at the end of each month.

The bandits made their plans as they waited for the appointed time to arrive. Mateo kept a sweat-soiled calendar on which he ticked off the passing days. On the evening of August 31, they stacked cross-ties high on the track where the curve was at its most acute and took cover in adjacent boulders. They were not disappointed.

The Red Rock Express arrived at 11 p.m., right on schedule. Firstly, they heard the hum and clack of wheels on the narrow-gauge roadbed, then the plaintive call of its whistle. Suddenly, as the train rounded the bend, the swinging beam of the locomotive's lamp, backed by the bloody glow from the firebox, cleaved the darkness. The panicking engineer, glimpsing the piled-up obstruction, slammed on his brakes and brought the train to a shuddering halt with its cow-catcher touching the wood.

Hoisting their bandannas into place, the Mexicans sprang into action, two men splitting off to discourage any vigilante passengers from trying to be heroes while at the same time relieving them of their valuables, and another departing to attend to the engineer and fireman. Meanwhile Mateo and his remaining two bandits pulled themselves up onto the vestibule of the express car. Mateo hammered on the slide door with his fist and yelled out, 'We dynamite you if you don't open up!'

Almost immediately the door was drawn back and a man barred the way, an angry-looking man in a blue cap and with a carbine in his hands. Before he could aim it, Mateo's pistol blasted off, killing the railroad man and clearing the way. All the bandits entered the car, where two company employees were staggering to their feet, their eyes wide with fear. They straight away dropped their guns and raised their hands, having no stomach for a fight.

'Open up the safe or you die!' Mateo snarled.

'Sure – don't shoot.'

Within seconds the safe was manipulated and its door swung open to reveal dollar bills, stack upon stack of them. Their hands trembling with excitement, the Mexicans scooped the money into the sacks they'd brought. As they prepared to leave, Mateo turned his hawk-eyes towards the two cowering railroad men. Fearing what was to come, they started pleading for their lives, but Mateo raised his gun and shot them both, killing them instantly. As he and his men were backing out, a shot sounded from the foremost passenger car.

Two bandits had gone to attend to the passengers; only one, a sack of valuables over his shoulder, reappeared. As he ran off into the darkness, another shot followed him but missed. A man in army uniform stood at the train's open window, brandishing his pistol. He'd already shot one bandit who was sprawled bleeding in the aisle behind him.

Mateo and his gang didn't waste further bullets, but sped off, carrying their spoils. They reached their horses, mounted, and then concentrated on putting as much distance as they could between themselves and the plundered train. As well as the two men that Mateo had killed, the engineer had also been gunned down. In the aftermath of the robbery, the railroad company confirmed that $100,000 had been stolen from its safe, and some $2,000 taken from the passengers – wealthy ranchers who had attended a stockmen's convention in Culver City. Four employees had been murdered.

The State Governor ordered out militia and cavalry. They curry-combed the territory, but to no avail. The birds had flown.

CHAPTER SIX

The boy Daniel Ramos had returned to his home by stagecoach, escorted by one of the Calico Springs deputies. His grateful step-parents and step-brothers and sisters welcomed him with open arms. During the following months, John Garfield would never let Ramos ride the range alone; he was always accompanied by himself or one of the ranch-hands. While Daniel had been missing, Garfield and his ranch-hands had combed the range and eventually concluded that the boy had been abducted. The matter had been reported to the law but no information regarding those guilty had been forthcoming. With the boy's return, a great deal was revealed. Garfield referred the matter once again to the local marshal; 'Wanted' notices for Mateo and his gang were circulated far and wide and a cash reward put up by the rail company, dead or alive.

As if to flaunt those who hunted them, news came through, by telegraph and newspaper reports, regarding the gang's hold-up of the Red Rock

Express and the killings that had taken place. Although the robbers' faces had been concealed, the passengers had no doubt as to the identity of their Mexican persecutors.

With the onset of winter, and a chilly wind blowing from the north, Daniel accompanied his stepfather on a tour of the line camps, dotted on the farthest ranch boundaries. These consisted of crude shacks where cowboys stayed alone. Their duties were to patrol the range in their area, to herd outfit cattle back, to chase strays away, to discourage rustling and to repair fences. Alone for so many hours, the cowboys were always anxious for a chinwag over a mug of coffee and Daniel loved to hear their stories and the exchange of humour with his stepfather.

John Garfield was normally a hale and hearty man, liked by all. But today Daniel noticed that he was quieter than usual. Of late, he had complained of not feeling well but had put it down to indigestion.

As they set out on the return journey he was sweating despite the cold wind and suffering from shortness of breath. When they were almost home, he suffered agonizing pain down his left side, radiating in to his arm. He slumped forward in his saddle, his face contorted. He collapsed heavily onto the ground. Daniel reined in and dismounted, running to his step father's side.

Garfield lived for only a few minutes more, long enough to reach out and clutch Daniel's hand. He tried to speak but a jolt of agony cut his breath, choking him.

'Don't die, Papa,' Daniel pleaded, but it was in vain. Tears were streaming down the boy's cheeks as John Garfield left for the next world.

Daniel's stepmother, Amelia, inherited the prospering ranch and its extensive stock. She grieved for her husband. Soon she found the duty of running the outfit too heavy for her. The new foreman, Buck Wallace, whom John had taken on shortly before his death, was paying her increasing attention. Indeed, he was soon taking over most of the chores.

Wallace sometimes seemed a rough customer, a burly, florid-faced man who liked his whiskey. But he knew the cattle business and towards Amelia he showed a kindness and gentleness to which she responded, prettifying herself and paying renewed attention to her hair and dress. Shortly he had moved in to the main house. Within a month they were married and she became pregnant.

As for Daniel and the other youngsters, Wallace showed them none of the kindness he reserved for Amelia. In fact, he clearly resented Daniel and allotted him the most menial tasks to do on the ranch. Furthermore, the boy grew fiercely jealous as his stepmother focused all her considerations on her husband.

By the time spring came round, Daniel's mood had plunged to deep melancholy and he became determined to run away.

Elmer had changed from the cool, prudent man he had once been. His wife and his friend had been murdered, and despite the cunning he had learned as a Texas Ranger, there now rose in him the impetuous and hateful rage of a man who had been deeply wronged. No people, no lawmen, could ever assume his responsibility of retribution. With his home destroyed he had no meaningful place to go now, but this did not bring an emptiness to his life. Any void was filled by the cold conviction that Mateo must die, and that he, Elmer Carrington, must do the killing.

In the first instance, after Doctor Hathaway had carried out his surgery, when laudanum still had him drifting in a dream-world, he found that he had his hands around Mateo's throat and the squeezing of his windpipe created a choking, and a bulging of the Mexican's eyes so that they looked like two onions. His tongue, purple in hue and coated with scum, hung loosely from his gaping mouth.

Elmer dragged himself from the dream and came round in a flurry of sweat.

In more rational moments, he tried to make plans as to how he could achieve such a situation. The immediate need was to regain some fitness. He was under no illusions as to the seriousness of his injury.

Doctor Hathaway had shown him a small and mangled piece of lead around which a fragment of cloth was still wrapped. 'You're a dead lucky man,' Hathaway had said. 'The bullet was deeply embedded. I probed into the wound, dug a great hole and got it out. It'd taken a scrap of your pants with it and it had all gone mouldy, but I swabbed away the poison.' He allowed himself a satisfied smile. 'I guess a less capable surgeon would never have reached it. It'd compromised your entire blood circulation, caused the infection.'

Elmer eyed his leg and grimaced, but he said, 'I'm right grateful to you, Doc. No words are enough to say how grateful.'

'I'm not promising you'll keep that leg,' the doctor cautioned. 'We'll let it drain for a few days, then I'll get a splint on it. It may still turn bad, but let's pray for the best.'

'I'll sure do that, Doc.'

And pray Elmer did, so emphatically that over subsequent weeks the wound healed and the splint straightened the leg, but he could not put his foot to the ground because it caused him considerable pain. Hathaway warned him he would never be pain free. 'But I'll be downright annoyed if you go and get yourself killed,' he added. 'I've not done all that surgery for nothing!'

Despite the wearisome, blistering travel, the bandits were gratified by thoughts that wealth was now theirs. By the time they made camp in a remote Maroma Mountain hollow, they had replenished their supply of liquor from a wayside cantina, and were in high spirits, particularly Mateo. They had fed on the juicy flesh of the goat they had killed and now they were downing snakehead whiskey to excess. They sat around, their greedy eyes glinting in the firelight, as Mateo took on the task of splitting the plundered cash. In the past, it had been his custom to keep the major share of any loot for himself, leaving them the minimum amount that would stave off their dissatisfaction. He'd relied on their fear of his explosive temper to quell complaint. But tonight everything seemed different as he smilingly doled out a more than fair allocation to each of his six remaining followers.

When the task was completed, the cash was stowed away in saddle-bags and the mood got riotous as more rot-gut was consumed. There was talk about the gang scattering and meeting in Mexico in a year's time, but any decision would have to wait till morning. One man produced a mouth organ he had lifted from a train passenger and this signalled a raucous sing-song, but after a while tiredness overtook them. A pine knot was placed on the fire, and three of them retired to their blankets, not giving a fig about the threat of waking with thick heads.

But Mateo was not tired. Excitement pulsed through his veins hotter than liquor. While giving the impression of drinking heavily like the others, he had downed only enough to satisfy his immediate lust. He surreptitiously removed his spare pistol from his saddle-bag and slipped it into his waistband, then he rose and stepped away from the campsite.

Once in the trees he took out both the spare Colt .44 and the one holstered at his hip. He checked that each was fully loaded. They were big six-shooters that could fire rapidly. He smiled his wolfish grin, feeling renewed exhilaration as he paced back to the campsite.

He opened up with a fusillade of lead. He fired from both hands, thumbing back the hammers, the guns booming like cannons. The only man still seated at the fireside took a bullet in the back, spurting blood as he was thrown headfirst into the flames. The remaining blanket-huddled Mexicans struggled up, but the heavy-calibre bullets tore into them, gunning them down before they could reach for their own weapons. The air was filled with the thunderous roar of the guns and the frantic screams of men, and everywhere was hazed in the swirl of acrid smoke.

At last Mateo, paused, breathing heavily from his efforts – but his work was not finished.

He inspected each body, checking for life. He saw faint movement in one man and groans came from another. He pressed a pistol to their heads and blew out their brains.

Afterwards, he holstered his guns. Kicking aside the corpses, piled one upon the other, he extracted from their saddle-bags the cash that he had so recently distributed. This he carefully packed into his own saddle-bags, buckling them tightly.

He retrieved his sombrero, took a final swig from a whiskey jug, then, his tack on his shoulder, he went to the spot where the horses were hobbled. They were still agitated by the recent gunfire but he soothed them with calming words. He cut the rawhide hobbles with a slash of his knife. He could not tolerate animals being left to suffer. It was better to let them roam free. He saddled his own big roan, mounted and rode out into the night, bound for Mexico, where US law had no jurisdiction. He was a wealthy man.

But he had overlooked one fact. When he had stepped away from the campsite, one of the gang, Luiz Prado, had also gone into the brush – to relieve himself. He had watched the killings, including that of his brother, with petrified eyes and then he had run off, thanking the Holy Saints that he had survived Mateo's treachery.

CHAPTER SEVEN

When Elmer was strong enough, he left Doctor Hathaway's small infirmary and took up lodgings at The Golden Sunrise Guesthouse on Main Street, Calico Springs. If he put his foot down, he suffered pain, could not move around far without the aid of a crutch. However, he worked hard on the exercises that the doctor recommended and he knew he was growing stronger each day. He needed to form a plan for his future. At least he had no financial worries. He had inherited a tidy sum of money from his father and this was safely deposited in the town's bank. But he found little satisfaction in this, for he was still burdened with sorrow, would always be, at the loss of Lauren.

Weeks after taking up residence at the guest house, he was visited by Bob Justin. He was jubilant. Notification had come through from the Texas Rangers Headquarters at Austin that he had been promoted to captain to replace Paddy McAfee. Elmer congratulated him, knowing the elevation was justly deserved.

As they were drinking coffee, the Ranger produced the lurid report of the train robbery in an old copy of *The Texas Chronicle*. Hatred burned deep in Elmer's heart as he read Mateo's name. The crime had been committed beyond the borders of Texas, and was not, therefore, within the Rangers' area of responsibility, but it cemented Elmer's resolve to kill his wife's murderer.

The thought that Lauren had died in the most hideous of circumstances and her remains dumped somewhere unknown had haunted Elmer's nightmares. The last point of contact had been in the canyon hideaway where Lauren had perished, and Justin agreed to help him find it.

Next morning they hired a springboard wagon and mare from the local hostelry and set out on their quest. It was a tedious and bumpy ride through rock-strewn canyons, some of which were choked with autumnal brush leaving a passageway too narrow to drive the wagon through; they were thus caused to divert. Despite the lateness of the season, the air was swarming with flies.

After hours of travel, both men recognized familiar rock shapes and canyon walls and knew they had arrived at the site of the gun battle. Elmer felt a shiver pass through him as he recalled the appalling events that had occurred here. Even now, he glanced at the high rims with apprehension, fearing that he might be within the sights of a hidden marksman. Could Mateo, knowing that he would return to this place, be waiting for him? He shrugged the thought away.

There was over everything a brooding silence. Not even a buzzard cruised on the high thermals. They halted the wagon at the side of the canyon and proceeded on foot, leaving the mare cropping at the thin grass. Elmer struggled bravely, using his crutch, crawling some of the way. Soon they were scrambling up the steep incline, clinging to outcroppings of rock for support. They reached a grassy plateau, backed by a gaping cave and Elmer knew immediately that this was where he'd been held captive and where Lauren had been murdered.

It was quite possible that his wife's body had been disposed of elsewhere, but he knew he would not rest until this place had been searched.

The two men separated, and for hours moved far and wide, seeking any sign of a burying, Elmer hobbling manfully. They even searched the gloomy depths of the cave.

Daylight was starting to fade and they were about to admit failure, when Elmer spotted a patch of earth that had been deeply scratched. At first he was puzzled but then concluded that this was where a coyote or other creature had attempted to dig, attracted by some scent. His heartbeat quickened. He called to Justin who joined him and agreed that this could be a grave.

The Ranger descended to the wagon and returned with a spade and a blanket. He began to dig, Elmer being too handicapped to assist, and presently the remains of a human hand were unearthed. The air thickened with the sickly stench of decay. Elmer waved away the swarm of flies that suddenly pestered them, and nausea enveloped him. They had found what he sought, yet the finding left him wanting to die.

He steeled himself, gritted his teeth and wiped away the tears that were blurring his eyes. Both men raised bandannas over their noses as Justin dug on. Soon the corpse was uncovered, seething with maggots and worms. It might have been unrecognizable had it not been for the familiar pattern of the rotting dress.

They raised what was left of his beloved Lauren from her makeshift grave and wrapped her in the blanket. Cradling her in his arms, finding her feather-light, Justin led the way down the treacherous slope, fanning away flies as he went. They gently rested her on the bed of the wagon and re-loaded the spade. Ten minutes later, with dusk deepening, they started back for Calico Springs. They arrived in the early hours of the following morning.

Elmer had Lauren attended to by an undertaker. He had a fine coffin made, and she was re-interred in the town's cemetery. Watched by a circle of friends, the local minister spoke words of tenderness and love and a hymn was sung. Elmer had a headstone erected with a simple inscription. He felt that a chapter had been closed.

But he swore it was not the *final* chapter.

The boy Daniel Ramos had come upon the farm late in the day. He was ravenous, not having eaten for forty-eight hours. He was also dog-tired. He had run away from home two weeks earlier, having left a note for his stepmother: *Gone to join Texas Rangers. Will make my own way from now on.*

He'd had no money as he set out on foot, camping rough or sometimes finding shelter in a barn or deserted shack. It was springtime, but summer warmth showed no sign of appearing and at night he shivered. He lived mostly off any scraps he could beg or steal from farms or smallholdings. Once, with an improvised catapult, he killed a squirrel and ate it raw. He had also tried to catch a snake but it eluded him. He drank from streams. He trudged southward across hills, sometimes finding sustenance and company in travelling pedlars who took mercy on the rail-thin youngster.

There were occasions when he regretted leaving his home, for there he had had a bed to sleep in and food to eat, but then he would recall that his stepfather was no longer there, his place having been taken by a man he could not abide – and he realized he would never go back.

And now he had come upon this large farm where there were a cultivated meadow, penned hogs and chickens and two horses in a corral. Utterly weary, his belly rumbling with hunger, he crept around a shadowy barn. Off to his left was a broken plough. Nobody seemed to be about. Dusk was deepening. He crossed the yard, approached the house. A door was standing open and he glimpsed the kitchen within.

He crept forward, desperation suppressing his fear. Through the doorway he could see a table on which a lamp glowed. There were also a half-eaten chicken, a loaf of bread and a large milk-jug. Nobody was in the kitchen, but he heard voices coming from another part of the house. Glancing around, he satisfied himself that he was unobserved, then he made his entry.

The proximity of the food crumbled his last hesitation. He lifted the jug and took a long swig of creamy milk. At that moment footsteps sounded, approaching from within the house. He grabbed the chicken and bread. He darted outside and spotted a man tinkering with the broken plough, his back turned. Daniel fled like a shadow across the yard to the only place of concealment he could see – the barn.

The light was dim inside; the smell of corn and manure was pungent. A milk-cow was looking at him inquisitively from her stall. He was frightened she might *moo* and raise the alarm, but her head dropped and she started to chew. He saw a ladder and, still grasping chicken and bread, he climbed to the loft. Apart from thin slivers of light coming from holes in the roof, he was in darkness, but he became aware that he was standing knee-deep in hay. This was obviously the store for the cow's fodder. He stumbled across to the far corner and dropped down. He immediately tore at the chicken with his fingers, stuffing it into his mouth. He had never tasted anything more delicious. With the flesh gone, he sucked the bones. The bread came next.

It was as he finished his last bite that voices and movement sounded from below and lantern-light was suddenly glimmering up through the trapdoor. The creaking of the ladder sounded as heavy weight was put upon it.

Daniel burrowed deeply into the straw, holding his breath and praying that his pounding heartbeat would not give him away. He saw light dancing over the beams and roof above him. Somebody was standing on the ladder and peering into the loft. They did so for what seemed an age, swinging the lantern back and forth. Suddenly it was withdrawn, the ladder creaked again, the light faded and Daniel sighed with relief. The threat seemed to be over – at least for the moment.

With people moving about outside, it would be futile to attempt escape from the barn tonight. He was too weary anyway. He snuggled deeper in the hay and closed his eyes, thankful that he was warm and no longer hungry. The morrow would have to take care of itself. Before long his breathing slowed and he slipped into sleep.

Daylight was streaming through the roof's holes when he was kicked to wakefulness. He groaned with fright. A burly man had snatched aside the covering of hay and was looming over him, his heavy-jowled face fierce. Chicken bones were scattered around. With a beefy hand the man grabbed Daniel's collar and dragged him to his feet.

'I think it good to look up here again,' he growled, his accent a guttural German. 'I teach you a lesson, you little thief!'

CHAPTER EIGHT

Luiz Prado, the only gang survivor from Mateo's killing spree, ran through the darkness, snatched at by low-swinging fronds from the pines and tripping over his spurs. He ran until his lungs were fit to burst. He trembled with the dread that Mateo might be pursuing him. He had just seen his young brother Ernesto, as well as his other *compadres*, murdered – and but for an intervention by the Saints, he would have been amongst them. They'd all been robbed of the cash that was rightly theirs – or almost rightly.

Now, he slumped against the bole of a tree, and his breath gradually calmed. He strained his ears for any sound of Mateo, but he heard only the normal nightly stirrings of the forest. He had consumed much liquor, had become light-headed, but horror had sobered him.

He himself had gunned down men in plenty, but he considered killing *Yanquis* was acceptable, almost a duty. Killing your *compadres* was the blackest sin.

He had never trusted Mateo, had always been

afraid of him. This night was the first time he had lowered his guard, and it had cost him dearly. Foolishly, he had left his cash, pistols and knife with his saddle-bags when he had stepped away to relieve himself. And his horse was still with the others. But as the intensity of his fear subsided, his cunning returned. He concluded that he would not miss his brother unduly, for he was argumentative and petulant. He lamented the loss of the cash more deeply. Now, Mateo had it all. Indeed, Mateo himself would be well worth robbing . . . and killing. Prado tried to suppress his fear of the man, set his mind to scheming.

His first action must be to return to the campsite and pray that Mateo had departed. He would hope to retrieve his weapons, saddle – and his horse, if that was possible.

Accordingly, he rose and stealthily retraced his steps, stopping frequently to listen for Mateo. All he heard was the hoot of an owl, the scurrying of mice and, further away, the yap of a coyote. Through the branches of the trees, he could see the cold white orb of the moon.

Twenty minutes later, he was back at the campsite. The fire was still burning. It had roasted Silvarez, who had fallen into it, a bullet hole in his back. The smell of his scorched flesh tainted the air. The hollow, bathed in light from the flames, presented a ghastly tableau of twisted corpses, including that of Prado's brother, but he paid them no heed. He found his gunbelt and bandolier and strapped them on. He also recovered his sombrero.

Moving cautiously, he located the clearing where the horses had been hobbled. None remained, but he heard them moving about in the trees and he soon found his own *grulla*. He led it back to the hollow, where it scented death and was agitated. He calmed it, got his saddle across its back, fastened the girth and mounted up.

He was sure Mateo would have headed south and that was the direction he took. He rode for two days, keeping to the foothills of the Maroma Mountains, finding cover in pine and oak scrub. He discovered no sign of Mateo; however, he felt certain that the man would be heading for Mexico. On the fourth day, from his high vantage point he spied the south-bound trail angling in from the north. His pulse quickened as he spotted movement, but then he relaxed. It was only an armadillo scuttling along . . . but something must have disturbed it. True enough, a lone horseman shortly came into view. There was no mistaking him. It was Mateo.

Luiz Prado knew that the trail curved around low, rocky hills, and any traveller thereon would pass from sight. He also knew that if he climbed over the crest, he would reach a point where he closely over-looked the trail. This would be an ideal place from which to bushwhack his prey.

Moving briskly he spurred the *grulla* upward through the pines and over the crest. Twenty minutes later, having tethered his animal in the brush, he emerged with an excellent, close-up view of the trail.

He hunkered down at the mouth of a cave, concealed by a rock buttress. He checked the
mechanism of his rifle and waited impatiently. A feral
lust to kill had the blood pounding in his ears. He
wondered how many bullets it would take to finish
Mateo. He licked his lips and thought of the fortune
that, the Holy Saints willing, would soon be his.

Mateo was an old hand at bushwhacking and trailing
an enemy. Yesterday, he'd watched birds circling in
the sky, sensed the focus of their attention and had
known that he was being followed, though by whom
he had no idea. He believed that nobody was aware
that his saddle-bags bulged with cash; he imagined
he had killed his entire gang and he had met no travellers since.

He realized that he was an easy target here on the
trail, and an instinctive hunch warned him that
danger was imminent, the way ahead being an ideal
spot for ambush.

He dismounted and led his roan to the trailside.
The animal was agitated as if sensing the proximity of
some menace. He tethered it and nose-wrapped it to
prevent it sounding off. He unsheathed his rifle, left
the trail and climbed into the trees on foot. If his pre-
monitions served him well, he would bushwhack the
bushwhacker.

Fifteen minutes later, he grunted with satisfaction,
for he could see the back of Luiz Prado. He didn't
know how he'd survived the shootings, but he was
sure he would die soon.

He had the man's back squarely within the sights of his rifle but he did not pull the trigger because a strange thing happened.

There was a loud roar. Luiz Prado came to his feet, glanced over his shoulder, his face contorted with terror. A dark, shaggy grizzly bear was rearing up only yards behind him. It had emerged from its cave, its musky smell pervading the air.

Prado raised his rifle, fired and saw dust kick out from the beast's chest. It didn't stop it but enraged it further. It straddled towards him on its hind legs, its fangs bared, saliva dribbling back from its flews, its claws looking like fistfuls of knives. Prado screamed, attempting to run, but he was struck by a monstrous swipe of a paw that ripped his poncho, shirt and flesh beneath, catapulting him forward. He hit the ground hard, the breath thumped from his body. The bear pounced upon him, lying heavily across his hips and legs, crushing him. He was helpless, suffocating in the beast's stench, suspecting his life was ebbing and having no strength to fight on.

Upslope, Mateo aimed his gun, intent on finishing Prado – but again he hesitated, fearing that he might hit the bear. Sensing his presence, the animal paused from biting Prado's shoulder. It cast a glance in the direction of Mateo who decided it would be wise to vacate his present position. Let the brute finish Prado off before it turned its attention on him!

He returned the way he had come, glancing backward to ensure that the bear was not chasing him. At that moment he heard the panicking whinny of

Prado's *grulla*. He changed direction, found the animal and freed it from its tether, then he ran on. He reached the roan, removed the nose-wrap, ripped the reins clear of the foliage and mounted up. He moved off straight away.

CHAPTER NINE

Six months after his shooting, Elmer still felt pain when he put his foot to the ground and he was obliged to rely on a crutch. Nonetheless, he was intensely grateful that he had kept his leg and he frequently thanked God that Doctor Hathaway had been blessed with such medical skill. Each morning he attended Lauren's grave, often bringing flowers, but he was not a man at peace. The old hatreds, lusts for retribution and impatience broiled in him more fiercely than ever.

The Texas Chronicle had reported the strange finding of bodies in the Maroma Mountains; six apparent *bandidos,* all killed by bullets. Assumption was that these were men of Mateo's train-robbing gang, though there was no sign of Mateo himself and no information had emerged as to his whereabouts.

The report fuelled Elmer's intentions to even greater heights. He longed for the day when he could walk unaided, and when he could strike the trail of the monster he wanted dead. Of course, that trail had gone cold. But no man could vanish completely; somebody must know where he was.

Otto Schmitt and his wife Olga were German immigrants who, twenty years ago, had come to Texas in search of greater personal freedom and better business opportunities than those afforded in their native Saxony. Through hard work, they had prospered and established the large farm into which Daniel Ramos had now stumbled.

Schmitt was a proud man with a short temper and he could not abide thievery. Grabbing the boy, he half threw him down the loft ladder and descended himself. 'We pass you over to the sheriff, that's what we do, and he can put you in jail – *Ja*!'

Still gripping Daniel, he hastened him across the yard to the scene of the boy's recent crime – the kitchen. There, awaiting them, was Olga, a plump *Frau* in an apron. She had just lifted a skillet of porridge from the stove.

Daniel looked at the woman, expecting to see her scowling and angry at the theft of the chicken and bread. To his surprise she gave him a kindly smile.

'Poor young boy,' she said. 'He's so thin. He must have been starving.'

'Starving or not,' Otto retorted, 'I hand him over to the sheriff. He will teach him not to steal from honest folk. I've heard he whips good-for-nothings.'

Olga shrugged her ample shoulders. 'Well, before

you do, let's feed him up. He can have some breakfast.'

Otto grunted his displeasure but let Daniel sit at
the table. A moment later a bowl of steaming porridge was placed before him. He'd never had
porridge before, but he blew on it and was soon
spooning it into his mouth. Next, the woman placed
a big sausage in front of him and some bread, which
he washed down with strong, black coffee. He could
hardly believe his luck.

To her profound regret, Olga Schmitt was a child-
less woman. She would have loved a son. Now, as she
looked at Daniel, her heart warmed.

'Are you running away from the law?' Otto
demanded.

'No,' Daniel said. 'I ran away from home. I'm
going to join the Texas Rangers at Calico Springs.'

'Texas Rangers, eh?' the farmer said. 'You are a bit
young, I think.'

'Perhaps he could stay here, till he is old enough
for the Rangers,' Olga suggested.

Otto shook his head stubbornly. '*Nein*,' he said.
'That would not be good.' He scratched his jaw
thoughtfully. 'Unless. . . .'

'Unless what, Otto?'

The German's mood had softened. 'Unless he
worked for his keep. We could do with an extra hand.
He'd have to work very hard, mind you.'

'*Ja*, that would be good.'

Daniel had listened with amazement. He had not
been consulted, but the prospect of cooked food

and maybe a bed to sleep in was too tempting to refuse.

'That *would* be good,' he nodded.

Over the next six months, Daniel worked hard on the farm. He helped the other farm-hand, an elderly German. The tasks were endless, but he loved the life – feeding the animals, cleaning out barns and pens, ploughing burrows and planting crops in the fields, collecting eggs and milking the cows and goats. Wholesome food had him putting on weight, his chest and shoulders broadening.

Otto Schmitt soon became fond of the boy and his industrious nature. He paid Daniel a wage, which he saved, his intention being to purchase a horse. Olga displayed unstinting, homely kindness to him, treating him as a son – but he still cherished the hope of one day becoming a Texas Ranger.

Elmer had cast aside his crutch a month ago, firstly using a stick and then discarding that. He concentrated on the exercises that Doctor Hathaway had recommended and he found his pain was greatly diminished. Shortly after this, he was in the saddle, pleased that he had lost none of his former skills.

One morning over breakfast, he was scanning through *The Texas Chronicle*, when he noticed a small footnote:

Carlos Viera, the former Mexican bandit, who was severely wounded and captured during a train robbery of a year ago, has recovered sufficiently to be transferred from an infirmary to the penitentiary in Culver City. He is expected to serve at least ten years.

Elmer's interest had quickened. The bandit might know something of Mateo's whereabouts. He immediately mailed a letter to the prison governor requesting permission to visit Viera. Three weeks later, the response came: *Permission granted.*

Within twenty-four hours he was on a train bound for Culver City.

The penitentiary was a foreboding grey-stone building with a watch-tower, turrets and battlements. Elmer entered through the main entrance, reported to the office and, after authority was granted, was conducted to the prisoners' living quarters. These consisted of small cells on three floors. As he was led along the gangway of the middle floor, inmates grasped their bars and shouted obscenities at him. Ignoring them, he followed the warder to the far end where he was ushered into a cell and the door locked behind him. A stale stench came from the slop-bucket which stood in the corner.

'Fifteen minutes,' the warder stated.

The Mexican, Carlos Viera, who had been sprawled on his pallet, sat up, a look of surprise on his face. His head was clean-shaven and showed an immense scar across its top. Elmer had learned that as well as being shot in the stomach, this man had cracked his skull when falling and been in a coma for weeks. Even now he looked decidedly weak. Viera

67

had probably been complicit in the murder of his wife, and Elmer felt in no mood for salutations. He did not even introduce himself, but got straight to the point.

'You speak English?'

'*Sí, señor* – a li'l.'

'Mateo gunned down all his gang and took the loot from that train robbery all for hisself. I guess he'd have killed you too, if you hadn't been lucky enough to get yourself captured.'

Viera spoke one word: '*Bastardo!*' He fell back onto his pallet.

Elmer said, 'If you ever wanna get released from this place, you best come clean and tell me where Mateo has his hideaway. Where is he now?'

The Mexican shook his head. 'I no understand.'

'Yes you do,' Elmer persisted. 'Where did Mateo go when he wanted to lay low? Mexico?'

'*Sí, señor*, Mexico.'

'Where in Mexico?'

Again, Viera shook his head, as if bewildered by events.

'You don't owe Mateo anythin',' Elmer said. 'He'd've killed and robbed you if he'd had the chance. He's a mean bastard, a murderer and double-crosser. I mean to kill him myself.'

Viera looked up, surprised. 'You will kill him?'

'That's what I said. That's what he deserves. But I've gotta find him first.'

'You can get me out of this stinking hole?' Viera asked.

'I can put in a good word for you.'

The Mexican gave an exasperated sigh. He spat at the bucket, missed, then he said, 'Go to Amerido, in Mexico. Kill the *bastardo*!'

CHAPTER TEN

Luiz Prado tried to open his eyes and could not. He was aware of crushing pressure on his chest. Also, an overwhelming stench that was nigh suffocating him – the stench of bear. He attempted to raise his eyelids again; this time he succeeded and light lanced into his eyes, paining him. Where was he? His mind grappled with recollections. He recalled seeing Mateo, and then running from the bear, and after that the agony before he blacked out.

He realized that he was lying beneath the brute. It appeared to be dead. He could hear flies buzzing. He recalled firing a shot, seeing it strike the animal's chest. At the time it had seemed to have little effect, but now he concluded that the bullet must have lodged somewhere vital. The heart maybe? The result had been a delayed action. The bear must have died while it tried to bite and claw him to death. And where was Mateo now?

He struggled to thrust aside the animal and agony shot through every part of his body. Gritting his teeth, he tried again and felt the weight give slightly. He paused, regaining what little strength he had. At the fourth attempt he was able to wriggle out – and now he realized how badly injured he was. His ribs felt broken. He was covered in blood, his clothing ripped to shreds. He tried to straighten up, but this caused him to cry out. He had never known such pain. He thought he might die.

Then Mateo came into his mind. He looked around. Where was the *bastardo*? He had gone. He had left him to the bear. Prado slumped back, ignoring the flies that swarmed around both him and the beast. He lapsed into unconsciousness.

When he regained his senses, the warmth had gone out of the day. Hatred of Mateo enveloped him. He longed to be able to kill him. He knew he must try to move, to drag himself away . . . but to where? In all his life, he had never needed help more. He recalled that he had left his horse tethered way back up the slope in the trees, but he doubted that he had sufficient strength to make the necessary climb. Maybe if he could get down to the trail, some traveller might come along. That seemed to be his best hope.

His progress down the punishing slope was snail-like. He weakened and was reduced to a crawl, dragging his lacerated body along using his elbows and knees, stopping to rest frequently. When, at last, he reached the trailside, night and a cold breeze had come. Wolves were sending their howls up to the pale moon.

Exhausted, he slept.

Black Hawk, a Comanche, found him lying at the trailside just after dawn on the following day. The Indian's ancient face was wrinkled like an old apple. While he was hunting for rabbits, he had stumbled across the dead bear and then the Mexican. Now, he saw that the man's clothing was soaked with blood and through its shreds, mutilations showed. Grandfather Bear must have been very annoyed with this man. At first, Black Hawk thought he had gone to the hunting grounds in the sky, but shortly he saw the rise and fall of his chest.

Black Hawk had always been a loner and three years earlier had been away in the hills when Chief Quanah Parker had led the Comanches onto the reservation in Oklahoma. Ever since, he and the White Eye girl whom he called Little Dove, had pitched their tipi in quiet valleys and the blue-coat soldiers had not troubled them.

Black Hawk sat quietly until the Mexican woke up and groaned with chagrin as he saw the Indian looking at him. Black Hawk lifted the canteen from his shoulder, uncorked it, and touched it to the lips of the man, who took a long gulp.

'I will help you to get up,' Black Hawk said in Spanish.

Surprised at being shown mercy, Prado nodded, and with the Indian's aid he clambered to his feet. He swayed but Black Hawk supported him. He had lost much blood. After a moment, with his arm across the Comanche's shoulders, he took tentative steps forward, wincing at his pain. He had no idea where he was being taken. They went slowly, stopping every few yards. Several times he nearly fell. After a torturous hour, they reached the tipi of Black Hawk where Little Dove was busy scraping the flesh from an antelope hide. She had long black hair and a sensuous body.

She had been kidnapped by the Indians when she was a child. She had soon grown used to the Comanche way of life and Black Hawk had treated her like a granddaughter. She had even attended the reservation school with Comanche children and had learned to understand the tracks White Eyes made across paper. But now, at nineteen, she was restless and capricious, and had secret thoughts that the old man would not have appreciated. Being white, she sometimes ventured into the town of Turtle Rock, traded rabbit skins for supplies and gazed longingly at clothes and jewellery in store windows. She wished she had money with which to purchase them.

Now, Black Hawk quickly explained to the girl in the Comanche tongue how he had found the Mexican. He asked her to clean and treat his wounds. Somewhat reluctantly, she nodded.

While Prado rested down on a pallet within the tipi, she cut away his tattered shirt, gasping as she saw his wounds. She left him and shortly returned with a bowl of water and cloth. With none-too-gentle hands she bathed him and presently she applied antelope fat over the claw and teeth lacerations.

Eventually Prado slept. He dreamed of killing Mateo.

On the following day Black Hawk gave him an old shirt and pants.

Over the next two weeks he rested a great deal and gradually his strength returned, fortified by rabbit stew. His ribs and wounds still hurt but less than they had previously.

He began to watch Little Dove. Her body was lissom and he yearned to see her naked. One day he asked her for a kiss.

'Kiss you!' she scoffed. 'I don't even know your name.'

'I am Luiz Prado, and women do not refuse me.'

'I do,' she said and turned away.

Next morning, she went to the town of Turtle Rock to get supplies. When she returned, she beckoned Black Hawk out of Prado's earshot.

'In town I saw many posters,' she said. 'They offer much money for the capture of Mexican bandits – dead or alive. I am sure the man we have looked after is a Mexican bandit. We could maybe get the reward for him.'

The old man frowned. 'That is not the Comanche custom,' he said. 'Once a person has been shown hospitality, made welcome in the tipi, it is not the Comanche way to betray him.'

'But I am not Comanche,' the girl said.

The following morning, she again went in to the town.

As he'd begun to recover from his injuries, Luiz Prado had grown uneasy and he felt vulnerable. Each day his desire to kill Mateo increased. Throughout his harrowing experiences, he had somehow retained his gunbelt and pistol and of late had kept them beneath his pallet.

Now, as he rested within the tipi, he heard the girl's voice coming from outside. She had returned from her absence. And then he became aware of the deeper murmur of a man's voice – a stranger's.

With desperate hands, Prado reached for his pistol, concealing it under his blanket. Almost immediately, the flap of the tipi was drawn back and Sheriff Harlock stepped inside, his gun in his hand.

'I'm arrestin' you on a charge of banditry,' he proclaimed.

Those were the last words he ever spoke. Firing through the blanket, Prado's gun blasted off, the lead cutting clean through the lawman's heart.

CHAPTER ELEVEN

The boy Daniel Ramos had left the farm with sadness. He had grown fond of the Schmitts; they had been kind to him and he had enjoyed the hard work, yet he now felt it was time to move on, to fulfil his ambition of becoming a Texas Ranger. When he left, Otto gave his hand a long shake and Olga cried, hugged him and kissed his cheek. He had saved his wages and he travelled by stagecoach to Calico Springs, arriving in the early afternoon.

Although the sun was shining and the streets were bustling with normal folk, he still shuddered as he recalled the fearful night when he'd fled from the Mexicans and hidden in a back street.

Today, he had no trouble in finding the office of the Texas Rangers. Steeling himself, he entered to find Captain Bob Justin sitting at his desk. When Justin looked up from his paperwork, Daniel said, 'Good afternoon, *señor*. I want to be a Texas Ranger.'

Justin smiled. 'It's a hard life, son. You've got to be real tough to stand up to it.'

'I am tough.'

The Ranger eyed him up and down, then said, 'I guess you are. How old are you?

'Sixteen-and-a-half.' It had never entered Daniel's mind to lie.

Justin frowned. 'Too young. Come back when you're eighteen.'

The boy looked utterly crestfallen and Justin took pity on him.

'If you wanted,' he said, 'and if you proved reliable, we could use you to run errands, clean out the stables and a lot of other jobs. The pay won't be great, but if you could do that until you were old enough to join as a grown man, then maybe we could employ you, that's if you qualified.'

Daniel gave him a wide smile and nodded vigorously.

Once again he had been offered work, just at the right moment.

In the days that followed Daniel heard that Elmer Carrington was staying at The Golden Sunrise Guesthouse, and one morning he visited him. To his delight, Elmer welcomed him warmly and set him up with coffee. Daniel expressed genuine sorrow on learning of Lauren's death. For a moment he was quite overcome. Elmer told him it was his intention to kill Mateo. The boy nodded sagely and expressed the opinion that death was too good for the Mexican. Presently he related his own experiences and his ambitions. Elmer listened with interest.

Eventually they parted, wishing each other well.

77

When Elmer got back from his visit to Culver City, he was excited. At last he might be able to pick up Mateo's trail. Of course there was no guarantee that the Mexican would have gone to the place called Amerido; nor that Carlos Viera was telling him the truth. But it was the only clue he'd unearthed so far and he had to follow it up.

Before he did so, he penned a letter to the governor of the Culver City Penitentiary explaining that Luiz Viera had given him useful information regarding the notorious Mexican bandit, Mateo. Although he felt no compassion for Viera, Elmer asked that he might be given some consideration. He had, at least, kept his word.

Elmer had never heard of Amerido. He sent away by mail-order for a map of Mexico and when it arrived he studied it and eventually spotted the name in tiny print,

Amerido was a village deep in Mexico. And that was where he intended going.

It took him three days to prepare, arming himself with his Henry .44 Repeater, a Colt pistol, ammunition and a Bowie knife. He purchased a compass and suitable clothing – poncho, shirt, and a sombrero.

On his last evening, Daniel came to him at the guesthouse while he was eating his supper.

'Captain,' he said, 'Captain Justin has told me that you are leaving in the morning, that you are going to Mexico to find Mateo.'

'Sure I am, Daniel,' Elmer responded.

'I have a favour to ask.'

'What favour?'

'A big favour.'

'What is it?'

'I want to come with you!'

Elmer dropped his spoon with a clatter.

After a moment he said, 'You can't. It'll be too dangerous. There ain't no place for a boy in what I'm gonna do.'

'I'm not a boy. I'm almost a grown man. And I hate Mateo real bad. Almost as bad as you. I have bought a pistol to take with me.'

Elmer saw the earnest glint in the boy's eyes. He scratched his jaw. He said, 'If anythin' should happen to you, I'd feel real bad.'

'I'll be very careful, Captain. I promise.'

'But the Rangers won't take kindly to you givin' up your job.'

'Captain Justin has given me leave of absence.'

Elmer took a mouthful of apple pie, then he said, 'All right, you can come, but don't expect a picnic.'

Next morning, Elmer took Daniel to the hardware store and kitted him out with the necessities he would need for the journey. At noon they boarded the stage and thus began a bone-jarring journey on the route known as Polecat Mail. It was to last for three days. The first night they stopped and slept at a way station; on the other nights they travelled on, sleeping on the floor of the coach.

They changed at several towns and finally disembarked at Polka City. Here, they enjoyed a bath at the Tonsorial Parlour, easing the cricks from their bones, stayed overnight at a guesthouse and the following morning bought, from a livery, two sturdy chestnut horses, a pack-mule and tack. Elmer's respect for the boy increased, for he remained cheerful and helpful, never once complaining.

After a final, hearty meal at a restaurant, they continued their journey, crossing into Mexico at a point ten miles south of Polka City. Elmer consulted his map, planning their route through the mountains and then onward into the desert. The compass would prove invaluable. They camped that night in a cave. Having checked for snakes, they lit a mesquite fire and enjoyed their supper despite the gnats that came to pester them. Before dawn, they had saddled up and were moving out, the day breaking before them. Presently, the sun became obscured by cloud and the air turned humid.

The mountains lacked crests, having flat uplands covered with saguaros. The floor of the world seemed cracked open with countless canyons and arroyos which trapped the heat, so that their energy was sapped.

By the time they descended from the mountains, the clouds began to multiply and merge.

'Soon we'll have a big storm,' Daniel opined, and sure enough within minutes thunder rumbled, causing the horses to whinny and rear, and lightning streaked like gunfire through the clouds. The smell of ozone tainted the air and the wind began to rise.

'There's cover over there.' Elmer gestured towards a rock overhang, but the rain came quite suddenly, a bludgeoning downpour with raindrops like bullets splattering on the rock, knocking the berries off junipers, and soaking man and boy. It plastered their shirts to their backs and filled the brims of their sombreros. They reached the sheltering rock too late to save them from a soaking.

For an hour the deluge continued, then trailed off as quickly as it had arrived. Elmer and Daniel looked at each other and suddenly they were laughing because they looked a sorry sight, like a couple of drowned rats. Elmer reckoned it was the first time he had laughed since Lauren had died.

They shook the water from their sombreros, climbed into their soggy saddles and moved on across the puddled ground. It was a half hour later, when they were crossing a shallow wash, that they heard a sound like an approaching freight train. The horses began to rear in alarm.

'What's that?' Daniel cried, his eyes round with fear.

They looked back to see a wall of water, advancing upon them in a crescent shape. It seemed to eat up the ground, coming at incredible speed.

Spurring their panicking animals, they rode up the bank to higher ground, arriving just in time to escape being carried away. They turned to watch the flood surge through the wash – a brown liquid avalanche, dragging trees, branches and debris with it. Two hours passed with the flood unrelenting, then the flow slowed; it gradually dwindled to a gentle stream, passing over bars of quicksand. Swarms of flies came to replace those that had been drowned.

'Best move on,' Elmer said. This was not the first flash flood he had experienced, but it ranked right up there amid the worst.

Again they started off, the animals sometimes hock-deep in mud. The heat and light were fading from the day and they went carefully over the treacherous ground, swatting at the mosquitos that seemed everywhere.

They did not foresee the disaster that awaited them.

They were moving over wet sand, which looked reasonably firm, when suddenly the ground seemed to turn to liquid, and the terrified horses and mule started to sink in what seemed a jelly-like substance. As they struggled frantically, they sank deeper.

Believing that horses and mules would sink more quickly than a man because of their greater weight and the smallness of their feet, Elmer lowered himself from the saddle and eased himself down. He immediately sank ankle-deep in the ooze, but, with tremendous effort, succeeded in drawing his booted feet clear, step by step, until he reached firmer ground. He was thankful that his boots had always been on the tight side.

He turned to see Daniel sliding from his animal, attempting to escape in the same way as he had, but the mud had taken hold of him, was now halfway up to his thighs.

Elmer got as close to the boy as he could without becoming bogged down himself, but their extended hands did not meet.

'Lean forward,' Elmer yelled.

'I am,' Daniel gasped.

'Then try to fall flat on your face.'

Daniel took a deep breath. He reckoned that if such a desperate measure failed, he would be doomed. But with great courage, he did as instructed and Elmer got a hold on his wrists. With a slow, steady pull he began to draw him out, but the quicksand was reluctant to let him go. It gurgled and made gasping noises.

Exerting every ounce of his strength, striving to ignore the pain in his leg, Elmer fought the quicksand for its prize and gradually dragged the boy clear. But his boots remained behind. It was impossible to recover them because the liquid sand oozed into the holes Daniel had left, covering them over, leaving the surface sleek and innocent-looking, just as it had done before they were ensnared.

Daniel sat head down on firm ground, breathing hard and thanking Elmer for rescuing him.

But the problem of the animals remained, and with the light fading, it was going to be difficult to overcome.

CHAPTER TWELVE

Elmer came up with a desperate plan. To stand any chance of saving the animals, they needed rope, and the only rope they had was attached to the saddles which were currently on the backs of the trapped mounts.

Elmer pulled off his boots, then his pants and shirt.

'What are you gonna do, Captain?' Daniel gasped anxiously.

'We need rope to get the hosses out,' Elmer responded. 'I'm goin' back into the quicksand. I guess if I spread myself, I won't sink.'

'*Madre mía*!' the boy exclaimed. 'I shall pray for you.'

Elmer grunted his appreciation, waded in to the mud and gently extended himself forward, arms outstretched, slowly pushing with his legs. To his relief he did not sink, but partially floated. Both horses had quieted, appearing resigned to becoming fully submerged.

Elmer reached Daniel's chestnut first. The animal snorted, but he soothed it with a rub of the still-exposed withers. He stretched his arm out and unhooked the rope from the saddle-horn. He uncoiled it, doubled the loop, passed the rope around the horse's neck and knotted it to prevent it sliding. Then, extending the rope as he went, he made it back to firm ground.

The chestnut had not moved, but now as the rope was drawn taut, man and boy heaved with all their weight. At first, all that happened was that the horse extended its neck, whickering with fear. At last, suddenly, it activated its front legs, striving to move forward . . . and slowly, aided by human brawn, it struggled into motion. A further ten minutes saw it on firm ground, shaking itself, its mud-caked body glinting in the moonlight.

The prospect of re-entering the quicksand was mighty daunting, but Elmer knew he had to do it if the other two animals were to be saved.

Daniel said, 'Let me go, Captain. I saw how you did it.'

Elmer shook his head. 'I'm bigger than you. I can spread my weight more.' With that he waded in again.

Rescuing the second horse was even harder than the first because it had sunk deeper. Pausing frequently, Elmer managed to float his way until he was in position to get the rope around its neck. Thereafter followed another monumental tug-of-war that at times appeared to be failing as the exhausted animal seemed reluctant to help. But at last it was goaded into motion and it, too, was drawn up onto firm ground. Once there, its legs gave out and it rested down on its side, its breath coming in great rasps. Elmer pulled off the saddle and tack and retrieved his Henry Repeater from the scabbard.

Now, there was only the mule to be pulled out. Utterly weary, Elmer waded into the quicksand for the third time. To his dismay, he found the beast had sunk almost up to its withers, weighed down by the packs it was carrying. It was exhausted, its eyes were closed and it seemed already to have given up the ghost. He got the rope around its neck, but soon realized there was no chance of rescuing it, nor the supplies on its back. With a heavy heart, he back-tracked to dry land, retrieved his gun from his belt and checked that it was loaded. He took careful aim and despatched the animal with a single shot to the head.

Daniel shed tears because he had grown fond of the mule.

They bedded down that night feeling crestfallen. Daniel lay awake for hours, watching the moon's mottled face float across the dark sky; he wondered what the future held. Would they find Mateo and give him the punishment he deserved?

Hatred of Mateo made him feel restless. He blamed him for all their misfortunes. Eventually, he rose from his blanket and went to where Elmer's horse was still lying on its side. Its breathing was now steady. Its eyes glinted up at him trustingly. He smoothed its neck and whispered soothing words in to its ear.

He checked his own chestnut, hobbled nearby. It seemed to have recovered from its ordeal. He returned to his bed and rolled into his blanket, aware of Elmer's gentle snore.

He speculated on how he would manage the remaining journey minus his boots. He consoled himself with the thought that he had travelled barefoot before, when he was running from Mateo. Now he was running to him. He slept.

When he awoke, the sun was already rising, burning off the mist from the mountain tops. He climbed up to find Elmer crouching over his prostrate horse. Elmer straightened up and turned, his face gaunt. 'He died during the night,' he said.

Neither of them felt in the mood for breakfast that morning.

When they moved on, they had no wish to burden their remaining mount with a double load, so they took it in turns to ride. They shared their one pair of boots, the walker having the benefit.

Elmer's compass had been lost with the mule, and this would make navigating the desert hard. The map was of little use because the country lacked landmarks. Elmer knew they had to head south and he told Daniel to watch for barrel cacti because they grew pointing south.

The heat became fierce and they urinated in their sombreros to make them cool.

In the afternoon they came to a derelict and deserted copper mine, and were glad to shelter from the heat in one of its shafts. They travelled on when the day became less torrid. That night they camped beneath a tall juniper tree.

After the moon had come, Elmer tried in vain to doze off, but he kept wishing that time would pass more quickly, so that they could find Mateo. Then a doubt occurred to him. Maybe he wasn't in Amerido. Maybe he had left or had never been there.

After the merciless heat of earlier, the night was downright cold. Daniel appeared already to be fast asleep. Suddenly blind instinct jerked Elmer out of his reverie. He glimpsed something moving on the boy's blanketed body, something that caught the moon's glint. Shock caused his heart to miss a beat as stark realization hammered into him – *rattlesnake!*

He was petrified that Daniel would move in his sleep and alarm the snake, causing it to strike. His hand closed over his Colt, but he decided he could not risk a shot for fear of hitting the boy. The snake was now motionless, half coiled, close to Daniel's head, perhaps relishing his warmth. Elmer debated whether to rush at the snake in an attempt to scare it off; the danger was that Daniel would be startled awake and attract the reptile's anger. But maybe it was a chance Elmer had to take. He was tensing his muscles, ready for a leap, when a miracle happened . . . the snake uncoiled itself and moved away, sidewinding in to the darkness.

Elmer exhaled in relief. Daniel suddenly grunted

and turned over, pulling the blanket tightly around him. He was none the wiser of the threat he'd just survived.

As they travelled on next morning, following the direction indicated by the barrel cacti, the desert became greener with grama grass and there were occasional stands of willow. At noon, they spied three *vaqueros* driving cattle. Elmer made Daniel dismount and they sheltered in trees, keeping out of sight until the herd had gone by. Later, they passed a village, saw peons working in fields, and a mile or so beyond, a big hacienda, all of which they gave a wide berth. They also steered clear of the well-worn trails that now appeared. They knew that *Yanquis* were never popular south of the border.

In the evening, a new danger loomed. They had stopped to rest the horse in a gully and Daniel had mounted guard while Elmer was filling their canteens from the stream that flowed through. Suddenly the boy came rushing back from his vantage point. '*Rurales!*' he cried.

Elmer cursed, corked the canteens, and the two of them scrambled back to the gully ridge, crouching down as they scanned the terrain. Riding about a quarter-mile away was a troop of *rurales* with their crossed bandoliers and kepis. Elmer knew that these half-wild *soldados*, so-called enforcers of the law, mostly consisted of killers and bandits released from prison. They had terrorized the *campesinos* of northern Mexico, and were to be avoided at all costs; they had the reputation of being as ruthless as the

Apaches. And their hatred of *gringos* was legendary. Thankfully it appeared they were bypassing the gully, moving back along the way Elmer and Daniel had come. That night they sat by their small mesquite fire, warming their toes and feeding on the gila monster lizard that Daniel had trapped. After it was skinned and the meat cooked, it provided a tasty meal.

'How long to Amerido?' Daniel asked, licking his fingers.

'We should make it in a couple o' days,' Elmer said. 'That's if we stay clear of trouble. Just think, in forty-eight hours we could be eatin' goat.'

After feeding, Elmer sat cleaning his Henry Repeater. Daniel looked at it admiringly. 'Maybe when I'm a Ranger,' he said, 'I'll have a gun like that.'

Another day of travel through the blistering heat came and went. It was after they had set up camp in a hollow, with daylight fading, that disaster struck. They were getting their fire lighted when they were startled by the metallic slotting of steel on steel as cocking pieces were levered. They glanced up in alarm to see four heavily moustached *rurales* standing on the rim of the hollow, their rifles pointed at them.

Elmer considered going for his gun, but then realized it would be futile. They'd been completely outwitted. One false move and they'd be riddled with bullets.

The foremost *rurale*, a giant with three chevrons

on his arm, gave an evil smile and spat out one venom-filled word: '*Gringos!*'

CHAPTER THIRTEEN

Within minutes, Elmer and Daniel were disarmed and their hands bound behind their backs. At rope's end they were led at a punishing pace by their mounted captors. Presently, as full darkness settled in, they linked up with the main column of *rurales*, which was under the command of a young officer. Elmer heard him called Lieutenant Baca. He viewed the prisoners with pitiless eyes and spat at them. They were given no time to rest as the march was resumed. No allowance was made for weariness. The ground seemed a mass of sand burrs and rocks. Elmer was bare-footed; soon his feet were a bloody mess and his weakened leg throbbed with pain. Daniel strove to stay upright as he was dragged onward. When he stumbled, the giant of a sergeant lashed him with his quirt.

Elmer had no idea where they were being taken but he knew that it would not be a good place. He felt sick with remorse at having brought the boy on this wretched journey.

The night was cold and the frosty moon and stars seemed distant and forbidding.

One brief stop was made and the men dismounted to rest the horses. The prisoners slumped to the ground, but all too soon the sergeant, whose name was Waaz, was lashing at them, cursing and blaspheming, and forcing them to stand. His quirt was made of rawhide and made heavy with lead. As the journey was recommenced, Lieutenant Baca rode at the head of the column, setting a murderous pace and not sparing a glance at the prisoners. At no time was there any attempt to communicate with them.

Stark dawn was painting the distant mountains with the first glimmer of day as they came in sight of a village – a straggle of single-storey, white adobe buildings lining a creek. From the biggest structure a Mexican flag of red, white and green fluttered in the strong breeze. This was clearly a headquarters of the *rurales*. The column speeded up as the horses sensed the nearness of water.

Elmer and Daniel, near dropping by now, realized that some form of rest might lie ahead, and they were goaded into a final effort.

As soon as they arrived amid the adobes, they were assailed by a pack of yapping, rib-thin dogs; Elmer felt sure the animals would have eaten them had they not been bludgeoned away with sabres by the *rurales*. The prisoners were hustled across a courtyard, passing a high adobe wall, aware that they were the centre of attraction for the numerous peons who stood around.

Shortly they found themselves in a tiny room – a cell. There were no windows and no light, apart from that coming through the doorway. A Mexican appeared and unfastened the ropes binding their hands. They dropped onto the dirt floor, working their arms to restore the circulation. A plump woman came in and threw a handful of corn down. She also provided a jug of water. 'For breakfast,' she said.

She and the man withdrew, the door was slammed shut and a key grated in the lock. They were in pitch darkness. They didn't know what to expect, but Elmer feared that they would be tortured, though he didn't reveal his suspicion to Daniel.

'You OK?' he whispered.

'I will be when we escape from this place,' Daniel replied.

'We better make the best of breakfast,' Elmer said, and they both felt about on the ground to pick up the corn. After they had eaten their scant share, they quenched their thirst from the jug. From outside, they could hear the shouts of the *rurales*. It seemed they were doing some sort of drill.

Eventually, they settled back on the ground, trying to sleep, but the heat in the cell was stifling. Presently they heard a scurrying movement across the floor; something bit Daniel's foot and he cried out.

'Rats!' Elmer exclaimed, and the thought was in his mind that when they had scooped up the corn from the floor and stuffed it into their mouths, they might have swallowed a ration of rat droppings. He tried to push the thought away.

He had just dozed off when the rattling of the key in the lock roused him. As the door was flung open, bright sunlight flooded in. Then it was partially blocked out as Sergeant Waaz and two of his men barged through.

The sergeant kicked Elmer and told him to get up. He struggled to his feet and his hands were again tied behind his back. He exchanged a despairing glance with Daniel as he was frogmarched out. He was escorted across the courtyard to the building above which the flag flew.

He was hustled through a doorway. Upon the door was a sign proclaiming CAPITAINE P. FAURY and he found himself confronted by an officer seated at a desk. He wore a smart grey uniform braded in silver.

It was a mystery how a Frenchman, Pierre Faury, had become a captain and a commandant in the Mexican *rurales*. Perhaps, Elmer concluded, he had come as a government adviser and had subsequently seen a chance of advancement in the country's military. However, it was obvious now that he was in no mood to enlighten his 'guest'.

Faury sprawled back in his chair, bit the top from his cheroot, spat it away and lit up. He had a thin moustache that curled at the ends to a fine point.

Elmer stood before him, his hands tied behind his back. His arms hurt from lack of circulation and his bare feet had left bloody marks on the earth floor. A guard stood on each side of him.

Faury took a long draw on his cheroot, then said, 'Why are you foolish enough to be in this country where Americans are despised, *mon ami?*'

From outside came the crackle of gunfire.

Faury smiled. 'My execution squads are at work,' he said. 'It is my duty to exterminate anybody who violates the law. Tell me why you are 'ere.'

Elmer cleared his throat. 'I came to Mexico to track down the man who murdered my wife.'

' 'Ave you succeeded?'

'No, but I know where he is.'

The captain's face hardened. 'Every condemned man pleads with me,' he said, 'and I know when they are lying. Now, I am too busy to listen to your pack of merde. You and the boy are spies and you will be shot.'

Elmer bristled with anger. 'We're not spies. But if you won't listen to reason, spare the boy. He is down-right innocent. He's Mexican anyway.'

Faury raised his hand impatiently. 'But he's 'elping you, therefore he's as guilty as you. Now enough talk!' he exclaimed. 'You will both die today. Now leave.'

Elmer felt a great surge of regret, not for himself but for Daniel. He should never have brought him.

He was grabbed by a guard who attempted to bundle him from the room, but he stood his ground. 'I'm tellin' you,' he cried. 'Me and the boy came to Mexico to kill Mateo. He raped and strangled my wife and he killed a good many other folks—'

'You say Mateo?' Faury snapped; his interest was

suddenly aroused.

The guard was dragging Elmer away, but the captain stopped him.

'Mateo?' he repeated.

'Yes,' Elmer answered, his voice tinged with desperation. 'He's wanted in the States. There's a big reward on his head.'

Faury stubbed out his cheroot. 'He's also wanted in Mexico for crimes south of the border.'

'Then let me kill him,' Elmer said. 'I guess I know where he is.'

'I also know where he is,' the Frenchman explained. 'I've 'ad my agents out. He is living under the name of Eduardo Anza in Amerido.'

'Then why ain't you arrested him?' Elmer asked.

For a long moment Faury didn't answer. He curled the ends of his moustache and assumed a crafty manner. 'I 'aven't arrested him for reasons of my own,' he said mysteriously. 'But I will make you a proposition. I will let you go if you promise to bring me Mateo's 'ead.'

'His head?' Elmer exclaimed.

'*Oui, mon ami.* The 'ead.'

'If you let us go, we will kill Mateo,' Elmer said.

'*Non.* I will not let you *both* go. The boy will stay 'ere. I want Mateo decapitated. If you do not bring me 'is 'ead within, say, two weeks, the boy will die . . . and so will you when we catch you!'

Elmer swallowed hard, trying to give himself time to think. 'One thing I need,' he said.

'What's that?'

'A pair of boots.'

Faury gestured to one of the guards. 'Fetch 'im some boots.' Then he swung back to Elmer. 'Two weeks from today, that's all,' he repeated. 'If you fail, the boy will be executed. I will shoot 'im myself!'

Elmer felt trapped. He didn't like the situation one iota; he didn't trust the Frenchman, but he had no alternative but to nod his compliance.

CHAPTER
FOURTEEN

He didn't see Daniel again. Elmer's arms were untied and he was led by the guards to where a cook was tending two huge cauldrons of what appeared to be stew. He was given a bowl of the steaming stuff and scalded his lips as he spooned it down. It was followed by a cup of coffee. He wished he had the means of getting food to Daniel but he was afforded no chance.

A young *rurale* brought him a pair of boots. Another, whom Elmer learned was called Alfredo, was assigned as his escort. Alfredo was about fifty, a tall silent man with blackened teeth and a drooping moustache. He was leading two horses. One was a big sorrel whose reins were handed to Elmer. In broken English Alfredo informed Elmer that he was to guide him to a point close to Amerido where he would give him his weapons and leave him to carry out his assignment. He also warned Elmer that if he tried any tricks, he would kill him. Elmer again wondered why Faury didn't send his own men in to seize Mateo, but could find no answer.

Soon, they were riding out of the village. Elmer was sickened at the prospect of leaving Daniel. He had no idea as to what the future held. All he knew was that he would have to come up with some plan and pray that Faury would keep his word to spare the boy if his conditions were fulfilled. Two weeks would pass rapidly. And now another concern troubled him: supposing Mateo was not in Amerido? He could be anywhere, on either side of the border, and locating him would be as difficult as finding an ant in an anthill.

They rode across the bleak, sun-baked landscape, and because he would no doubt have to make the return journey alone, he tried to memorize the route they were taking. It was not easy, for they were travelling through desert without landmarks apart from saguaro and mesquite, with only a thin ribbon of hills showing in the far distance.

Alfredo retained his silence, keeping in the lead, hardly sparing Elmer a glance. He knew that with the boy hostage, the *gringo* could not afford to attempt escape. The sun burned down upon them but they maintained a steady pace, stopping only rarely for respite.

It was late evening when they reached the hill overlooking Amerido and by then the heat had gone out of the day. Elmer gazed down at the jumble of low adobe structures. There were a few taller buildings including a church with two earthen towers, and a plaza. Beyond, he caught the glint of a river. Everything was rose-coloured in the sunset. Elmer took a deep breath, the ire in him rising. Was Mateo down there?

Alfredo looked at him and nodded, indicating that his task was done and this was as far as he would come. From his saddle-bag, he drew out Elmer's gunbelt, pistols and knife. He dropped them on the ground, as if fearing that if he handed them over directly, they might be turned against him. Then, with a wave of his hand, he turned and would have ridden off had Elmer not called to him, 'I want my rifle too!'

Alfredo swung back, frowning. He grudgingly drew Elmer's Henry Repeater from his scabbard and lowered it down. He'd hoped to keep it but maybe Sergeant Baca would have been displeased if he'd found out. He didn't delay further but spurred away. Soon he was lost amid the saguaros.

Elmer dismounted and retrieved the rifle and the belt, which he buckled on. He climbed back into the saddle and rode down the track that led towards the town. Everything seemed incredibly quiet. Not even a crow stirred in the sky. Again, he pondered on what his best course of action should be. If there was some form of guesthouse, he would book in and then start making inquiries. He wondered if his knife would be sharp enough to decapitate Mateo.

He was approaching the outskirts when he saw the tall wooden board. Big white letters were daubed across it forming three words.

Now he knew why Captain Faury had been unwilling to send his men in to arrest Mateo.

The three words were: *NO ENTRAR – PLAGA*! which translated to a blunt: Keep Out – Plague!

After Luiz Prado had gunned down Sheriff Harlock, he rapidly quit the lodge of Black Hawk, leaving the ancient Indian and the girl Little Dove in a state of shock. He left, expressing no thanks to them for reviving him from the dead, and he stole their horse into the bargain. His body was still scarred with lacerations that the bear had inflicted, and the pain from these sharpened his hatred for the man whom he blamed for his suffering and misfortunes – Mateo.

He drove the Comanche's old mare mercilessly, anxious to cover as much distance before the law realized that the sheriff had been murdered. On the third day his mount collapsed from exhaustion. He did not put her out of her misery with a shot to the brain; he was short of ammunition and he left her to expire in her own good time.

He did not intend to remain on foot for long. Also, he was armed with only his pistols and he felt the need for additional weaponry. When he crossed into Mexico and was satisfied that he was safe from pursuit, he remained concealed at the side of a trail while he contemplated further criminal activity.

He waited for two days until a perfect victim came along – a young *vaquero* clad in a fancy jacket, wide sombrero and *chaparreras* decorated with shiny brass buttons. He was astride a proud-looking palomino horse and there was a Springfield rifle in his saddle scabbard.

Prado couldn't trust the accuracy of his pistols at long range, so he walked out from his cover with his hand raised in a friendly gesture.

'*Buenos días, señor,*' he said. 'My horse has thrown me and bolted. I am now on foot. How far is it to the town?'

The *vaquero* eyed him, then smiled. 'Six miles,' he said. 'It's a long way to walk on a hot day. Do you want me to help you find your horse?'

'*Sí, señor.* That would be most kind.'

'In which direction did he go?'

Prado pointed vaguely to the hills behind him.

'Jump up behind me,' the *vaquero* suggested.

Prado nodded, accepted the man's helping hand and swung up onto the palomino's back. Once astride, he unsheathed his pistol, pressed the muzzle against his benefactor's spine and pulled the trigger. The detonation bludgeoned his ears.

The *vaquero* uttered no cry, but plunged from the saddle to the ground, the back of his jacket displaying a large, powder-blackened hole.

Prado struggled to control the panicking palomino. It took him several minutes before he was calmed. He eventually dismounted, led the animal to the side of the trail and tethered him.

He satisfied himself that the *vaquero* was dead, then dragged the body off the trail, hiding it in the bushes in case somebody else came along. The man was wearing a bandolier; slotted into it were a few bullets for the rifle, but unfortunately not many. Prado unbuckled the bandolier. He checked the man's pockets and found only a few pesos. From the corpse, he pulled off the clothing, boots and fitted spurs and replaced his tattered own. Sadly, the jacket was ruined with the gaping hole burned in its back.

Having assured himself that there was nothing else worth thieving, he returned to the palomino, untethered him and mounted, spurring forward. He patted the butt of the Springfield rifle and grinned, well pleased with the day's work. Now he must concentrate on his aim: to kill Mateo.

CHAPTER FIFTEEN

When Mateo had arrived in the sleepy little town of Amerido, he had assumed his real name: Eduardo Anza. Nobody knew that when he was away on so-called 'business' he indulged in banditry. He returned to the comfortable house he owned. Here, he employed as housekeeper the widow Señora Catalina Torrejon. For reasons known only to herself, she was fond of Mateo, or Eddy as she called him. She fussed over him, cooked tasty meals and even provided bedroom comforts when he was so inclined.

For his own part, Mateo, who was now a rich man, was content to enjoy the luxuries he could afford. At least for the time being. He gambled with the local gentry, showing an incredible lucky streak. He enjoyed his trips to the nearby town of Vallejo where there was excellent cock-fighting to bet on. In Amerido, he frequented the bordello and cantina, and even spent evenings with the padre, sipping his fine burgundy wine. Often he attended Mass on the

Sabbath, undertaking confessions, though he only recounted minor sins committed since his return.

It is debatable for how long this life would have satisfied him, because sometimes at night he dreamed of the old days, of riding roughshod over *gringos*, of lifting large amounts of loot. Maybe that would be for the future.

Matters continued in an agreeable fashion for a year, but then one evening, returning from a cockfight in Vallejo, the bullet came. He plunged from the back of his sorrel, landing in the thick cover of mesquite.

Luiz Prado cursed. For days he had dreamed of this sort of opportunity coming his way. The unmistakable figure of Mateo riding alone had made an excellent target, albeit a little further off than he would have chosen. Nonetheless, he had had him dead central in his sights It was as he was about to pull the trigger that the pressure of the rifle butt in his shoulder found a tender spot – a laceration that the bear's claws had left. The slightest of flinches caused his aim to move fractionally away from the intended target of Mateo's chest – but he believed he might have hit him in the head. He could not be sure. Mateo had dropped from his saddle like a sack of grain and disappeared into the brush, his horse galloping on. He might be dead.

But long ago Prado had reached the conclusion that Mateo was as crafty as sin, and he had the sort of luck that only a devil could boast.

Prado strained his eyes, scrutinizing the spot where Mateo had disappeared, but he could determine nothing. He was reluctant to quit his own cover, expose himself, and go to investigate. He gazed at the sky. The light was fading to twilight grey. Within an hour or so night would deepen. He would wait for darkness, then make his way down and hopefully find Mateo's corpse. The prospect excited him, though doubt still warned him that he would have to apply the utmost caution.

Time slipped away. Bats flitted above his head. His eyes ached with his constant surveillance of the mesquite, until at last dusk gave way to darkness. He made his move before the moon and stars came out. He crept down the slope with his Remington at the ready. He wished he had more ammunition. It grieved him that he had no money to purchase bullets, while Mateo had kept all the fortune they'd jointly stolen for himself. But now Mateo was dead . . . maybe.

He crossed the trail, reached the tangled mesquite. It loomed before him, the branches reaching out like ghostly claws. He forced his way into the thicket. All at once there was a great scurrying of movement before him and he nearly died of shock as the large black shape of a bird rose skyward, its wings beating the air like whipcord. He crouched down, his breath heaving. He was about to continue his search, when his hand touched something soft. He picked it up; it was a sombrero. A strange compulsion had him running his fingers around its brim, finding the hole

107

where the bullet had passed through. He wept tears of chagrin, knowing that somehow Mateo had eluded him in the darkness.

For days after his escape, Mateo remained in the town, reluctant to venture out and present himself as a target. He tried to determine who his assailant had been, giving no thought to Luiz Prado whom he believed had been killed by the bear. He knew he had many enemies, men who wanted him dead, but most of these were from north of the border. He decided to lie low for a while.

But then the plague hit Amerido and everything changed. It started with a few of the poorest peons falling foul of the disease and dying. When the town's doctor and mayor were smitten and passed away, matters became serious. Shortly deaths were commonplace amongst not only the impoverished, but the rich as well.

Mateo remained indoors with the blinds drawn, and Señora Torrejon boiled water furiously to kill infection. But she was obliged to leave the house on occasions to replenish supplies, and maybe that was when she caught the bug.

She was afflicted with malaise, pains in the limbs, headache and diarrhoea, together with a raging temperature. After five days, she developed a rash of red spots.

She lay in bed, twisting and turning. She kept crying out for him . . . 'Eddy . . . Eddy,' but it got on Mateo's nerves and he tried to ignore her. He chose not to frequent her room any more than necessary, for it smelt and he did not wish to become infected. He supplied water, but he was thankful she refused food.

She finally settled into a low, muttering delirium, and eventually, she died.

With absolute distaste, Mateo removed her body to the street for collection by the cart that gathered corpses.

He himself felt ill, but at first he put it down to his imagination. He checked himself over and over for red spots but found none. Even so, he took to his bed, inflicted by a shivering.

He lay for many hours, sometimes hearing women wailing in the streets outside as the disease claimed more victims. When he did lapse in to sleep a strange thing happened, for he was beset with dreams that were different from any he'd previously experienced. He saw again the contorted faces of people he'd tortured – men, women and children. He saw again the twisting bodies of those he had gunned down, or set afire or raped. He saw again the face of the Carrington woman as he strangled her. Their screams were ringing in his ears – their pleas for mercy. And he had spat at them and laughed. And in his dream, he now felt his own vulnerability because everything seemed to change. All his victims had risen from the dead, were chasing him, shrieking their hatred at him. He was running, stumbling and finally he fell.

He would wake in a lathering sweat, shouting his

own pleas, knowing that no mercy would come. It was in such a moment that he determined to make amends for all his sins. He would go to the padre, confess everything, and he would beg forgiveness no matter how many 'Hail Marys' he was obliged to recite.

As he rose from his bed and pulled on his clothing, a realization came upon him. He had no red spots and he was no longer shivering. In fact he concluded that he was not, after all, afflicted by the disease.

He left his house and passed along deserted streets, crossing the plaza. He was glad that the cart had recently done its rounds, clearing away the dead. He reached the padre's episcopal residence and stepped into the courtyard with its potted oleander trees. Everywhere was very quiet. Near the main door, the padre's surrey with its fringed canopy and brass lamps was drawn up, but it lacked a horse within its shafts.

He pulled on the big bell that hung at the main entrance. Twice he rang. There was no response. Gingerly, he turned the doorknob and stepped inside. No one was about, not even the major-domo.

'Father Almundo,' he called. He waited but there was only silence. He knew the padre's study-cum-bedroom was on the first floor. He mounted the narrow stairway and went along the landing. A knock on the door at the far end brought no answer, so he entered. The room was in semi-darkness, but the familiar smell of sickness hung on the air. He went to the window, raised the blind, allowing light to flood in. And then he saw Father Almundo.

The priest was lying on his bed, his face a mass of red spots. Mateo knew that he would be taking no confessions today or ever again. He was dead, his features twisted in anguish. Was meeting his maker such a torment?

Mateo was about to back out of the room, when he noticed the padre's vestments hanging from the picture rail – cassock with crimson piping, violet vest, coat and britches. An idea came to him, humility leaving him to be replaced by the old craftiness.

He quickly stripped off his own soiled clothing and pulled on that of the priest, together with the rectangular clerical cap. He drew a scarf across his face as a protection from infection, went down the stairs and back out into the courtyard.

He knew that the mare would be in the little stable at the side. He went to this and led the animal from her stall. Within five minutes, he had her between the shafts of the surrey.

CHAPTER SIXTEEN

Daniel was distraught when Elmer did not return after he was escorted out. He had heard shots from outside and wondered if he had been executed. The thought filled him with depression. He had no way of telling what had happened. For long, dreary hours he remained in the small cell, the monotony broken only by a *rurale* bringing him meagre food and water and emptying his slop bucket. He asked the man questions: What has happened to Elmer? What will happen to me? Why am I being kept alive? But the man did not answer and Daniel concluded that he was dumb.

At last Sergeant Waaz and another *rurale* appeared and ordered him to his feet. He scrambled up and his hands were immediately bound behind his back. He was then marched out into the sunlight – the fear that he was about to be shot had his heart pounding. But he was hustled past the grim execution wall to the office of Captain Faury. He stood before him just as Elmer had a few days earlier. This time the captain

112

had his feet on his desk.

'You are Mexican,' Faury said, 'so why were you 'elping the *gringos*?'

Daniel clamped back on his jangling nerves, forced his voice to sound steady. 'I was going to join the Texas Rangers.'

Faury contrived a wry grin. 'Why should a good Mexican boy want to join the *Americanos*?'

'My Mexican parents were killed by Comanches,' Daniel said. 'I was brought up by an American.'

Faury bit the end from his cheroot and spat it out. 'You are a strong lad. You should not have wasted your time wanting to join the Texas Rangers. It grieves me that I must now shoot you.'

Daniel stemmed his sudden surge of fear. 'What happened to my *compadre*, Captain Carrington?'

'He will not trouble you any more,' Faury said. He smiled to himself. The American would never return with Mateo's head within two weeks, of that he felt sure. 'I do not think we will keep you waiting,' he said. 'That would be unfair. You must be executed promptly.' He addressed the sergeant who gripped Daniel's arm. 'Take 'im out,' he commanded. 'I said I would shoot 'im myself. It will be a pleasure. Have 'im at the wall in one hour. I 'ave some paperwork to complete first.'

Sergeant Waaz said, '*Sí, Capitaine*,' and Daniel was dragged out. Five minutes later he was back in his cell with the door locked, his arms still bound. He collapsed onto the dirt floor and wept. The heat seemed more suffocating than ever. He tried to tell

113

himself that he wasn't afraid to die – but he was. And there was something else: their mission had ended in abject failure. He felt guilty. He believed that he had dragged all this misfortune onto Elmer and now there was no way he could redeem himself.

He felt he was battling a torrent as he struggled to prevent time from passing. He yearned to be free, to be alongside Elmer, who had been a good friend. His head and arms ached. He wondered what it would be like to be dead. Rats came to scurry about him in the darkness, and he felt almost in communion with them as they shared with him the last moments of his life. He wanted to make the most of every minute, but there was nothing he could do.

Eventually he gave up, lapsed into a stupor. He was roused from it when the key rattled in the door and he knew his time had come. It was Sergeant Waaz again; he hooked him beneath the armpit with his great paw and hoisted him up as if he had no weight. Another *rurale* placed a blindfold over his eyes. He was guided like a blind man to the outside and forced along at a pace far quicker than he would have chosen. The sun's heat felt as if it was broiling his brains. He stumbled but was held up. He sensed that many people were standing around, watching.

When they stopped, and Sergeant Waaz released his arm, he knew he had arrived at the wall.

'Where is the *capitaine*?' somebody inquired.

'He is coming now!'

There was a burble of excited voices. These were people who must have seen many executions, yet this one seemed to arouse particular interest.

He heard the sergeant say, 'All is ready, *Capitaine*.'

Faury's French voice came, though Daniel couldn't hear the exact words.

The metallic sound of a heavy pistol being cocked sounded. He was trembling, he couldn't help it.

Faury spoke again, and this time his voice came loud and clear. '*Adieu, mon ami.* This will teach you not to spy for the Americans.'

There was a lengthy pause, seconds that seemed like hours . . . then the gun exploded with a deafening 'crack!'

Daniel collapsed like a poleaxed calf. He lay on the baking earth, and as his ears recovered from the gun's blast, he was aware of laughter. He wondered if he was in heaven, but immediately knew he wasn't because dirt had ploughed into his mouth. He spat it out. The laughter was growing louder, not from one person but from many. He heard the crunch of boots beside him and the blindfold was suddenly tugged from his head. He was blinking in bright sunlight.

Captain Faury was standing over him, the pistol in his hand. He could hardly contain himself for laughing. 'Why did you fall down?' he asked.

Daniel forced himself into a sitting position. 'That is what people do when they are shot,' he mumbled.

'But you were not shot,' Faury said. 'My pistol fired only a blank. It was a test of your courage.'

Anger flared in Daniel's young eyes, but he held his tongue.

'I have been thinking,' the captain said. 'I think

115

you are too good for the Texas Rangers. I will give you two options. The first is that you join the *rurales*. The second is that you will die, and next time I will not use a blank.'

Daniel knew he had no choice. After a moment he said, 'I will join the *rurales*.'

Faury nodded with satisfaction. 'I must warn you. If you desert or betray the trust I will place in you, we will catch you and you will die the most hideous death imaginable.'

Daniel nodded.

The captain placed his hand on Daniel's shoulder, like a kindly father, and said. 'There is one more thing I must tell you. Before you join us, there is a test you must take. We need to make sure you are not a coward. It is quite good fun.'

'What test?' Daniel murmured. He felt he was beyond caring. Let them do what they liked to him.

'You must spend a night in the snakepit,' Faury said. He lifted his hand from the boy's shoulder, laughed again as a ripple of applause came from the onlookers.

Luiz Prado had just finished eating a raw lizard. It wasn't very wholesome, but it was all he had. Ever since he had been thwarted in his attempt to kill Mateo, he had camped, hidden in the mesquite brush overlooking Amerido. Once, he had ventured in close to the town but had turned back on seeing the sign proclaiming the plague. He wondered if Mateo would catch the disease and die a grisly death.

He hoped not. He still craved to kill Mateo himself and decapitate him. He would then be able to present his head to the Mexican authorities and claim any reward on offer and also satisfy his lust for revenge. One thing that grieved him currently, however, was his lack of ammunition for his rifle and handgun. He had used both in hunting game.

It was evening when a movement attracted his attention. A small, canopied surrey, pulled by a single horse, had left the town and was coming up the trail. As it drew closer, he saw that driving it was a figure in the unmistakable garb of a padre, complete with rectangular clerical cap.

Prado was desperate and frustrated. He had no wish to violate a man of the cloth; on the other hand, the padre might have a fat purse in his pocket. He decided against killing him and thus displeasing the Saints. Instead, he would simply relieve him of his money, which would only count as a small sin.

He stepped onto the trail, ahead of the approaching surrey, raising his hand in the friendly gesture he had used just before he had killed the *vaquero*.

The surrey pulled to a halt.

'*Buenos días*, Father,' he called. 'My horse threw me and I am on foot. I fear to go into Amerido because of the plague. Can I beg a ride with you?'

He gazed up at the padre. A scarf was drawn across, concealing his face, but there was something familiar about the eyes. At the same instant that Prado recognized this man he was hunting, Mateo snatched a pistol from beneath his cassock.

117

Simultaneously, Prado threw himself to the side, snatching out his own gun. Both men fired at the same time, but neither bullet found its mark. However, the blast was enough to have the horse rearing in panic, nearly tipping over the surrey and as its forelegs returned to the ground, the animal charged off at a crazy gallop.

Mateo fought desperately to retain his seat, but still managed to get off another shot. Again it went wide. Prado took a more measured aim. However, his hand was shaking and the bullet missed the hunched body on the surrey seat and sped onto hit the panicking horse, which plunged to the ground, dragging the wagon onto its side in the process.

Prado had a brief glimpse of Mateo falling clear, but he didn't linger. He ran headlong down the hill, kicking his way through the brush in giant strides. Perhaps Mateo had been badly injured in the fall; perhaps he was even dead. But Prado knew he had only one shot left in his own gun and, if Mateo had survived, he would stand little chance if it came to a shoot-out. Now all he could do was cover as much distance as possible because if further shots came his way they might not be so inaccurate.

Ten minutes later, he drew up, his breath heaving, and gazed back up the hill. He could see the canopy of the stricken surrey, even the bulk of the horse lying motionless – but there was no sign of Mateo. He shuddered.

He hurried on towards the town. He daren't return to his campsite and horse. Not with a nigh-empty gun.

Not with Mateo lurking. But as he continued the confidence grew in him that Mateo was out of the reckoning, that he had succumbed to the fall. Gradually his fear dissipated. An idea took root in his mind. He would chance his luck with the plague, go in to Amerido, find Mateo's house. And even more importantly, find the hoard of unexpended cash that was surely there.

CHAPTER SEVENTEEN

Elmer was stunned when he saw the sign proclaiming the plague. No wonder everything appeared so silent, and no wonder Captain Faury had set him free to attempt this crazy mission. He looked ahead at the jumble of buildings, all hazed now as dusk settled in. Many questions pounded at his mind: Was Mateo in the stricken town? Had he succumbed to the disease? If he, himself, didn't return to the *rurales'* headquarters within two weeks, would Faury really kill Daniel? If he ventured in to Amerido, would he fall foul of the plague? What hope would there be for Daniel then? He pondered long and hard and finally reached a decision. It seemed he had little option but to enter the town and chance his luck. But firstly he would wait for darkness.

He dismounted to rest the sorrel. He was desperately hungry, but he had no food. However, he had been given a canteen, which still contained some water. He poured a little into his sombrero and presented it to his animal to suck up. He finished the rest himself.

He hunkered down and wondered about Daniel. Had he been fed? Was he still surviving the cramped, rat-infested conditions of his cell?

So many questions made him dizzy, and the old pain in his leg still throbbed. The night seemed to take an eternity to come, but eventually he considered it gloomy enough to conceal his approach. He climbed into his saddle and urged his mount along the deserted trail towards the town. He went slowly, having no idea what he would do when he got there.

When he reached the outlying adobes, there were no lights or signs of life. Surely not everybody was dead!

He arrived at the head of the main street and saw the glimmer of candlelight showing from a window. His horse plodded on for some twenty yards, the clip of his hoofs on the cobbles sounding loud. Suddenly the moon drifted out from behind a cloud, a cold, white orb that cast grotesque shadows.

Off to his left he saw a faint light glowing from an adobe. Above its doorway he could just make out the words PABLO'S CANTINA. He pulled up and dismounted. He fastened his reins to a hitching post by a water trough, stepped onto the veranda and tried the door. It opened easily and he entered. On first glance, the place seemed deserted, but a lighted candle was set on one of the tables. It was burned halfway down.

He called, '*Hola*!' and after a moment there was a shuffling sound and a gaunt figure in an apron appeared from a back room. Elmer gasped. The man was a walking skeleton. His bones jutted out; the flesh seemed to hang loose from his bean-stick arms; his eyes glowed like burning coals. This must be Pablo, Elmer thought.

'*Señor*,' his voice was like the faint rasp of a saw, 'you should not come here. It is a place of . . . death.'

'I need food,' Elmer said.

Pablo started to protest, then gave up as if it was too much effort. 'I have very little,' he said. He moved out into the back room. Elmer sat on a chair and waited. From somewhere outside he could hear a woman sobbing with grief.

Presently the man returned with a chunk of mesquite bread and some corn tortillas on a plate, a jug of water and a cup. The food was stale; mould showed on the bread but Elmer was in no mood to be choosy and he rapidly devoured it. He was thirsty. He was tempted with the water. He poured some into the cup, raised it to his lips, but then put it back down on the table. He had heard that the plague was spread through water. Pablo stood watching him.

'You are *gringo*,' he stated in his rasping voice. 'You will die if you stay in this place. Why you come here?'

'I am here to see an old acquaintance,' Elmer replied. 'I don't know if he is still alive. His name is Mateo. Do you know him?'

Pablo looked puzzled. He shook his skull-like head. 'Nobody of that name in Amerido.'

122

Elmer felt perplexed. Was he on a fool's errand?

Somehow, he had retained some coins in his pocket. He drew a few out and placed them on the table. They were sufficient to pay for his meal and more besides. All at once he recalled what Captain Faury had told him. *He is living under the name of Eduardo Anza.*

'Do you know Eduardo Anza?' he asked, and saw Pablo's eyes widen slightly.

'No, *señor.* I know nothing.'

Elmer threw down some more coins. He was sure the man was lying.

'I don't want money,' Pablo said. 'I want what the Lord has taken from me – my woman and child.' And then he added, 'I'm dying, anyway. I have spots.'

'I'm sorry,' Elmer said, 'but I need to find the truth.' He placed the remaining coinage on the table. It was a generous sum. 'Eduardo Anza,' he repeated.

Pablo gazed at the money. He licked his lips.

'Where does he live?' Elmer persisted.

Pablo hesitated for a long moment, then he relented. He reached out with his skinny hands and scooped up the coins. 'Biggest house down the street, on the other side,' he said.

Elmer came to his feet, expressed his thanks and wished Pablo God's blessing. He left the cantina, but as he did so Pablo followed him to the door. '*Señor,*' he called.

Elmer halted and looked back.

'Maybe I should tell you,' Pablo said. 'You are the

123

second man to ask the same question tonight.

'You mean. . . ?'

'*Sí*. A half-hour ago. Another man, a stranger, a *vaquero*. I think he is an *hombre malo* – a bad man. He asked where Eduardo Anza lives.'

Elmer grunted with surprise. He touched the brim of his hat in recognition of the man's help.

He left his big sorrel hitched to the post and moved down the deserted street, keeping to the shadows and subduing the sound of his footfalls. There was no mistaking Mateo's house when he reached it – one of the few with a second storey. Treading quietly, he climbed onto the veranda and stood before the main door. No light showed through the windows. Who was the other man, and what business did he have with Mateo? He wondered if Mateo was inside, maybe asleep . . . or maybe dead from the disease.

When he touched the brass knob, he realized that the door was slightly ajar. Drawing his pistol, he eased it open and stepped inside. He was in a room that was dark, the blinds drawn. The air was tainted with a sickly staleness. He stood silently, straining his ears for sound. He heard nothing. Feeling his way, he crept to the two other downstairs rooms as well as the kitchen and found no sign of life. He tackled the staircase, climbing slowly, keeping to the side to prevent it creaking. In the first bedroom the blinds were raised, allowing the moon to shine in. There was an unmade bed but no other evidence of human habitation.

It was as he returned to the landing, moved along to the doorway of the second bedroom, that a pungent scent touched his nostrils ... unwashed body and stale sweat! He waited, holding his breath, his heart suddenly thumping. *Somebody was on the other side of the door.*

Impatience flared in him. He lunged, throwing his body against the half-open door, slamming it back with great force. Somebody yelled out and a gun blasted off – a deafening roar and a bright flash in the confinement of the room. The bullet smashed the far window, splintering the glass.

Elmer flailed with his arms, lost his hold on his pistol and found himself grappling with a shadowy figure. At first he thought it must be Mateo, but as they struggled he realized that was not the case. His opponent was a bigger man, and his hands were clawing for Elmer's throat. He brought his knee up to the man's groin and heard him yell with pain as he was thrown back, crashing against the metal bedstead in the process.

Elmer went after him but couldn't locate him in the darkness. However, his opponent found him with a vicious kick in the side. Ignoring the pain, Elmer grabbed his leg and twisted it, throwing the man down. He was on him like a catamount, ramming hard with fists and knees, pressing his weight down onto his body, ramming his head into his face.

His opponent was suddenly screaming with pain, screaming for mercy. Elmer relented slightly, still pinning the man beneath him. Both were slippery with sweat; they lay still, their breath coming in heaving gasps. Elmer knew that his opponent must be the *mal hombre* Pablo had mentioned. He also sensed that his own strength alone had not vanquished him . . . maybe he had another injury.

'*Señor*,' the Mexican hissed through clenched teeth, 'I can fight no more. I am badly hurt. I give in to you.'

'Who are you?' Elmer demanded.

'I am Luiz Prado. And I have . . . killed Mateo.'

'Killed him!' Elmer gasped.

'*Sí*. He was disguised as a priest, trying to escape this town. But he didn't fool me.'

'So you shot him?'

Prado grunted in assent. 'I think maybe he have cash on him . . . but he had nothing, so I come to his house, try to find where he had hidden it. Then you appear. . . .'

Elmer tried to absorb what Prado had said. He somehow couldn't believe that Mateo was dead. He suspected that the man was lying, but he had no way of proving it, not yet.

CHAPTER EIGHTEEN

Daniel gazed down into the pit. He was standing on its rim. His boots had been removed. His hands were no longer tied. A number of *rurales* were watching as Sergeant Waaz lowered a rope ladder over the side. The pit was some ten feet deep and fifteen feet across. Its sides were sheer – plastered smooth with adobe clay. There was neither hand- nor foothold.

It was dusk and although Daniel peered hard he could see no snakes in the shadowed depths. He suspected that they were hiding beneath the scattered rocks.

The sergeant gestured for him to climb down. For a second, Daniel considered making a run for it, to keep going until he was clear of this awful place, but when he glanced into the faces of the surrounding *rurales,* he knew it would be futile.

He swallowed hard and began his descent. It was then that he heard the loud buzzing sound from below, and he paused on the ladder, feeling sweat trickling down the nape of his neck. He had always feared rattlesnakes more than any other.

'Go on! Go on!' Sergeant Waaz snarled. 'Or I take the ladder away and you will fall.'

Daniel inched his way downward until his bare feet stepped onto the rocky floor of the pit and immediately the ladder was drawn up from his grasp. It was now quite gloomy. The buzzing had ceased, but he imagined that the air was pungent with the smell of snakes.

He crouched, making himself as small as possible. He was afraid that any movement would attract a strike. He glanced up, expecting to see faces staring down at him from above, but there were none. He felt deserted by humankind, left to die with only the companionship of rattlers.

He strained his ears, listening for slithery movement over rocks. He wondered how close they were. Perhaps some were coiled inches from where he cowered; perhaps they sensed the heat of his body.

Trying to grip his jangling nerves, he consoled himself with the thought that he had survived the first minutes of his ordeal. Maybe there was only one snake in the pit. Maybe it had gone to sleep. His hand closed over a small rock. He clutched it to him. It was, at least, a weapon of sorts.

Presently the moon drifted into view above the rim of the pit. Around him, everything was bathed in silver light and stark, black shadows. Then he saw the snake coiled so close that his breath was snatched

128

away. It was heavy-bodied, black-tailed, its diamond-shaped blotches blending with the ground. It raised its triangular head; its rattle was erect. This time the buzz was deafening.

In panic, Daniel erupted into life, slamming the rock with all his might into the reptile's head. It fell back. He was on it immediately, pinning its head to the ground with the rock, pressing with all his crushing weight. The snake threshed for an age; Daniel's arms ached with the effort of holding it. At last it lay still, its head nigh severed, and he shifted clear of it, panting and sweating. He returned to his original position, hunkering down. He listened for more buzzing, and sure enough he heard it, but this time from further away. However, his hope that there was only a single snake in the pit was false.

Presently the snakes quieted and the moon and stars became obscured by cloud, so that he was in total darkness. He knew that this would make no difference to the rattlers, for their sight was minimal, relying on their bodies to sense the warmth from other creatures. He remained as still as possible. If there were snakes nearby he didn't want to disturb them. He knew there was nothing else he could do but pray and this he did. Minutes lengthened into hours. He tried to doze, but suddenly he jerked to wakefulness. He felt something crawling over his foot.

He looked down and saw a big scorpion; it had pincers like a lobster and its body glinted with hairs. He jerked it away and crushed it with his rock.

Sometimes his ears seemed to play tricks on him and he heard again the deadly buzzing sound. Maybe he did or maybe he did not; he could not be sure. He wondered if Faury would keep his word and allow him out of the pit once the night was over. Or was it a trick, and he would be left here to die – if not from snakebite, from starvation?

At last he slept, fitfully at first and then more deeply. When he awoke a grey light was showing in the circle of sky that was within his vision. Gradually it filtered down into the pit. He gazed around for snakes but saw none. They must be hiding in the crevices. Shortly, he heard sounds coming from the village – the crowing of a cockerel, the clinking of breakfast pots, the murmur of voices, the barking of dogs.

Again, doubts assailed him. Was the plan to forget about him, to leave him to face a gruesome death?

An hour later, he looked up to see Waaz's face leering down at him. The sergeant tossed Daniel's boots into the pit, well away from the boy. He was laughing loudly. Daniel was obliged to cross amid the rocks, fearful that he might step on a snake, but he made it safely to his boots and pulled them on.

Meanwhile Waaz had dropped the rope ladder into the pit.

'Hurry up,' he called, 'unless you like it so much down there you want to stay!'

Daniel grabbed the ladder and, on stiff legs, climbed upwards.

A young *rurale* was assigned to watch over him. He was allowed to eat breakfast of eggs, tortillas and cornbread, washed down with coffee. After this he was marched over to the commandant's office. Captain Faury appeared to be in good humour. He congratulated Daniel on surviving his night in the snakepit and proving his courage.

'Per'aps you make a good *rurale*,' he smiled, smoothing the points of his moustache. 'You will get your uniform when you 'ave earned it, not yet. I 'ave decided that you will go on a patrol with Lieutenant Baca. You must be good and obey orders. I 'ave told 'im that if you misbehave in the slightest way, 'e is to whip you and bring you back to me. I will make sure you have a slow death, make you wish you 'ad never been born. But afterwards, I will show you mercy and decapitate you. You understand?'

Daniel said, '*Sí, Capitaine*,' But already his mind was dwelling on the prospect of escape.

In the afternoon, a column of a dozen mounted *rurales*, plus Daniel, set out on a patrol. They were all heavily armed with sabres, carbines and pistols, with the exception of Daniel, who was given no weapons. He had been supplied with a strong sorrel horse and he was positioned in the centre of the line in the charge of the veteran *rurale* called Alfredo.

The hours dragged by as they rode in a wide circle through searing heat. They searched the desert country for tracks of *bandidos* or Apaches, but they found none. They called at three villages where the peons showed them no hospitality and gazed at them with hateful eyes.

Lieutenant Baca frequently checked on Daniel, who watched out for any opportunity of escaping, particularly when they stopped for respite, but Alfredo remained close, even pissing alongside him, and no chance presented itself. He decided he would have to wait for another day.

He was weary when, that night, they returned from the patrol. He was glad to eat a hearty supper and retire to the cot he was allotted. For a while he thought of Elmer, wondering what had happened to him, but eventually he slipped into a sound sleep.

Next day he was set to work, peeling potatoes. He saw nothing of Captain Faury and Lieutenant Baca, though Sergeant Waaz watched him for a while and conversed with the cook.

On the third day of his 'enlistment', he was assigned to another patrol, which was commanded by Sergeant Waaz. Again, he was given no weapons – and a boyish *rurale*, Pedro, was put in charge of him. Once again hours of hard riding took them in a wide circle, following a different route from that of the previous patrol. This time they were drenched by a heavy summer storm. Thunder rumbled and lightning forked the sky, continuing for an hour.

By evening the sodden detachment was bone-weary. Dusk was seeping in as they reached a fast-running river and halted on its bank. Most of the men scattered into the adjacent cottonwoods to relieve themselves. Daniel, accompanied by his guard Pedro, did likewise. They found a small clearing, separated from the others by a screen of mesquite. Pedro was scarcely older than Daniel. He lacked the dedication of the previous guard, Alfredo. He sat down on the ground and within a minute was asleep. Daniel's heart began to race. Was this the chance he'd prayed for?

He didn't delay. Making sure he was out of sight of other men, he scrambled to the river-bank and immediately waded into the water. The current, strengthened by the recent rain, was soon drawing him downstream. He ducked beneath the surface for as long as his lungs would permit, coming up to snatch a breath before diving again. How long would it be before his guard awoke? He swam on with all the strength he could muster; it was made harder by the fact that he still wore his boots. He was glad that darkness had fallen rapidly. Presently, he quit the river, feeling the chill of the breeze, and, hearing no sound of pursuit, rested within a tiny cave beneath an overhang of rock.

His body ached with fatigue. He closed his eyes but did not sleep. Time passed.

He knew that so far he had been downright lucky. He wondered if Pedro had been reluctant to admit that he had lost his charge and maybe had carried out his own unsuccessful search, giving Daniel valuable time. However, sooner or later Sergeant Waaz would find out what had happened – and then there'd be hell to pay.

His fears were suddenly confirmed. Awareness gripped him and he whispered, 'Oh, God!'

He strained to listen. Beyond the cave's entrance, he could see the night sky silvered by moonlight. From close by came the clink of iron-shod hoofs and the blowing of horses . . . and Daniel died a small death. The ammonia-pungent whiff of horse urine tainted the air. And then he heard the maniacal voice of Sergeant Waaz blaspheming and cursing his men.

Daniel hugged against the rock, holding his breath, unable to stem his trembling. He wished the rock could absorb him

What would he do if they discovered his hiding place? The cave was a perfect trap. He fought back his fear. He bunched his fists, telling himself that he would die fighting, rather than submit to Waaz's wrath and the terrible torture that Faury had promised.

But within a minute, the sounds grew fainter, melting into the breeze, and he breathed again, guessing that the search party had passed over a ridge above him. How long would it be before they returned? Come daylight, they might find his tracks. He pondered on what he should do, and a vision of Faury's hate-filled face taunted him.

The thought somehow gave him renewed energy. He roused himself and crept from the cave. Then he set off, moving away from the route taken by the riders. He had no horse, no gun, and he had no idea where he was, but he was determined to make the most of his freedom.

Presently, he reached a shadowy mesquite thicket and plunged through it, not heeding the thorns that clawed at him.

CHAPTER NINETEEN

Elmer raised the blinds on the window, allowing moonlight to illuminate the room. The air that came in through the bullet-shattered glass was tainted with the sour stench of disease. He kept a careful watch on Prado. The Mexican remained on the floor, groaning. In the struggle, both pistols had fallen. Elmer retrieved them. He checked Prado's, found the chamber empty and tossed it aside. He levelled his own gun at the Mexican and said, 'You say you've killed Mateo. Where's his body?'

Prado struggled into a sitting position, cursing his pain. 'Sí, señor. His body … it is on the hill, outside of town.' In truth, he wasn't certain of this; he wasn't even sure Mateo was dead, though he hoped he was. He was intent on lulling the American into trusting him. He adopted a submissive manner.

'Take me to his body,' Elmer said.

Prado nodded. 'I may not be able to find it in the dark. We must wait till daylight.'

Elmer resigned himself to remaining there until

dawn. He had no desire to blunder about with this man in darkness. 'Why were you hiding up here?' he asked.

'I thought you were Mateo.'

'You said Mateo was dead,' Elmer said.

'I thought you were Mateo's ghost.' Prado replied.

Elmer grunted his disbelief. He asked, 'How come you know Mateo?'

'He killed my brother,' Prado said.

He looked at Elmer, the whites of his pleading eyes showing in the gloom. '*Señor*, I hurt badly. I was mauled by a bear . . . and now, the fight. Can I rest on the bed?'

Elmer said, 'Yes, but no tricks. I'm watching you.'

Prado rose from the floor and settled himself on the bed. Soon he was snoring.

Elmer was puzzled. This man was dressed as a *vaquero*, but he did not seem like a typical Mexican cowboy.

Elmer also felt weary. He seated himself on a chair, but he maintained his watch, his gun ready.

Time passed. He heard the church clock tolling the hours away. He was anxious to quit Amerido, for the place reeked of death. At last the first glimmer of dawn's light showed through the window. He heard the rattling progress of a wagon in the street outside. He rose, went across to the bed and touched the muzzle of his pistol to the Mexican's cheek.

Prado came awake and gazed around with alarmed eyes. Elmer found something familiar about the man, but couldn't determine what it was.

137

'Let's make a move,' he said. 'It's light enough now.'

Prado nodded and climbed stiffly from the bed. 'There's no need for the gun, señor. I will not run away.'

Elmer nodded but kept the gun pointed at the Mexican. They left the room and went down the staircase.

'Have you got a horse?' Elmer asked.

'*Si, señor.* Tethered in the trees at the top of the hill.'

They walked up the deserted street to where Elmer had left his own horse, tied by a water trough. Still keeping Prado covered, he mounted up. 'Lead the way,' he said. 'Take me to Mateo's body.'

The Mexican nodded. They left the ghost of the town, passed the sign warning them to keep out, and presently started to climb the hill. It was growing lighter. Prado was panting from exertion, but inwardly his mind was racing.

When they approached the wreck of the surrey, two turkey vultures rose into the sky. They'd been feeding on the dead horse that still lay between the shafts, its carcass ripped open, exposing ribs and guts.

'Show me Mateo's body.' Elmer demanded.

'*Sí.* It must be here somewhere.' Prado strode around in the long grass, searching. Suddenly he shouted with excitement, seeing a crumpled heap a few yards off. But as Elmer rode up, Prado groaned with dismay. Here was no body. It was just discarded

138

ecclesiastical clothes.

Gradually it dawned on Prado. Mateo was not here. He had eluded him yet again. Prado grew desperate. He noticed that Elmer had holstered his pistol. An idea came to him. He approached a hollow in the ground, a narrow hole and called out, 'Here!'

The way was too rugged for the horse so Elmer dismounted and joined him.

'Can you see it?' Prado said, pointing down. Elmer stepped forward, momentarily turning his back.

Prado sprang to life, made a grab for the holstered gun. Elmer felt the pistol catch leather as it was lifted. He felt the pressure of the barrel on his arm on the way up. He twisted around, ramming his elbow into the Mexican's belly, doubling him up in agony. The gun went off, the bullet whining harmlessly into thin air. He gripped Prado's pistol-holding hand. He squeezed, cracking the knuckles. Prado dropped the gun, stumbled and then went down. Elmer stooped to retrieve the weapon.

By the time Prado had regained his wind, Elmer had his gun pointed at him. 'You're too slow,' he growled.

The Mexican was sprawled helpless on the ground, his liquid dark eyes hysterical with fear. Elmer aimed his pistol at his head, his finger curled around the trigger. He could have killed him then and would have done so had he realized that he had been part of the gang that had murdered his wife. But his previous association with him had been mostly in the dark and recognition did not come to him.

With the man squarely in his sights, he paused, hearing the whimpered pleas for mercy. '*Por amor de Dios! No, señor!*' Elmer recalled the killings he'd been responsible for when he was in the Rangers and it gave him no pleasure. He had never killed in cold blood. He waited for half a minute, then he turned his gun to the side. 'Get away,' he said. 'I never wanna see you again!'

Prado scrambled to his feet, took one glance at Elmer, then ran off, stumbling, twice falling in his desperate haste. Soon he had disappeared into the trees further up the hill.

Daniel had been running for what seemed a lifetime. For a long while he kept mostly to the forest, welcoming its gloom, seeking cover wherever he could. He had swum across rivers; he had no idea where he was going. All he knew was that he had to put as much distance as he could between himself and any pursuers. He tried to convince himself that Sergeant Baca would not have spent too much time hunting for him. He would have had to lead his patrol back to camp. Faury would explode with fury when he learned of the boy's escape. Maybe he would send out a further search party. Daniel felt sorry for Pedro the young *rurale* who had gone to sleep when guarding him. He hoped he wouldn't be punished too severely.

He had quit the trees at mid-morning on the day following that of his escape. He constantly peered into the distance, fearing that he might see a column of *rurales*. Twice he swore he glimpsed riders bobbing up and down but when he blinked hard, he realized they were merely clumps of saguaro that he saw, shimmering in the heat. He prayed that he would soon come to a village where he might find a welcome, but he encountered nothing apart from sprawling desert and cactus, and far off, the hazy streak of hills which could have been a thousand miles away.

Towards noon, with the sun beating down on him, he was exhausted. There was no shade anywhere and he noted that overhead, a turkey vulture had been following him. At last he collapsed close to a towering cactus, curled into a foetus-like position and lapsed into a stupor. The vulture descended, landing a few yards from him, waiting.

A prod in the ribs roused him. He got his eyes open and looked up, but all he could make out, silhouetted against the bright sky, was a looming shadow. He thought: *Baca!* He glanced further afield and as his vision cleared he saw six mounted horsemen, sitting their animals, watching him. He cried out with despair, but then he realized that these men were not wearing *rurale* uniforms. His gaze swung back to the man standing over him. He was not Baca. Daniel saw the beard and the hard, weather-soiled features and the way his powerful shoulders bulged the seams of his sweat-dark calico shirt. He also saw the sheriff's badge pinned to his vest. His horror relented.

'What have we here?' the lawman demanded in a Texan voice.

Daniel struggled into a sitting position. '*Señor*,' he gasped, 'I am so hungry. Can I please have some food . . . and drink?'

The stranger emitted a deep laugh. 'Get up, boy.'

A minute later Daniel was wolfing down hard crackers and rashers of dried bacon, followed by water from a canteen. Afterwards he related his story to bemused listeners and presently he learned that his benefactors were Bannack County Sheriff Brad Wilshaw and his posse who had come south, having been granted authority from the Mexican government, in pursuit of Luiz Prado, murderer of Sheriff Harlock. Wilshaw was an old acquaintance of Elmer Carrington, and if this boy had been his sidekick, then he reckoned he warranted help.

The sheriff mounted his horse, pulled Daniel up behind him and the posse moved on, heading southward towards Amerido.

CHAPTER TWENTY

When Mateo had fallen from the surrey, the horse having been shot, he had hurt his back and had remained hidden in the grass for half an hour, cursing his luck that his disguise of wearing churchman's clothes had not fooled Prado. He was amazed that the man had survived the bear's attack. He guessed it was Prado who had shot at him days earlier.

At first he expected Prado would come looking for him but this did not materialize and he decided to make a move.

The night was flowing in about him.

Firstly he returned to the stricken surrey and retrieved his normal clothing into which he changed. Then he found his gunbelt and rifle that he had stowed beneath the seat, and, most importantly, the case in which he had crammed as much of the money as he could carry. The rest he had hidden beneath the floorboards of his house. He started up the hill towards the shadowy trees. He resigned himself to the prospect of the long walk to Vallejo where he had acquaintances who would help him in return for payment.

That was when a sound, coming from the forest, attracted his attention.

Hours ago Prado had left his horse close-hobbled in a clearing. Now, the prowling of some predator alarmed the animal and its nervous whinny carried clearly in the night air. Mateo grunted with satisfaction and changed direction, drawn by the sound. It took him some time to locate the horse, but when he eventually did he also found evidence of the campsite, together with the tack, that had been left.

He was about to gather up the saddle, when an idea came to him. His assailant was sure to return for his horse. Mateo would be ready for him. He extracted the lariat and knife from the tack, and uncoiled the rope. He tossed it up over the branch and adjusted the honda to create a hanging noose. Next, he cut out the narrowest of footholds in the trunk of the tree. He smiled to himself. The man would pay dearly for the inconvenience he had caused. He would walk into a trap from which there would be no escape, not from death, nor from the torture that would precede it.

Mateo waited impatiently through the dark hours. He adopted a position just outside the campsite's perimeter, his Springfield loaded and ready. He did not sleep but listened for sounds and heard the hooting of owls, the calls of coyotes and the occasional stirrings of the horse. Then, as the sun sent slivers of dawn's light through the tangled branches, he heard the blast of a single shot, fired by a handgun. It came from down the hill. He did not move but remained hidden in the undergrowth. Shortly, the panting breath of a running man became audible. When he burst in to the campsite clearing, he presented an almost point-blank target. In that instant Mateo recognized Luiz Prado.

He fired, the bullet slamming into Prado's shoulder, hurling him backwards. He lay upon the ground, screaming with pain. Mateo rose, walked to the writhing body. He pressed the muzzle of his gun against Prado's knee and pulled the trigger, shattering the leg and creating a spasm of agony in the fallen man.

Prado was raving as Mateo dragged him to the tree and slipped the lariat's noose over his head. He placed a further loop around his chest, beneath his armpits. He hauled Prado into an upright position and then hoisted him some two feet off the ground. He pushed his good foot onto the notch he had cut, forcing Prado to support his weight on this. As his blood seeped away, his strength would give out and he would drop, and experience a slow, choking death.

Well satisfied with his work, Mateo saddled the palomino and, gripping his case of money, rode off. He was slippery with Prado's gore but he did not care. His pleasure at stringing Prado up had been somewhat marred by the fact that he himself was not feeling well.

Twenty-four hours later, Sheriff Bradshaw, his six-man posse and Daniel stood in the clearing, gazing up with a mixture of satisfaction and distaste at the corpse dangling before them. On approaching Amerido, they had been drawn by the circling of buzzards above this spot and they had discovered Luiz Prado, or what was left of him after scavengers had been at work. His body was sodden with blood, but was now covered with a sheen of flies. His foot had slipped from its notch and the rope had strangled him. There was no way of telling the exact moment of death.

'You're certain that's Prado, Brad?' posseman Bud Wilson inquired.

Wilshaw nodded. 'It's him all right. I guess our hunt is over. We can go home.'

There were grunts of delight from his companions.

'We needn't have bothered comin',' another man commented. 'Somebody else did the job for us. But who?'

'It don't matter,' the sheriff said. 'It's not our concern. I guess he had plenty of enemies. At least we can confirm he's dead.'

'How will you prove it's him?'

Wilshaw smoothed his beard thoughtfully, then said, 'I'm gonna cut his head off, take it back. That'll prove we're not lying. I guess it'll still be recognizable.'

Everybody, except Daniel, agreed it was a good idea, although nobody volunteered to carry out the decapitation. However Bud Wilson was kind enough to hand the sheriff his big knife.

Later, there was some talk about going to the next town of Vallejo to replenish supplies, Amerido being a no-go destination, but Wilshaw decided against it, saying they would start back for home straight away.

Daniel was not happy with the situation. He had hoped that he could remain under the protection of the posse. He had also hoped that they would help him find Mateo – and even more importantly discover what had happened to Elmer. Now, with the prospect of the lawmen pulling out, he would have to make a decision. Either he could return across the border with the knowledge that his mission had been a failure, or he could stay in Mexico alone, pray that he could steer clear of the *rurales*, try to find his good friend and fulfil his original intention of bringing justice to the man he hated.

For a boy of sixteen the latter prospect would seem daunting. But Daniel no longer considered himself a boy, figuring that his experiences had matured him into a fully-fledged man.

Wilshaw tried to persuade him to return with them, saying it was crazy for him to stay in Mexico. However, Daniel could be stubborn, and the more they tried to talk him into going back, the more he insisted on staying. His intention would be to go to Vallejo where he felt he would be reasonably safe. Maybe he could earn some money while he formed a plan to complete what Elmer and he had set out to achieve.

Finally, Wilshaw reluctantly agreed to leave him. He and the other members of the posse had grown to like him, for he was a winsome companion. As a farewell token, they gave him a lariat and tack, and perhaps more portentously, a grullo horse that had been used as a pack animal but was equally reliable for riding. Daniel was profoundly grateful and bade them farewell with genuine sadness.

CHAPTER
TWENTY-ONE

After he had let Prado go, Elmer had remained close to Amerido for three days, watching the incoming trail in the hope that Mateo might show up, but he did not.

In the afternoon, he shot a turkey and, using the Indian method, he made a fire with sticks, cooked the bird and assuaged his hunger.

On the third night, he made camp in an oak thicket. He was tired and, with the onset of darkness, he bedded down. But in the small hours, he turned restlessly in his blanket, tortured by a dream that he was back in Amerido and victim of the plague. His body was covered in red spots. Soon he would die, his corpse left in the street for the death cart to collect, after which he would be consigned to a mass grave, forgotten and unmourned.

When a pain awoke him, it took a minute for him to orientate himself. Thank God the dream was nothing more than his brain torturing him. The morning was cool yet he was covered in sweat. Now, through overhead branches, he could see the glimmer of another dawn. *One more day's passed,* he thought, *and Daniel is getting closer to being shot.* And still he had come nowhere near to tracking down Mateo, let alone decapitating him. He shuddered. He ached all over. The fight he'd had with Prado had somehow left him drained. He figured maybe, at fifty-one, he was getting too old for such adventure.

Then he remembered his beloved Lauren, the torment she had suffered, and he knew he would never rest until either he or Mateo was in a grave.

He rose, stiff and cold, and pulled his poncho around his shoulders. He saddled the big sorrel horse and unbuckled the hobbles. It seemed an almighty effort. His legs felt numb and suddenly his breathing became laboured. He leaned against the horse. He tried to shrug off his grogginess, tried to convince himself that it was nothing serious. He knew he would need all his concentration if he was to keep watch on the trail into Amerido. His hope was still that Mateo would attempt to return to the town, go back to his house and the hoard of cash that was surely hidden within it. Mateo had to be stopped, preferably by a bullet in the head. No, Elmer told himself, not the head. That had to be preserved for Faury.

Nausea came upon him and he vomited up the food he had in his belly. Afterwards, he pulled the leg of his Levi's out of his boot and gazed at the inside of his knee. It was there that he saw the two red spots.

Now, his vision was blurred. He slumped to the ground, fell back and slipped into unconsciousness.

For a while the big sorrel waited, as if puzzled by events, but then a sparrow hawk flapped skywards from a nearby branch and this spooked the animal and he trotted off, gradually gaining speed. He was soon gone.

Daniel spotted the horse a half hour later, grazing on the sparse grass. He noticed that he was still saddled and this intrigued him. Every time he approached the big animal, he edged away but did not gallop off. He showed an interest in the *grullo*. Eventually Daniel got close enough to grab the trailing reins and was then able to pacify him with soothing words and a gentle pat of the withers.

He saw the weapon sheathed in the saddle scabbard. When he drew it out, his heart began to beat faster. He'd only seen one .44 Henry Repeater before and that had belonged to Elmer! His mind was suddenly racing. Did this mean that Elmer had fallen from his mount? Did this mean he was close by?

Daniel bridled his excitement as another possibility occurred to him. Maybe the gun had been stolen. Maybe Elmer was dead.

He led both animals to a nearby tree and tethered them. He circled around for ten minutes before he found what he sought – the tracks of the big sorrel. They showed clearly in the earth. If he followed them back . . . what would he learn?

He retrieved the two horses and picked up the trail. He lost it twice over patches of rock, but to his relief he found it again.

When he finally discovered Elmer sprawled on the ground, he didn't know whether to shout for joy or cry with despair. For a dreadful moment, he thought Elmer was lifeless, but then he saw the faint movement of his chest. He gripped his shoulder and to his relief Elmer's eyes opened and registered recognition.

'What's happened?' Daniel gasped.

Elmer attempted to respond but his words wouldn't come. His lips and tongue seemed swollen. He raised his arm, tried to wave Daniel away.

The plague, he thought, *he's caught the plague!*

He felt like dying himself, dying alongside Elmer. He felt utterly desperate. What could he do? But then he goaded himself into thinking. Sheriff Wilshaw and his men had discussed going to a place called Vallejo, which wasn't far off. If he could somehow get Elmer there, they might find a doctor.

Elmer was in no condition to ride a horse but an idea came to Daniel. For an hour he laboured, breaking off branches and tying them together with his rope. He checked Elmer frequently, but he only gazed at him with wide eyes and gestured for him to stay away.

Finally Daniel was satisfied with his work. He had fashioned a crude travois and he attached this to the big sorrel and spread his poncho across it. He returned to Elmer, dragged him up onto his unsteady legs and, ignoring his reluctance, persuaded him to take the few stumbling steps to the travois. Further effort had him lying back, tied to it.

Daniel mounted the *grullo* and, leading the sorrel, started off. Being dragged along, it was a rough ride for Elmer but he was in no condition to complain.

Presently, they passed a fingerpost indicating they were going the right way for Vallejo.

By the time they had passed through outlying fields where goats and sheep grazed, and Daniel saw the white buildings of the town ahead, the travois was disintegrating and he was afraid Elmer would fall off. Shortly they reached a half-ruined adobe. It was deserted, well out of town and standing alone. It had obviously been abandoned long ago. Beside it was a wrecked ox cart, its wooden wheels broken. Daniel decided to leave Elmer in the adobe, go into town and attempt to find a doctor. He explained this to Elmer, who now seemed much brighter and nodded his understanding.

Doctor Felipe Cabello served the community of Vallejo and was much respected by rich and poor alike. He was a tall, thin man with a studious manner who had qualified forty years ago at the Academy of Medicine, but he had learned more by treating *rancheros* and peons in poor communities. He was also a self-taught veterinarian and specialized in reviving birds injured in the popular local activity of cock-fighting.

When Señor Eduardo Anza called to see him, he

was horrified by the state of the man, who complained of vomiting and repeated diarrhoea. His appearance was ghastly; his colour was grey, his eyes sunken deep in their sockets. His heartbeat was rapid, as was his pulse. When Doctor Cabello saw the red spots, his worst fears were confirmed. Anza had the plague and must leave Vallejo immediately before contamination spread.

Anza accepted his orders to quit the town with a curt nod. His manner seemed to imply that he blamed the doctor for his sorry state of affairs. But Cabello showed professional patience. Perhaps he would have been less sympathetic had he realized that Anza was also known as Mateo.

'You must rest,' the doctor advised. 'Go to the derelict adobe outside of town. The one with the wrecked ox cart outside. Stay there and I will come and treat you this evening. You must avoid all contact with other people.'

Anza paid and staggered out, showing no gratitude. Cabello had felt a distinct dislike for him.

Elmer sat inside the adobe, his back against the wall, and waited for Daniel's return. A change had come over him. The swelling of his lips and tongue had gone down, the strength in his legs had returned, his vision had cleared and within him was the confidence that he would not die. He rose to his feet, and only after he had paced around within the walls three times did he feel the necessity to rest down again.

It was then that a figure appeared in the open

doorway. Mateo had heard movement inside the adobe, and, forever expecting trouble, came in gun first. The two men gazed at each other, both stunned as recognition dawned.

Elmer expressed his feelings first. The word burst from him as if of its own accord. '*Bastard*!'

Mateo swayed on his feet and despite his sickness a look of triumph spread across his face.

'Elmer Carrington,' he snarled. 'I have waited a long time for this. You escaped me once. You'll never do it again.'

'You raped and strangled my wife,' Elmer said. 'You'll rot in hell for that.'

Somehow, Mateo mustered a contemptuous laugh.

Elmer felt dismay. He had loaned Daniel his pistol in case he needed it in town. His Henry Repeater was leaning against the wall alongside him. He had no doubt that if he tried to grab it, Mateo would shoot him.

'I wish I could torture you, *amigo*,' Mateo leered. 'I wish I could slit you open, tie your guts to a horse's tail and watch you unravel – ha! But there's no time . . . no time. Say goodbye to this world.'

His look was insane as he raised his pistol and Elmer found himself gazing into the muzzle's unblinking borehole.

CHAPTER TWENTY-TWO

Daniel fired in haste, the big Colt kicking back in his hand. The squat, bandy figure of the man and the voice had been unmistakable. Mateo screamed as the bullet slammed into his back and he was catapulted forward, landing face down. Elmer grabbed his rifle and scrambled up. Blood was oozing from Mateo's wound and he was emitting a loud, groaning sound.

Elmer kept his gun pointed at him, never trusting him. He nodded his profound thanks to Daniel. 'You've saved my life twice today. I'll never forget that. Thank God you came.'

Daniel smiled, a proud glint in his eye. 'It was an honour, Captain.'

'Can you get me the rope?' Elmer asked.

The boy nodded, went outside, unhooked the lariat from the grullo's saddle-horn and returned. Elmer took the lariat, uncoiled it and then slipped the loop around the unresisting Mateo, passing it beneath his armpits. He pulled it tight. Daniel sensed what was coming and together they dragged the still-breathing Mateo outside to where the horses were grazing. Leaving some slack, Elmer fastened the end of the rope to the saddle-horn of the big sorrel. He was still unsteady, still faintly dizzy, but he got his foot in the stirrup and hauled himself onto the horse's back. Then he dug his heels in and they started off at a fast clip, soon becoming a gallop.

Mateo screamed once as the rope was drawn taught. He was dragged over the rugged ground, bumping up and down like a rag doll, leaving a trail of blood in his wake.

Elmer circled the adobe six times, when, panting, he finally reined in and fell from the horse. Daniel rushed to where Mateo lay, his pistol ready, but it was not needed. This evil man would never again terrorize innocent folk.

Elmer had risen to his feet, still unstable. He took no pride in killing Mateo, but the face of Lauren had been in his mind, and with it the terrible wrench of losing her and everything they had worked for. Revenge was not sweet, but it was something he'd sworn to do. Now perhaps her soul could rest in peace.

There was still the thought that the disease might be spread, so it was decided that Daniel would return to the town for food. Meanwhile Elmer sat in the adobe, the rifle slanted across his knees. The prospect of trouble still haunted him, but none came. A half hour later, Daniel was back, accompanied by Doctor Cabello.

Daniel had explained the entire situation to the medical man, who had at first been reluctant to believe that the person he had diagnosed with the plague and had since been killed, was a notorious bandit, but gradually he became convinced. He arrived at the derelict adobe fully prepared to treat another victim of the disease.

Elmer started to rise, but Cabello, speaking good English, told him to stay where he was.

'Please take off your shirt,' he instructed, and when Elmer complied, he listened to his chest with a stethoscope, then asked a number of quick-fire questions, nodding as the expected answers came. Next, he had him remove his boot and roll up his Levi's, exposing a single red spot.

'That's strange,' Elmer said. 'There were two spots last time I looked.'

The doctor smiled. 'A typical symptom. Your vision was blurred. You were seeing double.'

'Is it the plague?' Elmer inquired anxiously.

'No. You were the victim of *centruroides sculpturatus*.'

'What the hell is that, Doc?'

You were bitten by a bark scorpion, and a mighty vicious one by the look of things. I have never known such intense symptoms. It is not contagious. I will give you some opiates. You should feel completely better in a couple of days.'

As the truth sank in, Elmer sighed with relief.

Standing watching, Daniel was overcome, tears of joy streaming down his cheeks.

'The best thing you can do,' Cabello said, 'is go into town and have a good meal. I'll make sure you are made welcome.'

Elmer shook the doctor's hand, finding words inadequate to express his gratitude.

He and Daniel stayed in Vallejo for three days, enjoying rest and good food. True to the prognosis, Elmer recovered completely and, on his knees, he thanked the Lord for their salvation and prayed for those folk who had suffered in the plague. Cabello ensured his guests were treated with the utmost hospitality. They left with great sadness. The journey back was long. Mercifully, they encountered no *rurales*, nor any hazards that they could not overcome. They were jubilant, their mission completed. Daniel was to attain his ambition to become a Texas Ranger; Elmer would put flowers on Lauren's grave, maybe explain to her all that had happened, then he would open his soul to whatever the future might bring.

The aim of this book is two-fold: to meet the needs of students following the syllabus requirements of BTEC, the HCIMA examinations and City and Guilds courses; and also to provide a thoroughly up-to-date work of reference for all those engaged in tourist services.

The Business of Tourism

J. CHRISTOPHER HOLLOWAY

MSc, BEd(Hons), DMS, MInstM, FInstTT, FTS

Principal Lecturer in Business Operations (Travel and Tourism),
Department of Business Studies, Bristol Polytechnic

SECOND EDITION

PITMAN PUBLISHING
128 Long Acre London WC2E 9AN

© Macdonald & Evans Ltd 1985

Second edition first published in Great Britain 1985
Reprinted 1986, twice, 1987

British Library Cataloguing in Publication Data
Holloway, J. Christopher
 The business of tourism.—2nd ed.—
 1. Tourist trade
 I. Title
 338.4′791   G155

ISBN 0–273–02573–2

Printed in Singapore

Dedication

This book is dedicated to John O'Dell, former Head of the School
of Tourism at Bournemouth College of Technology and Principal
Lecturer in Tourism at Dorset Institute of Higher Education,
whose dedication to the cause of tourism education in Britain has
been second to none, and who I know would have written this book
himself if only time in his over-filled life had allowed him to do so.

1985   JCH

Preface to the Second Edition

Britain has a well-deserved international reputation for its success in marketing tourism, both as a destination for incoming tourism and as a country generating tourism to overseas destinations. Indeed, both the original concept of the package tour, introduced by Thomas Cook in the middle of the nineteenth century, and its modern equivalent using air charters, introduced in the middle of the twentieth century, were British in origin. The inclusive tour concept has since been emulated by the developed nations to a point where international tourism has become one of the strongest growth industries in the world. The potential for growth in this field, however, has hardly been tapped. Even in Britain, less than one in three of the population travels abroad in any one year, and the number of international tourists from the developing nations represents only a tiny minority of their populations.

Yet increases in leisure time, cheaper travel and rising curiosity about other lands, peoples and ways of life promise a bright future for the tourism industry in the twenty-first century. For developing countries, struggling to raise the living standards of their people and faced with the problems of competing with the developed nations in the fields of manufacturing and trade, the possession of attractive climate, scenery and other tourist resources offers the hope of economic stability and a better future for their citizens. For the tourist generating countries, the satisfaction of the tourists' curiosity about other countries and cultures should help to increase understanding and tolerance for others, reducing prejudice and international friction.

This rosy picture is not without its blacker side, however. The phenomenon of mass tourism in the second half of the twentieth century, with its accompanying pollution, congestion and human relations problems, is increasingly criticised by observers. Tourism is accused of trivialising the relationships between peoples of different lands and cultures, of degrading the artefacts and folklore of the less developed nations, even of neo-colonial domination by wealthy whites of the newly independent black nations. The image of a world in which the present developing nations themselves generate international tourists on the scale of the present developed nations—for example, 200 million Chinese travelling abroad each year—threatens to pose staggering logistical problems, quite apart from aggravating the present problems of tourism.

Whether tourism is to be seen as a force for good or evil in the world is a subject of endless debate. What is unquestionable, though, is that nations will have to come to terms with international tourism, and its effects must be taken into account in the planning of their economies. The needs of tourists and residents alike must be satisfied and their often conflicting interests reconciled. In this sense an understanding of tourism is essential for those involved in central or local government planning.

But tourism is also a business, like any other business, and one which has become increasingly multinational in structure and organisation over the past 20 years. It embraces accommodation, catering and entertainment; transportation; tourist sites and attractions ranging from historic homes to giant theme parks such as those of Disneyworld; and the organisers and distributors of tourism, the tour operators and travel agencies. Businesses in the generating countries have invested their capital in those destinations to which their tourists are attracted, and to take advantage of economies of scale they have diversified into other generating countries and across other sectors of the industry. The result is that tourism has also become a highly competitive industry, both within and between the generating countries.

To satisfy tourism demand competitively, to operate as an effective unit in the industry, and to plan for a future in which the needs of tourists and residents are met, all call for appropriate modes and levels of education and training for those who will work in the industry. This book is designed to provide the framework for the analysis of tourism, both as a business and as a new phenomenon in human relations in the latter half of the twentieth century.

The body of knowledge appropriate to tourism education is being continuously redefined. The Business Education Council has merged with the Technician Education Council to form the new BTEC which, working in close collaboration with the industry and its professional bodies, has refined its own approach to tourism-orientated courses, which have become more practically orientated and are finding greater acceptance and support from members of the industry.

The continuing growth of leisure and tourism during years of economic entrenchment in other industries has led to more demand for places on tourism-related courses. The industry, in turn, is coming of age professionally. Faced with a level of demand for employment which far outstrips the number of jobs available, employers are increasingly screening potential employees on the basis of sound vocational education qualifications. This has meant not only the wider acceptance of BTEC Diplomas in tourism, but also

a return to academic study of those in the industry who, frustrated
in their promotional prospects, are seeking to gain a knowledge of
first principles which will give them a competitive edge in an industry which during the past two years has been noticeably affected
by the growth of multiples. On the surface, at least, in terms of
current economic success, Big still means Beautiful.

The purpose of this book remains that of providing a sound
foundation for those interested in the serious study and analysis of
tourism as a business. It is designed to appeal particularly to those
following the Travel and Tourism options (stages I and II) on
BTEC Business Studies courses at Ordinary and Higher National
Diploma levels, but will also meet the needs of students following
other college diploma courses in tourism, and tourism option modules on professional courses such as those of the HCIMA or in the
BTEC diplomas in Hotel, Catering and Institutional Management.
The content will also be helpful for others already employed in
tourism, who wish to broaden their knowledge of the industry as
a whole and appreciate the relationship between their sector of the
industry and others.

The book's perspective is essentially British, but the(international
character of tourism requires also that a wider perspective be adopted
at times, and there are frequent references to, and comparisons with,
tourism in other countries) The writer of any textbook on tourism is
always in danger of falling between two stools in deciding the content
of his work. The material must not be treated so superficially that
readers do not gain the necessary grounding in the basic elements
and complexities of the industry; but at the same time, too detailed
treatment of the day-to-day activities of tour operators, travel agents
or other sectors can lead to the content becoming outdated almost as
soon as the book is in print. The tourism business itself is in almost
constant change and for this reason the training element in tourism
work—that is, aspects of the business such as the travel agency skills
of airline fare construction, ticket issuing and sales returns—are not
dealt with in this book. It is the author's belief that this need is best
met by specialist publications which can be continuously amended
and updated, complementing the work of skilled teachers in the
classroom. The author also takes the view that certain specialist
subjects applicable to tourism are best treated in separate texts, or
again they run the risk of superficiality. For example, marketing,
embracing skills such as salesmanship, promotion, advertising and
public relations, has important applications in tourism, but a knowledge of general marketing principles should first be gained from any
of the excellent marketing textbooks available, to be followed by
reference to the handful of specialist tourism marketing textbooks

dealing with this topic in depth. The same may be said for tourism planning, a subject essential for those planning to work in the public sector of tourism, and for travel geography, which will provide students with a more comprehensive background to the factors leading to the development of tourist resorts and attractions.

The structure of the book has been designed to help students in the systematic study of tourism as a business. The introductory chapters deal with the nature and significance of tourism and its historical development, with particular reference to the growth of mass tourism in the present century. This is followed in Chapter 4 by an examination of the business of tourism by reference to the general structure and organisation of the industry, and in the subsequent seven chapters by detailed examination of each sector of the industry in turn. The final two chapters are concerned with the role of public sector tourism and the impact of tourism in economic and social terms, with a look ahead to tourism in the twenty-first century.

It will be apparent to readers that a certain amount of repetition occurs throughout the chapters. This is intentional. Compartmentalising knowledge facilitates learning, so a sectoral approach has been taken in examining the industry and the way it operates. However, these sectors are interdependent and one cannot examine them entirely discretely. Rather than to cross-reference the material, which would require students to skim backwards and forwards through the book, wherever possible the issues are examined in their entirety as they arise.

Many earlier works have gone to influence the structure and content of this book. In particular, one must cite the important contribution to tourism education made by A. J. Burkart and S. Medlik in their *Tourism: Past, Present and Future* (Heinemann, 1981) which has become a standard text for tourism students over the past decade. My views and knowledge have also been shaped by my work in the tourism industry—in shipping, tour operating and retail travel—and in my subsequent teaching of tourism, and I owe a debt of gratitude to former employers and students, all of whom have in their own way helped to make this book possible.

My thanks go especially to Dr Adrian Bull, Senior Lecturer in Tourism at the Dorset Institute of Higher Education, who made a significant contribution to this book in the area of tourism economics, and to Neil Taylor, Managing Director, Regent Holidays of Bristol, for his comments and recommendations on the content of those chapters dealing with tour operations. Any errors or omissions, of course, are my own.

Contents

CHAPTER ONE

An Introduction to Tourism

CHAPTER OBJECTIVES

After studying this chapter, you should be able to:
* define what is meant by tourism, both conceptually and technically;
* explain the characteristics of the tourist product;
* list the various types of tourist destination, and identify the attractions of each;
* explain why tourist destinations are subject to changing fortunes;
* understand the purpose of statistical measurement of tourism and outline the main methods of gathering such data; and
* demonstrate the importance of tourism to a nation's economy.

DEFINING TOURISM

In a book dealing with tourism, it is sensible to begin by defining exactly what is meant by the term before we go on to examine the different forms which tourism can take. In fact, the task of defining tourism is not nearly so easy as it may appear.

While it is relatively easy to agree on technical definitions of particular categories of tourism or tourist, the wider concept is ill-defined. Firstly, it is important to recognise that tourism is just one form of recreation, along with sports activities, hobbies and pastimes, and all of these are discretionary uses of our leisure time. Tourism usually incurs expenditure, although not *necessarily* so; a cyclist or hiker out for a camping weekend and carrying his own food may contribute nothing to the tourism revenue of a region. Many other examples could be cited where tourism expenditure is minimal. We can say, then, that tourism is one aspect of leisure usually, but not always, incurring expense on the part of the participant.

Tourism is further defined as the movement of people away from their normal place of residence. Here we find our first problem. Should shoppers travelling from, say, Bristol to Bath, a distance of 12 miles, be considered tourists? And is it the *purpose* or the *distance* which is the determining factor? Just how far must people be expected to travel before they can be counted as tourists for the purposes of official records? Clearly, our definition should be specific.

One of the first attempts to define tourism was that of Professors Hunziker and Krapf of Berne University. They held that tourism should be defined as "the sum of the phenomena and relationships arising from the travel and stay of non-residents, in so far as they do not lead to permanent residence and are not connected to any earning activity". This definition helps to distinguish tourism from migration, but it makes the assumption that it must necessarily include both *travel* and *stay*, thus precluding day tours. It would also appear to exclude business travel, which *is* connected with an earning activity, even if that income is not earned in the destination country. Moreover, it is difficult to distinguish between business and pleasure travel since so many business trips combine the two.

In 1937 the League of Nations recommended a definition be adopted of a "tourist" as one who travels for a period of 24 hours or more in a country other than that in which he usually resides. This was held to include persons travelling for pleasure, domestic reasons or health, persons travelling to meetings or on business, and persons visiting a country on a cruise vessel (even if for less than 24 hours). The principal weakness here is that it ignores the movement of domestic tourists. Later the United Nations Conference on International Travel and Tourism, held in Rome in 1963, considered recommendations put forward by the IUOTO (now the World Tourism Organisation) and agreed to the term "visitors" to describe "any person visiting a country other than that in which he has his usual place of residence, for any reason other than following an occupation, remunerated from within the country visited".

This definition was to cover two classes of visitors:

(*a*) *Tourists*, who were classed as temporary visitors staying at least 24 hours, whose purpose could be classified as leisure (whether for recreation, health, sport, holiday, study or religion), or business, family, mission or meeting;

(*b*) *Excursionists*, who were classed as temporary visitors staying less than 24 hours, including cruise travellers but excluding travellers in transit.

Once again the definition becomes overly restrictive in failing to take domestic tourism into account. The inclusion of "study" in this definition is an interesting one since it is often excluded in later definitions, as are courses of education.

A working party for the proposed Institute of Tourism in Britain (now the Tourism Society) attempted to clarify the concept, and reported in 1976: "Tourism is the temporary short-term movement of people to destinations outside the places where they normally live and work, and activities during their stay at these destinations;

it includes movement for all purposes, as well as day visits or excursions."

This broader definition was reformulated slightly without losing any of its simplicity at the International Conference on Leisure-Recreation-Tourism, held by the AIEST and the Tourism Society in Cardiff in 1981: "Tourism may be defined in terms of particular activities selected by choice and undertaken outside the home environment. Tourism may or may not involve overnight stays away from home."

def

The above definitions have been quoted at length because they reveal how broadly the concept of tourism must be defined in order to embrace all forms of the phenomenon. Indeed, the final definition could be criticised on the grounds that, unless the activities involved are more clearly specified, it could be applied equally to burglary or any of a hundred other activities! Here, no guidance on the particular activities is offered, nor does it get us any nearer the solution as to how far away a tourist must travel from his home base before he can be termed as such.

Figure 1 illustrates the guidelines produced by the WTO to categorise travellers for statistical purposes. The loopholes in the definitions remain, however. Even attempts to classify tourists as those travelling for purposes unconnected with employment can be misleading if one looks at the social consequences of tourism. Ruth Pape has drawn attention to the case of nurses in the United States who, after qualifying, gravitate to California for their first jobs, since employment is easily found and they can enjoy the benefits of the leisure facilities which California offers. They may spend a year or more in this job before moving on, but the important point is that they have been motivated to come to that area not because of the work but because of the area's attraction to tourists. Many similar examples could be given, of secretaries working their way around the world (a kind of twentieth century Grand Tour?), or workers who seek summer jobs in the seaside resorts of the English South Coast or the French campsites.

Conceptually, then, to define tourism precisely is a difficult if not impossible task. To produce a technical definition for statistical purposes is less problematic. As long as it is clear what the data comprises, and one compares like with like, whether inter-regionally or internationally, we can leave the conceptual discussion to academics. With the advent of twentieth century mass tourism, perhaps the most accurate definition of a tourist is "someone who travels to see something different, and then complains when he finds things are not the same"!

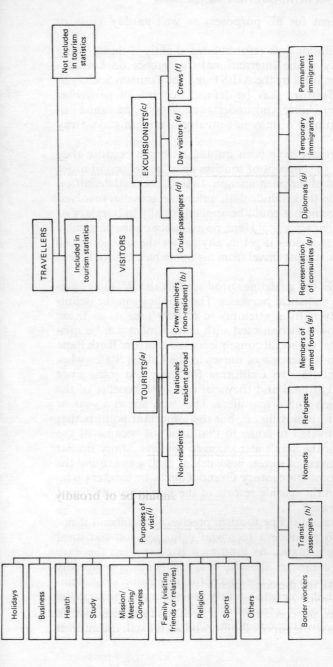

Source: WTO, Methodological Supplement to World Trade Statistics, 1978

Fig. 1 *Classification of travellers*

(a) Visitors who spend at least one night in the country visited. (b) Foreign air or ship crews docked or in lay over and who used the accommodation establishments of the country visited. (c) Visitors who do not spend at least one night in the country visited although they might visit the country during one day or more and return to their ship or train to sleep. (d) Normally included in excursionists. Separate classification of these visitors is nevertheless preferable. (e) Visitors who come and leave the same day. (f) Crews who are not residents of the country visited and who stay in the country for the day. (g) When they travel from their country of origin to the duty station and vice versa. (h) Who do not leave the transit area of the airport or at the port in certain countries, transit may involve a stay of one day or more. In this case they should be included in the visitor statistics. (i) Main purposes of visit as defined by the Rome Conference (1963).

THE TOURIST PRODUCT

Having attempted to define tourism, we can now look at the tourist product itself. The first characteristic of the product to note is that it is a service rather than a tangible good. Its intangibility poses problems for those concerned in marketing tourism. It cannot, for example, be inspected by prospective purchasers before they buy, as can a washing machine, a hi-fi or other consumer durable. The purchase of a package tour is a speculative investment involving a high degree of trust on the part of the purchaser.

It has often been said that selling holidays is "selling dreams", and this is to a great extent true. When a tourist buys a package tour abroad, he is buying more than a simple collection of services, i.e. aircraft seat, hotel room, three meals a day and the opportunity to sit on a sunny beach; he is also buying the temporary use of a strange environment, incorporating novel geographical features—old world towns, tropical landscapes—plus the culture and heritage of the region and other intangible benefits such as service, atmosphere, hospitality. The planning and anticipation of the holiday may be as much a part of its enjoyment as is the trip itself, and the later recalling of the experience and the reviewing of slides or photos is an added bonus. The product is therefore largely psychological in its attractions.

The challenge for the marketer of tourism is to make the dream equal the reality. The difficulty in achieving this is that tourism is not a homogeneous product; that is, it tends to vary in standard and quality over time, unlike, say, the production of a television set. A package tour, or even a flight on an aircraft, cannot be consistently of equal standard. A bumpy flight can change an enjoyable travel experience into a nightmare, and a holiday at the seaside can be ruined by a prolonged rainy spell. Because a tour comprises a compendium of different products, an added difficulty in maintaining standards is that each element of the product should be of broadly similar quality; a good room and service at a hotel may be spoiled by poor food, or the experience of an excellent hotel may be marred by a disappointing flight to the destination. An element of chance is always present in the purchase of any service, and where the purchase must precede the actual consumption of the product, as is the case with tourism, the risk for the consumer is heightened.

Another characteristic of tourism is that it cannot be brought to the consumer; rather, the consumer must be taken to his product. In the short term, at least, the supply of this product is fixed; the number of hotel bedrooms available at a particular resort cannot be varied to meet the changing demands of holidaymakers during a particular season. The unsold hotel room or aircraft seat cannot be stored for later sale, as is the case with tangible products; hence great efforts are made to fill hotel rooms and aircraft by, for example, heavily discounting the prices of these products at the last minute. If the market demand changes, as it does frequently in the field of tourism, the supply of tourism products may take time to adapt—a hotel is built to last for many years and must remain profitable over that period. These problems, unique to tourism, call for considerable ingenuity on the part of those responsible for marketing it.

THE NATURE OF A TOUR

To analyse the topic of tourism systematically, it will be helpful at this point to examine more closely the characteristics of a tour under five broad categories.

The motivation for touring

Motivation identifies first the purposes of the visit. There are a number of recognised categories of purpose, the most common of these being:

(a) holiday (including visits to friends and relatives, known as VFR travel);

(b) business (including meetings, conferences, etc.); and

(c) other (including study, religious pilgrimages, health, etc.).

It is important to distinguish between each purpose of visit because the characteristics of each will differ. Business travel will differ from holiday travel in that the businessman has little discretion in his choice of destination or the timing of his trip. Business trips frequently have to be arranged at short notice to offices and dealers overseas, and for brief periods of time. The businessman needs the convenience of frequent, regular transport, efficient service and good facilities at his destination. Because his company will be paying for the tour, he is less concerned about the price for these facilities; higher prices will not seriously impair his travel plans, nor would lower prices encourage him to travel more frequently—we can say, therefore, that business travel is relatively *price inelastic*. Holiday travel, however, is highly *price elastic*: lower prices *will* encourage an increase in the number of holidaymakers generally and will encourage other holidaymakers to switch their destinations. Holiday travellers will be prepared to delay their travel, or will book well in advance of their travel dates, if this means that they can substantially reduce their costs.

We therefore need to identify the reasons why a specific type of holiday or resort is chosen. Different markets look for different qualities in the same resort; a ski resort, for example, may be selected because of its excellent slopes and sporting facilities, because of its healthy mountain air, or because of the social life which it offers to skiers and non-skiers alike.

The characteristics of the tour

These define what kind of visit is made and to where. First, one can distinguish between *domestic* tourism and *international* tourism. The former refers to travel taken exclusively within the national boundaries of the traveller's country. The decision to take one's holiday within the borders of one's own country is an important economic one since it will affect the balance of payments and reduce the outflow of money from that country.

Next, the kind of visit should be determined. Is it to be to a seaside resort, mountain resort, country town, health spa, or major city? Is it to be a single centre visit, multicentre visit (involving a stopover at two or more places) or a touring visit involving extensive travel with brief overnight stays along the route? Or it could mean a sea cruise, in which case a decision has to be made as to whether to count this as international travel if the vessel visits foreign ports.

The length of time spent on the visit needs to be identified next. A trip that does not involve an overnight stay is termed a day trip or excursion. Expenditure by day trippers is generally less than that of overnight visitors and the statistical measurement of these forms of tourism is often collected separately. A visitor who stops at least one night at a destination is termed a tourist, as opposed to an excursionist, but he can, of course, in turn make day trips to other destinations from his base; indeed, a domestic tourist to, say, Eastbourne, may make a day excursion to France and in doing so becomes an international visitor for the purposes of the records of that country.

Again, for the purposes of statistical measurement we shall need to define some maximum length of stay, beyond which a visitor should no longer be considered a tourist for the records but take on the role of "resident". This maximum figure must of necessity be an arbitrary one, but is generally accepted as one year.

Mode of tour organisation

This further qualifies the form which the tour takes. A tour may be *independent* or *packaged*. A package tour (more correctly called an "inclusive tour") is an arrangement in which transport and accommodation is purchased by the tourist at an all-inclusive price and the price of the individual elements cannot be determined by the purchaser himself. The tour operator who organises the package tour programme purchases transport and hotel accommodation in advance, generally obtaining these at a lower price because he is buying them in bulk, and he then sells his tours individually to holidaymakers, direct or through travel agents. By contrast, an independent tour is one in which the tourist purchases these facilities separately, either making reservations in advance through a travel agent or *ad hoc* on route during his tour.

Tourists purchasing inclusive tours may do so on the basis of either individual or group travel. An independent inclusive tour is one in which the tourist travels to his destination individually, while on a group inclusive tour he will travel in company with other tourists who have purchased the same programme. The abbreviations IIT and GIT are used respectively to describe these two forms of package tour where scheduled airline flights are used.

The composition of the tour

This consists of the elements comprising the visit. All tourism involves travel away from one's usual place of residence, as we have seen, and in the case of "tourists" as opposed to "excursionists" it will also include food and accommodation. So we must here identify the form of travel—air, sea, road or rail—that will be used. If air transport is involved, is it charter or scheduled service? If an overnight stay, will this be in a hotel, guest house, campsite or self-catering facility? How will the passenger travel between airport and hotel—by coach, private taxi or airport limousine? A package tour will normally comprise transport, accommodation and transfers, but in some cases additional services may be provided in the programme, such as car hire at the destination, excursions by coach or theatre entertainment.

The characteristics of the tourist

An analysis of tourism must also include an analysis of the tourist himself. We have already distinguished between holidaymakers and businessmen. Now we need to identify the tourist by nationality, by socioeconomic background (social class and life-style), by sex and age. What stage of their life-cycle are they in? What are their personality characteristics?

Such information is valuable not only for the purpose of record keeping. It will also help to shed light on the reasons why people travel and how patterns of travel differ between different markets. The more that is known about these factors, the more effectively will those in the industry be able to meet the needs of their customers and develop appropriate strategies to promote their products in different markets.

THE TOURIST DESTINATION

We can now examine the tourist destination itself. The success of a tourist destination depends upon the interrelationship of three basic factors: its attractions; its amenities (or facilities); and its accessibility for tourists.

Attractions

The principal appeal of a destination is the attraction or aggregate of attractions which the destination offers. Cataloguing and analysing these attractions is no easy matter, especially when one recognises that what appeals to one tourist may actually deter another.

We can start by distinguishing between site and event attractions. A site attraction is one in which the destination itself exercises appeal, while an event attraction is one in which tourists are drawn to the destination largely or solely because of what is taking place there. A site attraction may be a country, a geographical region such as the Alps or the Lake District, a city, resort, or even a specific building. Examples of event attractions include exhibitions and festivals such as the Edinburgh Festival, sports events such as the Olympic Games, or an international conference)(The success of event attractions is often multiplied if the site is an attraction in its own right.

We must now distinguish between natural and man-made (or purpose-built) attractions. Natural attractions include beaches, mountains, open countryside or game parks; climatic features such as sunshine and pure air; unusual flora and fauna; and "spectacles" such as Niagara Falls or the Grand Canyon. Man-made attractions include buildings of historical or architectural interest; holiday camps; or "theme parks" such as Disneyworld in the USA or Thorpe Park in England.)

Obviously, the success of many tourist destinations will depend upon the combination of man-made and natural attractions which they have to offer; a rural manor house may be as much an attraction because of its setting as its architecture, and of course a holiday camp must be sited in an area which is also attractive for its climate and location. The success of the early spas rested on their ability to combine man-made attractions with the supposed medical benefits of the natural springs, and a ski resort requires both the good geographical features of weather and mountain slopes and the construction of adequate ski-runs, ski-lifts and "après-ski" entertainment.)

Site attractions may be *nodal* or *linear* in character. A nodal destination is one in which the attractions of the area are closely grouped geographically; although tourists may make day excursions out of the region, their holiday is centred on a particular resort or area which provides most of the attractions and amenities they require. Seaside resorts and cities are examples of nodal attractions, this making them ideal as destinations to be packaged by the tour operators. This has led to the concept of "honeypot" tourism development, in which tourism planners concentrate the development of tourism resources, whether in the construction of new resorts or the embellishment of existing ones. Aviemore in Scotland is an example of recent nodal tourism development—a purpose-built winter and summer holiday resort with all its attractions and amenities closely grouped. This development helps to preserve the natural beauty of the unexploited countryside.

Linear tourism is that in which the attractions are spread over a wide geographical area, with no obvious centres of interest. Examples include the Shenandoah Valley in the USA, and the natural beauty of the Highlands of Scotland or the Scandinavian countryside. Such destinations lend themselves best to touring holidays by coach or private car with accommodation in motels or private bed-and-breakfast facilities, since such mobile tourists are likely to stay only one or two nights at each stopover point.

Readers are reminded that much of the attraction of a destination is intangible, depending upon the image which the potential tourist has of it. India will be seen by one group of travellers as an outstanding attraction because of its unusual scenery and buildings, its strange culture and traditions, but others will reject the country as a potential destination because of its poverty or its alien culture. The image of a destination, whether favourable or unfavourable, tends to be built up over the course of many years. Thus for many continental Europeans, Britain is still seen as a fog-engulfed, rain-battered island noted for the reserve of its inhabitants, an image frequently stereotyped in the media, which increases the National Tourist Office's difficulty in selling the country.

Amenities

However attractive a destination, its potential for tourism will be limited unless the basic amenities which a tourist requires are provided. Essentially this means accommodation and food, but will include local transport and entertainment at the site. Amenities will differ according to the attraction of the site; at the Grand Canyon, for example, it would clearly detract from the beauty of the attraction to over-develop the rim with tourist hotels similar to those built in beach resorts. It should also be recognised that sometimes the amenity is itself the principal attraction, as is the case when a resort hotel is built to offer every conceivable on-site entertainment in a previously unexploited region. An area famed for its regional food may also attract gourmets to its restaurants, which then become not just amenities but the attraction themselves.')

Accessibility

A third factor which must be present to attract tourists is ease of access to the destination. While the more intrepid explorers may be prepared to put themselves to great inconvenience to see some of the great scenic attractions of the world, a destination will not attract mass tourists until it is readily accessible, regardless of the amenities it may have to offer. In this sense "readily accessible" means having regular and convenient forms of transport, in terms of time/distance, to the country from the generating country, and all at a reasonable price. If private transport is to be the means of access, tourism flow will depend upon adequate roads, petrol stations, etc. Here, the importance of amenities designed to facilitate accessibility becomes apparent—good railways and coach services, airports and sea ports.

On the other hand, if access becomes too easy this may result in over-demand and congestion, making the destination less attractive to tourists. The introduction of new motorways in Britain has opened up the Lake District and the West Country to motorists in a way not possible before, leading to increasing numbers of day trippers and severe congestion at resorts which are in high demand.

Now that we have looked at the factors motivating tourists to visit certain sites, let us look at two very different examples of resort destinations and explore what it is that makes them successful.)

Bath, England

This city firmly established its reputation as a spa over 200 years ago. Its attraction lay initially in the supposed healing properties of its mineral springs, and it became fashionable to "take the waters" for the sake of one's health at this and other contemporary spas in Britain. Over time it gradually passed from fashionable resort to fashionable place of residence as its social amenities increased. The fine buildings erected in the eighteenth and early nineteenth centuries in turn attracted the attention of the mass tourists of the twentieth century, making the town a popular venue for domestic and foreign tourists alike. Mass tourism has been aided by the provision of good hotels, guest houses and restaurants, a growing number of unique museums and cultural events such as the Bath Festival. Specialist shops and boutiques have added to the town's attraction. Its location close to the M4 and M5 motorways, on British Rail's Inter-city service only an hour from London and close to Bristol, have all heightened its attraction. It is close enough to London to make it an ideal destination for one day tours, and as a centre for the Cotswolds to the North and the Mendips to the South it is within easy access of some of Britain's best scenery, using private car or coach.)

Oberammergau, West Germany

This village resort in Bavaria manages to combine both site and event attractions. As a mountain resort in the Alps it lies at the heart of Europe, accessible through Munich by air from all over the world and with good road connections from north (Germany) and south (Austria). It is both a winter and summer resort, offering summer guests peace and tranquillity, healthy mountain air, outstanding alpine scenery and opportunities for hiking and mountaineering, with skiing in the winter. It offers unique wood-carving shops and the outstanding shopping centres of nearby Garmisch-Partenkirchen and Munich (less than an hour's drive away). A good range of accommodation is available at all prices and a recently-installed indoor and outdoor swimming pool complex has added to the amenities. But once every ten years, Oberammergau becomes the Mecca for hundreds of thousands of international tourists who wish to see the famous passion play which has been staged here since the middle ages. In other years the theatre where the play is staged still attracts countless day trippers.

These examples highlight another important point in relation to tourist destinations; the chances of their long-term success will be considerably enhanced if the attractions they offer are unique. Uniqueness is relative, however. There is only one Oberammergau passion play in the world, just as there is only one Grand Canyon, Eiffel Tower or Big Ben. But to draw tourists from the developed nations of Northern Europe and North America, mass tourism is based largely upon the attractions of sand, sea and sun, which the Mediterranean and Caribbean countries provide. Such attractions are seldom unique, nor do their customers require them to be so. These tourists will be satisfied so long as the amenities are adequate, the resort remains accessible and prices are competitive. If prices rise, however, or competing countries can offer similar facilities at lower prices, holidaymakers will switch their allegiance. Because of the singular properties of "heritage" tourism against those of seaside tourism, the former will retain its attractions for tourists to a far greater extent should prices rise, providing this increase is not exorbitant compared to those of other countries.

Tourist destinations have life cycles, as have all products; that is to say, they will enjoy periods of growth expansion, but will invariably suffer periods of decline or decay. If we examine the history of any well-known resort or destination we can see the truth of this.

Along the French Riviera, Nice, Cannes, Antibes, Juan les Pins, St Tropez, all have in turn enjoyed their period as fashionable resorts, but ultimately the early tourists have moved on to more fashionable resorts, often to be replaced by a new less fashion-conscious, less free-spending, market. In time this decline may become irreversible unless the resort can be regenerated by successful marketing. This may mean updating facilities as tourists become more demanding. In Britain's seaside resorts, failure to update many of the older hotels built in the Victorian era has meant that tourists who have experienced the improved facilities offered by foreign package holiday hotels are no longer attracted to British resorts. It may mean adding new attractions, such as indoor leisure complexes which cater for all-weather demand. In the late 1970s, when the steady rise of tourists to Spain's popular east coast resorts faltered, the response of Torremolinos, one of the coast's major resorts, was to build a conference centre to attract a new market. The success of the destination may depend upon the speed with which it responds to changes in taste and demand by its markets.

STATISTICAL MEASUREMENT IN TOURISM

Gathering data on tourism is a vital task for the government of a country, for its national tourist offices and for the providers of tourism services. Government needs to know the impact which tourism makes on the economy in terms of income, employment and contribution to the country's balance of payments. Concern with regional development requires that these statistics be sufficiently refined to allow them to be broken down by region. Governments will also wish to compare their tourism performance with that of other countries and to compare performances over a period of time.

Tourism organisations, whether in the public or private sector, require such data to enable them to make projections about what will happen in the future. This means identifying trends in the market, patterns of growth and changing demand for destinations, facilities or types of holiday. On the basis of this knowledge future planning can be undertaken; the public sector will make recommendations on the expansion or addition of tourist airports, road improvements or other services, while the private sector will recognise and react to changes in demand for hotel accommodation and develop new destinations or facilities. National tourist offices will plan their promotional strategies on the basis of these data, deciding where to advertise, to whom and with what theme. We can summarise the chief methods of research undertaken under the categories of international and domestic surveys.

International surveys

Although statistics of intra-European and transatlantic tourism flows were being collected before World War II, the systematic collection of tourism data on a world-wide scale developed in the early post-war years. This has intensified in recent years, particularly among the developing nations who have seen the introduction and rapid expansion of tourism to their shores. Global tourism statistics, dealing with tourism traffic flows, expenditure and trends over time, are produced and collated annually by the World Tourism Organisation (WTO) and the Organisation for Economic Co-operation and Development (OECD), and are published in the WTO's *World Tourism Statistics Annual Report and Tourism Compendium*, and in the OECD's annual *Tourism Policy and International Tourism*. Statistics, however, are not always strictly comparable, as data gathering methods vary and differences in definition of terms remain.

In Britain, information on travel into and out of the country is obtained in a variety of ways. Until the early 1960s most basic data on incoming tourism were obtained from Home Office immigration statistics, but as the purpose of gathering such data was to control immigration rather than to measure tourism, the data have major weaknesses, including failure to distinguish the purpose of travel—obviously a vital factor in measuring incoming tourism. The Government therefore decided to introduce a regular survey of visitors entering and leaving the country. The International Passenger Survey has enabled data to be collected since 1964, including the number of visitors, purpose of visit, geographical region visited, expenditure, mode of travel, transport used and duration of stay. This information is published quarterly, and compounded annually, in the Government's *Business Monitor* series (MQ6/M6 *Overseas Travel and Tourism*).

Numerous other surveys, both public and private, are undertaken, and these provide additional data on tourism volume and expenditure in Britain. The English Tourist Board carries out an annual Holiday Intentions Survey before Easter, which helps to forecast the anticipated level of tourism by British residents within Britain and overseas in the coming year. The same board also carries out regular hotel occupancy surveys. Private research organisations such as the BMRB (British Market Research Bureau) carry out interviews with consumers which include details of expenditure and volume of tourism consumption, although the details of such research are usually available only to subscribers.

National surveys

In Britain, as in other European countries, surveys producing broadly comparable statistics on tourism flows within the country are undertaken annually. Here the most important of these is the British National Travel Survey, which has been carried out since 1951 and is now administered jointly by the British Tourist Authority and the three national tourist boards of England, Scotland and Wales. This involves a random sample survey of British residents, including both those who take holidays and those who do not. Although the survey includes foreign holidays, it also enables statistics to be gathered specifically on domestic tourism, including the volume of such traffic, expenditure and characteristics of the market. The information it has produced has since 1971 been further supplemented by the British Home Tourism Survey, which takes into account travel other than for the purposes of holidays and includes holidays of less than four nights (unlike the BNTS). This is an ongoing survey, conducted among a random sample of British residents every month by the English Tourist Board on behalf of the three national boards. Detailed statistics for each of these surveys are again published annually.

While some information is available on regional tourism from these surveys, more sophisticated measurement of regional tourism is obtained through destination surveys which are carried out by the regional tourist boards, or in some cases by public bodies at county or local resort level. These are designed to produce a more accurate picture of tourism patterns, and will generally involve a combination of district accommodation surveys and a random visitor survey, designed to measure the contribution of both day excursionists and staying visitors within the region.

Techniques and problems of tourism measurement

From the foregoing it can be seen that tourism data collection has been largely quantitative in the past; that is, it has been designed to measure the volume of tourism traffic to different destinations, tourism expenditure en route and at those destinations, and certain other characteristics such as length of stay, time of visit, purpose of visit or mode of travel. These are questions which deal with the "how", "when", and "where" aspects of travel, and over time they have been refined so that additional data have been obtained. Expenditure, for example, can now be broken down by sector (shopping, food, accommodation, etc.), by nationality or by some other common variable. But recently the emphasis on travel research has shifted, and the aim has been to examine more qualitative aspects of tourism—questions as to *why* people behave as they do. Studies have been undertaken which are designed to reveal how and when holidays were planned and why a particular destination, time or mode of travel was selected.

Such data are less easily obtained through the medium of structured questionnaires and require the use of techniques such as motivation research, involving depth interviews, panel interviews and other qualitative methods which are time consuming to undertake and expensive. Nor can the results be subjected to tests of statistical probability, as can quantitative methods, in order to "prove their accuracy". Nonetheless, they do offer a valuable insight into the psychology of tourism behaviour which can advance our understanding of tourism as a phenomenon. Some researchers have argued, too, that quantitative methods may be too simplistic to be valuable, and it is often difficult to gauge the honesty and accuracy of answers elicited by the use of mailed questionnaires.

There are numerous other problems connected with the use of questionnaires for data gathering. Asking questions of arriving passengers at a destination is in reality an "intention survey" rather than an accurate picture of what a tourist will do or spend while at that destination, while surveys carried out on departing travellers involve problems of recall.

Using the results of such surveys for the purposes of comparison can be very misleading. An international journey requires an American resident to make a trip of many hundreds of kilometres, while in Europe day trips for the purposes of shopping or leisure are common experiences for those living near international borders. In some cases it is difficult to think of border crossings as international; no border control exists, for example, between Holland, Belgium and Luxembourg, nor are records available of crossings between these countries. Some countries still use hotel records to estimate visitors, these being notoriously inadequate; visitors travelling from one hotel to another are double counted while those visiting friends and relations will be omitted entirely. The author has experience of one hotel where records of nationality were based entirely upon the front office clerk guessing the origin of visitors' surnames! Accurate measures of tourist expenditure are equally difficult to make. Shopping surveys have problems in distinguishing between residents and tourists when shopkeepers are questioned, and tourists themselves will frequently under- or over-estimate their expenditure.

While international standards for methods of data collection and definition of terms have become widely accepted, variations still make comparisons difficult, not only between countries but within a country over a period of time, as a result of changes in methods of estimating data.

Some observers have argued that data should be collected not only to provide the economic impact of tourism on a country or region but also the social impact. Statistics on the ratio of tourists to residents, for example, or the number of tourists per square kilometre would provide some guidance on the degree of congestion experienced by a region. However, the social impact of tourism is also the outcome of many other variables, and statistical measurement is still a comparatively recent art which will require further refinement in the future for the purposes of both economic and social planning.

THE INTERNATIONAL TOURIST MARKET

We can end this chapter by looking at the business of international tourism today. Tourism is very big business indeed. Over 2,300 million tourists (approaching half the population of the world) travel away from home on a trip lasting four days or more in their own countries, and a further 290 million travel abroad. Direct expenditure on international tourism alone amounts to more than $100,000 million per annum, and accounts for over 5 per cent of all world exports. Although one of the fastest growing industries in the world, its potential for growth remains enormous; only one in fifty of the world's population actually travel across international borders in any one year (many of those who do travel, of course, make more than one such trip each year), and international travel is restricted largely to a handful of countries, with Europe responsible for some two-thirds of the traffic and North America accounting for most of the rest. The number of international travellers from the developing nations is minute, yet if one were to project increased living standards for these countries to a level equivalent to our present standard of living in the next century, the international tourism market would achieve staggering proportions. If only 5 per cent of the Chinese population were to travel abroad, this would inject a further 50 million travellers into the market! Such progression in living standards among the lesser developed nations is no longer certain, and indeed the strains that this development would impose upon the tourism industry and its impact upon the destination countries would be appalling. Nevertheless, although the increase in international tourism has slowed recently, the underlying expansion continues (see Table I).

Analysing the international tourism market, we must begin by distinguishing the countries which generate tourists, known as "generating countries", and countries receiving tourists, known as "destination", "receiving" or "host" countries. A few countries, of which Britain is one, play an equally important role in both generating and receiving tourists. For the most part it is the wealthier industrial nations, with their high per capita disposable income, which generate the tourists and the lesser developed nations, offering low living

TABLE I. A PROFILE OF INTERNATIONAL TOURISM, 1950–83

Year	International arrivals (millions)	International expenditure ($ millions)
1950	25.3	2,100
1960	71.2	6,800
1965	115.5	11,000
1970	158.7	17,900
1975	206.9	38,600
1980	279.0	95,300
1983	286.5	96,200

(*Source: WTO*)

costs, good climates and fine beaches, which receive tourists. The leading tourism generating countries include West Germany, USA, France, Canada, Holland, Belgium, Japan, Luxembourg and the United Kingdom; other countries with significant numbers of residents travelling abroad include Sweden, Switzerland, Denmark, Italy and Norway.

Within all these countries there are marked differences in the actual proportion of residents taking holidays abroad. Some four out of every five Swedish residents take a holiday of four nights or more each year (of which 50 per cent travel abroad), while only one in three Italians take a holiday (and only 5 per cent go abroad). We can say then that the *propensity* to take holidays is much higher among the Swedes, who live in a comparatively wealthy country, than among the Italians, although a significant number of the latter still do travel abroad.

We measure the *Gross travel propensity* of a nation by taking the total number of tourist trips per annum (or some other appropriate period of time) as a percentage of the population, while *Net travel propensity* reflects the percentage of the population taking at least one tourist trip. The *travel frequency* of a population is therefore defined as

$$Tf = \frac{Gtp}{Ntp}$$

where Tf = travel frequency; Gtp = Gross travel propensity; and Ntp = Net travel propensity.

In Britain, $14\frac{1}{2}$ million residents were estimated to have had a holiday abroad of four nights or longer in 1983 (of which nearly 9 million were travelling on package holidays), representing nearly

26 per cent of the population. This figure excludes business travel, which would substantially add to the total. Expenditure on holidays abroad amounted to £5,000 million (including fares paid to British carriers operating on international routes). In return, Britain welcomed some 12½ million foreign visitors in the same year, who brought nearly £4,600 million into the country.

Thus we begin to recognise the importance of international tourism for the economy of a country. Countries aim for a favourable balance of trade. They need to sell products abroad in order to obtain the foreign currencies with which to pay for their imports. Britain's visible trade balance has often been in the red in recent years—that is, we have brought goods abroad of a greater value than the goods we have sold abroad—but this situation can be rectified if we have a favourable surplus on our "invisible" trade, which includes services such as banking and insurance and also tourism. Britain has a good reputation for these services abroad and the balance of trade on invisible earnings has often been sufficient to make up for the deficit in the visible terms of trade.

Although there is no logical economic reason why the outflow of funds spent by British tourists abroad should be balanced by the inflow of foreign tourist expenditure (as long as other invisibles make up the deficit), successive governments have shown concern when the gap between incoming and outgoing tourist revenue becomes too marked. If the general terms of trade become too unfavourable this can lead to governments imposing a limit on the amount of foreign currency which residents are permitted to take abroad with them— the so-called "travel allowance". In the UK this has ranged, since World War II, from a low of £25 in 1952 to a maximum of £1,000 in 1979 (immediately prior to the lifting of all exchange controls in that year). While restricting the travel allowance does have some effect in reducing the demand for foreign travel, there is always the danger of retaliation by other countries. Such controls are also questioned on moral grounds, since they have the effect of restricting the freedom of movement of individuals which is regarded as a basic right in a democratic country. Fortunately, Britain has also been very effective in selling itself as a destination, increasing the number of foreign tourists from just over a million in 1955 to a high of 12½ million in 1983.

The role played by tourism in the economic development of the lesser developed nations is equally important. Many of these countries are turning to tourism as a means of improving their balance of payments deficits, attracting foreign investment and solving their unemployment problems. Because tourists are generally attracted to rural and comparatively undeveloped areas of these countries, where few alternative prospects exist for employment other than agriculture, tourism is seen as a viable industry. The fact that it is also labour-intensive, requiring only limited skills for most of its workforce, provides an additional attraction. However, substantial capital has to be invested initially to develop the infrastructure—roads, airports and other services—before capital can be attracted for the construction of hotels and other amenities.)

In addition to direct income and employment generated by tourism, there is also an indirect effect on the economy of a region. To measure the total impact of tourism on a region one must take account not only of the direct beneficiaries of tourists' money but also of the many indirect beneficiaries: farmers and wholesalers who supply food and drink to restaurants and hotels where tourists eat; the suppliers of hotel equipment and furniture; and the many other organisations and individuals who benefit to some extent by tourists visiting their area. Retail stores, banks, laundries, all derive some advantages from tourism in their area. Furthermore, since money spent by tourists is helping to pay the salaries of workers in these enterprises, these workers in turn are buying goods and services which they would not otherwise be purchasing. In this way money coming into the region is re-circulated and the total amount of tourist income generated is considerably greater than that spent by tourists alone. This phenomenon, known as the *multiplier effect*, will be discussed at greater length in Chapter 13.

The annual holiday represents a major expenditure in the year for most people, something to be saved for or to take out a loan for, but once on holiday people like to forget the normal financial restraints of daily life and they tend to spend more freely. In an earlier age, workers from the Lancashire mills would "blue" their annual savings in a glorious fortnight in Blackpool and this pattern is still prevalent among working-class holidaymakers in the popular resorts of the Mediterranean. However, the propensity to spend on holiday will differ not only according to socioeconomic background but also according to nationality. Tourists from certain countries are more prone to stay at self-catering apartments or campsites than are those from other countries, for example. In planning for tourism growth, therefore, tourist authorities must consider more than just how many tourists they can attract; they must also consider which types of tourist they can best attract, which are most desirable in terms of expenditure and acceptability to local residents, which will have least impact upon the environment, and they must then develop appropriate strategies to attract the markets for which they have targeted.

SELF-ASSESSMENT QUESTIONS

1. Why is it important to define tourism accurately? To whom is it important?

2. In what ways does tourism differ as a product from other products? How will this difference affect the way it is marketed?

3. Distinguish between the characteristics of business and holiday tourism. How do you think airlines will cater for the differences in these markets?

4. If you were responsible for promoting a seaside resort, what statistics do you think would be helpful to you?

ASSIGNMENT

Consider any tourist destination—town, resort or geographical region—known to you and analyse its strengths and weaknesses as a destination in terms of attractions, amenities and accessibility. In what life-cycle stage do you think it is at present? What would need to be done to boost tourism there?

CHAPTER TWO

The History of Tourism

CHAPTER OBJECTIVES

After studying this chapter, you should be able to:
* explain the historical changes which have affected the growth and development of the tourism industry, and the forms of travel and destinations selected by tourists;
* identify and distinguish between the enabling conditions and motivating factors encouraging the pursuit of travel;
* appreciate the historical and present-day role of tour operators in generating tourism;
* understand the major present-day trends affecting tourism in the UK and abroad.

EARLY ORIGINS

The term tourism dates from the early years of the nineteenth century, but this should not obscure the fact that what we would today describe as tourism was taking place much earlier in history. If one excludes travel for the purpose of waging war, early tourism can be said to have taken two forms; travel for the purpose of business (either for trading, or for business of state), and religious travel. Throughout history merchants have travelled extensively in order to trade with other nations or tribes. Such travel was often hazardous as well as arduous, relying on inadequate roads and uncomfortable transport, but the potential rewards were substantial. Both the Greeks and Romans were noted traders and as their respective empires increased, travel, often over great distances for the time, became necessary. There is also evidence of some travel for private purposes at this time; as an example, the Greeks hosted international visitors during the first Olympic Games, held in 776 BC, and wealthy Romans travelled on holiday not only to their own coast but as far afield as Egypt for enjoyment and, in some cases, to visit friends and relatives, thus setting the precedent for the substantial VFR market of the twentieth century. The Roman traveller in particular was greatly aided by the improvement in communications which resulted from the expansion of the Empire: first class roads coupled with staging inns (precursors of the modern motels) led to comparatively safe, fast and convenient travel unsurpassed until modern times.

Holidays, of course, have their origin in "holy days", and from earliest times religion provided the framework within which leisure time was spent. For most this implied a break from work rather than movement from one place to another. The village wakes of the Middle Ages, held on the eve of patronal festivals, provide an example of such "religious relaxation". However, by the time of the Middle Ages travel for religious reasons was also in evidence, taking the form of pilgrimages to places of worship (Chaucer's tale of the pilgrimage to Canterbury has popularised knowledge of such travel). Here, dedication or obligation were the motivating factors; travel occurred in spite of, rather than owing to, the prevailing conditions.

This generalisation can be made about most, if not all, forms of travel during the Middle Ages. Limited but varied travel did take place; adventurers seeking fame and fortune, merchants seeking new trade opportunities, strolling players, all moved freely around or between countries. All these, however, are identified as business travellers. There are certain preconditions to the development of travel for personal pleasure, and travel—certainly up to the time of the Middle Ages, if not until the nineteenth century—was something to be endured rather than enjoyed.

CONDITIONS FAVOURING THE EXPANSION OF TRAVEL

One can identify two categories of condition that have to be present before private travel is encouraged; *enabling* conditions (*travel facilitators*) and travel *motivators*. Of the former, two key conditions are time and disposable income (or better, *discretionary* income—that which is available after paying for essentials such as housing, food and clothing); throughout history, until very recent times, both have been the prerogative of a small elite in societies. Leisure involving the travel and stay of the vast majority of the population was out of the question in a world where workers laboured from morning to night, six days a week, in order to earn sufficient to stay alive. Sunday was expected to be treated as a religious holiday and was, of necessity, a day of rest from the week's toil.

Equally important, the development of pleasure travel depends upon the provision of suitable travel facilities. The growth of travel and the growth of transport are interdependent; travellers require transport that is priced within their budget and that is fast, safe, comfortable and convenient. Until the nineteenth century transport fulfilled none of these requirements. Prior to the arrival of the stagecoach (itself not noted for its comfort), the only form of transport other than the private carriages of the wealthy was the carrier's wagon, and this vehicle took two days to cover the distance between

London and Brighton. Road conditions were appalling—ill-made, potholed and in winter deeply rutted by the wagon wheels which turned the entire road into a sea of mud. The journey was not only uncomfortable but also unsafe; footpads and highwaymen abounded on the major routes, posing an ever-present threat to wayfarers. A significant breakthrough in terms of speed (though not in price) was achieved at the end of the seventeenth century with the advent of the stagecoach and, towards the end of the eighteenth century, the mail-coach which, through careful organisation and the establishment of suitable staging posts where horses could be changed, reduced the journey to Brighton to a matter of hours. Poor road surfaces continued to make such travel uncomfortable, but at least the discomfort was of shorter duration. Only with the introduction of macadamised surfaces after 1815 was this problem overcome. However within the next two decades the railways arrived, bringing with them the promise of a measure of comfort at an affordable price for the masses.

The development of transport is one side of the coin. The other is the provision of adequate accommodation at the traveller's destination. The traditional hospices for travellers were the monasteries, but these were dissolved during the reign of Henry VIII and the resulting hiatus acted as a further deterrent to travel for all those other than travellers planning to visit their friends or relatives. However, eventually the gradual development of and improvement in lodgings in the ale-houses of the day gave way to inns purpose-built to meet the needs of the mailcoach passengers. Not surprisingly, the inadequacy of accommodation facilities outside the major centres of population led to towns such as London, Exeter and York becoming the first centres to attract visitors for pleasure purposes, although clearly the social life of these cities acted as a magnet for the leisured classes.

There were other constraints for those prepared to overcome these drawbacks. In cities, public health standards were low and travellers risked disease, a risk compounded in the case of foreign travel. Exchange facilities for foreign currency were unreliable and rates of exchange inconsistent, so travellers tended to carry large amounts of money with them, making them attractive victims for the highwaymen. Travel documents were necessary, even in the Middle Ages, and political suspicion frequently made the issue of such documents subject to delay; merchants generally found such documentation easiest to obtain.

Enabling conditions will encourage the growth of travel by motivating the potential tourist extrinsically, but the more powerful motivating factors are intrinsic, that is, they arise out of a felt need or want on the part of the individual himself. The religious travel discussed earlier is an illustration of one such need, but a change of mental attitude towards personal travel had to come about before the secularisation of travel occurred on a wide scale. With this change of attitude. other latent wants and needs became established. These included concern with health, the desire to widen one's education, and curiosity about other cultures and peoples. Historically, as the opportunities for travel have increased, so have the expressed needs for travel expanded, as we shall see.

THE DEVELOPMENT OF THE SPAS

Spas were well established during the time of the Roman Empire, but their popularity, based on the supposed medical benefits of the waters, lapsed in subsequent centuries. They were never entirely out of favour, however; the sick continued to visit Bath throughout the Middle Ages. A regenerated interest in the therapeutic qualities of mineral waters has been ascribed to the influence of the Renaissance in Britain, with a parallel revival of spas on the Continent.

By the middle of the sixteenth century medical writers such as Dr William Turner were again drawing attention to the curative powers of the waters at Bath and at watering places on the Continent. Bath, along with the spa at Buxton, had been showing some return to popularity among those seeking the "cure", and by the early seventeenth century Scarborough and a number of other resorts were noted as centres for medical treatment. Over the following century, however, the character of these resorts gradually changed as pleasure rather than health became the motivation for visitors. The growth of the stagecoach services to these centres during the eighteenth century also further enhanced these resorts. Bath in particular became a major centre of social life for high society during the eighteenth and early nineteenth centuries; under the guidance of Beau Nash it became a centre of high fashion for the wealthy, and deliberately set out to create a select and exclusive image.

The commercial possibilities opened up by the concentration of these wealthy visitors were not overlooked; facilities to entertain or otherwise cater for these visitors proliferated, changing the spas into what we would today term holiday resorts rather than mere watering places. Eventually, towards the beginning of the nineteenth century, the common characteristic of almost all resorts to go "down-market" as they expand led to the centres changing in character, with the aristocracy and landed gentry giving way to wealthy city merchants and professional gentlemen in Bath. By the end of the eighteenth century the heyday of the English spas was already over.

Their decline can be traced to a number of factors. In the case of Bath, a rise in the number of permanent residents (coupled with an increase in the average age of the resident population) led to a change in the character of the town not dissimilar to that occurring in English seaside resorts during the latter half of the twentieth century. Commercial facilities became less popular as private entertaining in the home replaced the former public entertainment. However, it was the rise of the seaside resort which finally led to the demise of the inland spas.

THE GRAND TOUR

A parallel development in travel arose in the early seventeenth century as an outcome of the freedom and quest for learning heralded by the Renaissance. Under Elizabeth I young men seeking positions at court were encouraged to travel to the Continent in order to widen their education. This practice was gradually adopted by others lower in the social scale, and in time it became recognised that the education of a gentleman should be completed by a "Grand Tour" of the cultural centres of the Continent, often lasting three years or more—the term was in use as early as 1670. While ostensibly educational, as with the spas the appeal soon became social and pleasure-seeking young men of leisure travelled, predominantly through France and Italy, to enjoy the rival cultures and social life of Europe, with Venice, Florence and Paris as the key attractions. Certainly by the end of the eighteenth century the practice had become institutionalised for the gentry.

The result of this process was that European centres were opened up to the British cognoscenti. Aix-en-Provence, Montpellier and Avignon became notable bases for British visitors, especially those using Provence as a staging post in their travels to Italy. When pleasure travel followed in the nineteenth century, eventually to displace educational travel as the motive for continental visits, this was to lead to the development of the Riviera as a major centre of attraction for British tourists, aided by the introduction of regular steamboat services across the Channel from 1820 onwards.

THE SEASIDE RESORT

Certainly until the Renaissance sea bathing found little favour in Britain. Although not entirely unknown before then, such bathing as occurred was undertaken unclothed, and this behaviour conflicted with the mores of the day. Only when the sea became associated with certain health benefits did bathing gain any popularity, and this belief in seawater as an aid to health did not find acceptance until the early years of the eighteenth century.

It is perhaps to be expected that health theorists would eventually recognise that the minerals to be found in spa waters were also present in abundance in seawater. By the early eighteenth century small fishing resorts around the English coast were already beginning to attract visitors seeking "the cure", both by drinking seawater and by immersing themselves in it. Not surprisingly, Scarborough, as the only spa bordering the sea, was one of the first to exploit this facility for the medical benefits it was believed to offer, and both this town and Brighton were attracting regular visitors by the 1730s. But it was Dr Richard Russell's noted medical treatise *Concerning the Use of Seawater*, published in 1752, that is today generally credited with popularising the custom of sea bathing more widely; soon, Blackpool, Southend and other English seaside "resorts" were wooing bathers to their shores.

The growing popularity of "taking the cure", which resulted from the wealth generated by the expansion of trade and industry in Britain at the time, meant that the inland spas could no longer cater satisfactorily for the influx of visitors that they were attracting. By contrast the new seaside resorts offered almost boundless opportunities for expansion. Moral doubts about sea bathing were overcome by the invention of the bathing machine, and the resorts prospered.

Undoubtedly, the demand for seaside cures could have been even greater in the early years if fast, cheap transport had been developed to cater for this need. In the mid-eighteenth century, however, Londoners still faced two days' hard travel to get as far as Brighton, and the cost of such travel was beyond the reach of all but the well-off. The extension of mailcoach services in the early nineteenth century greatly reduced the time of such travel, if not the cost. As with the inland spas, accommodation was slow to expand to meet the new demand, although as the eighteenth century gave way to the nineteenth, a widening range of entertainment facilities (many associated specifically with the seaside) were developed alongside the new hotels and guest houses that sprang up to cater for the growing demand— a demand, as with the later stages of the life of the inland spas, now generated by pleasure seekers rather than health cranks.

The growth of the seaside resorts was spurred in the early nineteenth century by the introduction of the steamboat services. These were to reduce substantially the cost and time of travel to the resorts. In 1815 a service began operating from London to Gravesend, and five years later to Margate. The popularity of these services was such that similar services were quickly introduced to a number of other, more distant, developing resorts. One effect of this development was the construction in all major resorts of a pier to accommodate the vessels on their arrival. The functional purpose of the seaside pier was soon overtaken by its attraction as a social meeting point and "place to take the sea air" for the town's visitors.

Thus the first criterion for the growth of tourism was established; a fast, safe, convenient and reasonably priced form of transport made the resorts accessible to a large number of tourists. But a number of other factors closely related to the growth of tourism were also apparent by the early years of the nineteenth century.

One such factor was the rapid urbanisation of the population in Britain. The industrial revolution had led to massive migration of the population away from the villages and countryside and into the industrial cities, where work was plentiful and better paid. This migration was to have two important side effects on the workers themselves. Firstly, and for the first time, workers became conscious of the beauty and attractions of their former rural surroundings. The cities were dark, polluted and treeless. Formerly, workers had little appreciation for their environment—living among the natural beauty of the countryside, they accepted it without question. Now they longed to escape from the cities in the little free time they had—a characteristic still noteworthy among twentieth century city dwellers. Secondly, the type of work available in the cities was physically and psychologically stressful. The comparatively leisurely pace of life of the countryside was replaced by monotonous factory work from which a change of routine and pace was welcome.

This stress was accompanied, however, by a substantial increase in workers' purchasing power as productivity and the insatiable demand for more labour led to higher wages and greater disposable income. Worldwide demand for British goods also led to a rapid increase in business travel at home and abroad, and the greater wealth of the nation stimulated a population explosion, with better paid citizens demanding more goods and services, including travel. Only two factors were lacking for the launch of mass travel; holidays with pay and still faster, cheaper transport. The first was not to arrive on any scale until well into the twentieth century (although a fillip to the development of short-term travel was given by the granting of Bank Holidays in 1871), but the latter arrived in the first half of the nineteenth century in the form of the railways.

THE AGE OF STEAM: RAILWAYS

Two technological developments in the early part of the nineteenth century were to have a profound effect on transport and on the growth of travel in general. The first of these was the advent of the railway.

In the decade following the introduction of a rail link between Liverpool and Manchester in 1830, a huge programme of construction took place to provide trunk lines between the major centres of population and industry in Britain. Later, these were to be extended to include the expanding seaside resorts such as Brighton, bringing the resorts within reach of pleasure travellers on a broad scale for the first time. On the whole, however, the railway companies were slow to appreciate the opportunities their services offered for the expansion of pleasure travel, concentrating instead on meeting the demand for business travel generated by the expansion in trade. Competition between the railway companies was initially based on service rather than on price, although from the earliest days of the new railways a new market developed for short day-trips. Before long, however, entrepreneurs began to stimulate rail travel by organising excursions for the public at special fares. In some cases these took place on regular train services, but in others special trains were chartered to take travellers to their destination, setting a precedent for the charter services by air which were to become so significant a feature of tour operating a century later. Thomas Cook was not the first such entrepreneur—Sir Rowland Hill, who became chairman of the Brighton Railway Co., is sometimes credited with this innovation, and there were certainly excursion trains in operation by 1840—but Cook was to have by far the greatest impact on the early travel industry. In 1841, as secretary of the South Midland Temperance Association, he organised an excursion for his members from Leicester to Loughborough, at a fare of one shilling return. The success of this venture— 570 took part—encouraged him to arrange similar excursions using chartered trains and by 1845 he was organising these trips on a fully commercial basis.

The result of these and similar ventures by other entrepreneurs led to a substantial movement of pleasure-bound travellers to the seaside; in 1844 it is recorded that almost 15,000 passengers travelled from London to Brighton on the three Easter holidays alone, while hundreds of thousands travelled to other resorts to escape the smoke and grime of the cities. The enormous growth in this type of traffic can be appreciated when it is revealed that by 1862 Brighton received 132,000 visitors on Easter Monday alone.

Supported by a more sympathetic attitude towards pleasure travel by the public authorities such as the Board of Trade, the railway companies themselves were actively promoting excursions by the 1850s, as well as introducing a range of discounted fares for day trips, weekend trips and longer journeys. By 1855, Cook had extended his field of operations to the Continent, organising the first "inclusive tours" to the Paris Exhibition of that year. This followed the success of his excursions to the Great Exhibition in London in 1851, which in all had welcomed a total of three million visitors.

Cook was a man of vision in the world of travel. The success of his operations was due to the care he took in organising his programmes to minimise problems; he had close contacts with hotels, shipping companies and railways throughout the world, ensuring that he obtained the best possible service as well as cheap prices for the services he sold. By escorting his clients throughout their journeys abroad he took the worry out of travel for the first-time travellers. He also facilitated the administration of travel by introducing, in 1867, the hotel voucher; and by removing the worry of travel for the Victorian population, he changed their attitudes to travel and opened up the market. The coincidental development of photography acted as a further stimulus for overseas travel, both for prestige and curiosity reasons.

The success of these early forays abroad led the railway companies to recognise the importance of their links with the cross-channel ferry operators. The management of the ferries gradually came under the control of the railways themselves, so that by the 1860s they dominated ferry operations to the Continent and to Ireland.

The expansion of the railways was accompanied by a simultaneous decline of the stagecoaches. Some survived by providing feeder services to the nearest railway stations, but overall road traffic shrank and with it shrank the demand for the staging inns. Those situated in the resorts were quick to adapt to meet the needs of the new railway travellers, but the supply of accommodation in centres served by the railways was totally inadequate to meet the burgeoning demand of rail travellers. A period of hotel construction began, leaders in which were the railways themselves, building the great terminus hotels which came to play such a significant role in the hotel industry over the next hundred years. The high capital investment called for by this construction programme led to the early formation of the hotel chains and corporations in place of the former individual hotel proprietors.

Coincidentally with this technological development, Victorian society was undergoing social changes which were to boost pleasure travel for the masses in Britain and for the better-off minority abroad. The new-found interest in sea bathing meant that the expanding rail routes tended to favour the developing resorts, accelerating their growth. At the same time, Victorian society placed increasing importance on the family as a social unit. This led to emphasis on family holidays for which the seaside resorts were ideally suited, offering as they soon did a range of entertainment for adults and children alike. The foundation of the traditional seaside entertainment was soon laid—German bands, "nigger minstrels" and pierrots, Punch and Judys, barrel organs, donkey rides, and the seaside pier as the central focus of entertainment. Resorts began to develop different social images, the result in part of their geographical location; those nearer London or other major centres of population developed a substantial market of day trippers, while others deliberately aimed for a more exclusive clientele. These latter generally tended to be situated further afield, but in some cases their exclusivity arose from the desire of prominent residents to resist the encroachment of the railways for as long as possible; Bournemouth, for example, resisted the extension of the railway from Poole until 1870. Some areas of early promise as holiday resorts were quickly destroyed by the growth of industry— Swansea and Hartlepool, for example, and Southampton, where beaches soon gave way to developing docks.

Health continued to play a role in the choice of holiday destination, but emphasis gradually switched from the benefits of sea bathing to those of sea air. Climate became a feature of the resorts' promotion. Sunshine hours were emphasised, or the bracing qualities of the Scarborough air, while the pines at Bournemouth were reputed to help those suffering from lung complaints. Seaside resorts on the Continent also gained in popularity and began to develop their own social images—Scheveningen, Ostend, Biarritz and Deauville became familiar names to British holidaymakers who ventured overseas. Some overseas resorts flourished as a reaction to the middle-class morality of Victorian England; Monte Carlo, with its notorious gambling casino, was a case in point. This desire to escape from one's everyday moral environment was as symptomatic in its way in the nineteenth century as it was to become by the middle of the twentieth.

Other forms of holidaymaking, opened up by the advent of the railways on the Continent, arose from the impact of the "Romantic Movement" of mid-Victorian England. The Rhine and the French Riviera benefited from their romantic appeal, while the invigorating mountain air of Switzerland offered its own unique appeal which was firmly established by the 1840s. The additional interest in mountaineering, which began as a popular English middle-class activity in the 1860s, secured for Switzerland its role as a major Continental holiday centre for the British, boosted still further when Sir Henry Lunn, the travel entrepreneur, introduced winter ski holidays to that destination in the 1880s. The railways made their own contributions to these developments, but above all they encouraged the desire to travel by removing the hazards of foreign travel that had formerly existed for travellers journeying by road.

THE AGE OF STEAM: STEAMSHIPS

Just as the technological developments of the early nineteenth century led to the development of the railways on land, so was steam harnessed at sea to drive the new generations of ships. Here, necessity was the mother of invention. Increasing trade worldwide, especially with North America, required Britain to develop faster, more reliable forms of communication by sea with the rest of the world. Following the development of the short sea ferry services in the 1820s, deep-sea services were introduced on routes to North America and the Far East. The Peninsular and Oriental Steam Navigation Company (later P & O) are credited with the first regular long-distance steamship services, beginning operations to India and the Far East in 1838. They were soon followed by the Cunard Steamship Company which, with a lucrative mail contract, began regular services to the American continent in 1840. Britain, by being first to establish regular deep-sea services of this kind, dominated the world's shipping in the second half of the century, although it was to become challenged increasingly by vessels of the other leading industrial nations, especially across the north Atlantic. This prestigious and highly profitable route prospered not only from mail contracts but also in terms of both passenger and freight traffic as trade expanded. This traffic was boosted later in the century by the advent of substantial emigrant traffic from Europe and the steady growth of American visitors to Europe. Thomas Cook was to do his part in stimulating British tourist traffic to North America, operating the first excursion to the USA as early as 1866.

The Suez Canal, opened in 1869, stimulated demand for P & O's services to India and beyond, as Britain's empire looked eastwards. The global growth of shipping led, in the latter part of the century, to the formation of shipping conferences which developed cartel-like agreements on fares and conditions applicable to the carriage of traffic to the various territories to which these vessels operated. The aim of these agreements was to ensure year-round profitability in an unstable and seasonal market, but the result was to stifle competition by price and eventually led to excess profits which were enjoyed by most shipping companies until the advent of airline competition in the mid-twentieth century.

LATE NINETEENTH CENTURY DEVELOPMENTS

As the Victorian era drew to a close, other social changes came into play. Continued enthusiasm for the healthy outdoor life coincided with the invention of the bicycle, and cycling holidays, aided by promotion from the Cyclists' Touring Club which was founded in 1878, enjoyed immense popularity. This movement not only paved the way for later interest in outdoor activities on holiday but may well have stimulated the appeal of the suntan as a status symbol of health and wealth, in marked contrast to the earlier association in Victorian minds of a fair complexion with gentility and breeding. The bicycle offered for the first time the opportunity for mobile rather than centred holidays and gave a foretaste of the popularity of motoring holidays in the early years of the twentieth century.

As tourism became organised in the later years of the nineteenth century, so the organisation of travel became an established institution. Thomas Cook and Sir Henry Lunn are two of the best known names associated with the development of tours at this time, but many other well-known companies trace their origin to this period. Dean and Dawson appeared in 1871, the Polytechnic Touring Association in the following year and Frames in 1881. In the United States, American Express (founded by, among others, Henry Wells and William Fargo of Wells Fargo fame) initiated money orders and travellers' cheques, although the company did not become involved in booking holiday arrangements until the early twentieth century.

Mention has already been made of the impact of photography on nineteenth century travel. As the nineteenth century drew to a close, the vogue for photography was accompanied by the cult of the guidebook. No British tourist venturing abroad would neglect to take his guidebook, and a huge variety of guidebooks, many superficial and inaccurate, were available on the market, dealing with both Britain and overseas countries. The most popular and enduring of these was Baedeker which, although first published as early as 1839, became established as the leading guide for European countries at the end of the century.

TRAVEL IN THE FIRST HALF OF THE TWENTIETH CENTURY

In the opening years of this century pleasure travel continued to expand, encouraged by the increasing wealth, curiosity and outgoing attitudes of the post-Victorian population and also by the increasing ease of such movement. By now travellers were safer from both disease and physical attack, the Continent was relatively stable politically, and documentation for British travellers uncomplicated— since 1860 no passports had been required for any country in Europe.

World War I proved to be only a brief hiatus in the expansion of travel, although it led to the widespread introduction of passports for nationals of most countries. Early post-war prosperity, coupled with large-scale migration, boosted the demand for international travel. Interest in foreign travel was further boosted by the first-hand experience of foreign countries that so many had gained during the war. New forms of mass communication spurred curiosity about other countries; to the influence of posters and the press were added the cinema, then radio and ultimately television, all playing their part in widening knowledge and interest.

After World War I, however, forms of travel began to change radically. The railways went into a period of steady decline with the introduction of the motor car. Motorised public road transport and improved road conditions led to the era of the charabancs in the 1920s and renewed popularity for outings to the seaside, but it was the freedom of independent travel offered by the private motor car which destroyed the monopoly of the railways as a means of holiday travel in Britain, although continental rail travel survived and prospered until the coming of the airlines. In an endeavour to stem the regression, rail services were first rationalised in 1921 into four major companies—the LMS, LNER, GWR and SR*—and later nationalised following World War II.

The arrival of the airline industry signalled the beginning of the end, not only for long distance rail services but, more decisively, for the great steamship companies. British shipping lines in particular had been under increasing threat from foreign competition throughout the 1920s—French, German and US liners challenged British supremacy on the north Atlantic routes especially—but before World War II commercial air services did not pose a significant threat to the industry as a whole. Air services introduced in the 1930s were expensive, unreliable, uncomfortable and necessitated frequent stopovers for distant destinations. Partly for these reasons commercial aviation was more important for its mail-carrying potential in these years than for the carriage of passengers. It was not until the technological breakthroughs in aircraft design achieved during World War II that airlines were to prove a viable alternative to shipping for intercontinental travel.

Among the major travel developments of the 1930s the holiday camp deserves a special mention. Aimed at the growing low-salaried market for holidays, the camps set new standards of comfort when they were introduced, offering 24-hour entertainment at all-in, reasonable prices, backed by efficiency in operation and including the all-important child-minding services which couples with young families needed so badly. This was in marked contrast to the lack of

*London, Midland and Scottish Railway, London and North Eastern Railway, Great Western Railway and Southern Railway.

planned activities and often surly service offered at seaside boarding houses of the day. The origin of these camps goes back to earlier experiments of organisations such as the Co-operative Holidays Association, the Workers' Travel Association and the Holiday Fellowship, but their popularity and general acceptance by the public can be ascribed to the efforts and promotional flair of Billy Butlin, who built his first camp at Skegness in 1936, supposedly after talking to a group of disconsolate holidaymakers huddled in a bus shelter to avoid the rain on a wet summer's day. The instant success of the concept led to a spate of similar camps built by Butlin and other entrepreneurs in the pre-war and early post-war years.

It was during the between-wars period, however, that the seaside holiday became securely established as the traditional annual holiday for the mass British public. Blackpool, Scarborough, Southend and Brighton consolidated their positions as leading holiday resorts, while numerous newer resorts—Bournemouth, Broadstairs, Clacton, Skegness, Colwyn Bay—grew annually in terms of residential population as well as in number of annual visitors. Up to the time of the Depression in the early 1930s hotels and guest houses proliferated, both in the seaside resorts and in London. In the latter some of the leading West End hotels were constructed, largely to satisfy demand from overseas tourists.

At this time Britain experienced the first stirrings of government interest in the tourism business as a whole. In this respect Britain was well behind other European countries; Switzerland, for example, had long recognised the importance of its inward tourism and was actively involved in both tourism promotion and the gathering of tourism statistics by this time. The British Travel and Holidays Association was established by the government in 1929, but with the theme "Travel for Peace" its role was seen as essentially promotional in nature and its impact on the tourism industry was relatively insignificant until its change in status forty years later. By the outbreak of World War II the British government had at least recognised the potential contribution tourism could make to the country's balance of payments; equally, they had recognised the importance of holidays to the health and efficiency of the nation's workforce. The Amulree Report in 1938 led to the first Holidays with Pay Act in the same year, which encouraged voluntary agreements on paid holidays and generated the idea of a two-week paid holiday for all workers. Although this ambition was not realised until several years after the end of World War II, by the outbreak of the war some 11 millions of the 19 million workforce were entitled to paid holidays—a key factor in the generation of mass travel.

THE SECOND HALF OF THE TWENTIETH CENTURY

As had occurred after World War I, World War II also led to increased interest in travel. The extensive theatre of war had introduced combatants not only to new countries but to new continents, generating new friendships and an interest in diverse cultures. Another outcome of the war, which was radically to change the travel business, was the advance in aircraft technology which led for the first time to a viable commercial aviation industry. The surplus of aircraft in the immediate post-war years, a benevolent political attitude towards the growth of private sector airlines, and the appearance on the scene of the early air travel entrepreneurs such as Harold Bamberg (of Eagle Airways) and Freddie Laker, aided the rapid expansion of air travel after the war. But more significantly for the potential market, aircraft had become more comfortable, safer, substantially faster and, in spite of relatively high prices in the early 1950s, steadily cheaper by comparison with other forms of transport. Commercial jet services began with the ill-fated Comet aircraft in the early 1950s, but already by then advance piston-engine technology had ensured that air travel prices would fall substantially. With the introduction of the commercially successful Boeing 707 jets in 1958, the age of air travel for the masses arrived, hastening the already apparent demise of the great ocean liners. In terms of numbers carried, air travel overtook sea travel across the north Atlantic in 1957 and although the great liners were to continue Atlantic operations for a further decade, their uncompetitive costs and length of journey time resulted in declining load factors from one year to another.

While the scheduled operations of the state airlines were commercially successful, private airline operators broke new ground with their development of charter services which proved highly profitable. Initially, government policy ensured that these charters were restricted to troop movements, but as official airline policy became more lenient the private operators sought new forms of charter traffic. The package holiday business resulted from co-operation between these carriers and entrepreneurs in the tour operating business. Vladimir Raitz is credited with being in the forefront of this development; in 1950, under the banner of Horizon Holidays, he organised an experimental package holiday programme by air to Corsica. By chartering his aircraft and filling every seat instead of committing himself to a block of seats on scheduled air services, he was able to reduce significantly the unit cost of his air transport and hence the overall price to the public. While carrying only 300 passengers in that first year, he repeated the experiment more successfully the following and succeeding years. The potential profits of this operation soon attracted other travel agents to move into tour operating, and by the early 1960s mass-market package tours were a major phenomenon of the European travel industry, contributing to an escalation in coastal tourism development on the Spanish mainland and the Balearic Islands, as well as in Italy, Greece and other Mediterranean coastal resorts.

Although Britain took the lead in developing package tours to the Mediterranean, other northern European countries soon followed in packaging their own sun, sea and sand holiday programmes, competing with Britain for accommodation in the hotels of the Mediterranean coast. During the 1970s Britain further liberalised its air traffic regulations and this, coupled with the growth in second holidays resulting from longer paid holidays, led to the development of a new winter package tour market for which both skiing and winter sunshine holidays were provided. By spreading demand more evenly throughout the year in this way tour operators were able to lower their prices still further, increasing the off-season demand.

After the post-war recovery years, standards of living rose sharply in the 1950s and there was a simultaneous increase in private car ownership. Holidaymakers switched to the use of private cars and this change affected both coach and rail services. In 1950 about two out of three domestic holidays in Britain were by rail, but this figure had fallen to about one in seven by 1970. Private car ownership rose during this time from 2 million to over 11 million vehicles. This change in travel behaviour led to the return of the "transit hotel" or motel, in the tradition of the old staging inns, serving the needs of long-distance motorists. The flexibility of travel arrangements which the private car offers also encouraged the growth of excursions and short-stay holidays, and resorts close to major centres of population benefited considerably. Road improvements, especially the network of fast motorways constructed on the Continent and in Britain, following the American pattern, brought other more distant resorts closer in travel time to the major cities, changing in some cases both the nature of the market served and the image of the resort itself. The ever resourceful tour operators met the private car threat to their package holiday programmes by devising flexible packages aimed at the private motorist at home and abroad. Hotels, too, spurred on by their need to fill off-peak rooms, devised their own programmes of short-stay holidays tailored for the private motorist. The demand for hired cars on holidays overseas also increased substantially, producing a major growth in this sector of the travel industry.

In other sectors the shipping lines, hit by air competition and rising prices during the 1960s, were forced to abandon many of the traditional liner routes. Some companies attempted to adapt their vessels for cruising, not entirely successfully; vessels purpose-built for long-distance fast deep-sea voyages are not ideally suited to cruising, either economically or from the standpoint of design. Many were incapable of anchoring alongside docks in the shallow waters of the popular cruise destinations such as the Caribbean. Companies that failed to embark on a programme of building new vessels more suited to the needs of the cruise market, either through lack of foresight or of capital, soon ceased to trade. However, many new purpose-built cruise liners, of Greek, Norwegian and later Russian registry, appeared on the market, filling the gaps left by the declining maritime powers, and based predominantly in the popular Caribbean or Mediterranean cruising waters. British shipping was not without its innovations, however; Cunard Line initiated the fly-cruise concept, whereby their vessels were based in the Mediterranean and aircraft were chartered to fly cruise passengers direct to the sun to join their cruise ships.

If the rapid escalation of fuel and other costs during the 1970s placed a question mark over the whole future of deep-sea shipping, ferry services have by contrast been outstandingly successful since the 1950s. Again, this largely resulted from the increased demand of private motorists taking their cars abroad for their holidays, although operational profitability depended also on continuous usage of vessels, fast turn-rounds in port and much lower levels of passenger service than would apply on cruise vessels. Cross-Channel and trans-Mediterranean services in particular have flourished in a pattern of expansion which is likely to continue unabated for the foreseeable future. New marine technology has led to the development of new forms of cross-Channel vessels, although so far hover-craft and jetfoil vessels appear to have operating limitations that have prevented their posing a serious challenge to the more traditional craft plying the short sea routes.

Private car holidays have given a fillip to camping and caravanning. By 1980 there were 600,000 caravans in Britain, producing severe congestion on the holiday routes and in key holiday centres at peak seasons. The visual despoilation of the landscape by caravan sites was just one form of pollution caused by tourism about which central and local governments have become increasingly concerned.

In Britain the 1970s were marked by a new direction in government policy towards tourism, initiated by the Development of Tourism Act 1969. This Act, the first in the country devoted specifically and uniquely to tourism, established a new framework for public sector tourism which formally recognised the growing importance of the industry to the British economy. Government and quasi-government agencies have shown themselves concerned with their role in conservation as well as promotion as tourism from overseas leapt. The former largely laissez-faire attitude of successive governments changed to one of recognising the need for adequate planning and control, to balance supply and demand, to maintain the quality of the tourist product and to safeguard tourists' rights. Thus tour operators became government licensed for the first time in the 1970s, government incentives were provided for the construction of hotels and other tourist facilities, and the first hesitant steps were taken to register and categorise the accommodation sector. The failure of public sector tourism planning and control in other countries, most notably Spain, has added fuel to the government's policy-making in Britain during the past decade.

As business and trade prospered in the developed countries, business travel has also flourished, leading to demand not only for individual travel but also for conference and incentive travel on a world-wide scale. The 1970s have also seen the emergence of new patterns of tourism. As economic power has shifted between countries, so have new tourism-generating countries come to the fore, notably the oil-rich Arab countries and Japan. Europe has benefited from this influx, as have the developing tourist-based economies of the Far East—Indonesia, Malaysia and Thailand have all strengthened their tourism attractions to appeal to these new markets.

Changing social patterns have given rise to new patterns in holiday-taking; special interest holidays to cater for the expanding range of interests of a leisure-orientated society, e.g. activity holidays for those whose sedentary occupations encourage more energetic forms of travel experience. As prices soared in the 1970s the keynote in Britain became "value for money", and millions turned to self-catering holidays. Economy, however, was only part of the reason for this change. Tourists in the free-and-easy 1960s and 1970s rebelled against the constraints imposed by package holidays in general and the accommodation sector in particular. Set meals at set times gave way to "eat when you please, where you please, what you please". The package tour industry responded by providing the product to meet the need; self-catering villas and apartments flourished across southern Europe, while in the UK resort hotels gave way to self-catering flats.

By the 1970s, the annual overseas holiday had become a habit for millions of Britons. When the recession came, consumers revealed that they were more disposed to forego durable goods than holidays. The annual holiday had become a habit seen by many as a necessity of life rather than a luxury.

SELF-ASSESSMENT QUESTIONS

1. Distinguish between enabling conditions and motivating factors in tourism.

2. What were the main effects of urbanisation on the demand for travel in the nineteenth century?

3. Why did Switzerland become an important holiday resort for the British in the second half of the nineteenth century?

4. True or false? (a) The spas were the first centres in England to attract tourism. (b) No travel documentation was needed for foreign travel by Britons in Europe prior to World War I. (c) Seaside piers were initially built as landing stages for steamers. (d) The main factor delaying Bournemouth's development as a seaside resort was its distance from London.

ASSIGNMENT

Outline the factors encouraging international tourism, and indicate why they were generally absent prior to the nineteenth century.

CHAPTER THREE

The Age of Mass Tourism

CHAPTER OBJECTIVES

After studying this chapter, you should be able to:
* outline the growth of mass tourism;
* define different forms of tourism and their motivation;
* describe the origins and development of the package holiday;
* analyse the factors influencing the general demand for tourism;
* identify the main tourist areas and countries;
* analyse the factors influencing individual choice of destination, accommodation and mode of travel;
* identify the main methods by which tourist products may be purchased.

MASS TOURISM AND MODERN TECHNOLOGY

The origins of mass tourism

Although the nineteenth century produced a considerable change in the size and nature of tourism, it was not until well into the twentieth century that "mass" tourism can truly be said to have come about. There were two main periods of growth.

(a) Firstly between the two World Wars the European countries in particular underwent a period of social upheaval out of which came higher expectations by the masses of holiday entitlement, incomes and material living standards. This led to demands for more and longer holidays. Coupled with this was the development of mass transport by road, whilst railway services were also at the end of their peak. The rate of tourism growth was itself increasing until interrupted in 1939 by World War II.

(b) In the 1950s and 1960s pre-war growth was resumed but spread much more widely so that international tourism began to reach mass markets in many countries. This was stimulated by the development of relatively cheap and fast air transport, and by the application of sophisticated marketing and management techniques by producers in what was now recognised to be the tourism "industry".

Mass tourism in the 1930s and early 1950s was largely a domestic business. In Britain, for example, residents took 26½ million long holidays in 1951 of which only 5½ per cent were foreign holidays (by 1979 out of 58 million long holidays 20 per cent were abroad). The mass destinations were the seaside resorts, using transport by rail, coach or car, and accommodation mostly in guest or boarding houses or staying with relatives. In North America tourists increasingly used private cars for summer camp holidays in national parks and similar destinations.

Holiday camps and holiday villages

During the 1930s there emerged the holiday camp which, whilst in itself never having been a major form of accommodation, has had a major impact on the way destination facilities for tourists are provided and operated.

The concept of a holiday camp arose in different ways. For example, in Britain Butlin opened his first camp in 1936 to provide cheap purpose-built accommodation with mass catering facilities and a tremendous range of entertainment and amusement all on one site, preferably by the sea. In pre-war Germany the concept of highly organised and often militaristic health and recreation camps provided holidays for many who would otherwise have been unable to afford them. Political and social influences of the time had similar effects, such as the development of villages de vacances in France.

The main attribute of holiday camps to have won widespread adoption is the principle of accommodation and entertainment all in one place. Operators such as Butlin and Warner appreciated early on that in resorts where entertainment was lacking, especially in wet weather, a full programme of activities was a very attractive product. This was particularly true if they were packaged and on-site with accommodation. This idea has spread to some resort hotels, particularly new ones, so that in many destinations it is unusual to find a hotel without games rooms, swimming pool, tennis, dancing and so on.

The concept of the holiday camp or village has changed; it is now less regimented, more flexible, offering mainly self-catering accommodation in tents, caravans or chalets, together with optional catering. One of the most successful operators is Club Méditerranée, a French company whose 50,000 beds in "holiday club villages" are spread throughout countries around the world. These are now virtually the "total resort" where the tourism product is packaged into one place. This theme is taken up in Chapter 7.

Movement to the sun

Creating a "total resort" is symptomatic of the tourism industry's increasing commercial ability during the mid-twentieth century. As mass tourism became established, suppliers of tourism products expanded and developed their marketing expertise. In so doing, increasingly sophisticated market research revealed the motivations of different groups of tourists. One of the most important motivations proved to be the attraction of sunshine and warmth, particularly to the mass of relatively well-off people living in the cool and variable climates of North America and Northern Europe. As time, money and technology have permitted, so the pressure of demand from these markets has moved south, as shown in Fig. 2.

Major firms in the tourism industry have identified and provided for this demand. For example, large hotel chains such as Sheraton and Hyatt in the USA have built considerable resort properties in Florida, Mexico and the Caribbean, British and German tour operators such as Thomson and TUI have developed bulk inclusive tours to the Mediterranean and north Africa; and charter airlines have opened up increasingly longer-distance routes south.

Expertise in dealing with such mass tourism has spread to other types of tourism where large numbers of people are involved: tours to centres of culture such as London or Rome; winter sports holidays; incentive travel for businessmen. The mass tourism product has thus become available to many different market sectors.

Jet aircraft

At the core of this longer-distance movement of people to destinations lies the jet aircraft. The first commercial passenger jet services began in the 1950s using Boeing 707 and Comet aircraft. This had two main effects.

(a) Average speeds of 800–1000 kph, compared with older propeller driven aircraft travelling at 400 kph, meant that an air traveller could reach a far more distant destination in a given time. This was particularly useful for business journeys where time is valuable.

(b) More importantly for mass holiday tourism, airlines scrambled to purchase new jets, leaving a large supply of good, secondhand propeller driven aircraft which were often purchased cheaply by small companies to undertake charter operations. These were able to carry tourists to "sunshine" destinations faster than trains or coaches. Many of these companies had started operations after 1945 with war surplus aircraft and had developed business during the 1948 Berlin airlift (e.g. Laker).

A second upheaval in air transport occurred after 1970 when the first wide-bodied jets (Boeing 747s), able to carry over 400 passengers appeared in commercial service. The cost of carrying one passenger one kilometre was considerably reduced and the result was an increased supply of air seats at potentially cheaper prices. At the same time earlier jets were sold to charter operators in the same way that propeller driven aircraft had previously been released.

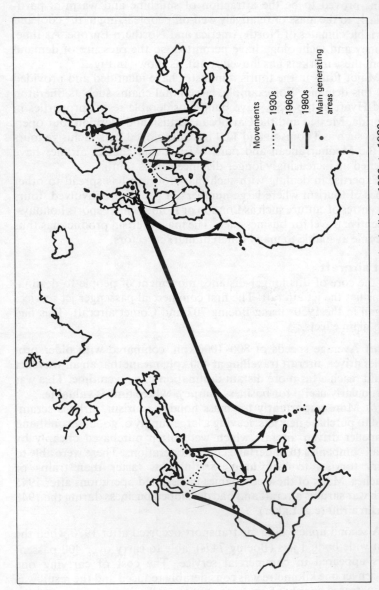

Fig. 2 Changes in destination trends for mass market holidays, 1930s to 1980s

Aircraft in use by scheduled and charter airlines are now not dissimilar (*see* Chapter 5), and technology has provided a range of relatively cheap, fast and efficient aircraft capable of intensive services on routes of various lengths.

Identikit destinations

The net result of recent developments in tourism for the mass markets has been the establishment of destinations for particular market segments which, in all but their location, are very often remarkably similar. A convention centre, for example, may contain a conference building which may be usable for other purposes, with committee/ lecture rooms, modern single- or twin-bedded hotel rooms with private facilities, restaurants with banqueting rooms, bars, exhibition space, indoor and outdoor sports facilities, and good scheduled transport links. The location may be Portsmouth, Basel or Rio— once inside the delegate may not even notice where he is.

The larger the mass market, the less distinctive destinations are likely to be, especially if the destination is small and recently developed. One can find 1970s-built "marina" type resorts with yachting basins, hotel/apartment/villa accommodation, similar restaurants, cafes and shops, and golf, tennis, watersports, folk singers and barbecue nights in any one of a dozen countries around the Mediterranean, the Caribbean, north Africa and the south Pacific. These "identikit" destinations are the result of comprehensive market research amongst various generating markets to find products with guaranteed mass demand. They may be compared with the piecemeal development of resorts two or three generations ago which may have had purely local or domestic attractions.

Not all destinations are similar, of course. Whilst many may be "down-market" in attractiveness, that is they may offer cheap tourism to a large number of people, with the image of great popularity, others may be identikit "up-market" destinations, allegedly offering higher quality and thus more expensive services to fewer people. So in the former category we may think of Benidorm, Miami or perhaps Niagara Falls, or Seefeld in Austria; in the latter Bali, Fiji or Barbados. Many identikit destinations have been developed through the activities of multinational tourism companies such as Sheraton Hotels, Rockresorts, Club Mediterranée, Club Robinson or THF. Within their establishments a tourist will find a comforting degree of uniformity.

Mass tourism has therefore demanded and received products designed specifically for its needs as revealed through market research, i.e. products which are *user-orientated* as opposed to *resource-*

orientated (that is, based on the resources available at a destination). We must now break down mass tourism into its various forms.

FORMS OF TOURISM

It is important to understand that there are a very large number of reasons why tourism takes place, that is different *purposes* for tourism. Sometimes it is the destination itself that provides the purpose for the visit, sometimes its characteristics and sometimes the destination is merely incidental to the purpose of travel. To simplify the pattern of reasons we can classify tourists into a number of *purpose-of-travel markets* which give rise to different forms of tourism.

Relaxation and physical recreation

Destinations catering for these forms of tourism demand include coasts, countryside and mountainous regions (including so-called "wilderness regions"). The markets for this form of tourism, however, can be broadly divided between consumers who demand attractive scenery and a sense of "communing with nature", and those seeking the attractions of sun, sea and sand.

The appeal of countryside and mountains has exercised a strong influence over British tourists for more than a hundred years, as we have seen in the chapter dealing with the history of tourism. Demand for this type of holiday is still substantial, but relatively stable, and is met by the tour operators in the form of "Lakes and Mountains" package holidays. However, within Europe the major attractions of this kind are situated in countries which have become relatively expensive for the British over the past three decades— Switzerland, Norway, Austria, Southern Germany—and as the currencies of these countries harden against the pound sterling, demand levels off or falls.

By contrast, since sea bathing first became popular during the nineteenth century there has been a consistent demand by tourists for destinations which offer the attractions of the sea with access to a beach—preferably sandy—and hopefully good weather to enjoy it. This demand is common to almost all nations with temperate or cold-temperate climates. The tourist's expectation of his holiday is of clear warm sea, easily accessible, supported by warm sunshine to enhance the pleasure. Sunbathing in itself is a relatively newer objective, and is one that was not common in the last century.

If the above factors provide an indolent person's holiday, then activity is increasingly in demand through a range of entertainment and sports facilities. Destinations which fail to offer sun, sea, sand

and these facilities tend to suffer loss of demand. Hence a poor summer in a British seaside resort may drive tourists towards the Mediterranean; pollution in the sea and overcrowded beaches at an Italian resort may drive them to Yugoslavia or north Africa.

The popularity of this kind of holiday seems constant. About 40 per cent of all British tourists in Britain go to the seaside and perhaps some 25-30 per cent of those going abroad do so too.

Touring, sightseeing and culture

A second major form of tourism is also concerned with leisure. This involves the "wandering" tourist who, not content to remain on a beach, may travel around sightseeing and possibly stay in a different place each night. He may wish to see as much of a country or area as possible and to visit notable cultural monuments or attractions. In part this may be from a desire for self-education, but may also be for his self-esteem or to be able to show off to his peers that he has visited the places concerned. The camera is the main accessory for this kind of tourist, and the destinations the tourist selects are most commonly urban centres.

An excellent example of this type of tourism is the American tourist who makes the "circus" or "milk-run" around Britain. Typically this may be the trip: London-Oxford-Stratford-Chester-Lake District-Edinburgh-York-London, as shown in Fig. 3. (Frames Tours and White Horse are two operators who provide this very circuit.)

The destinations visited by sightseeing tourists are likely to be far more widespread than for the sun, sea and sand people. They are likely to need far more transport services in order to travel to a different place each day or two; this is called a "linear tour", as opposed to a "nodal tour" where tourists are based in one place, perhaps making excursions from there. Hotels in destinations on these linear tours can have quite a difficult time as they may have to change rooms and receive/bill different guests daily.

There are so many different types of attraction and so many motivations for visiting them that it is difficult to identify a "mass market" for this type of tourism. Nevertheless the products purchased—the transport, accommodation, tickets to attractions, and so on—are sufficiently similar to claim that this is an identifiable market segment.

About 20 per cent of British domestic tourists take this kind of holiday and also about 25 per cent of those going abroad.

Visiting friends and relatives

It is sometimes claimed that those visiting their friends or relatives

Fig. 3 *The linear tour. An example of the "milk-run" around Britain*

(VFR) are not really tourists at all in the conceptual sense. They do not usually purchase accommodation nor much food or drink or other services at the destination, certainly not on their own account. They are therefore seen as of little economic value to the destination.

To the transport operator, however, this is a very important market. British Airways, for example, runs a number of overseas reunion clubs specifically to encourage people to fly for VFR purposes. One in six of overseas tourists to Britain come for this reason, and from some countries such as Canada and Australia it is more like one in two.

The motivations for VFR are self-evident, but the effects less so. In a way these tourists are like business travellers in that the destinations are not chosen by them but predetermined and they are not often likely to buy holiday attractions. Most of them go to destinations which may not necessarily possess tourist attractions but which are population centres where friends or relatives live. Tourists are therefore visiting "non-tourist" areas.

In 1983 about 25 per cent of British domestic tourists were VFR.

Business travel

An area of tourism frequently ignored in planning is travel for business purposes. The business person may travel for a variety of purposes, and in doing so will buy the same, or similar products as do holidaymakers. Business people also spend money on entertainment and recreation while at their destinations, so that it is difficult, if not impossible, to separate the "business" element of their travel from the "tourist" element. For this reason, business travel is usually counted along with other forms of tourism in the official statistics for tourism in most countries.

The nature of business travel demand, however, is significantly different in many ways from that of holiday travel demand, and this must be recognised and catered for by suppliers of tourist services. Firstly, business travellers frequently travel to destinations not usually seen as tourist destinations. Cities such as Birmingham, Aberdeen, Brussels, Frankfurt and Geneva are important magnets for the business traveller: we can say, therefore, that demand is largely *city-orientated*. Also, demand is not dependent upon seasonal factors such as variation in climate or temperature. It is also less dependent upon economic factors such as a relative decline in the value of the pound sterling against foreign currencies, or the on-set of a recession (indeed, business travel activity may even rise as customer demand falls off, because companies may have to market their products more aggressively abroad).

Business travel is also less seasonal than holidaymaking. The comparative stability of business travel year-round is a boon to transport services, which can accurately forecast and plan their scheduled services based on known levels of demand.

Business people take relatively short, but frequently occurring, trips, which call for regular and frequent travel connections to the major business destinations. Reservations have often to be made at short notice, and the traveller must be able to obtain confirmation in advance of travel and stay arrangements.

Business travel is relatively price-inelastic; business people cannot be encouraged to travel more frequently by the offer of lower prices, nor will an increase in price dissuade most from travelling. While this general principle holds true, it must be added that during a prolonged depression such as we have recently been experiencing, companies—particularly the self-employed business people—have become more cost-conscious, and the more progressive travel agency chains have responded to this need by identifying discount air travel opportunities for their business house clients.

Within their destinations, business tourists will demand different services. They may require car hire, communications facilities or secretarial services at their hotel; their overall demand for recreational activities may be less than that of holidaymakers, and will focus on evening activities, but it should also be remembered that business travellers are often accompanied by their spouses, who may wish to make use of the tourist attractions of the region.

While seasonality is less apparent in business travel, the problem is replaced by one of *periodicity*. Demand for business flights is particularly high at peak periods of the morning and evening to allow business travellers to optimise their time at their destination. Also, few business travellers wish to remain at their destination over a weekend, posing particular problems of spare weekend capacity for those hotels catering largely for business markets, who must market their rooms to different clients over the weekends.

One important social change affecting the business travel market has been the growth of female business travellers. This calls for special consideration in hotels, such as additional bathroom fittings (make-up mirrors, bidets) and security measures to protect the single woman traveller.

Business travellers expect, and generally receive, a level of *status handling* less apparent in other forms of travel. Much business travel is first class, with a consequent high level of service from the suppliers of travel, including their intermediaries the travel agents. Senior executives, and frequent travellers, receive VIP treatment ranging from the use of special lounges at airports to the placing of complimentary flowers or fruit in hotel bedrooms.

Special forms of business travel

Two forms of business travel deserve special mention here. The first of these is travel for conferences or special events.

The term "conference" is often rather loosely applied to describe all forms of formal meetings between groups of people with similar interests. These can in fact range from international congresses (dealing, for example, with subjects such as air pollution or nuclear energy) to association conventions such as those of the American Bar Association, down to individual company meetings. Conferences, or conventions as the Americans usually call them, are an important element in the business and professional world, enabling participants to up-date their knowledge and mix socially with others of like interests. Many are arranged on an annual basis, such as those of political parties, trade unions or professional bodies. Participation is often encouraged by arranging these conferences in an overseas location, and this has been stimulated in recent years by the construction of purpose-built conference centres in many major business or tourist resort centres throughout the world, such as those of Berlin, Copenhagen, Hamburg or Las Vegas. The United States has led the field in the development of conference facilities, and has built some of the biggest conference centres in the world, accommodating up to 10,000 delegates. Major conferences may involve as many as 25,000 delegates, with closed circuit television relaying events in the main hall to other centres. In Britain, a number of large purpose-built conference facilities have been built in London and leading resorts such as Harrogate, Brighton and Bournemouth during recent years.

Although attracting large-scale conferences to a resort can be highly profitable (the average spend per day by delegates is substantially higher than that of other forms of tourist), there are relatively few international events of this size, and the scale of competition between centres makes it difficult to ensure year-round usage of such facilities unless they are multi-purpose. Consequently, such centres tend to double as exhibition centres, where fairs, pop concerts and similar mass-appeal functions can be mounted to draw markets year round.

While conference and exhibition travel demand is related to the health of the economy, there has been a steady underlying rise in the number of conferences, due to increasing job specialisation and the need for greater communication on an international scale.

More recently, a second business travel phenomenon has

appeared, in the shape of incentive travel. This is travel given by firms to employees, or to dealers and distributors, as a reward for some special endeavour or as a spur to achievement. A good example is the American car company which flies two planeloads of sales executives and showroom managers to the Caribbean for the launch of their new model (British Leyland went one better, hiring a cruise liner for the launch of their Metro). Travel has been found to have greater motivating power than rewards of cash or other incentives, and the growth of incentive travel in the past decade, both in the UK and abroad, has been substantial.

Both conference traffic and incentive travel are influenced by government policies on the taxation of income and business expenses. When policies favour conference travel as an allowable expense against corporate taxation, this form of travel will flourish. A short while ago, the United States Government decided to restrict such allowances to conferences taking part in the United States and its immediate neighbours (such as Mexico), causing European conference centres considerable consternation. Fortunately for the development of the international conference market, the policy was soon countermanded.

Reference should also be made here to the development of specialist package tours catering to the needs of the business world. Some specialist operators have chosen to concentrate on arranging highly lucrative industrial tours—such as trips for groups of European farmers to see the latest agricultural technology in operation in the United States. These programmes exercise strong appeal, especially where this becomes an allowable expense in the generating country.

Specialist motives

In addition to the above major forms of tourism, there is a variety of specialist needs giving rise to travel demand. We can take four examples.

(a) Study is an important motive. Students travelling to centres of learning or training for short or vacation courses may be legitimately regarded as tourists. For example, many hotels and operators offer holiday tuition courses in the arts or sports; London, Oxford and Bournemouth are just three destinations which provide English language education.

(b) Many tourists travel for sport. This may be participant sport, such as skiing or mountaineering, or spectator sport, such as attending the Olympics or World Cup series.

(c) Then there is health tourism. Ever since the development of spas in the eighteenth century there have been visitors to centres of medical treatment. The continuing popularity of spas on the Continent, with well-used, up-to-date facilities is evidence of this. This tourism can also be aided by government policy. In West Germany, for example, visits to spas can be treated as legitimate claims against medical insurance (providing such treatment is carried out at spas within the Federal Republic).

(d) Religion may be a strong motivator. There have been pilgrims as long as there has been religion, so that the tourist demand for destinations such as Lourdes or Mecca is constant.

THE PACKAGE HOLIDAY

What is an inclusive tour?

The term package holiday is a popularly used expression for what the tourism industry technically calls an inclusive tour or IT. In a way an IT is a total tourism product as it generally consists of transport from the generating area to the destination, accommodation at the destination and possibly some other recreational or business tourist services. These products are purchased by a firm called a *tour operator*, combined and sold as a package at a single price to tourists. So in many ways the term package holiday may be a better description than inclusive tour, if technically incorrect.

For many, the IT has become identified particularly with the inclusive holiday by *air*. Because of the geographical position of the UK, a generally greater proportion of tourists going abroad use air travel from the UK than from most other major generators. This has allowed air tour operation to be more swiftly developed from the UK than from elsewhere. However, land- and sea-based packages have an equal right to be recognised as ITs.

The origins of ITs

In a sense the operations of Thomas Cook in the 1850s and 1860s were inclusive tours. Cook put together all the elements of his excursions and sold them as a single package and other "tour organisers" followed his example. Most of these excursions were linear tours, going from place to place, rather than holidays centred in just one destination.

Tour operation proper got under way after World War II and flourished, particularly in Europe, for several reasons.

(a) Economic and social conditions were conducive to mass tourism generation. In the post-war world of promised social and economic equality, more people wanted to take the kind of holidays that previously only a few had been able to enjoy. However, they were often chary of making their own arrangements, even to places which the men of the family may have visited in wartime.

(b) A surplus of aircraft converted from military to civilian use existed, which created the conditions for air charter services. At the same time, owing to technical and cost/price problems with scheduled transport which will be seen in Chapters 5 and 9, transport operators frequently had surplus seats available on their services which they were willing to sell en bloc at almost any price. A tour operator who could buy cheap transport and also use bulk purchasing power to secure large discounts from hoteliers could put together an IT at a very attractive price.

(c) Conditions were right for marketing ITs. During the 1950s and early 1960s cheap pricing was important to consumers who had been through years of austerity and now wanted to improve their material living without spending too much. Also, American ideas on packaging and advertising had reached Europe, so that consumer acceptability of the packaged IT was high.

(d) Legal and economic controls on tourism were often conducive to IT development, such as the easing of post-war foreign exchange controls and the policy in the UK of restricting private airlines to a virtually all-charter operation.

ITXs and ITCs

In air tour operation, two main forms of IT developed, both of which will be investigated more fully in Chapter 9 but which are described briefly here.

Where scheduled services operate with aircraft never fully loaded, airlines may sell blocks of seats to tour operators very cheaply, in fact at any price which more than covers the small extra costs of providing for passengers in seats that would otherwise fly empty. The airlines impose conditions on the tour operator that make it difficult for the operator to resell to travellers who would be using the flight anyway (booked direct with the airline at the normal fare). These seats must be sold on a return or round-trip basis, which in airline terms means an *excursion* ticket for each passenger. The tour operator then builds this into a package called an inclusive tour by excursion or ITX.

Where a tour operator charters a plane, or part of a plane, for a special flight, the resulting package is called an inclusive tour by charter or ITC. In the 1950s and 1960s there were usually two sorts of charter operation: those wholly of charter companies using older secondhand aircraft on a constant basis; and those of scheduled airlines which happened to have expensive aircraft scheduled to do nothing on some days and therefore available for hire. In either case aircraft were often available for the same return flight at the same time each week. This enabled a series of charters to the same destination, where one week's returning flight brings back the previous week's outgoing passengers. This is known as a *back-to-back* operation.

Modern charter operations, which use aircraft identical to those used by scheduled airlines, still fly series returns on the same system.

Selling the IT
One of the great advantages of the IT is the neatness with which it can be sold, particularly in markets which are mass generators of tourists. In the sense that it is almost a complete tourism product, the customer has no problem in putting together elements of a complete cohesive package. It also has a special appeal to those who are rather unsure about travel, especially iong-distance travel, in that it offers both ease of booking and a degree of security to the tourist.

Generally, the ITC has tended to be associated with mass-market travel in the cheaper price ranges. This is inevitably because of the circular pattern of price, cost and demand (see Fig. 4). An efficient

Fig. 4 *The relationship between price, cost and demand*

charter requires a high load factor, that is aeroplanes and accommodation as full as possible, to keep cost per passenger down. This is passed on as a very cheap price, which in turn assures high demand and therefore a high load factor. This situation is exactly right for the mass-market tourists prepared to go to destinations in 'large numbers.

The ITX has tended to be identified with slightly more expensive packages, since the air ticket is more expensive and price does not depend so directly on numbers of passengers. As choice with scheduled services is also usually more flexible, tour operators can combine this flexibility with higher-priced accommodation to create a more exclusive IT for smaller numbers of people.

Travel agents like to sell ITs, as they receive commission on single transactions, rather than having to arrange separate services for tourists to make the same total commission. Destination areas that are attempting to develop new resorts or accommodation have also supported tour operators strongly, as they can reach a large market of tourists very quickly.

The IT product therefore has many advantages in selling tourism to mass market generators.

What has happened to tour operators?

We need to paint here a very brief picture of recent tour operators' development in order to review the full scene in Chapter 9. The formative years of air tour operation, and to some extent coach tours, were the 1960s. Firms such as Clarksons, Thomson, Cosmos and Wallace Arnold in the UK, Neckermann and Touropa in Germany or Vingresor in Scandinavia grew fast.

In the early 1970s, four separate but connected series of events took place.

(a) Major growth occurred in foreign ITs, particularly by air. This was partly due to reasonable economic growth, partly to the availability of better and more economic aircraft, and partly (from the UK) to the easing of foreign exchange controls (1966-70 £50 per head, 1970-77 £300).

(b) Considerable integration took place, both between tour operators (horizontal integration) and where tour operators became involved with other sectors of tourism such as airlines or hotels. This process has continued.

(c) There was ruthless competition which caused the failure of some companies, notably Court Line (controlling Clarkson's Holidays) in 1974.

(d) Regulations and controls on the industry were progressively introduced. In the UK, for example, the 1971 Civil Aviation Act provided for a system of licences to control air tour operators, and after the failures of 1974 the current bonding schemes to protect customers were started. In Germany and Switzerland the governments initiated similar controls.

More recently trends have developed and altered. Very strong links exist between tour operators and airlines such that now virtually all major European and Japanese tour operators are airline-owned or airline owners. Selling activities have become more international, with companies like Airtours expanding from Germany and France into Switzerland, Belgium, Holland and elsewhere, or Tjaereborg from Denmark into Germany and the UK. The idea of the package has also become more popular in domestic tourism. Hotel companies such as Grand Metropolitan and Holiday Inns, local authorities and tourist boards, have all realised the potential of a packaged product to boost flagging domestic tourism, and have frequently used "themes" to develop their ITs.

Anything can be packaged

In fact the idea of a package can be linked to virtually any theme and any type of tourism. Almost all sectors of the industry contain firms who are prepared to combine their services with others into an inclusive holiday or an inclusive business trip. This may take almost any form and may or may not be theme-based.

Some ITs are designed for particular groups, sometimes known as special-interest or affinity groups (although this title is dropping out of use). Equally, enterprising travel agents can make use of special arrangements to construct a tailor-made individual IT to a customer's specification if he has a special requirement. The IT is therefore capable of being almost a universal tourism product.

DETERMINANTS OF TOURISM DEMAND

So far, this chapter has outlined some of the facts and structures of tourism generation. For a fuller understanding of how and why tourism originates it is necessary to examine some of the theory underlying tourism demand. In this section we shall look only at factors affecting *total* demand, whilst in Chapter 4 we look at the allocation of that demand.

Psychological/social factors

Is tourism a Good Thing for the tourist? Is it a desirable product that consumers may wish to have, either as an end in itself or as a means to an end (as in business travel)? Most research assumes that tourism is such a product or group of products but often ignores the psychological and social motivations of tourists. Marketing textbooks examine this area but usually only in terms of consumer choice.

Some psychological determinants are obvious. For example, the social need to visit one's friends or family living in another place dominates the VFR market, although for some tourists VFR may only be ancillary to another motive. More complex are the psychological determinants of holiday demand. The psychological and physiological need for a break from work is recognised, almost as a medical need, on a par with the first reasons for visiting spas and the seaside. This implies relaxation and often an environment completely different from that of the tourist's home surroundings. The social pressures towards tourism, however, are far greater than this. A consumer, or consuming family, is likely to be influenced by many different sources, for example work colleagues, neighbours and friends. If such people take a holiday, there may be strong social pressure on the individual consumer to conform also.

Fashion also plays a major role. It may become fashionable to take a holiday at a certain time of year or to take a certain type of holiday; equally it may become fashionable business practice to reward employees by incentive travel. Many people are influenced by fashion in tourism just as they are by fashion in clothing, and resorts have in turns benefited and suffered from a sequential rise and decline of their appeal to trend-setting holidaymakers and later to the mass markets.

The desire for a sun-tan is a relatively recent example of the pull of fashion in tourism. In Victorian times, a white skin reflected high status associated with the leisure classes who were able to stay at home while labourers working out of doors accumulated an unfashionable tan. As the leisure classes took to travel abroad, fashion turned about face, with the wealthy cultivating sun-tans as evidence of their exotic travels, and this was in turn emulated by other travellers.

Psychology also influences tourism through habit. People frequently stick to habitual activities through a preference for security and no desire for change. In leisure time use this means they may simply become accustomed to taking a holiday or business trip at a fixed time and maybe always to the same place. Tourism buying can easily become as habitual as always buying the same make of car or brand of coffee. Many seaside resorts in Britain depend heavily on the traditional demand for their attractions by holidaymakers whose parents and grandparents visited the same resort.

Sociopolitical factors

Tourism demand is also influenced by the society and the political system in which the tourist lives. Many societies actively encourage tourism, mostly as a break from work to provide physical and mental relief and as a reward for effort. In the countries of Eastern Europe, for example, there are policies on *social tourism* where tourism entitlement is deliberately rationed out by the state for everybody, almost regardless of means. The Soviet worker therefore knows exactly when and what his holiday entitlement will be. In West Germany, as we have seen, medical insurance schemes often allow the jaded worker to take a long break in a spa resort, ostensibly for medical treatment but in practice also as a holiday. In any event the worker can be regarded as a tourist since the spa resorts are normally residential and well away from the generating areas.

Most countries have a system of public holidays for all. In Britain the first bank holiday (August) was introduced in 1871, and gradually the number of holidays has grown to the current eight days a year (in England). Many other countries have more public holidays, such as twelve in Japan and thirteen in Spain. Pressure to have these holidays may come from various parts of society, such as governments, religious groups or trades unions. The holidays may be patriotic, religious or ceremonial, yet almost invariably become part of popular holiday expectations.

In general, sociopolitical systems influence more especially the choice of tourism destinations, and this will therefore be discussed more fully in the next chapter.

Economic money-related factors

Undoubtedly the main factor governing tourism demand is the constraint of money. The psychological and social pressures discussed above tend to make tourism a desirable product which will satisfy consumer or business needs; thus we may see the purchase of tourism products as a consumer *objective* (some economists may refer to this as providing the maximum *utility* for the consumer). In most countries products are allocated in exchange for money, and so the possession of money can be seen as a *constraint* on achieving the consumer's objective.

Since most individuals make purchases out of their incomes, the size of those incomes is likely to be very important for tourism demand. In fact there has been much research which shows that, typically, when a person's income rises 1 per cent he or she is likely to spend about $1\frac{1}{2}$ per cent more on tourism (this is called an income elasticity of $+1\frac{1}{2}$). So, for a country which is developing fast and increasing its income, the effect on tourism generation is likely to be great. West Germany and Japan, for example, have generated very large numbers of tourists since the war as their economies redeveloped.

It is important to qualify this by adding that the distribution of incomes within a country is also important. If higher incomes are concentrated in the hands of a few people, as in some Middle Eastern countries, certainly the "haves" will travel, but with so many "have-nots" there will be no mass tourism generation.

Business tourism is also constrained by cash. While the income elasticity is likely to be less strong, much business tourism spending such as incentive travel and conference attendance depends on the business having sufficient cash income from its operations. This usually depends on the state of the economy, so buoyant economies generate business tourism.

Tax policy is important here. If governments allow all business tourism spending to be allowed as a business expense, companies may be equally willing to spend on tourism as on stationery and communications. Sometimes governments wish to curtail such spending and place limits on tax deductibility, so forcing businesses to spend out of profits—not a pleasing prospect. Over the last few years US government tax policy has fluctuated with their presidents, and business travel there has changed accordingly.

Equally significant with income is price; and clearly, the relative price of a tourist product against other similar products will be a key factor in tourism demand. Most tourists seek sun, sea and sand and this, as we have seen, has led to the development of "identikit" destinations. Choice between these destinations is dependent very largely on the relative value for money which each is seen to offer. Two factors are at work here in deciding price: the relative exchange rates between the generating country's currency and that of the destination country, and the inflation rates in these countries. Thus if a country such as Spain, which is heavily dependent upon the tourist trade, suffers inflation at a higher level than that of its leading competitors, or higher than the rate of inflation in its main generating countries, tourists will switch to countries such as Greece or Yugoslavia. The high inflation country may eventually be forced to devalue its currency in order to attract back its tourists.

Sometimes, however, inflation rates may be so low in a destination country compared with the generating country that even unfavourable exchange rates will not discourage travel. Such has been the case in recent times with Switzerland, which, with inflation rates typically averaging less than 3 per cent per annum, has been able to attract British tourists experiencing up to four times this level of inflation.

Relative prices of overseas and domestic holidays are also key pointers to tourism demand, and will be monitored closely by governments seeking favourable tourism balance of payments. The English Tourist Board, concerned about the image of cheap holidays abroad which is generated by tour operators, has taken steps to promote England as a country offering prices comparable with, or cheaper than, holidays in leading Mediterranean destinations.

Finally, the price of tourism relative to other products must be considered. For an individual, tourism competes with other items such as a car or home improvements for a share of the budget. Thus if someone is debating whether to take a holiday or buy a new car, a special offer on cars coupled with a threat of later price rises will probably stop him from being a tourist. If this price relationship is widespread within a country there could be many car buyers and few tourists!

Economic time-related factors

Especially for people at work or in education, time may be as great a constraint on tourism as money. Whereas buying, say, furniture is only limited by cash, buying tourism involves both cash *and* time, both of which may have limited availability. Holiday entitlement at work or school can then have a spectacular effect on tourism. Over the last few years many schools in Britain have introduced one-week half-terms, rather than two or three days, and families increasingly use these periods to take a second holiday.

Holiday entitlement at work is generally increasing in most countries. In Europe the average allowance is now around twenty-two to twenty-five working days per year, and in many countries there is a legal minimum. As these lengths increase, more people are prepared to take second holidays or may extend the duration of their main holidays.

Whilst the timing of holidays may not affect the overall demand it does have an influence via prices. Holiday timing is not simply governed by the weather but is also controlled by public holidays, factory closure and school/college vacations. These often combine to build a peak season where demand often exceeds tourism supply so that prices are high. This then leads suppliers such as hoteliers and airlines to influence demand through price adjustments at different seasons. Despite such action, about 80 per cent of all European tourism still takes place during the months of June to September.

Technical factors

There are a number of other, largely technical, influences on tourism demand. The needs of businesses affect business tourism, such as the necessity of maintaining business contacts, attending exhibitions or important conferences. Demand in the VFR market is affected by the need for family reunions, for example at weddings and funerals, or simply for a get-together for a group of old friends. Students may need to travel for foreign language education, whilst pilgrims may need to visit a holy centre at least once in their lives. All of these are examples of factors which stimulate a constant demand for tourism services.

THE MAIN GENERATORS

Which countries generate tourism?

Over a third of the world's international tourism spending is by West Germans or Americans. The factors discussed above have combined in these two countries to produce large numbers of tourists every year. Germans particularly place a high value on tourism as part of their pattern of living. Major generating countries are shown in Table II.

TABLE II. MAIN TOURISM-GENERATING COUNTRIES (1982)

Country	Expenditure (US$m)
West Germany	16,218
USA	12,347
United Kingdom	6,376
France	5,157
Japan	4,113
Holland	3,302
Canada	3,202
Austria	2,685
Switzerland	2,216
Belgium and Luxembourg	2,191

Source: OECD

Domestic tourism is greatest in the United States as it has easily the largest population of the above countries and, with its large land area, can be considered in travelling terms as the equivalent of several European countries. It is estimated by the US Travel Data Centre that about 480 million domestic visits are made by Americans each year. In Britain for comparison the figure is about 131 million visits of which 48 million are major holiday trips of four or more nights.

Domestic tourism is also high in the Soviet Union and other countries where the political system discourages outgoing foreign tourism. Reliable statistics of travel in these countries are rarely available.

Which areas of countries generate tourism?
Urban centres and conurbations are the obvious main generators of tourism, but for more reasons than may be readily apparent.

(a) In most developed and industrialised countries the bulk of the population lives in urban areas. In the UK, for example, 90 per cent of people live in large towns and conurbations. Pressures of urban living may also act to make travel a more necessary and desirable purchase for the town dweller than for the countryman.

(b) In many countries incomes in urban areas, from industry and commerce, are higher than those in rural areas, from agriculture and other primary production. We must qualify this by adding that incomes will be especially favourable for tourism in newer urban areas than in older ones more dependent on declining industries where there may be lower wages and higher unemployment.

(c) The country dweller, perhaps engaged in agriculture or fishing where machines cannot be stopped or offices closed at will, may find it more difficult to travel than the town dweller. Thus, for example, farmers are amongst the groups of people least likely to be holiday-makers and have far less need to travel on business than say salesmen.

To the urban pattern of population must be added the effects of factors already discussed, principally the regional distribution of income and wealth. A country dweller in northern Italy for example is more likely to be a tourist than a town dweller from southern Italy because income differences are so marked. Social and psychosocial patterns also differ from one part of a country to another.

In the UK the result of the above factors is that the prime tourist-generating area is London and the South East. Then, in order of importance, come the mainly urban areas of the West Midlands, Yorkshire–Lancashire, south Wales and lowland Scotland, followed by the prosperous but less urban areas of southern and central England. A good guide to the relative importance of these markets is the location of travel agents, 28 per cent of whom are in the London area.

Changing patterns of generation

Within the UK the pattern of tourism generation has changed only slowly as some areas become more prosperous and tourism-oriented, such as many new town areas, and others decline, such as inner cities.

Change is more marked internationally, however. Fifteen years ago the USA was easily the main generator of tourism; today it has been overtaken by West Germany. More spectacular has been the increase in the number of Japanese tourists, joined recently by Koreans, Taiwanese and Thais. Political disturbances have reduced tourism from countries such as Czechoslovakia and Iran, but those countries which discover new industrially-based and well-distributed wealth together with stable political systems will undoubtedly produce the tourists of the future.

INDIVIDUAL CHOICE IN TOURISM

Up to this point we have looked at the overall or aggregate picture of tourism demand which reveals how and why tourism is generated in certain places and by certain groups of people. We can now go on to look at how decisions are made by individual tourists, whether consciously or unconsciously, on where to go, where to stay, what mode of travel to use and where they will purchase their product. In short, we are looking at the factors leading to individual choice in tourist behaviour.

In many instances choice may be limited or even non-existent. The British businessman wishing to conclude a contract this evening in New York for example has no choice of destination and little choice of transport—he must use a British Airways Concorde flight. His choice is therefore limited to various accommodations and booking methods. A Soviet worker may not even have that flexibility—his holiday may be fixed entirely by the state.

Choice is influenced by many factors, but as we shall see there are the recurring ones of money, time and what may loosely be termed fashion. As already seen in connection with overall demand, some factors may make a particular tourism product a desirable consumer objective, whereas others may act as constraints on consumers trying to reach their objective. The constraining factors such as time and money may limit the consumer to a less desirable objective, perhaps one that is less fashionable.

All the time it is important to remember the tourist's overall objective, i.e. for the businessman the contribution to the business's policy and for the holidaymaker the purchase of a (hopefully) satisfying experience. These objectives colour the tourist's view of choices available. It is also important to bear in mind that tourists do not always have full information about choices available, so that they may make a selection which the better-informed employee in the tourism industry would regard as silly.

DESTINATIONS

It is possible to define destinations in different ways. A destination may simply be a resort or a business centre which the tourist visits and where he stays. It may be an area or even a country within which he travels. It may be a cruise ship which visits several ports. It is therefore useful to define a destination as *a place or set of places to which tourists go, and in which they may stay, as a prime objective of their visit.*

Tourists with no choice

Sometimes, as seen above, consumers may have no choice in determining their destination. This is especially true with business travel and with the VFR market, where to stay with friends or relatives means going to where they live. In this latter case it is possible that there *is* a choice, between a holiday elsewhere using paid-for accommodation and staying free with family or friends. The choice is therefore partly controlled by money constraints, although this may be unimportant compared with the desire or need to renew acquaintances.

Low-income groups may also have relatively little choice of destination in that money and/or time limit the range of alternatives. Thus the excursionist from London with limited means and only public transport available may want to go to the seaside and be limited to reaching either Southend or Brighton. Whilst both are excellent resorts, in many ways superior to others farther afield and more expensive to reach, the excursionist has no opportunity to choose elsewhere.

Attractions

The main reason for choosing a destination must be its attractions. The effect of the attractions on tourists is psychologically complex and is depicted in Fig. 5.

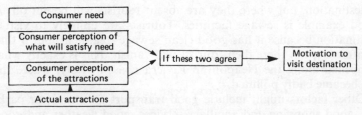

Fig. 5 *The motivation process for a destination*

In Chapter 1 we explored the importance of attractions at a destination which, in aggregate, will act as a magnet for mass tourism. We will now explore this further. The attractions must be things which provide positive benefits or characteristics to the tourist. They might be such things as proximity to seas or lakes, mountain views, safari parks, interesting historical monuments or cultural events, sports events or pleasant and comfortable conference surroundings. The list of possible motivational attractions is very large, but there are many pitfalls in the motivation process.

(*a*) The intending tourist needs to be *aware* of all the attractions. If he is not the process cannot begin.

(*b*) He may *perceive* the attractions in different ways. One person may perceive the bingo halls in Blackpool as escapist fun which give hours of pleasure, whilst to another they may be a boring waste of time and money. Perceptions are coloured by experience and attitudes, which are different for everybody.

(c) The intending tourist may not *know or recognise* his needs very well. If he does know them, he may not correctly diagnose the benefits which could satisfy his needs. For example, Mr A at home in New York wants to sample everyday British culture, but books a holiday in London in high summer. He probably finds no-one who speaks English and certainly little typical British culture!

(d) The perceptions of need and attraction must correspond for there to be motivation to visit a destination.

Overcoming these pitfalls is the job of advertising. A good advertising programme makes consumers aware of destinations, allows for the different factors affecting their perceptions and tries to relate benefits to needs in consumers' minds.

Distractions

One can argue that just as important as the positive attractions of a destination are the negative effects of distractions; that is, there are some factors which do not positively motivate tourists to visit a destination, but where they are absent tourists will be put off. A good example is sewage facilities. Tourists are unlikely to visit a destination because it has good clean sewage treatment, but if that treatment is not there then tourists will vanish. This is exactly what happened along the Neapolitan Riviera coast in Italy, where the sea became badly polluted.

Other factors might include good transport links and car parking, good shopping and ancillary services, good weather and good relations with the resident "host" population. The absence of these has inhibited tourism in many places ranging from wet, cold northern English seaside resorts to some Spanish destinations with accusations of unfriendliness.

It is not always possible to divide clearly attractions from distractions. For example, the existence of good accommodation and food might, for a British family visiting America, be only incidental to choice but for an American family visiting France it might be a major motivating attraction. Similarly, "fashionable" resorts such as St Tropez or the Costa Smeralda of Sardinia may be primary attractions to some tourists but only secondary to others.

Money and time

If asked to solve a problem, a computer may frequently act by working out an "ideal" solution, but then have constraints imposed on it that force it to seek a next best, or third or fourth best alternative. The same is often true for tourists. The major constraints as we have begun to see already are likely to be time and money. Ideally, a very long holiday in an exotic destination might satisfy a tourist's needs, but he is severely constrained by his income or wealth and by his holiday entitlement from work or school.

Obviously these constraints act in different ways for different people. The old-age pensioner may have no time constraint whatever but be restricted by having only a small pension which limits him to a cheap holiday. A senior company executive or a busy successful farmer may have plenty of money to spend but very little time available. For most of us a combination of time and money dictates the "optimum" destinations available. Of course, as incomes rise and holiday entitlements increase, then the constraints are progressively relaxed. Equally, if prices in a destination rise or the foreign exchange rate for it becomes more expensive, then the constraints on that destination become tighter.

The main control exercised by these constraints is on the distance a tourist travels. Distance in this sense is a combination of time and cost rather than actual kilometres. For example, London to Bath, London to Boulogne and Glasgow to Skye are all similar point-to-point distances, but the long time necessary for the latter two, and particularly the extra cost associated with crossing water, would make them less popular for a day's excursion. This is where new direct or cheaper transport links could bring destinations within constraints, as when motorway links are opened or as when Miami became a cheap destination for British tourists in 1979–81.

There is an interesting relationship between distance to destinations, measured by time/cost, and the number of tourists to travel for a visit of given length. This is shown in Fig. 6. As one might expect, in general the more time and money it takes, the less people are prepared to travel. There is however a form of *minimum* distance, below which people do not think they are getting away from home and are therefore not very likely to travel. So there tends to be an "average" travel time (represented by the peak in Fig. 6) which is related to the total length of time/money available. Excursionists spend on average about $1\frac{1}{2}$–2 hours travelling to a destination, one-

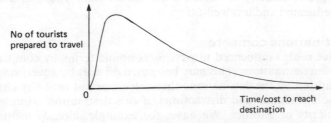

Fig. 6 *How far tourists go to reach destinations*

week tourists about 4-6 hours, and two-week tourists about 8-12 hours.

These constraints, then, directly relate likely destinations for particular groups of tourists to the generating areas in which they live.

Repeat visiting

For many products, purchasers frequently continue to buy the same type. This is often true for example with instant coffee, where a consumer may always buy the same brand (brand loyalty). In many cases it is also true for tourism destinations. This situation is known as *repeat purchasing* or *repeat visiting*.

There are varying reasons why purchasers, faced with a choice of destinations, may continue to choose the same one many times.

(*a*) It is possible that the constraints mentioned above continue to operate in the same way so that only one destination is ever attainable. Thus a trade association might invariably choose the same centre for its annual conference because it is the only one which all delegates can easily reach within a reasonable time.

(*b*) The attractions of a particular destination to certain tourists may be so strong that no other is ever considered. This often seems to apply to cruising; P & O have found that for some cruises on the SS Canberra repeat visiting was 90 per cent or more, that is 90 per cent of the passengers took a similar cruise previously.

(*c*) Security and comfort may motivate a tourist to choose the same destination time after time. If a family, once having found a destination, likes its attractions, has an enjoyable time and maybe meets new friends, the chances are high that the visit will be repeated. This may extend to using the same accommodation in the same resort, at the same time each year, and therefore meeting the same like-minded people each year.

Sociologists and psychologists have undertaken research to distinguish between people who like this extreme security and those who prefer adventure, new faces and a new destination each time. Those who prefer security are often older rather than younger, are less well-educated and less well-off.

Destinations compete

Choice is also influenced in psychoeconomic terms by competition between destinations. This may be caused directly by advertising and promotion by the destinations themselves, or indirectly by changes in the attractions and distractions of one destination affecting the popularity of another. We have, for example, already mentioned the influence of prices and fluctuating exchange rates on aggregate demand for destinations. Equally, given two sun, sea and sand destinations with very similar attractions, if political conditions in one of these deteriorate, or if it gets a reputation for lawlessness, overcrowding or pollution, we can expect a proportion of tourists to switch to the other destination in preference. Economists refer to this as a cross or cross-price effect.

Obviously the degree of competition depends on the similarity between destinations, so if a destination wants to avoid losing out on cross effects it may attempt to stress its uniqueness in its publicity. The choice of destinations offering an Eiffel Tower is rather limited!

MODES OF TRAVEL

For most tourists the choice of travel mode follows on from the choice of destination. Once again there are "attractions" of particular modes, including convenience, comfort and perhaps speed, as well as "distractions" such as safety, and the same constraints of time and cost. The resulting pattern of tourist transport within Great Britain is shown in Fig. 7.

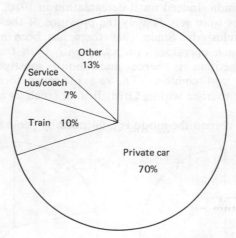

Fig. 7 *Transport modes used by tourists within Great Britain, 1980*

Private or public?

The main choice traditionally has been between private transport (mostly private car) and public transport. In the 1950s public transport by train, bus or coach was predominant, but the 1960s and 1970s produced a major change to private transport. With increased car ownership, tourists have much greater convenience and flexibility with car travel. If a car is owned anyway, the perceived cost of using it for a tourist trip is only the variable cost, mostly petrol, so that for family use in particular it is likely to be considerably cheaper than using public transport. For those who do not have a car, or who decide not to use their own car, the choice may be between public transport and hire cars.

There are two main types of supplier of hire cars.

(a) The large international companies or consortia such as Hertz, Avis, Europcar, Budget or InterRent all charge similar high prices but offer a wide choice of cars, hiring locations and flexibility. They are therefore of most use to business travellers for whom the price constraint is not so significant.

(b) There are many small, local hirers who may be cheaper but who perhaps operate from only one or two locations. These may be more useful for the holiday tourist or excursionist.

Public transport can be divided into regular service and charter/ excursion. Most trains are scheduled services, whereas bus and coach travel for tourism within Great Britain is about 50 per cent by charter/excursion. Indeed until deregulation in 1980, long-distance coach services were very largely the province of the National Bus Company exclusively. Since 1980 there has been a much wider choice of coach operators competing with both trains and each other. Competition is fierce and choice mostly dictated by speed, price and comfort. The use of other forms of public transport for tourism within Great Britain (such as air or ships) is negligible.

For travel abroad the mode is influenced by geography. There is

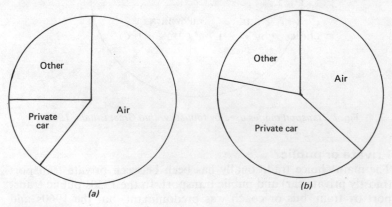

Fig. 8 *Transport modes used by tourists going abroad from (a) Great Britain and (b) West Germany*

an interesting comparison between travel abroad by the British and the West Germans, shown in Fig. 8. Because Great Britain is an island, more than half of all outgoing British tourists choose air travel, presumably for speed and convenience. Only one in six take a private car, because of the delay and cost of sea crossings, compared with nearly half of all Germans.

Choosing between airlines or between ferry companies may be related more to the convenience and availability of routes than to comfort or price. It is only when "price wars" develop, such as on transatlantic air routes between 1977 and 1982, instigated by Laker, or on cross-channel car ferries from 1980, that price seems to become a very significant factor.

Time, delays and frustration

These are factors often ignored in looking at choice of transport, but which are very important in influencing choice, especially for repeat purchasing.

Air travellers have frequently complained about delays and over-crowding at London Heathrow, and this has led to attempts by airlines and other airport authorities to develop alternatives. Air UK and Amsterdam Schiphol airport, for example, co-operate to enable travellers from the Midlands and the North of England to avoid London when en route to long-haul destinations.

The same applies to virtually all other forms of tourist transport. Users of road bottlenecks for example may choose to visit a different destination or use rail. Ferry companies operating in the western English Channel benefit when there are queues and delays on Dover and Folkestone routes. Strikes or undue red tape at some African gateway airports sometimes cause holiday tourists to change desti-nations next time. These may all be seen as further constraints on travel mode choice which can only be altered by the competent authorities.

ACCOMMODATION AND ATTRACTIONS

Switching to self-catering

Thirty or forty years ago the majority of tourists stayed with friends and relatives or in guest-house type accommodation. Hotels were used by business tourists and the better-off holidaymakers, whilst at the other end of the price spectrum holiday camps were developing their popularity. There have been two major movements in consumer demand since then:

(a) the upgrading of standards of serviced accommodation, which will be looked at below; and

(b) the switch to self-catering accommodation.

This switch is common to all the main generating countries. It can be seen as a logical consequence of the use of private cars for travel and the growing desire for freedom of choice during a tourist visit. At the same time labour costs have generally risen faster than other costs in destinations, causing serviced accommodation to become relatively more expensive.

Since choice in accommodation is inevitably bound up with money constraints, and tourism is a large item in many budgets, many tourists have recently sought long-term ways of maintaining the characteristics of their most desired accommodation but reducing the cost. This has led to many people owning caravans/tents, second homes, and to timesharing.

A caravan or tent may be purchased because, although it involves a high initial outlay, in subsequent times the cost of accommodation is very small and the quality known. Also it may be possible to let it when not required and so regain some of the cost. Pioneers in the use of towed caravans, motor homes and so on are the Americans, whose main concern is often freedom of destination choice and flexibility of movement.

Second homes have a further advantage in that they will probably also appreciate in value. A tourist with savings available may therefore be able to have accommodation virtually free if the appreciation of the property covers the costs of services and maintenance. Many German, French and Dutch tourists buy second homes, often in the country or by the sea, and this is reflected in the nature of the newest Spanish or French resorts where 80 per cent or more of the accommodation available is likely to be for outright sale.

For those who cannot afford these purchases, the fastest growing demand is for timesharing. In this case a property such as an apartment or villa is sold to several co-owners who each buy a week's or a month's use of it at different times of year. Thus to buy a week in high summer may be very expensive, but a week in low season may be very cheap. The co-owner may then sell his week or month at whatever price he can negotiate (and prices usually appreciate). In many cases he may also use a scheme where he can "swap" his week for one in another property elsewhere and thus have a choice of destinations. Because of this flexibility, timesharing is continuing to be a major growth area in the 1980s. There are now estimated to be some 20,000 timeshare owners in the UK and over 40 timeshare resorts.

Requirements in serviced accommodation

As living standards advance, so tourists have raised the requirements necessary to satisfy their consumer objectives in buying accommodation, i.e. they want higher standards of rooms and facilities. This demand has been spearheaded by American tourists who, being used to high living standards, naturally wish these standards to be maintained on a holiday or business trip.

At the same time technology has spread, enabling better quality accommodation to be provided without a great increase in cost. Perhaps the most notable improvement over the last few decades has been the spread of en suite facilities—rooms with private bath and WC. To take one example, a well-known guide listed the facilities shown in Table III for a British holiday resort. This is just the change in one ten-year period.

TABLE III. IMPROVEMENTS IN FACILITIES IN SERVICED ACCOMMODATION

	No of hotel rooms	No of rooms with private bath	% with private bath
1972	1440	656	45.5
1982	1394	816	58.7

Demand has also caused hoteliers to install such things as radio and television, central heating and air conditioning, fitted carpets, swimming pools, in-house entertainment, well-equipped meeting rooms and so on. In these respects large modern hotels in business centres or newly developed resort areas such as Hong Kong, Hawaii or the north African coast have a distinct advantage over older hotels in traditional destinations. Many of these older hotels have been forced into expensive re-equipping and modernisation programmes or faced closure.

To be a desirable choice, then, the modern business hotel should contain en suite rooms equipped to this year's standards, conference and meeting rooms with up-to-date communications and information systems, and whatever relaxation facilities are in vogue, such as jacuzzi pools or squash courts. A resort hotel is likely to need a full entertainments programme, either in-house or arranged by the hotel, together with the appropriate indoor and outdoor places for it.

Sightseeing and sport
Choice of attractions is closely linked to choice of destination. However, once a destination has been selected, consumers may have a range of amenities and activities open to them during their stay. As with destinations, their selection is likely to be based on motivation

caused by positive attractions, tempered by distractions and regulated by constraints, notably time and money.

There may be no choice at all, as where a coach tour runs to a fixed itinerary with no free time, or limited choice, as in a specialist sports or arts weekend. Apart from activities which *must* take place, such as business meetings or visiting mandatory sights, choice is determined by individual and changing requirements. There has been considerable research into what tourists do with their time, showing that frequently major activities include relaxation, sightseeing, sport, shopping and joining in somehow with local life.

Here, constraints come into play. For example, a tourist staying in Tunisia for a week may want to go sightseeing in the Sahara, but the only available way might be a four-day package trip. The tourist may feel that this does not allow sufficient time for other activities and therefore limits sightseeing to local half-day excursions. A tourist in the Caribbean might like to spend a day big-game fishing or learning to water ski, but if on a limited budget may not be able to afford either. So choice of activity is restricted.

Fashion is a major determinant of demand. During the 1970s and the 1980s some trends in activities undertaken by tourists have emerged. One is the increase in demand for participant sports so that for example many German tourists may be found learning or playing tennis in Mediterranean resorts, whilst Japanese tourists are increasingly keen to play golf. Another is the growth of general activity holidays based around themes of sport, arts and crafts or hobbies. Followers of these fashions not only choose destinations to suit but select appropriate and complementary attractions at the destinations.

CHOICE IN PURCHASING METHOD

Finally, consumers may exercise choice as to how they buy tourism products. The distribution channels for these products are varied, and will be discussed more fully in Chapter 8, but it is important here to follow briefly through the paths a consumer may use.

Use an agent?

In most countries the majority of tourism products are not sold through travel agents, although some products may be entirely or almost entirely sold this way. International air tickets are mostly sold through agents, with a minority of customers purchasing directly from airline offices. ITs in Britain, for example, are mostly sold through agents. The use of the agent is largely dictated by control exercised by the principals themselves, such as airlines, or by retail organisations, such as the Association of British Travel Agents.

In some cases consumers have a choice between direct booking and using an agent. Since the price is likely to be the same for buying the same product, choice would be determined by convenience, custom and advice.

Most people are of course likely to choose a convenient booking method. If there is a travel agency next door they will use it. They may also be accustomed to buying through an agent, so that is the first place they will call when going out to buy. On the other hand, if they ordinarily buy direct from suppliers such as hotels they may not think of visiting an agent at all. An agent may be used if the consumer requires (hopefully) impartial advice and wants to know about other products available.

This last factor is also important in determining choice between travel agents. Even in a country like Britain with over 5,500 travel agents, most people have a feasible choice of no more than three or four agents to approach. Since with fixed prices and commission rates there is no price advantage, selection will probably depend on who gives the best service, advice and friendliness.

Use a package?
Another question for the consumer is whether or not to buy an IT. Again tradition and convenience are major factors. Of British tourists going abroad, 50 per cent use an IT, whereas only 10 per cent of domestic British tourists do so. This is partly because tourists within the country have traditionally booked their accommodation directly and provided their own transport, and partly because an IT is a convenient way of overcoming the unknown problems likely to be encountered on a foreign trip.

The main influence tour operators can bring to bear is price advantage based on buying accommodation and transport cheaply in bulk. This is difficult in domestic tourism, but often valuable in overseas travel.

In choosing between packages offered by different operators, price and the perceived advantages such as better service or closer departure points are determining factors. Most tour operators also try to encourage repeat purchasing and to maintain customer loyalty.

Alternative channels
Apart from using a travel agent or direct booking, there are a number of alternative ways for the tourist to buy his tourism products. These include clubs and societies, mail order, electronic booking methods and so on.

Choice between these is largely a matter of convenience, assuming that the distribution channel concerned offers the products required. These again are discussed more fully in Chapter 8.

SELF-ASSESSMENT QUESTIONS

1. Identify the economic, geographical, social and psychological factors accounting for the fact that "sun, sea and sand" tourism is the dominant form of present-day mass tourism.

2. What types of tourism does Britain cater for and to what markets do you think these are most likely to appeal abroad? Analyse the attractions of Britain in terms of both aggregate and individual choice.

3. Distinguish between the characteristics of tourists who are more likely to choose package tours and those preferring to travel independently.

4. How do governments influence (a) business travel and (b) holiday travel?

5. Explain why the pattern of tourist transport within Britain (Fig. 7) is broken down as it is.

6. What is "time-sharing"? Explain its appeal to tourists.

ASSIGNMENTS

1. Produce a diagrammatic map to show: (a) the main tourist generating areas of the world; (b) the main destinations; (c) the links between them. Account for the main findings in a short report.

2. Construct and undertake a short questionnaire survey among fifty or sixty friends and colleagues to find out: (a) where their last holiday was; (b) why that destination was chosen; (c) what accommodation or package was used, and why; (d) where their next holiday is likely to be.

CHAPTER FOUR

The Structure and Organisation of the Tourism Industry

CHAPTER OBJECTIVES

After studying this chapter, you should be able to:
* identify the integral and associated sectors of the tourism industry;
* understand the chain of distribution and how this is applied to the tourism industry;
* distinguish between different forms of integration among tourism organisations and analyse the reasons for such integration.

THE CHAIN OF DISTRIBUTION IN THE TOURISM INDUSTRY

Introduction

Tourism demand is met by the concentrated marketing effort of a wide range of tourist services. Together these services form the world's largest and fastest growing industry. Because some of these services are crucial to the generation and satisfaction of tourists' needs, while others play only a peripheral or supportive role, it is not easy to determine what constitutes the "tourism industry". Furthermore, some services, such as catering and transport, provide for the needs of others besides tourists. Some simplification is necessary, and Fig. 9 provides a framework for the analysis of the industry based on a central *chain of distribution* supported by specific public and commercial sector services.

The term "chain of distribution" is used to describe the methods by which a product or service is distributed from its manufacturing source to its eventual consumers. Traditionally, this is achieved through the intercession of a number of *middle men* who buy the products and sell them to other links in the chain. The middle men may be wholesalers, buying large quantities of the product and selling in smaller quantities to others, or they may be retailers, representing the penultimate link in the chain, buying from the wholesaler and selling to the consumer (*see* Fig. 10).

A producer, of course, is not obliged to sell his products through the chain. He may choose to sell direct to the consumers or direct to retailers, thus avoiding the wholesalers. Wholesalers in turn sometimes sell products direct to the consumer (as in "cash and carry"

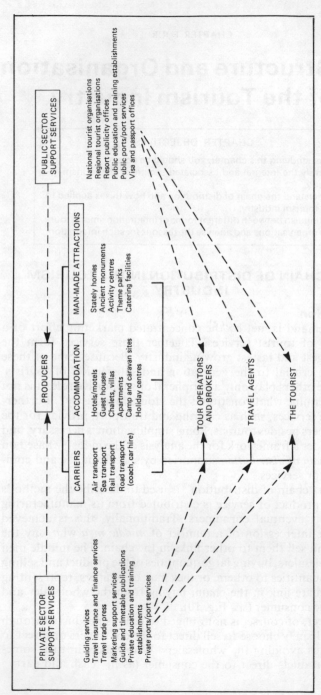

Fig. 9 The tourism industry

PRIVATE SECTOR SUPPORT SERVICES

Guiding services
Travel insurance and finance services
Travel trade press
Marketing support services
Guide and timetable publications
Private education and training establishments
Private ports/port services

PRODUCERS

CARRIERS

Air transport
Sea transport
Rail transport
Road transport
(coach, car hire)

ACCOMMODATION

Hotels/motels
Guest houses
Chalets, villas
Apartments
Camp and caravan sites
Holiday centres

MAN-MADE ATTRACTIONS

Stately homes
Ancient monuments
Activity centres
Theme parks
Catering facilities

PUBLIC SECTOR SUPPORT SERVICES

National tourist organisations
Regional tourist organisations
Resort publicity offices
Public education and training establishments
Public ports/port services
Visa and passport offices

TOUR OPERATORS AND BROKERS

TRAVEL AGENTS

THE TOURIST

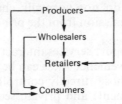

Fig. 10 *The chain of distribution*

companies), avoiding the use of a formal retailing outlet. These alternatives are illustrated in Fig. 10, and all these methods are to be found in the tourism industry.

As we have seen earlier, the tourism product consists essentially of transport, accommodation and attractions, both natural and man-made. The producers of these services include air, sea, road and rail carriers, hotels and other forms of tourist accommodation, and the various man-made facilities designed to attract the tourist, including stately homes and other buildings, catering facilities, amusement parks and activity centres such as skiing resorts. These services may be distributed in a variety of ways to tourists, either direct, through travel agents (the *retailers* of the tourism industry) or through tour operators or brokers.

Brokers are most actively involved in the distribution system in the field of air transport, although they may also bulk-purchase hotel accommodation or certain other services. By purchasing these products in quantity they are able to negotiate lower prices and in turn sell individual air seats or hotel rooms to consumers or travel agents at a mark-up that allows them an acceptable level of profit.

Tour operators buy a range of tourist products in bulk—airline seats, hotel accommodation and coach transfers, for example—and "package" these for subsequent sale to travel agents or to consumers direct. By buying a number of individual items of tourist services and packaging them into a single product—the "package holiday"—tour operators are seen by some theorists as *producers* of a new product rather than wholesalers of existing products. This is a fine point, and a debatable one, but in the author's view their role is rather one of "bulk purchaser" of tourism products and they are better described as middle men. (This is especially true as recent developments in the industry have led to tour operators selling "seat only" aircraft flights to top up their load factors. Here the function of tour operator and broker becomes increasingly indivisible.)

Travel agents form the retail sector of the distribution chain, buying travel services at the request of their clients and providing a convenient network of sales outlets catering for the needs of a local catchment area. They do not normally charge for their services, receiving instead a commission from the principals for each sale they negotiate.

A wide variety of support services interact with this central distribution system. For convenience these can be divided between public sector organisations (those directly controlled or operated by national or local government) and private sector organisations. The former include the various public tourism bodies in Britain, government-operated airports and seaports and their support services, passport and visa services, and public authority educational institutions providing courses of education and training for the tourism industry. The private sector includes guiding services, travel insurance and finance services (including foreign exchange and travel credit cards), the travel trade newspapers and journals, institutions providing private courses of education and training for the tourism industry, any private port or port services, travel guide and timetable publishers, and various specialist marketing services such as travel consultants and brochure design agencies. In the following chapters each of these areas will be examined in turn, to explore their role, their functions and the interrelationships that exist between them and which together create the dynamics of the tourism industry.

Common-interest bodies

A feature of the tourism industry is the extent of association, voluntary or otherwise, that has taken place between businesses that share similar interests or complement one another's interests in some way. Such association can take different forms, but typically three forms can be identified: that based on the interests of a particular sector of the industry (or *link* in the chain of distribution); that based on a concern with specific tourism destinations; and that based on a concern with tourism activity as a whole. These may be referred to in turn as *sectoral*, *destination* and *tourism* organisations, any of which may be regional, national or international in scope.

A further subdivision may be identified between professional and trade bodies. Professional bodies are made up of individuals whose common interest is likely to be based on objectives which include establishing educational qualifications for the industry or sector, devising codes of conduct guiding the standards of behaviour of members, and limiting or controlling entry to the industry or sector. Membership of such bodies is associated with the drive for status and prestige on the part of its members. Trade bodies, by contrast, are groupings of independent firms whose objectives are likely to include the exchange of views, co-operation (especially in the area of marketing), representation and negotiation with other organisations, and the provision of services for members. At times such organisations may also include an interest in activities with which the professional associations are concerned, such as entry to the industry and the provision of appropriate education and training.

Sectoral organisations

Probably the most numerous organisations are those which reflect sectoral interests. As we have seen, there are a wide range of sectors making up the tourism industry and each of these can be expected to have at least one common-interest association. Professional bodies catering for sectoral interests include the Chartered Institute of Transport (CIT), the Hotel Catering and Institutional Management Association (HCIMA), the Institute of Travel and Tourism (ITT) which is concerned with the educational standards of travel agents and, to a lesser extent, tour operators, and the Guild of Guide Lecturers (GGL). Sectoral trade associations include the Association of British Travel Agents (ABTA), which represents both travel agents and tour operators, the Tour Operators' Study Group (TOSG), a consultative body representing the leading tour operators in the UK, and the British Hotels, Restaurants and Caterers' Association (BHRCA).

Similar bodies are to be found in other countries with a developed tourism industry. The American Society of Travel Agents (ASTA), for example, fulfils a similar role to that of ABTA, but because of the international impact of the United States as a tourist generating country it is an influential body worldwide.

Destination organisations

A destination organisation is one drawing its membership from public or private sector tourism bodies sharing a common interest in the tourist development or marketing of a specific tourism destination. That destination may be a resort, a state or region, a country, or an area of the globe. Membership of such bodies is open to firms or public sector organisations rather than individuals. These will have two common objectives:

(a) to foster co-operation and co-ordination between the various bodies that provide or are responsible for the facilities and amenities making up the tourism product; and

(b) to act in concert to promote the destination to the trade and to tourists generally.

These organisations are therefore trade rather than professional bodies by nature, and their structure will range from public sector consortia such as the East Asian Travel Association (EATA) to the

Pacific Area Travel Association (PATA) (a mixture of private and public sector bodies), or to the Travel Industry Association of America (TIAA), a wholly privately sponsored body whose aim is to market the United States.

Tourism organisations

The activities of some bodies transcend the sectoral boundaries of the industry. Such organisations may have as their aim the compilation of national or international statistics on tourism or the furtherance of research into the tourism phenomenon as a whole. The World Tourism Organisation (WTO) is perhaps the most significant public body concerned with the collection and collation of statistical data. The organisation represents public sector tourism bodies from most countries of the world, and the publication of its data makes possible comparisons of the flow and growth of the tourism business on an international scale.

Similarly, the Organisation for Economic Co-operation and Development (OECD) has a tourism committee composed of tourism officials drawn from all member countries, and this committee produces regular reports comprising comparative statistical data on tourism development to and within these countries.

By contrast, at a national level, in Britain the recently formed Tourism Society is composed of individuals from both the public and private sectors who are concerned with the professionalisation of their industry through improved standards of research and education.

INTEGRATION IN THE TOURISM INDUSTRY

The rationale for integration

A notable feature of the industry over recent years has been the process of integration that has taken place within and between the sectors of the industry. If we refer to our model of the chain of distribution, we can identify this integration as being either *horizontal* or *vertical* in character. Horizontal integration is that taking place at any one level in the chain, while vertical integration describes the process of linking together organisations at different levels of the chain.

All business is highly competitive and the tourism industry is no exception to this rule. Such competition, often encouraged by government policy of the day, has been evident in the industry ever since the development of mass market tourism in the 1960s, and the process has accelerated in the 1980s following policies of government deregulation in the airline and coach sectors. Competition forces companies to seek ways to become more efficient and integration offers significant advantages, not least that of benefiting from economies of scale; by producing and selling more of a product the company reduces the unit cost of each product, since the fixed costs incurred are spread over an increasing number of units, whether these be hotel bedrooms, aircraft seats or package holidays. The savings achieved can then be passed on to passengers in the form of lower prices.

Most companies, asked to identify their organisational goals, would cite market expansion as a major objective. Growth in a competitive environment is a means to survival, and history testifies to the fact that few companies survive by standing still. Integration is a means to growth by enabling a company to increase its market share and simultaneously reduce the level of competition it faces.

Greater sales mean more turnover and therefore potentially more reserve funds for reinvestment in the company and thus more profit. This in turn enables the company to employ or expand its specialist personnel. Nowhere is this more true than in companies whose branches are individually quite small. For example a small chain of travel agents or hotels may for the first time, through mergers, be able to employ specialist sales or marketing personnel, or their own legal or financial advisers. More money becomes available too for the marketing effort—a programme of national advertising in the mass media may become a real possibility for the first time.

Perhaps the greatest benefit offered by integration, though, is the negotiating power that the larger company achieves in its dealings with other organisations. By expanding the scope of its operations in this way the tour operator secures purchasing power in negotiating for low prices for hotel rooms or aircraft seats; it ensures that handling companies at the destinations to which its tourists fly are eager for the company's business and will provide attractive quotations in order to secure that business; it reduces the operational risks in its business by ensuring that, where holidaymakers may be at risk in a resort due to the hotels' tendency to overbook its guests, it will be the rival clients rather than its own who are turned away. Similarly, hotels uniting in larger groups will be able to negotiate better deals through their suppliers for the bulk purchase of, for example, food and drink, and airlines will bring more bargaining strength to the negotiating table in their dealings with foreign governments for landing rights or new routes.

In addition to these broad benefits offered by integration generally, there are other advantages specific to horizontal or vertical integration which will now be examined in turn.

Horizontal integration

Horizontal integration can take several forms. One form would be the integration resulting from a merger between two companies offering competitive products. Two hotels may merge, for example, or two airlines competing on similar routes may unite. Such mergers may result from the takeover of one company by another or it may be a voluntary union between two consenting companies. If the association is a voluntary one, however, it need not entail total ownership; arrangements can be made to maintain individual identities while uniting in the form of a consortium—an affiliation of independent companies working together to achieve a common aim. For example, a marketing consortium may be formed to derive the benefits of economies of scale in the marketing effort through, for example, the publication of a joint sales brochure. Alternatively, a common interest may be the purchase of bulk supplies at discount prices. Both of these advantages are shared by consortia such as Best Western Hotels or the Prestige Hotel chain.

A second form of integration occurs between companies offering complementary rather than competitive products. Tourism, as we have seen, is defined as the travel and stay of people. Close links therefore form between the accommodation and transport sectors, who are interdependent for their customers. Without hotel bedrooms available at their destination airline passengers are unlikely to be prepared to book their airline seats with the air carriers. Recognition of this fact has led many airlines to buy into or form hotel divisions, especially in those regions of high tourist demand where bed shortages are commonly experienced. This trend was given impetus when the "jumbo jet" era arrived at the beginning of the 1970s and the airlines realised the consequences of operating aircraft with 350 or more passengers aboard, each requiring accommodation over which the airlines had little or no control. This was to lead to the integration of Pan American Airways with Intercontinental Hotels (although Pan American has since divested itself of this hotel chain to cover losses sustained after the deregulation of air transport in the USA), and between TWA and Hilton Hotels International, while in Europe a consortium of five European airlines, with the financial backing of leading banks, developed the Penta Hotel chain.

For similar reasons airlines may link themselves together. A route operated by one airline company may, for example, provide a logical *feeder* service for another airline's services and, in the sense that the two services are complementary rather than directly competing, a merger is formed for this reason.

The changing nature of tourism demand may also encourage companies to diversify their interests horizontally. A few years ago shipping companies, faced by a decline in demand for their services as their prices rose and airline prices fell, began buying their way into the airline business, in the short term in order to offer alternative forms of transportation, but ultimately to survive as liner services were phased out. Thus in the early 1960s, Cunard Line first bought British Eagle Airways for the North Atlantic operation and later, as government policy on route operations became more restrictive, a share of BOAC's north Atlantic airline operations.

At the retailing level integration also occurs, but because the traditional development of travel agencies has led to regional rather than national strengths, such integration has tended to take the form of regional rather than national expansion. As tourism moves into the 1980s the pattern is beginning to change to programmes of national expansion as the large chains buy out smaller ones. Thus, we have recently seen the rapid expansion of the Hogg Robinson travel agency chain, which has absorbed Wakefield Fortune, Renwicks and Ellerman's along with other small companies in a very short space of time. Similar expansion has taken place at Pickford's and Lunn Poly (itself a wholly owned subsidiary of Thompson Travel). The tendency is for the retail travel business to become increasingly concentrated among a handful of multi-branch major retailers, a trend that is likely to continue.

Vertical integration

As we have seen, vertical integration is said to take place when an organisation at one level in the chain of distribution merges with that at another level. This integration can be *forward* (or *downward*) where an organisation merges with another lower in the chain than itself (as would be the case where a tour operator buys a group of travel agents), or it is described as *backward* (or *upward*) where the initiating organisation is higher in the chain (e.g. a tour operator buying its own airline or hotel chain). Forward integration is obviously found more commonly since it is more likely that organisations at the production level, rather than the sales level, will have the necessary capital available for such expansion. The higher in the chain the firm being purchased, the greater is the likelihood that high capital investment will be required.

As with horizontal integration, organisations can achieve significant economies of scale through vertical expansion. Where total profits available in each individual sector may be insufficient, taken overall a satisfactory level of profit may be made for the parent organisation to thrive in a strongly competitive environment, while the organisation may also stand to improve its competitive position in the market place.

As with the linking of complementary services in horizontal integration, many companies are concerned to ensure the continuation of their supplies. A tour operator, dependent upon a continuing supply of aircraft seats and hotel beds and facing competition on an international scale for such supplies, can best ensure their provision through direct control, i.e. by "buying backwards" into the airline sector as did Thomson Holidays with Britannia Airways. It has to be borne in mind, however, that Thomson is in turn a part of a much larger organisation whose interests extend far beyond the tourism industry and whose capital reserves are substantial for an investment of this kind. Many other tour operators have followed this pattern, either by integrating backwards or by starting their own airline division. Thus we find Cosmos Holidays (itself part of a large Swiss parent company) linked with the charter carrier Monarch Airlines, and more recently Horizon Holidays has established Orion Airways, while Intasun have set up Air Europe.

Such integration offers the added advantage of improved quality control. Ensuring that standards are uniform, consistent and of the required quality is no easy matter where the product is composed of diverse, disparate services, as in tourism. Clearly, the task is greatly facilitated where such services come under the management of a single parent company.

Equally, the production sector will attempt to exercise control over the merchandising of its products. Airlines, shipping services and hotels represent multi-million pound investments, yet curiously these services rely on fragmented, individual and frequently inexpert retail agencies to sell their products. Travel agents carry no stock and therefore have little brand loyalty to the companies whose products they sell. It is logical for the producers to seek to influence the retail level by buying into travel agencies, as Cunard have done with the purchase of Crusader Travel (now Cunard Crusader Travel).

Air carriers can also help to ensure an even flow of demand for their seats by controlling the tour operations. The former BOAC purchased ALTA Holidays (now Speedbird Holidays) and later, as British Airways, bought the direct-sell operator Martin Rooks, as well as forming their own tour operating division under the Sovereign and Enterprise banners. In the same way, British Caledonian controls Blue Sky Holidays, and Laker, before its demise, took control of Arrowsmith, the North Country operator.

There are grounds for believing that vertical integration of this kind would be less subject to scrutiny by the Monopolies Commission than would horizontal expansion, where a significant sector of the industry may eventually come under the control of a handful of powerful companies. An organisation committed to growth and seeking to expand its operations in the tourism field is likely to see vertical integration as a logical means to its end.

In the long run some danger is posed to the travel agents themselves by the process of vertical integration into the retailing sector. Airlines or tour operators opening their own retail outlets may, by competitive pricing or other marketing strategies, be able to attract the market to these outlets rather than the traditional agencies. A possible counter-move on the part of travel agents would be to form consortia to operate and sell exclusively their own package tours. Numerous efforts have been made since the 1960s to form such a consortium, but so far with only limited success in Britain, although on the Continent rather more success has been achieved in this direction.

Conglomerates

No discussion of integration in the tourism industry would be complete without reference to the role of the conglomerate. A conglomerate is an organisation whose interests extend further than a single industry. By operating in a number of diverse business spheres such a company spreads its business risk; losses in any one year in one industry may be offset against profits in another.

The continuing pattern of growth which the tourism industry has exhibited in the past, and the long-term growth prospects for leisure services, have attracted many businesses outside the tourism field. Thus the breweries have expanded into the hotel operating and holiday camp fields, Thomsons has interests at all levels of the chain of distribution, and even at the retailing level external interest is now apparent, with the development by W. H. Smiths of in-store travel agencies. This pattern is by no means limited to the UK; throughout the world banks, finance houses, department stores and many other organisations are turning to leisure as the demand for consumer durables levels out. The purchase of Thomas Cook by the Midland Bank perhaps marks the start of substantial bank investment in the tourism industry in this country.

SELF-ASSESSMENT QUESTIONS

1. Define: (a) consortia; (b) chain of distribution; (c) horizontal integration; (d) common-interest groups.

2. List three reasons for vertical integration in the tourism industry.

3. Distinguish between backward and forward integration.

4. True or false? (a) Middle men are essential to the chain of

distribution. (*b*) National tourist offices, hotels and air carriers are all producers in the tourism industry. (*c*) ABTA is a sectoral trade organisation.

ASSIGNMENT

Discuss the benefits of a policy of growth for a firm in the tourism industry.

CHAPTER FIVE

Passenger Transport I: The Airlines

CHAPTER OBJECTIVES

After studying this chapter, you should be able to:
* understand the role that airlines play in the development of tourism, and the effect of government policy on this role;
* understand how air transport is organised and distinguish between different categories of airline operation;
* understand the reasons for air regulation and the systems of regulation in force, both within the UK and internationally;
* appreciate the role and functions of IATA;
* appreciate the role of the air broker as intermediary in the air transport industry.

INTRODUCTION

Tourism is the outcome of the travel and stay of people, and, as we have seen, the development of transport, both private and public, has had a major impact on the growth and direction of tourism development. The provision of adequate, safe, comfortable, fast, convenient and cheap public transport is a prerequisite for mass market tourism. A tourist resort's accessibility is the outcome of, above all else, two factors; price (in absolute terms as well as in comparison with competitive resorts) and time (the actual or perceived time taken to travel from one's originating point to one's destination). Air travel, in particular, over the past 20 years has made medium- and long-range destinations accessible on both these counts, to an extent not previously imaginable. In doing so it has substantially contributed to the phenomenon of mass market international tourism, with its consequent benefits (and drawbacks) for the receiving nations.

Public transport, while an integral sector of the tourism industry, must also provide services which are not dependent upon tourist demand. Road, rail and air services all owe their origin to government mail contracts, and the carriage of freight, whether separate from or together with passengers, provides a significant (and sometimes crucial) contribution to a carrier's revenue. It should also be recognised that many carriers provide a commercial or social service which owes little to tourism demand. Road and rail carriers, for example, provide essential commuter services for workers travelling between their places of residence and work. These carriers (and sometimes airlines, as in the remoter districts of Scotland) provide an essential social and economic service by linking outlying rural areas with centres of industry and commerce, thus ensuring a communications lifeline for residents. The extent to which carriers can or should be commercially orientated while simultaneously being required to provide a network of unprofitable social routes poses a continuing problem for government transport policy.

Most forms of transport are highly capital intensive. The cost of building and maintaining track in the case of railways and of regularly re-equipping airlines with new aircraft embodying the latest advances in technology requires massive investment, available only to the largest corporations, and may call for financial subsidies from the public sector. At the same time transport offers great opportunities for economies of scale, where unit prices can be dramatically reduced. There is a high element of fixed costs, for example, for an airline operating out of a particular airport, whether that airline operates flights four times a day or once a week. If these overheads are distributed over a greater number of flights, individual seat costs per flight will fall.

The question of economies of scale is one for caution, however; there comes a point where the growth of organisations can result in diseconomies of scale which may offset many of the benefits resulting from size. The inability of some major airlines to compete with leaner, more efficient carriers is a case in point. Major airlines, for reasons of prestige, are likely to opt for expensively furnished high-rent city-centre offices, imposing an added burden on overheads.

The air carriers

In Chapter 2 we explored the way in which the development of air transport in the second half of the twentieth century contributed to the growth of tourism, whether for business or for pleasure. Travel by air has become safe, comfortable, rapid and above all cheap for two reasons.

The first reason is the enormous growth of aviation technology, especially since the development of the jet airliner. Since the introduction of the first generation jet (the Comet) in the early 1950s, seat cost per kilometre has fallen in absolute terms and against other forms of travel. Engine and aircraft design has been continuously refined and improved, reducing drag, increasing engine efficiency and lessening fuel consumption. At the same time increases in carrying capacity for passengers and freight have further reduced average unit seat cost. The current third generation, wide-bodied jets, spear-headed by the introduction of the Boeing 747 "jumbo" jet in 1970, have reduced seat costs still further (although the sudden escalation of seat availability in such aircraft, from the previous typical 130 seats to a massive 350 seats plus, posed serious marketing problems for the airlines equipping their fleets with jumbos).

Following the huge increases in fuel costs after the oil crisis in 1973/4, research was stepped up to find ways of improving fuel economy. This has been achieved by a combination of improved engine efficiency and reduced weight (even to the extent of cutting down the number of pages in in-flight magazines!). However, the jet engine has now reached a stage of evolutionary sophistication which makes it increasingly difficult (short of a revolutionary breakthrough such as the development of new forms of fuel) to produce further economies, and cost-cutting exercises have largely replaced techno-logical innovation as a means of stabilising prices.

The second factor in the development of mass travel by air has been the enterprise and creativity demonstrated both by air transport management and by other entrepreneurs in the tourism industry. The introduction of net inclusive tour basing fares for tour operators and variable pricing techniques such as advance purchase excursion (APEX) and "stand-by" fares have stimulated demand and filled aircraft seats. The key factor though has been the chartering of aircraft by tour operators, first on an *ad hoc* basis for weekly depar-tures and later on a *time series* basis (with the chartered aircraft being placed entirely at the disposal of the tour operator throughout the season or year). Chartering in this way, coupled with very high load factors on each aircraft, reduced unit seat cost to a point where low cost package tours (especially to such destinations as the east coast of Spain and Majorca) brought foreign holidays within reach of millions in the UK and Western Europe.

THE ORGANISATION OF AIR TRANSPORT

It is convenient to think of air transport operations under three broad headings:

(a) scheduled air services;
(b) non-scheduled air services (charter services);
(c) air taxi services.

Scheduled services are those which operate on defined routes, whether domestic or international, for which licences have been granted by the government or governments concerned. The airlines are required to operate such services on the basis of published timetables, regardless of passenger load factors (although flights and routes which are not commercially viable throughout the year may be operated during periods of high demand only).

Such services can be further categorised as *public* (state-operated) or *private*. In most countries the public airline will be the national flag-carrier (as with Air France) but the extent of public versus private ownership will vary in air transport according to a country's form of government. In planned economies such as those of the Soviet bloc, all airlines will be run by the state, while in the USA, by contrast, all airlines will be operated by the private sector. British Airways, a publicly owned carrier, is at the time of writing expected to become privatised as a consequence of Conservative government policy, with the result that all civil aviation in the UK will be in the hands of private companies.

According to their route network and relative importance within the air transport business, carriers other than the national flag-carrier may be identified as either *second force* or *third force* airlines. Leading airlines providing competitive or complementary services to those of the national flag line on domestic or international routes, or sometimes those providing substantial inter-regional services, are termed second force airlines. Those providing a network of regional or local services are usually termed third force, or *feeder* airlines. The relationship between these levels of carrier and the determination of government policy towards each level (as well as between the public and private sectors) have shaped the present pattern of air transport in Britain.

The economics of scheduled airline operations

The development of an airline route is something of a "Catch 22" situation. Airlines require some assurance of traffic demand before they are prepared to commit their aircraft to regular service on a new route, while air travellers in their turn require regular and frequent services in order to patronise a route. There is usually an element of risk involved in initiating a new route, especially since seat prices are likely to be high to compensate for low *load factors* (seats sold as a percentage of seats available on an aircraft) and high overheads (in both operational and marketing costs) before traffic builds up. When a route has proved its popularity, however, the pioneer airline is faced with increasing competition (as other airlines are attracted) unless this is strictly controlled by the respective governments. This in turn results in lower load factors and either higher prices or reduced profit margins. Key routes such as those across the north Atlantic attract a level of competition which can make it difficult to operate any services profitably, especially since the deregulating policies of the United States and British governments in the late 1970s, which have supported open competition.

The selection of suitable aircraft for a route is the outcome of the assessment of the relative costs involved, of which there are two kinds, and the characteristics of the aircraft themselves.

(a) *Capital costs.* When supply outstrips demand, as is the case currently with many second-hand aircraft on the market and intense competition for sales between the remaining aircraft manufacturers, airlines can drive very hard bargains in purchasing new equipment. It must be remembered that costs for new aircraft are usually a package embracing not only the sale of the aircraft itself, but the subsequent provision of spares. Loan terms can be a key issue in closing a sale, and some manufacturers are prepared to offer very favourable trade-ins on old aircraft to sell their new models.

(b) *Operating costs.* Aircraft are not easily interchangeable between routes. Broadly speaking, they are designed to operate efficiently on either short-haul (up to 1,500 miles), medium-haul (1,500–3,500 miles) or long-haul (over 3,500 miles) routes, but not on any combination of these. Mile for mile, short-haul routes are more expensive to operate than are long-haul, due to two factors. First, short-haul travel requires a greater frequency of take-offs and landings, and in take-offs an aircraft consumes substantially more fuel than it does once it has attained its operational ceiling during flight. Second, short-haul aircraft spend a proportionately greater amount of their time on the ground. Aircraft earn money only while they are in the air, and depreciation of their capital cost can only be written off against their actual flying hours. For this reason it is important that they are scheduled for the maximum number of hours' flying each day. Ground handling charges can be reduced by speeding up the turn-around of an aircraft, and airlines will aim to turn their aircraft around in as little as 50–60 minutes. This time will include off-loading and on-loading passengers and baggage, preparing cabins for the coming flight and refuelling.

Long-haul aircraft usually operate at a ceiling of 30,000–40,000 feet (supersonic flights, between 50,000 and 60,000 feet), while other aircraft operate at lower ceilings. While the cost of getting the long-haul aircraft to their operating ceilings is high due to the length of climb, once at these heights there is little wind resistance and therefore the rate of fuel usage falls considerably.

(c) *Aircraft characteristics.* These will include the aircraft's cruising speed and "block speed" (its average overall speed on a trip), its range and field length requirements, its carrying capacity and its customer appeal. In terms of passenger capacities, airline development tends to occur in leaps rather than through slow progression. While the introduction of jumbo jets led to an overnight tripling of seats on jet aircraft, increase in demand was naturally more gradual. While average seat costs fell sharply with the advent of the jumbos, it was to take some time before passenger demand caught up with the new availability.

Carrying capacity, however, is also influenced by the payload which the aircraft is to carry, i.e. the balance between fuel, passengers and freight. An increased payload in fuel will enable an aircraft to travel further without stopping for refuelling, but this will be at the expense of the numbers of passengers that can be carried. Sacrificing both fuel and some passenger capacity may allow aircraft to operate from smaller regional airports with short runways.

The customer appeal of an aircraft depends upon such factors as seat comfort and pitch, engine quietness and the interior design of cabins. In a product where, generally speaking, there is a great deal of homogeneity, minor differences such as these can greatly affect the marketing of the aircraft to airlines.

Corporate objectives and government policy

Airlines, as are all transport companies, are inevitably faced with conflicting pressures in establishing their objectives. In the case of private airlines, the interests of shareholders may lie in the maximisation of profits, or at the very least in ensuring a reasonable rate of return for their investment. This may be constrained by the need to ensure long-term growth for the airline, and by political or social obligations such as support for the nation's aviation industry, or pressures to reduce noise pollution, or to keep fares down. Public airlines, too, face conflicting pressures in setting objectives. British Airways during the 1970s was paradoxically required to meet target returns on capital invested by the government while simultaneously forced into non-competitive purchasing, and the operation of uneconomic routes as a social service.

Airlines will often be subject to the dictates of government in the use of their aircraft for defence purposes, or for the operation of air routes seen as politically expedient (such as the London–Peking route of British Airways). Similarly, the development of a new holiday destination may be the outcome of public sector objectives rather than the commercial policy of the airline concerned.

Marketing of air services

It is for marketing to determine the destinations to be served (although, as we have seen, government policies, particularly in the field of regulation, will strongly influence these), flight frequencies and timings (based on traffic potential to the destination, the nature of market demand and current levels of competition). Routes are of course dependent upon freight as well as passenger demand, and a decision must be reached on the appropriate mix between freight and passengers, as well as the mix of passenger markets to be served—business, holiday, VFR, etc.

Flight frequencies and timings may also be subject to government controls. For example, it is common to find countries limiting the number of flights permitted into and out of airports at night. Where long-haul travel, and hence time zone changes, are involved, this can severely curtail services. The congestion of traffic at major international airports will have a further "rationing" effect on flight operations.

It is particularly important for business travellers that they are able to make satisfactory connections with other flights on comprehensive itineraries. To gain a strategic marketing advantage, an airline will want to coordinate its flights with other complementary carriers, leading to *interline* agreements between carriers (the free interchange of documents and reservations between carriers). In long-haul planning, the carrier must also decide whether the company is likely to maximise its revenue by operating non-stop flights to the destination, or providing intermediate stop-over points to cater for passengers wanting to travel between different legs of the journey (known as "stage" traffic). This will permit the airline to cater for, or organise, stop-over holiday programmes, and the appeal of duty-free shopping facilities in the stop-over airport.

Following the planning stage, the airline must determine its pricing policy. Fixing the price of airline seats is a complex process, involving consideration of:

(*a*) the size and type of aircraft operating on the route;

(*b*) the route traffic density and level of competition;

(*c*) the regularity of demand flow, and the extent to which this demand is balanced in both directions on the route;

(*d*) the type of demand for air service on the route, determining the mix between first class, economy class, inclusive tour-basing fares and other discounted ticket sales;

(*e*) the estimated break-even load factor (the number of seats which must be sold in order to recover all costs), typically set at somewhere between 50 and 60 per cent of capacity on scheduled routes. The airline's aim is to achieve this level of seat occupancy, on average, throughout the year.

Demand for air travel can change at short notice, depending upon such factors as the state of the economy of the generating country or the political stability of the destination country. This instability can have a serious effect upon the overall viability of airline operations. This uncertainty can be mitigated by leasing aircraft for a route rather than buying. Most airlines will, from time to time, lease out aircraft to unload surplus capacity, and conversely other airlines will take up a lease on an aircraft to cope with sudden increases in demand or to cover a service when their operations are hit by maintenance problems or a crash. Airlines who have specialised in leasing arrangements may well buy new equipment specifically to lease this to other carriers. In most cases such leases are *wet leases*, i.e. they include the lease of the operating crews. Aircraft under lease in this way are painted in the appropriate livery of the carrier for which they are to operate.

Most scheduled services are operated on the basis of an advanced reservations system, with lower (APEX) fares being made available on many routes for bookings taken substantially (2–3 months) in advance and low "stand-by" fares offered to prospective passengers without reservations who are prepared to take their chance on seats being available an hour or so before flights. An alternative system which has been developed for high density traffic routes is the "shuttle", for which no advanced reservations are needed and for which all passengers are guaranteed a seat, with an extra flight being added if need be to handle surplus demand. This type of service can only be commercially viable for routes which experience a high level of regular (typically business) demand in both directions. Such services were first operated in the United States in the 1960s, but British Airways introduced a shuttle service in Britain in 1975 between London and Glasgow and has since extended this to other domestic routes in the UK. Sir Freddie Laker introduced the first international "no reservations" service between New York and London (later modified to provide a traditional booking service), and a plan has been unveiled to form a new airline operating a shuttle service between five European capitals (London, Paris, Brussels, Amsterdam and Dublin).

Non-scheduled (charter) services

These have grown at the expense of the scheduled services since the 1960s. Their appeal has been essentially one of price; by setting a very high break-even load factor (typically 85–90 per cent) and by keeping overheads low, prices have been dramatically reduced compared with those of the scheduled services. Charter airlines save on marketing costs (they do not advertise their routes to the public), on operational costs (they provide a less elaborate service, both in the air and on the ground) and on head office costs (being less concerned with status and the need to keep a high profile before the travelling public, they settle for simpler administrative offices away from high-rent central-city areas). But above all they have one great advantage over scheduled airlines in that they are not obliged to operate to a timetable; they can choose to withdraw their less fully booked flights and either transfer their passengers to other charter airlines or *consolidate* their flights with others experiencing similar low loadings. In this way passengers benefit from the lowest possible air fares while sacrificing the guarantee of a specific flight (or even a flight from a specific airport, since a consolidation may involve a switch to a different airport.) This sort of "trade-off" would not suit the business traveller but is acceptable in the holiday market.

Until the mid-1960s the British government permitted charter carriers to operate out of the UK on only a limited scale. Charters were restricted to *closed groups* known as affinity groups, consisting of members of a club or other organisation whose principal purpose was not that of obtaining low-priced air travel. This led to the formation of a large number of bogus "clubs" and the rules governing the operation of affinity charters were flagrantly ignored. Policing "bent" charters proved difficult and from the 1960s onwards the government liberalised its policies regarding charter regulations. Tour operators, already experiencing strong growth in demand for the new package tours, were quick to develop the charter market, at first chartering on an *ad hoc* basis but soon turning to time series charters to minimise costs.

The scheduled airlines feared dilution of their traffic by the new charter services, but in fact the charters succeeded in tapping an entirely new market for foreign holidays. Prices tumbled and there was a huge growth in numbers carried, especially from northern Europe to the Mediterranean. On the lucrative north Atlantic services charters made impressive gains paralleling those of the scheduled services between 1965 and 1977 with the advent of advance booking charters (ABCs), to which the scheduled carriers responded by introducing advance purchase excursion (APEX) fares. However, scheduled airlines had to exercise caution that they did not dilute normal revenue by introducing discounted fares of this kind.

One notable development in the industry has been the tendency for tour operators to form or take over their own charter airlines, predominantly to ensure seat availability for their own passengers.

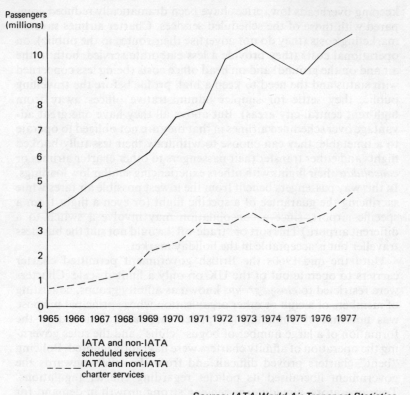

Source: IATA World Air Transport Statistics

Fig. 11 *Growth of charter and scheduled air services across the north Atlantic, 1965–77. After 1977 figures were inflated by the inclusion of flights through the Miami gateway*

Surplus capacity on these charters is then made available to smaller-scale tour operators mounting their own programmes to the same destination. This development has had the effect of creaming off much of the charter business formerly obtained by the independent airlines, forcing these to seek alternative markets for their aircraft.

Air taxis

These are private charter aircraft accommodating small groups (typically from four to eighteen persons) and are used particularly by business travellers. They offer advantages of convenience and flexibility; routings can be tailor-made for passengers (for example, a feasible itinerary for a business day using an air taxi might be

London-Paris-Brussels-Amsterdam-London, a near impossible programme for a scheduled service), small airfields close to a company's office or factory can be used (there are some 350 of these in the UK alone, with a further 1300 in western Europe) and flights can be arranged or routings amended at short notice.

Aircraft in use as air taxis range from helicopters seating three or four, with a range of some 400 kilometres, to Bandeirantes flying eighteen passengers within a similar range. Some small aircraft such as HS125-600s can carry ten passengers up to 2500 kilometres but most air taxi work entails journeys of up to 800-1000 kilometres and is therefore an ideal medium of transport for travel between the commercial centres of Europe.

Some corporations which formerly ran their own fleet of executive aircraft have switched to using air taxis since purchase is difficult to justify unless aircraft have very high usage rates.

Development is now in progress on short take-off and landing (STOL) aircraft, capable of operating from runways much shorter than those previously in use. This will make it possible in many cases to operate aircraft with smaller passenger capacities directly between city centres, thus adding a new dimension to business travel in particular. Proposals already exist for the construction of a STOL airport in London's dockland.

Air brokers

One further sector of the airline industry must be mentioned here, that of the air brokers. These are the middle men who act as intermediaries between aircraft owners and their potential charter market. They act both in an advisory and a sales capacity and their task, which is often overlooked in discussions of the air transport industry, is to find suitable aircraft at the right price, both for *ad hoc* and series charters. To do so they must maintain close contact both with airlines and with the charter market.

They play an important role in securing aircraft seats at times of shortage and in disposing of surplus capacity at times of over-supply, and are also active as intermediaries in tour operators' flight consolidations. The body representing their interests in the industry is the Air Brokers' Association.

Reference should also be made here to the middle men, commonly known as "consolidators", who play an increasingly important role in the industry by purchasing surplus flight seats in bulk from miscellaneous scheduled carriers and disposing of these through non-ABTA non-IATA "bucket shops" at illegally discounted fares (see p. 107).

THE REGULATION OF AIR TRANSPORT

The need for regulation

With the growth of the industry, regulation, whether of national or international routes, has become necessary for a number of reasons. First and foremost there is the question of passenger safety, which requires that airlines be licensed and supervised. For reasons of public concern other controls will be necessary, such as those designed to reduce noise or pollution.

Since air transport has a profound impact on the economy of a region or a country, governments will take steps to encourage the development of routes which appear to offer prospects of economic benefit and to discourage services on those routes already suffering from over-capacity. While the policy of one government may be to encourage competition or to intervene where a route monopoly is forcing prices up, another government's policy may be directed to rationalising excessive competition in order to save energy waste or to ensure profitability for the national flag-carrier. One characteristic of such involvement is the *pooling* arrangements made between airlines operating on certain international routes whereby all revenue accruing on that route is apportioned equally between the carriers serving the route. This may appear to circumvent competition on a route, but is also one means of safeguarding the viability of the national carrier operating in a strong competitive environment.

In some areas air transport is an essential public utility which, even if commercially non-viable, may be socially desirable to provide communication with a region where geographical terrain may make other forms of transport difficult or impossible (as is the case with some areas of the Hebrides in Scotland). In this case, financial subsidies may be provided to maintain the service. Such services would be required to operate on a regular rather than intermittent basis.

The question of balance between public and private air transport will depend upon the political viewpoint of the party in power, and this will also be reflected in a government's regulatory activities.

Systems of regulation

Broadly speaking, air transport operations are regulated in three ways.

(*a*) Internationally, scheduled air routes are assigned on the basis of agreements between the governments of the countries concerned.

(*b*) Internationally, scheduled air fares are established (for member airlines) by the mutual agreement of the airlines concerned and through the mediation of the traffic conferences of the International Air Transport Association (IATA), a trade body. Agreed tariffs are then subject to ratification by the appropriate governments. Nationally, air fares within the UK are also subject to the formal approval of the Civil Aviation Authority (CAA), acting as the regulatory agent of the government. Similar bodies exist in other countries.

(c) National governments will approve and license the carriers which are to operate on scheduled routes, whether domestically or internationally. In the UK the CAA has this responsibility, and is also responsible for the licensing of charter airlines and of tour operators organising package holidays by air abroad.

Air transport regulations are the result of a number of international agreements between countries dating back over many years. The Warsaw Convention in 1929 first established common agreement on the extent of liability of the airlines in the event of death or injury of passengers or loss of passenger baggage. Then at the Chicago Convention on Civil Aviation held in 1944, eighty governments were represented in discussions designed to promote world air services and to reach agreement on standard operating procedures for air services between countries. There were two outcomes of this meeting: the founding of the International Civil Aviation Organisation (ICAO), now a specialised agency of the United Nations; and the establishment of the *five freedoms* of the air. These comprised the privileges of:

(a) flying across a country without landing;

(b) landing in a country for purposes other than the carriage of passengers or freight, e.g. in order to refuel aircraft;

(c) off-loading passengers, mail or freight from an aircraft of the country from which those passengers, mail or freight originated;

(d) loading passengers, mail or freight on an aircraft of the country to which those passengers, mail or freight are destined;

(e) loading passengers, mail or freight on an aircraft not belonging to the country to which those passengers, mail or freight are destined, and off-loading passengers, mail or freight from an aircraft not of the country from which these originated.

These privileges were designed to provide the framework for bilateral agreements between countries and to ensure that carriage of passengers, mail and freight between two countries would normally be restricted to the carriers of those countries.

The Anglo-American agreement which took place in Bermuda in 1946, following the convention, set the pattern for many of the bilateral agreements which have followed. This *Bermuda Agreement*, while restricting air carriage between the two countries to national carriers, did not in fact impose restrictions on capacity for the airlines concerned, but this was modified when the Bermuda Agreement was renegotiated in 1977 (and ratified in 1980), in line with the tendency of many countries in the intervening years to opt for an agreement which would ensure that a percentage of total traffic on a route was guaranteed for the national carriers of the country concerned. It was Britain's intention, in this renegotiated agreement, to avoid over-capacity on the route by restricting it to two British and two American carriers.

Carriage on routes within the national territory of any one country (known as *Cabotage* routes) is not subject, of course, to international agreement and is normally restricted to the national carriers of the country concerned. In some cases, however, this provides opportunities for a country's national carriers to operate exclusively on international routes in cases where countries have overseas possessions. This is the case, for example, on routes out of the UK to points such as Gibraltar and Hong Kong. More significantly, air fares on such routes are not subject to ratification by IATA.

The role of IATA

For many years effective control over air fares on international scheduled routes has been exercised by the International Air Transport Association, a trade association comprising some 80 per cent of the world's airlines which operate on international routes. The decreed aims of the organisation, which was restructured in its present form in 1945, are to promote safe, regular and economic air transport, to provide the means for collaboration between the air carriers themselves, and to co-operate with the ICAO and other international bodies for the promotion of safety and effective communications. However, it is IATA's fare-fixing role which has aroused most controversy since the association has in the past acted in effect as a legalised cartel. Fares have been established at the annual fare-fixing IATA Traffic Conferences by common agreement among the participating airlines; while subject to ratification of the governments concerned, in practice such approval has been largely automatic.

Critics of IATA have argued that fares as a result have been unnecessarily high on most routes and the effect has been to stifle competition. In many cases agreed fares are the outcome of political considerations in which the less efficient national flag-carriers have been able to push for prices unrelated to competitive costs. IATA also controls many other aspects of airline operation in addition to fares (such as the pitch of passenger seats, which dictates the amount of leg room a passenger may enjoy, and the kind of meals that may be served on board flights), and as a result airlines have had to concentrate in their marketing on such ephemeral aspects of the product as service, punctuality or the design of stewardess's uniforms, rather than providing a genuine measure of competition.

It is widely felt that this has led to inertia among the participating carriers, with agreements resulting from a desire to avoid controversy among fellow members. Nor has the cartel ensured profitability for its members, since they face open competition from non-IATA carriers who have successfully competed both on price and added value.

Because of this, and because of governmental commitment to the concept of free competition (especially in recent years in the United States), IATA restructured its organisation in 1979 to provide a two-tier structure: a tariff section to deal with fare-fixing, membership of which is voluntary for member airlines; and a trade section to which all members must belong and participate. A number of airlines, notably US carriers, chose to withdraw from the tariff-fixing section, but continue to gain from the benefits of membership of the trade section.

These benefits are considerable and trade activities occupy most of IATA's time. Among the achievements of IATA one may cite the provision of a central clearing house system which makes possible quick financial settlements between members; standardised tickets and other documents which are interchangeable between carriers; compatibility on the basis of air fare constructions and changing exchange rates; and the general standardisation of operating procedures (such as the licensing of travel agents). If IATA were to be wound up it would lead to considerable inconvenience for the travelling public; already in the United States the lack of *interlining* facilities (which permit through fares on a single ticket on multi-stop journeys) on non-IATA carriers can be a serious drawback for travellers.

Domestic regulation of air transport

Internally, each country will develop its own regulatory machinery. In the USA, where regulatory authorities have influence far beyond the confines of that country's borders, licensing is the responsibility of the Civil Aeronautics Board (CAB). This body has been until recently concerned with applications for new routes and approval of airline fares. However, under the administration of President Carter, plans were introduced to phase out this organisation's functions gradually, beginning in 1980. CAB authority over domestic routes ended in 1981, and two years later government control over domestic airline fares within the USA was terminated, at which time the decision was also made to deregulate the distribution of airline tickets, allowing for outlets other than approved travel agents to sell air tickets. The US airlines, however, appear content to retain their existing network of agency distribution points. The Federal Aviation Agency (FAA) remains responsible within the USA for air traffic control, and the efficiency and safety of air travel.

In the UK the Civil Aviation Authority (CAA) has assumed most of these responsibilities since its formation in 1971. Specifically, this body is concerned with the provision of air navigation services (including the management of certain Scottish airports and advising the government on the strategic planning of national airports) and all forms of economic, technical and operational regulations (including airworthiness, operational safety and the licensing of both air carriers and air travel organisers).

The CAA was set up under the requirements of the Civil Aviation Act 1971. Prior to this Act no clear long-term government policy had been discernible; as governments came and went, policies with respect to competition or to the balance between public and private carriers changed. With the idea of providing some longer-term direction and stability a committee of enquiry into civil air transport, under the chairmanship of Sir Ronald Edwards, was commissioned by the government to prepare a report on the future of British air transport. This report, *British Air Transport in the Seventies*, appeared in 1969. The gist of their recommendations was that the government should periodically promulgate civil aviation policy and objectives; that the long-term aim should be to satisfy air travellers at the lowest economically desirable price; and that a suitable mix should be agreed as between public and private sector airlines. The state corporations (BOAC and BEA) were confirmed in their role as the flag-carriers for the scheduled services, but were recommended to merge and to start charter and inclusive tour operations. The idea of a major *second force* airline in the private sector, to complement and compete with the new public airline, was proposed, as was the suggestion that a more liberal policy be adopted towards the licensing of other private airlines. Finally, the report proposed that the economic, safety and regulatory functions carried out by the previous Air Transport Licensing Board, the Board of Trade and the Air Registration Board should thereafter come under the control of a single Civil Aviation Authority.

The Civil Aviation Act, which followed publication of this report in 1971, accepted most of these proposals. BOAC and BEA were merged into a single corporation, British Airways; British Caledonian was confirmed as the new second force airline, following the merger between Caledonian Airways and British United Airways; and the new Civil Aviation Authority was formed.

Government policy since 1971

In introducing the concept of a second force private airline, the Edwards Report had clearly seen this as being designed to compete with the public flag-carrier across the north Atlantic. After the formation of British Caledonian, the government granted the carrier north Atlantic routes in 1973. Within two years, however, government policy was changing to one of "spheres of influence", with the second force airline licensed for complementary rather than directly competitive routes. Ignoring British Caledonian's claim that two British carriers on the North Atlantic would have the effect of increasing the British share of the total market by taking away business from the American competition, the CAA redistributed routes, giving British Caledonian South American routes and restricting the north Atlantic largely to British Airways. A White Paper in 1976, *Future Civil Aviation Policy*, indicated the prevailing policy to end dual designation—a policy that has since been eroded by the 1979 Conservative government in their support for the deregulation of the air transport industry. Recent years have seen the award of US routes to British Caledonian and later an "open skies" policy across the North Atlantic, with first the licensing of Laker's ill-fated "Skytrain" service to New York and Los Angeles, and later the launch of two cut-price airlines, the US carrier People's Express and its British competitor Virgin Atlantic. Unprofitable former routes of British Airways have been delegated to smaller UK airlines.

The equivocal attitude of successive governments regarding the "commercial" versus "public utility" aspect of air transport has apparently hardened in favour of the former, with British Airways engaged in a massive cost-cutting exercise in order to get back into profitability in the face of the air price war of the 1980s. Plans have been announced by the Conservative government to denationalise British Airways directly the carrier has established a firm financial footing, and this is likely to occur during 1985, although at the time of writing it has yet to be determined whether the airline is to be sold off as a single entity or broken up into "parcels". The charter airlines associated with the leading British tour operators have claimed that a privatised British Airways which is permitted to hold on to its large and well-established charter division (British Airtours) would represent unfair competition for small carriers.

DEREGULATION

In 1978 the United States passed its Airline Deregulation Act which called for the abolition of commonly agreed air fares and the ending of CAB control within five years. In the same year the CAB itself issued a "show cause" order to IATA requiring that association to justify its policy of fixing prices by international agreement between carriers, in violation of US anti-trust laws.

Collusion on the setting of North Atlantic fares ended in 1980, preceded by the withdrawal of a number of US carriers from IATA's tariff-fixing conference. The British government has supported the drive for a more liberal approach to air fares within Europe, and in particular within the EEC, where artificially high air fares are contrary to the free trade clauses in the Treaty of Rome. Agreement was reached with the Dutch government in 1984 to remove constraints on capacity and fares between Britain and Holland, and should the new services on this route generate substantial new traffic, it could cause other carriers to reappraise their own policies, especially in the case of carriers operating to contiguous destinations, who may experience traffic loss from this cut-rate competition. There could also be a marked effect on cross-channel ferry services resulting from the new low air fares between Britain and the continent.

Those supporting airline deregulation have argued that price-fixing through IATA has had the effect of keeping fares artificially high and of insulating less efficient carriers against their competitors. Unfortunately the introduction of deregulation coincided with a period in which airlines were going through extreme economic difficulties—rapid inflation (particularly in fuel and labour costs), high capital investment for new aircraft and a stagnant market. The result was huge losses for most airlines, especially across the Atlantic, and the scramble to get passengers to fill seats at any cost led to price wars in which all carriers, large or small, suffered. There is a similar fear that reduced prices on European scheduled air services will threaten the now well-established charter routes.

However, deregulation has undoubtedly encouraged airlines to become more efficient by cutting costs. The danger is that such cost-cutting exercises may affect maintenance and other ground services, posing a threat to passenger safety. Air passengers, while benefiting from lower fares in the short term, will gain little in the longer term from the collapse of airlines and the closure of uneconomic routes or a return to monopoly on other routes. They (or their travel agent) suffer the added inconvenience of having to "shop around" for the lowest applicable air fares on a route. Travel agents are being required to provide more services for a lower return, since they earn their income in the form of a percentage of the airline fare applicable. This situation has been eased by the introduction of electronically computed air fares, and already most straightforward domestic, and the major international, fares are available to travel agents through closed user group systems.

In their efforts to obtain bookings at whatever cost, the airlines have expanded their strategy of selling off unsold seats at short notice at heavily discounted fares through non-appointed travel agents. These *bucket shops* have multiplied in Britain, aided by the fact that the government has felt itself powerless to prosecute such illegal discounting for lack of evidence. The problem of attempting prosecution is that only airlines which are required to file their fares with the CAA (such as the British carriers and certain others such as the US carriers under the terms of the Bermuda Agreement) are in breach of the law. Off-line carriers (those not having a service into the UK) are not obliged to file their fares with the British government, a fact that places these airlines at an advantage in competing with other carriers. The success of the bucket shops in providing discounted tickets to businessmen as well as holidaymakers poses a serious threat to the viability of IATA-appointed travel agencies, who are not permitted under the terms of their agreement with IATA to sell such discounted tickets.

Airlines have argued that they should be permitted to sell discounted seats openly through any distribution system they choose, and British Airways, towards the end of 1981, experimentally introduced the sale of discounted tickets to the Far East through IATA travel agents, risking prosecution. The evidence suggests that the airline regulatory system, at least as far as fares are concerned, is ineffective because it is unenforceable. Recent developments such as the decision by one large multiple travel agency chain, Pickfords, to provide their outlets with price saver counters, while simultaneously launching a series of "Travel Mart" shops selling cheap air tickets in competition with the bucket shops, is further evidence that cut-price airline tickets have become respectable and are here to stay.

SELF-ASSESSMENT QUESTIONS

1. Explain the terms: (*a*) load factor; (*b*) wet lease; (*c*) cabotage route; (*d*) consolidation.

2. How are the air transport policies of the Conservative Party likely to differ from those of the Labour Party?

3. Distinguish between flag carriers, second force and third force airlines.

4. What marketing advantages do charter operators have compared with scheduled service operators?

5. Why are short-haul routes more expensive to operate than long-haul ones?

ASSIGNMENT

Argue the case for and against deregulation in the airline industry.

CHAPTER SIX

Passenger Transport II: Sea, Rail and Road Services

```
CHAPTER OBJECTIVES
After studying this chapter, you should be able to:
* identify the differing categories of water-borne transport, and
  analyse the reasons for their growth or decline;
* understand the role and scope of public and private railway
  and coach organisations in Britain;
* understand the importance of marketing and market segmen-
  tation for public transport companies;
* understand the consequences of regulation and deregulation
  of transport, and evaluate the case for or against open com-
  petition;
* recognise the impact that private car ownership has had on
  tourism and the tourist industry.
```

INTRODUCTION

Although air services today play the leading role in providing tourism transport, sea, road and rail services continue to play an important part, both domestically and internationally, in meeting travellers' communication needs. While air transport clearly offers the fastest links over long distances, other methods of travel have their own unique advantages. Coach travel still remains the cheapest means of travel almost universally; the introduction of new technology on the railways has seen the advantage of speed that air services have enjoyed over the railways gradually eroded on short and medium-length journeys; and the relaxation and entertainment of a voyage by sea goes a long way towards making up for slower speeds and greater costs. Technology in shipping has enabled new forms of water-borne transport to be developed in recent years—vessels such as the hovercraft (technically an aircraft, since it travels above the surface of the water) and the hydrofoil, with its derivatives the jetfoil and the twin-hulled jet cat. These, too, have provided faster communication over short sea routes and in difficult terrain.

The pleasure that people still enjoy in being afloat has spawned many recent tourist developments, including yacht marinas, self-drive motor craft, dinghy sailing in the Mediterranean and canal barge holidays in Britain. Similarly, the fascination with steam engines has led to the renovation of lake steamers in England and paddle steamers in the USA, as well as the regeneration of private steam railways in Britain and elsewhere. The division is blurred between transport and entertainment, between public and private means of transport; the journey or the vehicle becomes an end in itself for the tourist as much as a means to an end.

WATER-BORNE TRANSPORT

It is convenient to use the generic term "water-borne transport" in this chapter since this will include not only sea-going vessels, but also river, canal and lake craft, all of which are playing a growing role in tourism. We are faced then with four categories of water-borne transport services:

(a) ocean-going line voyages;
(b) cruises;
(c) short sea voyages (or ferry services);
(d) inland waterway services.

The history and fortunes of these differing forms of transport reveal strong contrasts, and each will be dealt with separately here.

The ocean liners

Line voyage services are those offering passenger transport on a port-to-port basis. Such services have declined over the past 30 years to a point where today very few exist anywhere in the world, and even these are generally operated on a seasonal basis only. The reasons for this decline are not hard to identify.

From the 1950s onwards advances in air transport technology, as has been shown, resulted in the price of air transport falling on most routes, and especially across the Atlantic, to a point where it became cheaper to travel by air than by sea. Shipping lines found themselves unable to compete, faced as they were with rising labour costs and a labour-intensive product. Many vessels were old and outdated and the cost of replacing them prohibitive; at the fares passengers would be prepared to pay it would be difficult if not impossible to write off the capital cost of a new vessel during its normal life expectancy of 15–20 years. Other operating costs were also escalating and this, coupled with the advantages of improved speed, safety and comfort standards offered by the airlines, signalled the demise of worldwide shipping. During the 1960s and 1970s the major shipping companies reduced or discontinued their long-established routes out of the UK—P & O to the Far East and Australia, Union-Castle line to South Africa and Cunard across the Atlantic.

The resulting shake-ups in shipping management led to attempts to regenerate traffic or to use existing vessels for cruising, but the large liners' days were numbered. A small but continuing demand for transport by sea remains for those with money and leisure time, or others who suffer from fear of flying or airsickness; and a very limited number of services continue to operate, but on a highly seasonal basis. The Queen Elizabeth 2 provides a connection between Southampton and New York (via Cherbourg) during the summer months, and cruises for the balance of the year. The South African Shipping Corporation—Safmarine—have recently reintroduced services between Southampton and South Africa, successfully building on the nostalgic goodwill still felt for the old Union Castle Line vessels on this route: but once again the demand is concentrated on winter sailings out of the UK (to take advantage of the summer months in South Africa).

With hindsight it is easy to pinpoint the inevitability of shipping's decline. However, it must be said that shipping management must bear some of the blame for failing to adapt their product to changing needs. Ships built or operating in the 1950s failed to meet the needs of the post-war market. Insufficient cabins with private bathrooms were available to meet the needs of the American market in particular, and the vessels' specifications and size made them inflexible and unsuitable for routes other than those for which they were built. Because shipping companies did not recognise early enough the threat that the airlines posed for the future of their companies, they did not respond soon enough by moving into that sector of the industry themselves.

For years the shipping business was saddled with a series of cumbersome and bureaucratic "traffic conferences" whose rules governed the operation of freight and passenger shipping in various geographical regions. Conference membership offered many advantages (as with IATA, members' tickets and other documents were interchangeable), but it also imposed restrictions on operation which tended to inhibit creative marketing by individual members. Prices were strictly controlled and no individual tour-based fares were available; travel agency appointments were limited and sanctions were imposed on agents dealing with non-conference lines.

With the decline of shipping the influence of these conferences waned, and the withdrawal of Cunard from the Trans-Atlantic Passenger Steamship Conference in 1971 signalled their end as an effective power in the regulation of shipping. Shipping associations today are less concerned with regulation and more with co-operation and marketing. In Britain the Passenger Shipping Association concerns itself with marketing and training, but also takes a growing interest in the protection of shipping, whether of line voyages, cruising or ferry operations.

Cruising

Since the late 1950s the passenger shipping industry has steadily shifted its emphasis from line voyages to cruises. Initially this transition proved difficult; vessels in service at the time were for the most part too large, too old and too expensive to operate for cruising purposes. Their size limited them in the number of ports they could visit and they were built for speed rather than leisurely cruising. Some savings in fuel were possible by cruising at reduced speed, but ideally cruise vessels must be purpose-built to maximise their operational efficiency. The ideal cruise ship is a vessel of some 18,000–22,000 tonnes, carrying 800–850 passengers (although the former French Line flagship "France" has been extensively renovated and now, as the 66,000 tonne "Norway", operates successfully on the New York/Bahamas cruise run). The ratio of staff to passengers is reduced for cruises (per diem prices for cruises are substantially below those of line voyages) and cabins are generally smaller, with larger areas given over to deck space and public rooms. Further economies on fuel are obtained by spending more time in port and by making a greater number of port calls, which incidentally satisfies cruise clients more.

Cruising was severely hit by the rapid rise in fuel prices during the oil crisis of 1973/4, but the decline in the fleets of the established maritime nations such as Britain was to some extent compensated for by the growth of new maritime powers, most noticeably the Greeks and Russians, whose operating costs are lower.

The centre for international cruising remains the United States, with about 1.7 million passengers sailing from US ports each year. Miami (including Port Everglades and Fort Lauderdale nearby) has become the principal embarkation point for cruises from the USA, with most vessels travelling to the nearby Caribbean Islands. The British cruise market has experienced a pattern of slow decline over recent years, to some 75,000 passengers today, of which about a third are *fly-cruise* passengers. Forecasters predict a further fall in this number, as costs increase relative to other holiday opportunities.

Fly-cruises were developed in Britain in the late 1960s, and have helped to off-set some of the general decline in cruising. On this form of cruise, passengers are flown from the UK (or other originating point) to a cruise port in the Mediterranean (or other convenient starting point), and return by air at the end of their cruise, thus avoiding the lengthy period at sea which is necessary before a cruise vessel reaches warmer climes. The shipping companies can offer attractive all-in prices for these packages by chartering aircraft for outbound and return flights. The traditional cruise passengers, who are typically older and more conservative, many of them unprepared to fly, initially resisted this innovation, but the concept has helped to attract a new, younger market. Recently, attempts have been made to attract the British market to US-based fly-cruises to the Caribbean and other destinations. However, the Mediterranean remains far the most important destination for the European markets. Another significant cruising market is in Australia, with a strong programme of cruising to the Pacific islands (*see* Fig. 12).

The dominance of the Americans in the world cruising market has resulted in strict standards being imposed on all foreign flag carriers operating out of US ports. All ships sailing ex-USA are subject not only to stringent hygiene and safety inspections, but their companies are required to be bonded against financial collapse. This has had the effect of hastening the demise of older vessels unable to meet these standards.

Innovations in cruising have continued over the last decade, with the introduction of new ports of call. More adventurous destinations have been introduced (such as cruises to the Antarctic), shipping companies have organised cruises with specific themes to appeal to a specialised market, such as archaeological and horticultural cruises, or the "Jazz" cruises run by Holland–America Line, and, most importantly, the mass tour operators have moved into cruise operating. During the 1970s a number of British tour operators began chartering cruise vessels to sell fly-cruise programmes as part of their package holiday operations. These early charters ran into a number of problems; standards of service and operation suffered as the tour operators attempted to attract a new market for cruises at unusually low prices. More recently the larger tour operators have co-operated with the cruise companies by bulk-purchasing cruise berths on a regular cruise and marketing these as part of their overall tour programme.

In spite of ever-increasing costs, cruising has remained remarkably resilient. Both cruising and specific cruise vessels draw on very loyal markets with a high pattern of repeat purchasing—P & O claim as many as 60 per cent of Canberra's passengers are regulars. Although the world fleet of cruise vessels is less than 100, shipping companies believe that a small but stable world market will remain. This confidence is reflected in recent orders for new tonnage, which includes the launch of Hapag Lloyd's 27,000 ton "Europa" in 1981, the purchase by Cunard of the former Holland America Line ves-

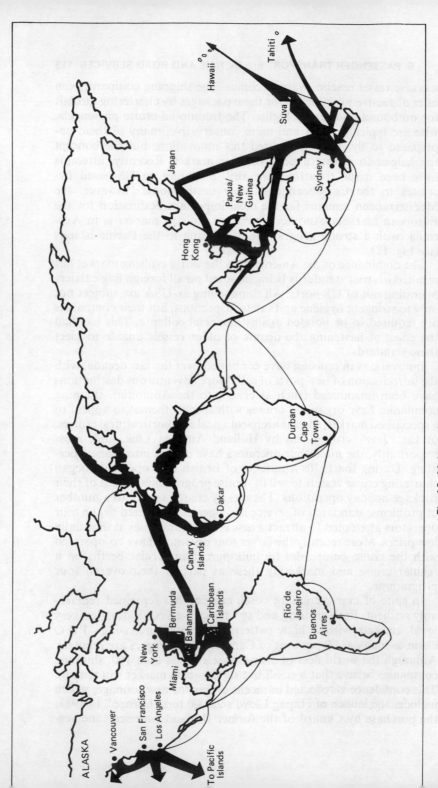

Fig. 12 *Major cruise routes in the world*

sels "Vistafjord" and "Sagafjord", and the launch of P & O's new 40,000 ton "Royal Princess" in 1984. Carnival Cruise Line has recently placed an order for two 48,000 ton liners for delivery in 1986.

Cruise vessels are both capital- and labour-intensive, and western shipping companies are increasingly concerned about the rapid escalation of costs in cruise operations. There is increasing competition from lower-cost operators who can undercut prices. Greek operators have the benefit of lower labour costs (although some British companies have retaliated by employing a high proportion of foreign marine staff to reduce costs). The Russians, too, can substantially undercut western prices (some critics argue that these prices are uneconomic and reflect the Soviet Union's desire to earn foreign currency rather than make profits). Recent plans have been revealed for the Russian fleet to be augmented by a further five 750-passenger vessels by 1990.

Another prominent development in cruising has been the introduction of comparatively small cruise vessels which would formerly have been considered uneconomic. The 3,000 ton "Vacationer", which provides basic facilities for 150 passengers at low per diem rates, has successfully attracted the cheaper end of the market, while at the same time similar size vessels aimed at providing yacht-like facilities for a small number of passengers, have managed to attract the luxury end of the market, especially where the destinations have been exotic and unique. The "Lindblad Explorer" is an example of such a vessel, which has been in operation for a number of years, offering a very high level of service and accommodation, and this is now being emulated by a new generation of small cruise vessels.

A problem faced by cruise operators in the UK has been that of selling such a sophisticated travel product through mass market retailers. In Britain, less than one in ten travel agents are productive in terms of cruise sales; many counter sales staff lack the expertise or experience to sell cruises, and in spite of the potential high levels of commission to be gained by such sales, more training is needed for this side of the industry.

Ferry services

The success story of shipping is undoubtedly the growth of the short sea voyages within Europe in the last decade. This is attributable to the general growth of tourism in the region, to the growth of trade (especially membership of the EEC) and, perhaps most of all, to the increase in private car ownership which has led to demand for flexible, mobile holidays. From Britain alone some 2½-3 millions of the 15 million private cars in use are taken abroad each year. Notwithstanding the growth of the centred package holiday business, there has been a continuing demand for independent holidays by private car, especially by those who have been abroad on a number of occasions.

In the UK and elsewhere the tour operators—and indeed the ferry companies themselves—have responded to this demand by developing and marketing more flexible *self-drive* packages. Ferry companies have been notable for their creative marketing; new ships have been introduced, with new standards of comfort, offering faster loading and unloading facilities; new services have been introduced which provide a wider geographical spread of routes to tap regional markets (such as Plymouth-Roscoff and Sheerness-Vlissingen). The ferry companies are co-operating with the growing number of coach operators who are expanding their long-distance intra-European services (a process greatly aided by the deregulation of the coaching industry in 1980), and have themselves packaged tours to the Continent in conjunction with their cross-Channel sailings. Today an extensive network of ferry services operates throughout Europe to meet the demand for intro-European travel by sea (*see* Fig. 13).

Since 1968, new forms of water-borne craft—the hydrofoils and hovercraft—have provided an added appeal for those seeking novelty or those in a hurry but disliking to fly. The hovercraft, a vehicle which rides on a cushion of air just above the surface of the water, offers the advantage of speed, and its ability to travel over land as well as water avoids the usual capital costs of dock facilities, since the vessel can be docked on any convenient obstacle-free foreshore. Unfortunately, the vessel has been bedevilled by technological problems in its development. It offers its passengers a somewhat bouncy and noisy ride by comparison with traditional ferries, and cannot operate in high seas. Recent development has concentrated on enlarging the passenger and cargo carrying capacity of the hovercraft, with the current SRN-4 Mark 3 capable of carrying 55 cars and 424 passengers. There are plans to stretch this to a payload of 75 cars and some 600 passengers. However, some transport economists are doubtful whether the hovercraft offers a viable means of cheap transport in the future, other than over difficult terrain.

The hydrofoil is by contrast thought to offer substantial opportunity for future development, even though it, too, has suffered from technological teething problems. This vessel operates with a conventional hull design, but when travelling at speed this hull is raised above the surface of the water on blades, or "foils". This

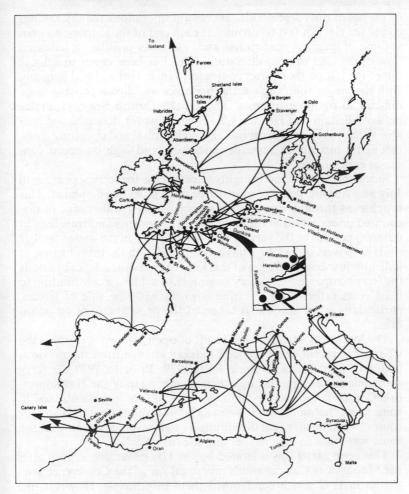

Fig. 13 *Major passenger and car ferry services in western Europe*

enables the vessel to travel at speeds of up to 60 knots. Recent models have been powered by jet engines (jetfoils), and these have been operated experimentally on cross-channel services, but have yet to prove themselves economically viable over routes of this length. They are, however, widely used on shorter crossings in many parts of the world.

Operating short sea services is expensive both in terms of capital investment and direct operating costs. Profitability is achieved through a combination of maximum usage of equipment and sales of on-board duty-free goods. Successful operations require sailings round the clock, a fast turnround at each end of the journey, an even volume of business year-round and, as far as possible, a balanced flow of demand in both directions. This has been easier to achieve out of the UK on the shorter routes to France, Holland and Belgium, with the longer routes to southern France and Spain proving more difficult to optimise revenue. The DFDS Danish Seaways service between Britain and Denmark/Sweden, however, has achieved notable success in spite of exceptionally high capital and operating costs, through a mixture of versatile marketing and high on-board consumer expenditure.

Since holiday demand is highly seasonal for the ferries, peaking in July and August, demand at other periods must be stimulated. This is achieved through competitive pricing, with a wide range of discounted prices aimed at different market segments and travelling at different periods of the year. Quick round-trips on the same vessel or short stopovers of 1–3 days have multiplied with the introduction of judicious low-cost packages of this kind. At extreme off-peak periods the ferry companies' aims may be simply to achieve a contribution to fixed costs rather than ensuring a profit with the sale of tickets, particularly when account is taken of the profitability of on-board sales.

The low prices which are the result of open competition across the Channel in recent years reflect a marked change from the previous policy of fixed prices in force until 1979. Prior to 1979 the ferry companies, operating through their membership of the Harmonisation Conference, united to negotiate annual fare agreements, and in some cases "harmonisation" went as far as revenue pooling on major routes (whereby an equal distribution of all revenue accruing on the route was made to the lines serving the route).

This open cartel was tolerated by the UK government, even after the Monopolies Commission's investigation of the Conference's activities in 1972 which condemned them in principle. However, the system of negotiating tariffs through the Conference broke down in 1979 when a number of carriers decided to opt for an "open fares" policy. Pooling arrangements were ended and a two-year price war between the companies led to large losses on operations in 1980 and 1981. This is unlikely to mean a return to the old Harmonisation process—indeed, the Office of Fair Trading has expressly forbidden it—but prices had to rise significantly in 1982 to offset former losses, and the lesson learned at the time suggests that any widespread cross-channel price war is unlikely in the near future. Rather, competition is tending to focus on the development of larger and more luxurious vessels, with facilities similar to the smaller cruise liners. At the time of writing, the Conservative Government's policy of privatisation in the transport sector has resulted shortly in British Rail divesting itself of its Sealink cross-channel services (which were operated jointly with French, Dutch and Belgian railways).

Inland waterways
The inland waterways of Britain—lakes, rivers and canals—provide opportunities for the growing demand among tourists for water-borne holidays. The many small private boat-owning companies in Britain have formed consortia in order to market their services more effectively. The leading marketing consortium is that of Blakes, which has been operating more than 70 years and today represents some 40 boat companies operating on the Norfolk Broads and other domestic and foreign waterways. Hoseasons and Boat Enquiries offer similar consortium services, the most important of which is the production of a single brochure for mass circulation. The British Waterways Board has played its part in encouraging the use of British waterways for pleasure purposes, and has been in the forefront of efforts to reopen the old disused canals to provide a network of interconnecting waterways throughout the country. Major rivers such as the Thames in Britain, the Shannon in Ireland and the Rhône in France have been well exploited by the private hire companies.

But public craft also play an important role in inland waterway tourism, either in the form of day excursions or longer cruises by river or lake steamer. The lake steamer is a familiar sight and an important tourist attraction in such areas as the Scottish lochs, the English Lake District and overseas on the US/Canadian Great Lakes and the Swiss or south German lakes. The great rivers of the world also provide notable cruising services, many of which have been successfully packaged for the international tourist market. These include such diverse services as paddle steamers on the Mississippi, cruises along the Rhine, China's Yangtse River boats and services up the Amazon, which is navigable to ocean-going vessels as far as Iquitos in Peru.

Many of these services seem to have particular appeal to the British market and the package tour operators, in their search for new attractions overseas, can be expected to incorporate a greater range of inland waterways programmes in their specialist tours of the future. Another noticeable trend is towards greater luxury on board small craft, as boat owners go up-market to beat the competition.

THE RAILWAYS

Public railways

Considering their long lead over other carriers in providing public service transport, it may be considered surprising that the railways in Britain have taken so long to adapt to the needs of mass market tourism in the late twentieth century. Certainly the railways played a major role in providing tourist transport throughout the first half of the century, but as ownership of private cars grew so tourist traffic on the railways fell. This process, which was already notable before World War II, accelerated after 1947 when the railways were nationalised in Britain. The switch to private passenger transport, coupled with the rapid expansion of freight transport by road, meant severe financial difficulty for British Rail in the 1950s and 1960s, which they attempted to solve by a huge reduction in their route operations, especially on unprofitable branch lines. As far as the tourist was concerned this resulted in many smaller resorts and tourist destinations being no longer accessible by rail. The alternative of coach links connecting with the rail termini makes tourist travel inconvenient and time-consuming and this, coupled with continuing fare increases on the railways, has made rail an unattractive contender for tourist transportation to many destinations (although the railways have continued to serve the needs of many major resorts such as Brighton, Bournemouth and Torquay).

In the 1970s and 1980s, however, British Rail became more marketing-orientated in an attempt to win back the tourist traffic. In this they were helped by the enormous increase in petrol prices which changed the patterns of car usage for domestic holidays. Package holidays in the form of "Golden Rail" tours, operating in conjunction with British hotel companies, enabled the railways to increase their share of the domestic holiday market. British Rail's "Merrymakers" programme, launched at the beginning of the 1970s, was aimed at railway enthusiasts who were mainly interested in the rail trip itself. These excursions were originally organised using charter trains, but later British Rail provided similar day trips on scheduled services and longer "short break" packages were introduced.

More recently the railways have furthered their market segmentation policy by providing substantial discounts on specified routes for day and period return travel, and this has boosted short break traffic as well as competing effectively with the new low coach fares introduced by the road transport companies after deregulation was introduced in 1980. In the field of product innovation, the High Speed 125 train, operating on key Inter-City routes, offers a service competitive in time, city centre to city centre, with those of the airlines. The future of the Advanced Passenger Train (APT) is still uncertain after serious technical problems were encountered during trial runs, but British Railways believe that these problems have now been overcome, and further tests have been announced. If successful, the combination of greater speed and increased comfort will strengthen the appeal of rail services in the UK. Abroad, express services such as the TGV (Train à Grande Vitesse) in France and the Bullet Train in Japan provide similar high standards of speed and comfort which offer viable alternatives to air services.

Internationally, although routes and standards of service have declined in many countries, the railways continue to exert a fascination for the growing market of rail enthusiasts, especially on the long transcontinental routes. Tour operating entrepreneurs have taken advantage of this and organised special programmes incorporating long-distance rail journeys, for example, on the trans-Siberian route and overland from Europe to Hong Kong. Recently, too, the old Orient Express was introduced as a private venture after extensive renovation, admittedly now operating only as far as Venice, but regenerating the standards of luxury and service enjoyed in the heyday of the railways during the 1930s. Whether this appeal to nostalgia is a short-term market vagary or a longer-term tourism feature remains to be seen.

The private railways

With the electrification of the railways in Britain, the nostalgia for the steam trains of the pre-war period has led to the re-emergence of many private steam railways. Using obsolete track and former British Rail rolling stock, enthusiasts have painstakingly restored a number of branch lines to provide an alternative system of transport for travellers as well as a new attraction for domestic and overseas tourists. In Britain alone, some forty such lines are in operation (*see* Fig. 14), with 400 other projects either in hand or under consideration. Some of these depend largely on the tourists' patronage, while others also provide a convenient commuting service for local residents; their profitability however is frequently dependent upon a great deal of voluntary labour, especially in the restoration of track, stations and rolling stock to serviceable condition. Since these services are generally routed through some of the most scenic areas of Britain, they attract both railway buffs and tourists of all kinds, and undoubtedly enhance the attractiveness of a region for tourism generally.

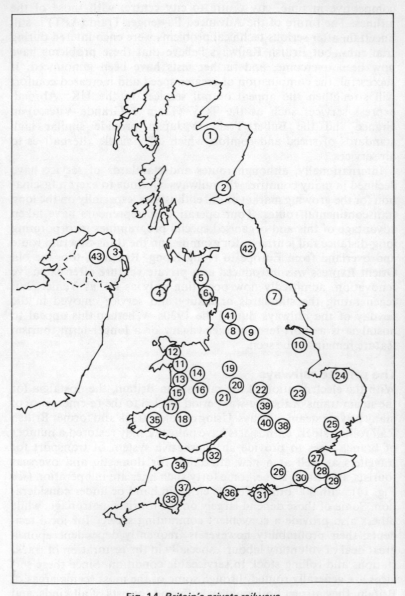

Fig. 14 *Britain's private railways*
(1) Strathspey Railway; Aviemore to Boat of Garten, 8 km. (2) Lochty Private Railway; Lochty to Knightsward, 3 km. (3) *Railway Preservation Society of

COACH TRAVEL

Coach operators today offer a wide range of tourist services to the public, both directly and through other sectors of the industry. These services can be categorised under the following general headings:

(a) express coach routes, both domestic and international;
(b) private hire services;
(c) tour and excursion operating;
(d) transfer services.

Long distance coach services provide a cheap alternative to rail or air travel, and the extension of these both within the UK and from the UK to points in Europe and beyond has drawn an increasing number of tourists at the cheaper end of the market, particularly among the young (50 per cent of National Bus Company's express service passengers were reported to be under 35 years of age in 1979).

Ireland; Whitehead and special runs. (4) Isle of Man Railway; Douglas to Port Erin, 11 km. (5) Ravenglass and Eskdale Railway; Ravenglass to Dalgarth, 11 km. (6) Lakeside and Haverthwaite Railway; Haverthwaite to Lakeside, 5½ km. (7) North Yorkshire Moors Railways; Pickering to Grosmont Junction, 29 km. (8) Worth Valley Railway; Keighley to Oxenhope, 8 km. (9) Middleton Railway; Turnstall Road to Middleton Park Gates, 3 km. (10) Lincolnshire Coast Light Railway; Humberstone, 1½ km. (11) Snowdon Mountain Railway; Llanberis to Snowdon, 7½ km. (12) Llanberis Lake Railway; Gilfach Ddu to Penllyn, 3 km. (13) Festiniog Railway; Porthmadog to Tanygrisiau, 19 km. (14) Bala Lake Railway; Llanuwchllyn to Bala, 7 km. (15) Fairbourne Railway; Fairbourne to Barmouth, 3 km. (16) Welshpool and Llanfair Light Railway; Llanfair Caereinion to Sylfaen, 9 km. (17) Talyllyn Railway; Tywyn to Nant Gwernol, 11½ km. (18) Vale of Rheidol Railway; Aberystwyth to Devil's Bridge, 19 km. (19) Foxfield Light Railway; Foxfield to Blythe Bridge, 6½ km. (20) Chasewater Light Railway; Chasewater Lake circuit, 3 km. (21) Severn Valley Railway; Bridgenorth to Bewdley, 20½ km. (22) Great Central Railway; Loughborough to Rothley, 8 km. (23) Nene Valley Railway; Wansford to Orton Mere, 9 km. (24) North Norfolk Railway; Sheringham to Weybourne, 4½ km. (25) † Stour Valley Railway; Marks Tey to Sudbury, 18½ km. (26) Mid-Hants Railway (Watercress Line); Alresford to Ropley, 5 km. (27) Sittingbourne and Kemsley Light Railway; Sittingbourne to Kemsley Down, 3 km. (28) Kent and East Sussex Railway; Tenterden to Wittersham Road, 5 km. (29) Romney, Hythe and Dymchurch Light Railway; Hythe to Dungeness, 22 km. (30) Bluebell Railway; Sheffield Park to Horsted Keynes, 8 km. (31) Isle of Wight Steam Railway; Haven Street to Wootton, 3 km. (32) East Somerset Railway; Cranmore. (33) Dart Valley Railway; Buckfastleigh to Staverton Bridge, 11 km. (34) West Somerset Railway; Minehead to Bishops Lydeard, 32 km. (35) Gwili Railway; Carmarthen, 3 km. (36) Swanage Railway; Swanage to Herston Halt. (37) Torbay and Dartmouth Railway; Paignton to Kingswear, 10 km. (38) *Leighton Buzzard Narrow Gauge Railway. (39) *Market Bosworth Light Railway. (40) *Cadeby Light Railway. (41) *Yorkshire Dales Railway. (42) *Bowes Railway, Tyne and Wear. (43) *Shane's Castle Railway. * All have short track for passenger steam haulage. † Planned (1982).

Younger passengers in particular have been attracted to the adventurous transcontinental coach packages which provide, for a low price, transport plus minimal food and lodging en route (often under canvas). However, for the most part coach travel remains the medium of transport for the elderly, in spite of efforts by the coach operators to attract a younger market for coach tours and excursions. In 1979 only 23 per cent of coach tour passengers in the UK were under 44 years of age. This is perhaps unsurprising in view of the advantages which coach travel offer to the elderly—not only low prices (which reflect comparatively low operating costs *vis-à-vis* other forms of transport) but the convenience of door-to-door travel when touring, overcoming baggage and transfer problems, and courier assistance, especially in overseas travel, where the elderly avoid problems of documentation and language. One result of this is that coach tour companies have a high level of repeat business. The operation of coach tours is a highly seasonal one, however, and companies, unless able to obtain ad hoc charters or contract work (such as schools bussing), are forced to lay off many drivers and staff.out of season.

Most coach companies specialise in certain spheres of activity. While some operate and market their tours nationally, others may specialise in servicing the needs of incoming tourists and tour operators by providing excursion programmes, transfers between airport and hotels, or complete coach tours for overseas visitors. These coach companies must build up close relations and work closely with tour operators and intermediaries abroad and in the UK.

Legislation in coaching

Under the terms of the Transport Act 1980, in order to set up or continue to operate a coach service, an operator must apply for a coach operator's licence. This is granted by the Traffic Commissioners, with conditions which limit the operation to a specified number of coaches. Licences normally run for five years, although under some conditions the term can be shorter. Before granting a licence, the Traffic Commissioners must be satisfied that the applicant has a good financial record and adequate resources to operate the number of coaches for which he has requested a licence. At least one responsible member of the company must hold an individual transport operator's licence, which is essentially a certificate of professional competence based on management experience and appropriate educational qualifications (for example, Membership of the Institute of Transport). The Commissioners must also satisfy themselves that the operator will provide satisfactory maintenance facilities (or in lieu, a contract with a supplier of such facilities), and the operating centre where vehicles are to be garaged must be specified.

The government has recently submitted proposals for the abolition of road service licensing throughout Great Britain (with the exception of bus services within London), in order to free road services from restriction or competition. However, the supervision of quality and safety standards of public service vehicles and operators will be maintained and tightened. It is also proposed to reorganise the National Bus Company into smaller free-standing parts, which will be transferred to the private sector. Legislation for these changes is likely to take effect in 1986.

Coach operating conditions now fall into line with EEC directives, which are designed to ensure adequate safety provisions for passengers. The concern with safety has been highlighted by recent incidents in the coach industry, most noticeably a series of serious accidents on the continent involving holiday coaches. The EEC regulation governing drivers' hours (No. 543/69) dictates the maximum number of hours' driving permitted for each driver per diem. These regulations apply automatically to all express journeys by coach with stages over 50 kilometres.

The controversial tachograph, introduced in the EEC in 1970 and adopted by Britain in 1981, following the Passenger and Goods Vehicles Recording Equipment Regulations 1979, provides recorded evidence of hours of operation and vehicle speeds by individual drivers. While there can be little doubt that implementation of these regulations has led to higher safety standards in the industry, the effect has also been to increase the cost of long-haul coaching operations, thus making it more difficult to compete with rail and air services. To permit through journeys without expensive stopovers, two drivers must be carried; or increasingly, since rest periods must be taken off the coach, drivers are exchanged at various stages of the journey. With the constraint of a limited number of seats on a coach, this has the effect of pushing up costs per seat by a significant amount.

The financial security of coaching operations has been increased through introduction of the Bus and Coach Council bond, under the terms of which member operators pay 10 per cent of their touring turnover each year as insurance against the financial collapse of any member. This bond has been accepted by ABTA in lieu of that Association's own bonding arrangements. It is worth noting, however, that public sector operators, who are covered by Treasury guarantees against failure, are exempted from payment of this bond, providing a useful boost to the cash flow of, among others, the National Bus Company.

Deregulation and its aftermath

Recently, substantial changes have occurred in the coaching industry in the UK as a result of the 1980 Transport Act which ended the licensing regulations affecting express coach services on routes of more than 30 miles. Prior to this the licensing system favoured the development of national and regional oligopolies; the trunk routes were effectively controlled by three major carriers, the National Bus Company, Wallace Arnold and Ellerman Bee Line, with National dominating the market. Elsewhere, some 220 licensed coach operators dominated regional routes, the result of historical development of the coach industry. Companies wishing to compete with the established carriers had to apply for a licence to the Traffic Commissioners, who were generally prepared to consider the granting of this only where a new service was to be offered or a new market tapped. Applications could be refused on the strength of existing operators' complaints that their business would suffer. This obviously limited competition and there was little incentive for creative marketing. Similar restrictions applied to all coach tour operations (with the sole exception of tours operated by coach companies on behalf of overseas tour operators on which all passengers had been pre-booked abroad).

With the ending of regulation a spate of new coach services of all types was introduced in 1981. A number of important regional coach companies came together to form British Coachways, a consortium designed to compete with National on their express trunk routes. National responded to this challenge by expanding into the formerly restricted regional territories to compete with the monopolies there. British Rail became the immediate target of the coach operators, who introduced new, low-priced express services between major city centres and initially attracted a considerable amount of traffic away from British Rail, until that organisation introduced its own highly competitive discounted fares.

At the time of going to press one can judge only the short-term effects of the 1981 price war in the British coach industry. Where prices become uniformly low, passengers seek other benefits in choosing between competitive companies. National appears to have made substantial gains at the expense of its rivals through its ability to offer greater frequency of service and flexibility. With its huge fleet of coaches and a national network of routes, it can at short notice replace a defective vehicle with little inconvenience to its passengers, an advantage denied to its smaller rivals. However, smaller companies operating newer or more "unusual" vehicles (such as luxurious foreign-built coaches) may offer effective competition to the larger companies; but a picture is now beginning to emerge of companies experiencing severe under-utilisation of such equipment, as the high capital investment (up to £100,000 a coach) depreciated over a period of five years, drives seat prices out of reach to all except a small, highly selective market. The British Coachways consortium proved unable to challenge National as effectively as they had hoped and, after the withdrawal of some of its founder members, added problems over their terminus location in London led to the collapse of the consortium in October 1982. Fear has been voiced that cut-throat competition could lead to falling maintenance standards and the failure of smaller, less efficient companies without the resources to survive a major price war.

Before deregulation, the market for coach services had been virtually static. The deregulation of the industry led to increased demand, but at the same time increased the capacity available on the market, resulting in lower average load factors for many operators. If one omits the largely short-haul services of the Transport Executives and municipal operators, National Bus now holds about three-quarters of the UK market for stage and express services, and carries more than one in ten of the 1.75 million passengers taking coach holidays in the UK each year. Although National has continued to strengthen its market share of UK coaching operations, the Monopolies Commission has shown no inclination to investigate coach operations since deregulation, working on the premiss that National's major competitor is in fact British Rail, and the competition between these two has held down fares.

In spite of this domination of the market by National, isolated examples of successes by private British coach services should be recognised. Trathens, operating luxury express coaches between Plymouth and London, have formed a successful working partnership with National on this route. Another formerly well-established company, Cotters, have expanded their operations through takeovers of Scottish coach companies and have held on to their market leads on selective long-haul express routes, using high-quality air suspension coaches—a forerunner of National's own "Rapide" service on key express routes which have been so successful in winning traffic away from British Rail. The development of these express services, which use vehicles of advanced design (often continental) with on-board video, toilet facilities and hostesses serving drinks and snacks, is one of the most significant in recent coaching operations.

On the international scene, an interesting development has been the growth of "shuttle" services between Britain and the Continent. These international stage journeys enjoyed a huge boom between 1981 and 1983, and estimates have indicated some 650,000 seats were available to the market in summer 1984. However, the profitability of these routes declined sharply in 1983, as the differential between coach and air travel prices fell. The collapse of Magic Bus at the end of 1982 (quickly absorbed into the National Bus organisation) was followed by the failure of a number of operators in 1983. More recently, the declining value of the Belgian Franc against sterling has resulted in fly/bus operations (in which passengers are flown to Ostend to pick up coaches hired in Belgium) undercutting British through-coach prices. Both shuttle and coach camping package holiday operations were badly affected in 1984, and a question mark hangs over the long-term viability of these operations—although world events which would lead to large increases in fuel prices could restore the profitability of these routes.

Also on the international scene, mention should be made of the importance of coach operations in North America. Notwithstanding the size of the continent, which has led to the development of the greatest network of domestic air routes in the world, and the high level of private car ownership, coach services both nationally and regionally have flourished at the expense particularly of the railways. The two major national coach operators, Greyhound and Continental Trailways, have built up a giant network of regional and transcontinental routes, including services into Canada and Mexico. Effective marketing, concentrating on value for money, package holidays linked to scheduled coach services, and unlimited travel within specified periods, have attracted widespread demand among domestic and international travellers. In the field of coach excursions, Gray Line, using a franchise system, has built up a network of city-based excursion operators not only within the USA, but also in numerous overseas countries.

THE PRIVATE CAR

Undoubtedly the increase in private car ownership has done more to change travel habits than any other factor in tourism. In Britain this phenomenon occurred after 1950 and had a significant impact on coach and rail load factors. It also gave families a new freedom of movement; not only were costs of motoring falling in relative terms, but car owners tended to perceive only the direct costs of a motoring trip, ignoring the indirect costs of depreciation and wear and tear. Thus car travel was favoured over public transport. This perception of low cost coupled with greater flexibility led to a great increase in motoring holidays and in particular to day excursions and short-break holidays.

The effect of this on the travel industry has been considerable; the hotel and catering industry has responded by developing motels and transit hotels, roadside cafes and restaurants, geared to the needs of drivers, while hotels and restaurants in more isolated areas away from public transport routes welcomed a growing market of private motorists. Car ferry services throughout Europe expanded and flourished and countries linked by such services experienced a visitor boom (France remains, for the British, the leading independent holiday destination).

Camping and caravan holidays have also grown with car ownership. The tour operators have fought back against this trend to independent holidays by creating flexible self-drive package tours suited to the needs of the private motorist, along with optional car hire packages for tourists on regular package holidays seeking something more adventurous to do abroad than lying on the beach. The car hire companies themselves have developed their services to cater for the needs of businessmen and other tourists without cars, and rail/drive and fly/drive packages have appeared on the scene. In the United States a market has been tapped for "motor homes" or motorised caravans. Even the railways have adapted to motoring needs, providing *Motorail* services for motorists to take their cars by rail with them to their holiday destinations.

In the 1980s the desire for greater freedom and flexibility on holiday suggests that, providing energy costs do not become exorbitant, the demand for private motoring holidays is likely to remain buoyant, at least for family travel. This expansion of motoring has brought, and will amplify, the problem of congestion and pollution. Small holiday resorts and scenic attractions cannot expand sufficiently to meet the demand for access and parking facilities without damaging or destroying the environment which the motorist has come to see. Inevitably, greater controls will be required in the future through action such as "park and ride" schemes, introduced at St Ives, which require visitors to park their cars outside the resort and travel in on public transport. Extensions of such schemes may ease the problem but will not entirely solve the growing crisis of private car saturation in small countries.

SELF-ASSESSMENT QUESTIONS

1. List the factors that led to the decline of line voyage shipping in the 20-year period 1950–70.

2. What are the relative merits of coach and rail travel for different markets in the UK?

3. How has a wider market been attracted to cruising during the past few years?

4. True or false? (*a*) Line voyages have been entirely displaced by cruising today. (*b*) Cruises are more expensive to operate than line voyages. (*c*) Demand for cross-Channel ferry services is fairly evenly balanced throughout the year. (*d*) The Harmonisation Conference was responsible for ensuring agreement on cross-Channel fares.

ASSIGNMENT

How has the tourist industry responded to the travel demands of the private motorist?

The Accommodation Sector

INTRODUCTION

In this chapter we are principally concerned with examining the commercial accommodation sector. It must not be forgotten, however, that this sector must compete with a large non-commercial supply of accommodation which is equally important in the tourism business; the VFR (visiting friends and relatives) market is a substantial and growing one in tourism. In addition to this there is a wide variety of other forms of private accommodation used by tourists; that used by campers and caravanners, in privately-owned yachts, in second homes, in the growing market for "exchange homes" and the swopping of timesharing accommodation. Even a strict distinction between commercial and non-commercial accommodation is difficult to make since the range of accommodation on offer is a continuum between profit- and non-profit-making sectors of the industry. Among the latter, youth hostels and YMCAs may be concerned only with recovering their costs of operation, while the use of educational institutions for tourist lodgings during holiday periods is designed chiefly to make a contribution towards the running costs of the institutions. And to what extent should sleeping facilities on board hired yachts or cruise ships in port be counted towards the sum of the stock of commercial accommodation available to tourists? There are even long-distance coaches in operation which provide specially fitted sleeping accommodation, and in certain parts of the world tour operators charter trains for inclusive tours in which the train acts as a hotel throughout.

these forms of overnighting can be ignored by those
the tourism industry. Quite apart from the fact that even
staying in private accommodation away from home is
nonetheless making a contribution to the tourism revenue of a region
(through local travel and entertainment) and must therefore be
counted in the tourism statistics of that region, he may also be
commercially exploited by other sectors of the industry. Tour operators, for example, have provided flight "packages" designed to meet
the needs of villa and apartment owners on the Continent; the airlines, recognising that home exchanges can represent a healthy source
of flight revenue, have developed and commercialised the home
exchange business by founding centralised directories (such as the
British Airways "Homex" scheme to which individual subscribers
have access); and national tourist offices keep directories of home
owners prepared to make exchanges or willing to welcome overseas
tourists into their homes for meals (a particular feature of United
States hospitality).

THE STRUCTURE OF THE ACCOMMODATION SECTOR

The accommodation sector comprises widely differing forms of sleeping facilities which can be conveniently categorised as either *serviced*
(in which catering is provided) or *self-catering*. These are not water-
tight categories since some forms of accommodation, such as holiday
camps or educational institutions, may offer serviced, self-service or
self-catering facilities, but they will help in drawing distinctions
between the characteristics of the two categories. Figure 15 provides
an at-a-glance guide to the range of accommodation which a tourist
might occupy.

A feature of the industry is that, as mass tourism has developed,
so have the large chains and corporations in the accommodation
sector. Hotels and motels are reaching a stage of development in
which a few major companies have come to dominate the international market. This expansion has been achieved not only through
ownership but also through franchising, whereby hotels and motels
are operated by individual franchisees paying royalties to the parent
company for the privilege of operating under the brand name. This
form of expansion has been used with great success around the world
by the largest hotel company in the world, Holiday Inns. Since these
chains market their products more aggressively, advertising extensively at home and overseas and establishing links with the tour
operators, they tend to play a more significant role in the industry
than even their market share might suggest.

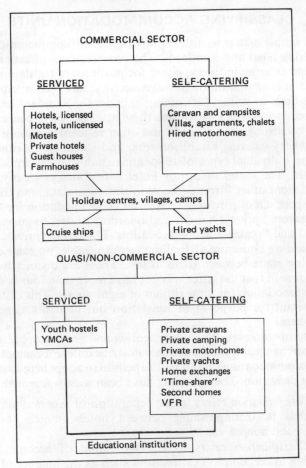

Fig. 15 *The structure of tourist accommodation*

In an effort to counteract this influence, a number of independent hotels are now banding together to form marketing consortia to provide a more effective and centralised marketing effort. Consortia such as Best Western Hotels, Inter Hotels and Prestige Hotels provide a strong marketing challenge to the large hotel chains and an attractive alternative to the tour operators.

In recent years a similar pattern of ownership by large corporations is evident in the field of holiday camps and holiday centres, with none of the leading companies in Britain still in private hands (*see* p. 140). Similar trends are beginning to emerge in the caravan and campsite sectors.

CLASSIFYING ACCOMMODATION UNITS

It is no simple matter to differentiate between accommodation units of differing types and standards. The process of classification of the hotel and catering industry, either for purposes of legislation or for systematic examination of business activity, has been attempted at various times in Britain (for example, under the Standard Industrial Classification system). However, these attempts have concentrated largely on distinguishing hotels and other residential establishments from sundry catering establishments, and statistical or other data based on individual types of residential establishment are less than adequate. The motel or motor hotel is not always clearly distinguished from other forms of hotel in statistical data, and there is a broad spectrum of privately controlled accommodation for tourists ranging from "private hotels" and boarding houses to guest houses and bed and breakfast accommodation. The terms "private hotel" and boarding house are virtually interchangeable, no clear distinction being made between them in law. These are distinct from the guest house in that the latter will not have more than four bedrooms or accommodation for a maximum of eight guests. This distinction is important for purposes of legislation but need not concern us further here.

The terms *categorisation*, *classification* and *grading* are also often used interchangeably, and since they describe different characteristics of the accommodation units it will be helpful to adopt here a standard range of definition. The following have been widely accepted.

(a) *Categorisation* refers to the separation of accommodation by type, that is, distinguishing between hotels, motels, boarding houses, guest houses, etc.

(b) *Classification* refers to the separation of accommodation according to certain physical features such as the number of rooms with private bath, etc.

(c) *Grading* refers to the separation of accommodation according to *verifiable objective features of the service offered* such as the number of courses served at meals, availability of night porters, etc.

There is as yet no common agreement within the industry regarding these terms, nor has any term yet been devised which satisfactorily covers the subjective assessment of the accommodation's facilities such as quality of food and service, or atmosphere.

Provision was made under the Development of Tourism Act 1969 for the compulsory classification and grading of the hotel industry in Britain, but this has been widely resisted by the industry itself and the British Tourist Authority has made no attempt to impose it, choosing to rely instead on a system of voluntary registration first introduced in 1975. The weakness of this system is that it relies on facts provided by the hoteliers themselves without inspection and control from the public sector. Being voluntary it omits a large proportion of the accommodation sector for which there is still no composite listing. The pressure for compulsory registration, in line with other European countries, continues.

Of the private classification and grading systems, those operated by the AA and RAC in Britain are probably the best known. These provide for a star-rating of hotel units, the AA's assessment being based on three characteristics:

(*a*) statements of fact on the nature of the premises and the services provided;

(*b*) the number and extent of the premises and services;

(*c*) the subjective assessment of their quality.

Premises are graded from "approved" through one to five stars, with rosettes being awarded for standards of catering. There are also a number of guides on the market dealing with the subjective assessment of catering in hotels and other establishments, of which Egon Ronay's and the *Good Food Guide* are perhaps the best known.

THE NATURE AND DEMAND FOR ACCOMMODATION FACILITIES

Hotels and other residential establishments share a number of marketing problems. In the first place, what is sold to the tourist is not a single product but the sum of a variety of different products, each of which could be the principal factor accounting for the customer's choice.

First and foremost, a customer's choice is likely to be based on location, a key factor in the profitability of the unit. Location implies both the destination (resort for the holidaymaker, convenient stop-over point for the traveller, city for the businessman) and the location *within* that destination. Thus the businessman will want to be at a hotel close to the company he visits, the seaside holidaymaker will wish to be as close as possible to the seafront, and the traveller will want to be close to the airport from which he is leaving. In economic terms a "trade-off" will occur between location and price; the tourist, unable to afford a seafront property, will opt for the one closest to the front which fits his pocket. Location is, of course, fixed for all time. If the resort loses its attractions for visitors, the hotel will suffer an equivalent decline in its fortunes.

The fact that high fixed costs are incurred in both building and operating hotels compounds the risk of hotel operating. City centre sites are extremely expensive to purchase and run (estimates for central London have ranged as high as £130,000 per room for hotel construction), requiring very high room prices. The market may resist such prices but is nevertheless reluctant to be based at any distance from the centres of activity, even where good transportation is available.

The demand for hotel rooms will come from a widely distributed market, nationally or internationally, whereas the market for other facilities which the hotel has to offer will be highly localised. In addition to providing food and drink for its own residents, the hotel will be marketing these services to tourists or residents within only a short distance of the site. Clearly a very different market segment will be involved, calling for different advertising, promotion and distribution strategies.

Another characteristic of the product is that it is seldom uniformly in demand throughout the year. Tourist hotels in particular suffer from levels of very high demand during the summer and negligible demand in the winter months. Even hotels catering chiefly to businessmen, while they may experience consistent demand during the year, will find that demand is largely for Monday–Thursday nights and they will have a problem in attracting weekend business, a problem known as *periodicity* as apart from seasonality. This lack of flexibility in room supply and the fact that the product itself is highly perishable (if rooms are unsold there is no opportunity to "store" them and sell them later) mean that great efforts in marketing must be made to attract off-peak customers, while potential revenue has to be sacrificed during the peak season because demand is greater than supply. Even with creative selling, such as discounted winter-breaks which the hotels have now introduced, many tourist hotels in seasonal locations such as seasides will be lucky to achieve average year-round occupancy of more than 50 per cent. These hotels are then faced with the choice of staying open in winter, with the hope of making sufficient income to cover their direct operating costs for the period, or closing completely for several months of the year. The problem with the latter course of action is that a number of hotel costs, such as rates and depreciation, will continue whether or not the hotel remains open. Temporary closure also has an impact on staff recruitment, with the attendant difficulties of obtaining staff of the right calibre for jobs which are only seasonal. In recent years more and more of the larger hotels have opted to stay open year-round, with special packages designed to attract the off-season market. The increase in second holidays in Britain has helped in this endeavour.

We have talked chiefly in terms of the physical characteristics of a hotel which attract its market, but no less important are the psychological factors such as service, "atmosphere", even the other guests with whom the customer will come in contact. Any or all of these factors will be taken into consideration by customers in making their choice of hotel.

Some patterns of demand

Less than a third of British holidaymakers stay at hotels in the UK, although some 60 per cent will do so when holidaying abroad. This obviously reflects the large VFR market in the UK, as well as the growing camping, caravanning and self-catering market. About a quarter of overseas visitors stay at hotels when in the UK, but the pattern will vary considerably between nationalities, and other socioeconomic variables such as class, age and life-style will also have an influence on choice of sleeping accommodation. In particular, the nature of, and consequent demand for, the large hotel will be quite different from that of the small guest house or bed and breakfast unit. A large hotel may well provide attractions of its own, distinct from the location in which it is situated; indeed in some cases the hotel may be a more significant influence on choice than is the destination. This is often true of the large hotel/leisure complex providing a range of in-house entertainment such as is found in a number of American and, increasingly, European hotels. This type of hotel is still rare in Britain.

This range of attractions helps to offset the impersonality which is inescapable in the very large hotels. However, less than 5 per cent of hotels in Britain have more than fifty bedrooms and outside London the 100-bedroom hotel is a rarity. The British hotelier therefore tends to concentrate on personal service in his appeal to the market.

Elsewhere, large hotels have been more sensitive to market changes than have smaller units. In the USA, where change and novelty is a feature of market demand, hotels have deliberately "themed" their architecture and interior decoration to emphasise their uniqueness, and budget for regular redecoration to keep up to date. More traditional hotels, particularly in Britain, have responded by re-emphasising their traditional values and style. There is now some evidence that even in North America the market is moving away from the vast, monolithic 1,000-bed hotels to the smaller, more intimate ones.

The point here is to emphasise that in neither case is the product seen by the customer as purely a "room in which to sleep". Rather, it is a "total leisure experience" comprising a range of different services and emotional experiences which together go to make up the holiday or the business stay.

The small guest house, farmhouse or bed and breakfast establishment provides a valuable service to the tourism industry and its consumers. Being largely family-run, it provides a unique, personal service at a low price which is welcomed by a particular segment of the holiday market. It caters effectively for the impulse purchaser in touring holidays and it conveniently expands the supply of tourist accommodation during peak periods of the year in areas which are highly seasonal and where hotels would not be viable.

The traditional domestic holiday in a small seaside guest house or hotel faces competition which threatens the whole future of the smaller accommodation units. First, there is the gradual process of the British market switching from seaside holidays in the UK to overseas package holidays at similar prices and often offering better value for money than the accommodation provided in Britain. The lure of guaranteed sunshine is of course the key factor in this change, but as a result of the experience package holiday tourists have had abroad they have come to demand higher standards on holiday in Britain too—accommodation with swimming pools, private bathroom, better food and wider entertainment. The traditional accommodation sector has not responded to this new demand quickly enough or to the extent necessary. Whatever the reasons for this—margins are often too low to provide for this kind of reinvestment in the property and up to the end of 1982 public sector financial assistance was restricted to the Economic Development Areas—there is little doubt that a substantial number of small hotels and guest houses will be forced to close their doors during the next few years. The present pattern of closures suggests that the decline is affecting unlicensed properties most severely. Licensing laws, particularly the restraints on drinking hours, are a liability in the promotion of tourism to Britain and there is continued pressure from the tourist boards and others in the industry for a liberalisation of these laws.

A second challenge faced by these institutions is the shift towards self-catering. This has come about partly in an effort to hold down holiday prices, but of at least equal importance is the demand from tourists for more flexible types of accommodation and catering than have formerly been available in the smaller British hotels and guest houses. The once-popular fully inclusive holiday comprising three meals a day, taken at fixed times of day in the hotel, no longer meets the needs of the modern tourist who may wish to take day trips by car to the surrounding area and will therefore want to eat irregularly and perhaps omit a midday meal. Self-catering apartments fulfil this need and their popularity abroad with British tourists has led in turn to a fast expansion of similar facilities in the UK, at the expense of the boarding houses. Many smaller hotels have adapted their premises to provide self-catering units in order to survive. The motels have also expanded in number to meet the need for flexibility in touring holidays—it has been estimated that there are some 150 motel units in Britain today—but these units are ideally suited to larger countries where they serve the needs of long-distance motorists travelling on the motorway networks.

Farm holidays have also enjoyed considerable success in recent years, both in the UK and on the continent. This arises from the recognition by farmers (and the tourist boards) that tourism is a less "seasonal crop" than are many other more traditional farming activities. Farm-based accommodation is popular, too, among the growing number of holidaymakers whose life-style orientation is towards healthy food and natural outdoor life. Within the Economic Development Areas, and particularly in Wales, the tourist boards have provided financial assistance and training for farmers interested in expanding their accommodation for tourists. On the continent, Denmark in particular has been notably successful in packaging farm holidays for the international market in conjunction with the tour operators and ferry companies.

THE HOLIDAY CENTRES

Holiday camps were very much a British development, introduced in the 1930s by three noted entrepreneurs of the day, Billy Butlin, Fred Pontin and Harry Warner, with the aim of providing "all-in" entertainment for the family at a low price in chalet-style accommodation which would be largely unaffected by inclement weather. The Butlin–Pontin–Warner-style holiday camps were enormously successful before World War II and in the early post-war years, but all three organisations have now been absorbed into large corporations. Of the hundred or so camps in Britain today, the leading companies now share 70 per cent of the market, which is believed to be close to 4 million holidaymakers a year (*see* Table IV). The balance of the market is largely split among a number of independent companies operating a small number of sites, although some larger operators have recently taken an interest in this area of the accommodation sector; Trusthouse Forte, for example, have one holiday village.

The market for this accommodation is almost entirely between May and September, with most camps closing in the winter months, although there is increasing emphasis on filling accommodation in the fringe months of spring and autumn.

Holiday centres have been affected as much as any other accommodation facilities by changes in public taste for holidays. Before the

TABLE IV. THE LEADING COMPANIES IN BRITISH HOLIDAY CENTRE
OPERATING, 1984

	Ownership	No of UK centres	Estimated No of visitors
Pontin's	Bass Charrington	30	850,000
Butlin's	Rank Organisation	6	815,000
Ladbroke's	Ladbroke Group	16	500,000
Haven Holidays	English China Clays	18	350,000
Warner's	Grand Metropolitan	10	150,000
Total			2,665,000

war they attracted a largely lower-middle class clientele, but in the
post-war period their market became significantly more working
class and the canteen-style catering service and entertainment provided reflected this market segment's needs. Bookings were made
invariably on a Saturday to Saturday basis, with clients booking
direct with the companies concerned (each company attracting a
high level of repeat business from a loyal market). Guests travelled
independently to the camps.

More recently these camps have gone up-market, changing their
names to holiday centres, holiday villages, holiday parks or estates.
The former working class entertainment orientation has been modified to cater for wider social tastes. Large chalet blocks have given
way to smaller units with self-catering facilities. A choice of catering
styles has been introduced, ranging from fully serviced, through
self-service to self-catering, but the latter form of service reflects the
highest growth rate (Butlin's is now 70 per cent self-catering).

Billy Butlin's early attempts to introduce his holiday camp concept
abroad failed but the holiday village concept has been successful on
the continent, with the Club Méditerranée an outstanding example
of such success, largely attracting a young market. More recently
Pontin's (under the Pontinental banner) have succeeded in extending the British market overseas, and Butlin's has followed by taking
over and marketing camp and caravan centres on the continent
under the "Freshfields" brand name.

THE DISTRIBUTION OF ACCOMMODATION

/Large hotels and hotel chains have considerable advantages in gaining access to their markets. Many international chains have close

links, through ownership or financial interest, with the airlines, a situation brought about in the early 1970s when the airlines, introducing their new jumbo jets, hastily set about establishing connections with hotels to accommodate their passengers. This gives hotels access to the airlines' computer reservations systems, important in reaching the international market.

Large hotels depend upon group as well as individual business to fill their rooms, so they must be in a position to maintain contact with tour operators, conference organisers and others bulk-buying accommodation. The tourist boards can play a part in helping such negotiations by organising workshops abroad to which the buyers of accommodation and other tourist facilities will be invited.

Increasingly the larger hotel chains are installing their own computerised reservations systems to cope with worldwide demand for immediate confirmation on availability and reservations. Some chains maintain their own offices in key generating countries (and of course each hotel will recommend business and take reservations for others in the chain), while independent hotels reach the overseas markets through membership of marketing consortia or through representation by a hotel representative agency.

These hotel representatives are not merely booking agents; they are on contract to the hotels they represent and will offer a complete marketing service. Some agencies, such as William R. Galley Associates, R. M. Brooker or Utell International, generalise in their representation, while others specialise, either by representing hotels within a specific geographical area such as the Caribbean or smaller "character" hotels.

Sales made through hotel representatives are normally commissionable at 10 per cent to the representative. This does not prejudice the commission normally allowable to travel agents, so a hotel being represented abroad may well find that a high proportion of its sales are costing 20 per cent of the room price to obtain. A small hotel must carefully consider whether it can set prices at a level which permits it to pay out commissions of this magnitude.

Sales through travel agents
Patterns of sales through travel agents are inconsistent. Within the UK few agents, other than a handful of specialist business house travel agents, deal regularly with hotel bookings. This is partly the result of the traditional pattern in Britain for tourists to book direct and partly because agents feel that the income accruing in commission for such sales is too small to merit the cost of servicing the business. There is also no common agreement between the hotel associations and ABTA on payment of commissions to agents, so

each arrangement must be negotiated individually. Some hotels are prepared to pay a standard commission of 10 per cent on all sales, but these are the exception rather than the rule. Others will set a lower rate of commission or will not pay commission on sales for peak holiday periods.

However, hotels incorporated in domestic package tours, such as British Rail's "Golden Rail" holidays, or those which have produced a package tour programme which is easy and convenient for agents to sell, such as the weekend bargain break type of programme, do pay commission to domestic agents and sales through this source are increasing, although still relatively small in terms of hotels' overall turnover. Agents do undertake international hotel bookings more readily, especially where the hotel concerned has a UK representative or where the agent is arranging an independent package tour for his clients.

The pattern of agency sales for UK holiday centres is similar. Traditionally these have been booked direct, but the leading companies, especially Butlin's, have made a conscious effort to increase their sales through travel agents in recent years, partly as a means of reaching a wider market than the one they have traditionally drawn on in the past. About one in six such sales are now made through agents in Britain.

Finally, mention should be made of the sale of accommodation through public sector tourism outlets. This has been undertaken for some years on the continent—in Holland, for example, the Dutch tourist offices (VVVs) provide a reservations service for tourists, charging a fee for doing so—and some recent innovations in the UK have resulted in a number of seaside resort hotels selling through regional tourist board offices in the Midlands, a policy which, if successful, is likely to be extended. There has been some initial resistance to this idea from travel agents, but until agents show themselves willing to become more involved in such sales the accommodation sector is bound to seek new outlets for its products as the battle for the accommodation market becomes more acute.

SELF-ASSESSMENT QUESTIONS

1. How is changing taste affecting the market for accommodation?

2. What must a seaside resort hotel take into account in deciding whether or not to close in the winter?

3. Discuss how the holiday camps have changed in the period 1930–80.

4. What must a hotel do to try to increase its sales through travel agents in the United Kingdom?

ASSIGNMENT

Produce a brief report which demonstrates how the various types of accommodation unit reach their market in the UK and abroad.

CHAPTER EIGHT

Travel Retailing

CHAPTER OBJECTIVES

After studying this chapter, you should be able to:
* explain the role of travel agents as a component in the tourism business;
* list the functions that a travel agent is expected to perform;
* identify the strengths and weaknesses of existing agents;
* be aware of the requirements for setting up a travel agency, for obtaining membership of ABTA and for securing licences from principals;
* understand the threats an agency faces from alternative forms of distribution;
* be aware of the growing role of computer technology in travel agency operations.

INTRODUCTION

Most travel principals sell their products to consumers through the medium of travel agents. Such agents have been in existence for over a hundred years (selling mainly shipping and rail services before World War II), but their major growth has coincided with the growth in air travel and package tours. Before these two forms of travel became common the shipping companies had also provided a reservations and ticketing service in their own offices situated in the leading ports and cities, and likewise the railways and coach companies, with transport terminals close to their markets, could also offer a convenient direct sales service to the public. With the development of air transport the airlines found that, since the airports were away from market centres and there was already established a satisfactory network of travel agents to handle sales, the additional costs involved in setting up a chain of direct sales offices were not justified. In turn, agents expanded in number to meet the demand for air tickets.

The origin of package tours can be traced to certain travel agent entrepreneurs who began operating their own programmes of foreign tours (*see* Chapter 9). Historically, of course, Thomas Cook had originated as a tour operator and expanded to sell a range of travel services later; the mass market tour operations by air that we know today owe their origins as much to the handful of travel agents with vision, who recognised the opportunities for mass travel in the 1950s, assuming that air prices could be reduced, and who began putting together their own holidays. These "packages" were sold in turn through other travel agents, becoming eventually the agents' largest source of revenue. Today the vast majority of airline tickets and eight out of ten package holidays abroad are purchased through travel agents. There are today some 5,500 "recognised" travel agents (i.e. members of the Association of British Travel Agents) in the UK and perhaps a further 2,000 non-members.

THE ROLE OF TRAVEL AGENTS

The role of a travel agent is dissimilar to that of most other retailers in that an agent does not purchase travel for resale to his customers. Only when a customer has decided on a travel purchase does the agent approach the principal on his customer's behalf. The travel agent therefore does not carry "stock" of travel products. This has two important implications for the business of travel distribution. Firstly, the cost of setting up in business is comparatively small compared to other retailing businesses; and secondly he is under no obligation to dispose of products he has purchased and therefore has less brand loyalty towards a particular product or company than do other retailers.

The latter characteristic can be an advantage to the consumer since it aids the impartiality of advice that agents will give their customers (assuming that commissions on sales are equal). On the other hand, it poses a marketing problem for the principals in their need to count on travel agency support to sell their products.

The main role of agents is to provide a convenient location for the purchase of travel. At these locations they act as booking agents for holidays and travel, as well as a source of information and advice on such services. Their customers look to them for expert product knowledge and objectivity in the advice they offer.

Although the range of services that an agent may offer will vary according to the nature of demand in an area, the specialisation of the agency in question and the preferences and marketing policies of the proprietor, these will usually include air, rail, sea and coach transport, car hire, hotel accommodation, and package tours. Ancillary services such as travel insurance, travellers' cheques and foreign exchange may also be offered, and some agents will undertake the arranging of travel documentation for their clients.

Travel agents can be classified in a number of ways. There is firstly the distinction between those who are members of ABTA and those who are not—an important one for purposes of trading, as we shall see. Agents can also be differentiated by the type of business in which they specialise and by the location of their office; these two characteristics influence each other.

Travel agents are located in major city centres, in the suburbs of large towns, and in smaller towns and villages. To be successful they need to be sited close to the centre of the shopping district. With other similarly sited agents they compete for travel business within a catchment area which, in the case of a large city, may extend only to the surrounding streets or, in the case of an important market town, may draw on residents within a radius of 30 or 40 miles. Those agents whose location is close to important city centres or centres of business and industry (such as industrial estates) will usually try to take advantage of the opportunity their location offers to develop the business travel requirements of companies in the area. Some agents who specialise in business house travel may go to the extent of providing an *implant* (or *in-plant*) office in which members of travel agency staff are based within the business house client's premises to handle the company's travel needs exclusively.

It should also be remembered that agents in city centres will draw on business not only from residents in the area but also from workers employed in the area, who may find it more convenient to make their travel arrangements close to their place of work rather than to their homes. This is particularly true of central London.

TRAVEL AGENCY OPERATIONS

The vast majority of travel agents are small, family-run organisations in which the owner acts as manager and employs two or three members of staff. In such an agency there is little specialisation in terms of the division of labour; staff will be expected to cope with all the activities normally associated with the booking of travel, which will include:

(*a*) advising potential travellers on resorts, carriers, travel companies and travel facilities worldwide;

(*b*) making reservations for all travel requirements;

(*c*) planning itineraries of all kinds, including complex multi-stopover independent tours;

(*d*) accurately computing airline and other fares;

(*e*) issuing travel tickets and vouchers;

(*f*) corresponding by telephone and letter with travel principals and customers;

(*g*) maintaining accurate files on reservations;

(*h*) maintaining and displaying stocks of travel brochures;

(*i*) interceding with principals in the event of customer complaints.

In addition to product knowledge, therefore, the main skills that counter staff require will include the ability to read timetables and other data sources, to construct airline fares, to write tickets, and to have sufficient knowledge of their customers to be able to match customer needs with products available. There is also today a growing need for staff who can operate computer reservations systems.

The correct construction of airline fares and issue of airline tickets is a far more complex subject than might be apparent to the uninitiated, and entails a lengthy period of training coupled with continuous exercise of these skills. However, computer ticketing is already available (albeit presently only on a small scale) and many of the more common airline fares are also now accessible by computer; it is therefore likely that these particular skills will not be required in the near future to the same extent as they have been in the past.

In addition to these counter staff functions, agency managers must arrange to protect and maintain stocks of tickets and other negotiable documents, record sales and complete sales returns for travel principals, although again many basic accounting procedures are now becoming computerised. Marketing skills are called for in the in-shop and external promotion of travel services, and additionally the normal administrative skills of efficiently running a small office are needed.

Agents earn their revenue in the form of commissions on sales. Levels of commission payable vary over time and according to the travel product, but typical commissions at present are 7–7½ per cent for shipping services, 9 per cent on airline reservations and 10 per cent on package tours, with incentive commissions of 2½ per cent or more sometimes payable by tour operators for the achievement of pre-established targets.

The scope and depth of functions which an agent is called upon to perform pose problems for the marketing of travel. First and foremost there is the problem of product knowledge. No individual agent, however knowledgeable, can be expected to have a complete knowledge of all resorts and hotels worldwide. While tour operators and others arrange regular educational trips abroad for travel agents, these are more widely available to short-haul destinations, and product knowledge of the more exotic long-haul travel destinations is difficult to acquire. For this reason the tour operators' brochures become not only the chief sales tool but also the major source of information about resorts. The problem for the consumers, however, is that this can hardly be treated as an unbiased source of information. The agent's role becomes one of knowing where to find unbiased information, and to cater for this need a comprehensive selection of travel guidebooks is available for agency use (those most commonly used appear in Chapter 11).

Again the introduction of computer systems into travel agencies is about to ease considerably the burden of product knowledge for agents. Already Prestel, British Telecom's viewdata service, provides a very wide range of information on travel products, and as more extensive data-banks come on-line in the future, this aspect of the agent's role will decline. The question arises as to whether travel agencies will continue to play an important role in the future if travel information is readily available through other public sources such as reference libraries.

One curious omission from the services provided by travel agents up to now is that of domestic holiday arrangements. Traditionally holidaymakers in Britain have made their own arrangements direct with principals. In the past holidays have been neither as conveniently packaged nor as remunerative for agents to sell as have foreign tours. This is beginning to change as inflation in Britain pushes domestic holiday prices up and as travel companies in Britain, anxious to exploit new sources of revenue, are making a more concerted attempt to woo business from agents by providing packages that are easy to sell. A consortium operating under the "Holiday UK" banner now provides a range of package holidays available through some 1,800 agents in Britain and this is beginning to have an impact on traditional British buying habits.

TRAVEL AGENCY APPOINTMENTS

ABTA membership

In the UK there are no legal licensing requirements to set up as a travel agent, but in some countries governments do exercise licensing control over agencies and the EEC is currently looking into this issue for its members. However, most principals license the sale of their services through the issue of an *agency agreement*, or contract. Without such an agreement the principal will not pay commission on sales, although some companies do dispense with the formal procedures for recognition—it is unusual, for example, for hotels to insist on a formal agreement before they will pay agents' commission on sales.

To sell the services of tour operators who are themselves members of ABTA, the travel agent is required to belong to ABTA as well as entering into a formal agreement with the company concerned. Membership of ABTA is required because of a ruling (recently challenged by the Office of Fair Trading, but upheld by the Restrictive Practices Court in 1982) that only ABTA travel agents may sell services of ABTA tour operators, and in turn these agents refrain from selling package tours of companies who are not ABTA members. This reciprocal booking agreement, which amounts to a closed shop, is known as *Operation Stabiliser* and was introduced by ABTA in 1965 as a means of protecting the travelling public. In the event of the collapse of an ABTA member, the Association was to draw on a *Common Fund* provided from membership subscriptions, which would compensate customers for lost holidays and ensure that those stranded abroad as a result of the collapse would be repatriated. Later, with the introduction of alternative bonding arrangements for tour operators (*see* Chapter 9), this Common Fund became the Retailers' Fund and operates today to protect consumers against the consequences of a retail agent collapsing.

Thus, ABTA membership provides considerable trading advantages, but it also imposes certain obligations on its members. Premises are open to ABTA inspection, agents must abide by a strict code of conduct, and at least one qualified member of staff must be employed. "Qualified" is defined as having two years' experience, or one year's experience together with training equivalent to the Certificate of Travel Agency Competence (COTAC), level 2. However, ABTA's conditions which formerly restrained agents from discounting travel and prevented their selling non-travel products ("mixed selling") have now been overturned by the Restrictive Practices Court.

The individual agency agreements drawn up by tour operators lay down terms of trading. Perhaps the most important of these is that (with rare exceptions) agents are required to sell the principals' services at published prices. Technically it is illegal to impose such a constraint uniformly on all agents but there is no restriction on the introduction of such clauses in individual agreements between agent and tour operator.

IATA appointments

A licence is required for commission to be payable on the sale of services of members of the International Air Transport Association (with the exception of domestic services). Since IATA travel makes up a substantial proportion of a typical travel agency turnover, it is important for travel agents who wish to offer a full range of services (and doubly so for those developing business house traffic) to obtain the necessary appointment.

Travel agency approval is controlled by IATA's Agency Administration Board, acting in the UK through an Agency Investigation Panel (AIP) made up of a number of IATA members operating out of the UK. The AIP investigates financial standing, security (for control of ticket stock) and suitability of premises, staff qualifications and the applicant's ability to generate new business. If approved, a Passenger Sales Agency Agreement is issued and a numeric ticket validation code is provided which will be stamped on all tickets issued by that agent. This approval enables the agent to sell the services of all IATA members. The process of obtaining approval can be lengthy and agents will in the meantime be expected to generate business without remuneration (IATA rules prohibit the splitting of commission between agents). Proof of turnover is no longer specifically required to obtain approval, but there can be little doubt that evidence of healthy support for an IATA carrier will assist in obtaining a sympathetic hearing for agency approval.

Other appointments

Approval is also required to make commissionable sales on the services of British Rail, National Coaches, domestic airline services and other principals such as shipping and car hire companies. Obtaining approval for most of these is largely a formality, especially for ABTA and IATA appointed agents.

Non-ABTA agents

It is estimated that there are some 2,000 travel agents in Britain who are not ABTA members. Some of these are content to sell "fringe" services of non-ABTA tour operators and similar companies, but from the point of view of their effect upon the industry the *bucket shops* are the most important sector of non-ABTA retailing.

These, as discussed in Chapter 5, act as convenient outlets for airlines intent on dumping unsold seats on the market at short notice and at heavily discounted fares. This reduces the revenue opportunities for ABTA/IATA agents, who are fighting for a change in the legal position which would make it possible for these tickets to be sold through officially appointed agents. At the end of 1981 a breakthrough was achieved whereby British Airways was authorised to sell discounted tickets to certain selected destinations through ABTA/IATA agents. This scheme, however, appears to have made little impact on the growth of "bucketed" tickets sold through non-ABTA outlets.

RETAILERS OUTSIDE THE UK

While most countries generating mass-market tourism have similar procedures and organisations which need not concern us here, mention should be made specifically of the trade body for travel agents in the United States, the American Society of Travel Agents (ASTA), mainly because this body has influence far beyond the confines of that country's borders.

Because of the huge market for overseas tourism in the United

States, ASTA has become an organisation which draws its membership not only from travel agents and principals in that country but also from principals throughout the world who have an interest in stimulating the American market to their country. Thus the affairs of ASTA, and the annual conference especially, have particular interest for many British tour operators and other operators of tourism plant in the UK.

Individual national travel agency associations such as ABTA also belong to an international travel agency body known as the Universal Federation of Travel Agency Associations (UFTAA). This organisation plays a valuable role in representing the interests of travel agents worldwide in such international issues as the negotiation of travel agency commission rates with IATA.

THE EFFECTIVENESS OF TRAVEL AGENTS

A subject of considerable controversy in the industry is the relative effectiveness of the travel agent as a medium for the distribution of travel services. As has been explained, agents receive their remuneration in the form of commissions on sales and for this they provide a convenient sales point for the travelling public. Their role as providers of information is, as we have discussed, more questionable, with the evidence pointing to serious gaps in product knowledge among many agents, particularly in the area of long-haul travel.

Travel agency work still has something of a glamour image for young people and the prospect of cheap travel is an attractive lure for new staff. However, levels of pay in agencies are generally below those to be found in other areas of retail distribution and it is hard to attract and retain the calibre of staff best qualified to provide the sophisticated level of sales effort needed to deal with travel enquiries.

A number of attempts have been made in recent years to compensate for the lack of basic travel knowledge among young staff. The earlier work of the Institute of Travel and Tourism, and the more recent introduction of the Certificate of Travel Agency Competence, validated by City and Guilds, have undoubtedly helped to increase travel sales and management skills, supported by in-service courses run by the Air Transport and Travel Industry Training Board (until wound up in 1982) and, more recently, the ABTA National Training Board. However, well qualified staff in travel agencies remain the exception rather than the rule. ABTA's requirement of two years' experience in lieu of formal training has done little to encourage agency managers to ensure that their staff obtain more formal qualifications.

The growth of the travel agency multiples may well change these attitudes; alternatively, the process may lead to the demise of the small, unqualified agents. The large chains, spearheaded by Thomas Cook, Pickfords, Lunn Poly and Hogg Robinson are in the process of rapid expansion in the number of branches they operate; there are, at the time of writing, eight chains operating over 100 outlets, and several of these have plans to add substantially to their total over the next few years. Their increasing efficiency, coupled with superior in-service training, poses a threat to the continuing existence of the small agent. Multiples also offer great opportunities for the application of specialist expertise (both functional and, for those staff serving on the counter, geographical), and they provide career prospects which are sufficiently attractive to recruit "high flyers" for the first time to this sector of the industry.

The rapid increase in computerisation of travel retailing favours the multiple, which has the resources to develop these facilities innovatively. Thomas Cook in particular has exploited this opportunity by recently introducing a mechanism by which customer needs are matched to specific destinations through a computer databank. Customers are reassured of their selection by a money-back guarantee of satisfaction.

This type of computer may help to overcome one important problem associated with the advice offered by agents—its questionable impartiality. Principals—tour operators in particular—attempt to encourage agency support by setting targets for sales or offering higher levels of commission for sales increases. With the prospects of bonuses for individual counter staff it is difficult for an agent to maintain complete impartiality.

Finally, travel agents are expected to play an active role in the promotion of travel services—indeed, they are specifically required to do so under the terms of their code of conduct—but some will go no further than displaying promotional material in their shops and windows. Others will advertise in local press or cinema or run film shows for potential customers. However, it is questionable whether in doing so they are actually increasing the propensity for their clients to travel, or whether they are merely competing one with another for a share of the travel market which is actually generated and stimulated by the principals' own advertising and promotion. Nor is there much evidence (at least in Britain) to suggest that agents exercise much influence over their customers' decisions regarding destination or product; by far the most significant factors in these choices are the influence of travel brochures and word of mouth recommendation. In fairness, the picture does seem to be a little different in the United States where research suggests that agents appear to have greater influence over their customers' decisions such as the choice of hotel or airline.

DIRECT SELL

Can a travel principal sell its products direct to the public at lower cost without losing sales? This is a vital question for carriers and tour operators. Organisations which have sold direct traditionally, such as British Rail, and others who are newcomers to the industry and who have adopted a policy of selling direct exclusively, do not have to reckon with the retaliatory forces of ABTA and can base their decision purely on the economics of the situation. Selling direct cuts out the high cost of servicing the middle men as well as paying a commission on each sale. On the other hand it involves considerable capital expense in setting up sales offices, and direct marketing costs can be heavy, especially for the programme of national advertising which is necessary to reach the travelling public.

However, for principals who presently deal through the travel agency network, the decision to sell direct for the first time or to attempt to increase the proportion of direct sales has to be tempered with discretion, since to antagonise agents might result in a significant loss in sales through traditional channels, especially for a product as homogeneous as travel. Thus British Airways decided to abandon the decision, taken a few years ago, to expand their "in-plant" booking desks in the headquarters of large businesses following a strong reaction from ABTA, whose members threatened to switch sales to competitive carriers. The airline has, however, cautiously expanded its network of city centre sales offices, as much to maintain control over its product sales as to save commission.

Tour operators depend upon agency support for up to 90 per cent of their sales (although most small companies licensed to sell less than 10,000 holidays a year cannot afford to distribute through travel agents nationally and will either develop a policy of selecting a number of key supportive agents or will opt to sell all holidays direct). Within the last few years, however, a number of tour operators have entered the direct sell field with some success. The three largest of these, Martin Rooks (175,000 holidays a year), Portland Holidays (128,000) and Tjaereborg (120,000), claim to offer holidays which are substantially cheaper than those sold through agents, simply by cutting out agency commissions. There is evidence to suggest that this claim is justified in many cases (though not in all) and this, coupled with the appeal of strong product knowledge among the company's staff, appears to have overcome the traditional resistance of the British public to purchasing holidays direct. Direct sell now approaches some 20 per cent of the total market for package tours in Britain and it is thought that this figure may rise to some 30 per cent before levelling off.

The success of Martin Rooks and Portland does not appear to have been affected by the fact that both are divisions of travel organisations which sell largely through agents (British Airways and Thomson Holidays respectively). ABTA is disturbed by the trend but has so far not sought confrontation on the issue with these companies (perhaps on the grounds that they would not wish to threaten their own sales of market leaders' products).

OTHER ISSUES IN DISTRIBUTION

In general, it has been tour operating policy to sell products through the entire network of ABTA travel agents. In 1971, however, Cosmos Holidays, among the brand leaders in package tours, adopted a policy of limiting outlets on the basis of their productivity, dropping a large number of their relatively unproductive agents. This policy was soon followed by Global and Thomson Holidays after analysis of sales which revealed that a large number of agents were producing only a handful of bookings while 90 per cent of bookings were achieved through some 100 highly productive agents. It is interesting to note that Cosmos has since decided to reverse this policy decision, returning to a pattern of limited support for all agents, and an increasing measure of support for agents who are more productive.

In turn, travel agents who do represent a full range of principals' services are in practice fairly selective in the services they recommend; a decision based not only on what they believe to be in the consumers' interest but on their own self-interest too. Commission levels will be a factor to be taken into consideration, but of equal importance is the efficiency of the principal's reservations system; an agent who has difficulty in making telephone reservations for his client will be less inclined to favour that principal's services. The personal relationship that exists between travel agent and tour operator or other principal provides another dimension; here the role of the sales representative can be of immense importance in creating an image for his company and cultivating the goodwill of that company's travel agents.

THE ECONOMICS OF TRAVEL AGENCY OPERATION

Setting up as a travel agent in Britain requires little capital investment (since no stock has to be purchased), no formal qualifications and no government licence. This led to the rapid proliferation of agencies after the early 1960s, with the process accelerating in the 1980s, much to the concern of ABTA and its members. Agencies have outpaced the growth in travel demand so that, in spite of price inflation and small increases in commission levels paid by principals, a larger number of branches are now fighting for a smaller share of the cake. With the number of agencies in a region multiplying, IATA licences become more difficult to obtain and this has the effect of pushing up the prices at which agencies changed hands (a change of ownership does not automatically ensure the retention of an IATA licence but it does make retention easier than trying to obtain a licence when starting from scratch). The future potential for the travel market has also forced prices up as newcomers are prepared to pay high prices for good locations, in the expectation of maintaining existing custom ("goodwill" in the accountant's terminology).

Strong demand does not, however, guarantee profitability. This is geared to the commission payable by principals which, with small variations according to the travel "mix" sold, will average around 9 per cent of turnover. Out of this gross profit on turnover the agent must pay all the running expenses of his agency (see Fig. 16). Only after these expenses are deducted can an agent ascertain whether he has made a net profit or loss. If we assume—and it is a big "if"— that agents do not themselves have the ability to increase the overall size of the travel market in their region, and again assuming all agents within the region are equally sales- and service-orientated (another big "if"), then the only means of improving profitability is to increase efficiency by achieving higher turnover at the same cost or similar turnover at reduced cost.

There have been few studies in Britain of travel agency productivity and profitability, although the EIU (Economist Intelligence Unit) report on travel agency profitability (see Bibliography) made an attempt to do so in 1968. This survey has shortcomings in methodology, but suggests that at that time some two-thirds of agents responding to the questionnaire were making profits, although 75 per cent of all agents were generating just 22 per cent of the total travel revenue. Clearly, many of these were making substantial losses and conversely some agents were achieving very high revenue figures.

The report did not make clear that profitability may be as much a factor of location as of efficiency; nor is fast turnover necessarily commensurate with a professional standard of advice and sales assistance. A case may be made for emulating the American approach to retail agency operations; providing a fast and efficient sales service for package tours and simple point-to-point travel reservations, and at the same time offering a more specialised advisory service for complex travel arrangements through an expert in product know-

Sales:	1,121,801
Less cost of sales	1,012,488
Gross profit	109,313
Expenditure:	
Administration [a]	8,747
Rent and rates	6,807
Light and heat	1,009
Cleaning	480
Insurance	713
Postage, printing and stationery	3,019
Telephone, telex, computer rental	12,244
Advertising and sales promotion	8,975
Salaries [b]	34,438
Expenses [c]	2,294
Repairs and renewals	1,011
Bad debts	60
Subscriptions [d]	583
Bank charges, interest on loans	2,010
Professional charges, legal costs	1,225
Total expenditure	83,613
Operating profit	25,700
Add interest receivable	7,095
Net profit before tax	32,795

Fig. 16 *Operational costs of a travel agency. A monthly profit and loss account to show typical expenditure in a branch of a small travel agency chain*
(a) Including proportion of head office expenditure, directors' salaries and fees, etc. (b) Including national insurance contributions, etc. (c) Including travel, entertainment, etc. (d) Including timetables and guides, trade and professional membership fees, etc.

ledge (known as a certified travel counsellor) who may charge a fee for his services in addition to earning commission on the travel sold.

Another failure of the EIU Report was in not making clear which were the profitable and non-profitable services sold by travel agents. Harry Chandler, of Chandler's World Travel, tried to correct this omission by publishing in 1969 an analysis of his own company records which sought to identify the average costs applicable to each service in terms of labour units for commission earned. He found at that time that package tours and long-haul air travel was subsidising the other travel services sold by agents; a re-evaluation of the records in 1973 found much the same results.

This raises the question of whether an agent should continue to provide a full range of travel services for his clientele or concentrate only on those which he finds profitable. Many adopt the former course on the grounds that customers buying unprofitable services will be tempted to return to the same agent later to buy more profitable travel arrangements. Nevertheless, a growing number feel that the latter course is the more sensible to adopt. If their approach becomes widespread it will cause the principals affected to rethink their distribution methods, either by organising alternative distribution outlets or by improving the efficiency of existing ones, for example, by the introduction of cost-effective computer reservations systems.

The system of bonus payments by which principals reward highly productive agents with increased rates of commission is also encouraging agents to become more selective in the products they display and actively sell. This trend is also likely to have an impact on principals' distribution systems, and lead to more specialised travel agents offering a more selective range of travel "brands".

Agents must also assess their means of increasing their own efficiency. Many, for example, are eager to obtain business house accounts because of the high revenue yield such accounts promise. However, many such accounts are notoriously slow to settle their debts and an agent can find himself in the position of subsidising the company's cash flow, since he is under an obligation to settle his own accounts within two weeks. In this case the agent must carefully evaluate the costs and benefits to his company of this account.

THE IMPACT OF COMPUTER TECHNOLOGY ON TRAVEL RETAILING

Profound changes are already under way in the retailing of travel services. Technology's impact on travel retailing has made itself felt since the beginning of the 1980s with the introduction of the first generation agency computer systems. To discuss the merits of differing systems in this volume will be of little value, since systems are being modified and improved almost daily and costs in real terms of "going computer" are falling steadily, to a point where even the smallest agencies will find it profitable to invest in some computer hardware.

The tourism industry in general is ideally suited for computer technology. It requires a system of registering availability of transport and accommodation at short notice; of making immediate reservations, amendments and cancellations on such facilities; of quoting complex fares and conditions of travel; of rapidly processing documents such as tickets, invoices, vouchers and itineraries; and of providing accounting and management information. All of these functions are now available, to a greater or lesser extent, in agency computer systems which are designed either to operate in isolation or to link with the reservations systems of travel principals.

At the time of writing a number of independently designed systems are in operation with individual agents, but the lead in agency computers is being taken by two competing systems: that of Travicom, a company formed by a travel consortium which includes British Airways and British Caledonian among its members; and that of Modulas, a system under development by Tourism Technology (a company part-owned by a consortium of travel agents).

Travicom is a multi-access reservations system which interfaces with Prestel to provide a link with airline and other principals' reservations computers. Coupled with the subsidiary functions offered by DPAS (data processing and accounts system), it provides all the functions that an agency requires, including air fare quotations and air ticket printouts.

Modulas, which has been introduced more recently, has been designed as a modular system which can be adapted to meet the needs of agents of all sizes. The objective was to introduce, for the smaller agent, a unit with a basic range of functions at reasonable cost, but with the facility for the agent to add extra units gradually to increase the capacity and range of functions as the business grew. Eventually it is planned to incorporate facilities to cope with the electronic transfer of funds, which is expected to be in use in retailing before the end of the 1980s (*see* Chapter 10).

The Modulas programme has been beset by developmental problems and reluctance on the part of agents themselves to commit themselves to a system as yet largely untried.

The full potential of British Telecom's Prestel as an information provider is only beginning to be tapped, although most travel agents in the UK have now installed it. Prestel presently gives the general public access to a limited range of travel information, including certain fares and data on availability. Travel agents, on the other hand, as members of closed user groups (CUGs), can access a much wider range of information, and, interfacing directly with principals' reservations systems using private viewdata gateway, can make, alter or cancel reservations. A key system for agents using Prestel is "Skytrack", which enables agents to interface directly with many airlines' reservations computers, to make bookings and to obtain fare quotations. While many agents are still expressing misgivings about the value of Prestel (the information it provides is only as good as the frequency with which it is updated), there can be little doubt of the potential value of the system as the scope of its operations widens. Prestel, too, will ultimately enable funds to be transferred electronically from agent or customer to principal. Just as computers offer great promise for agents, so they also pose a serious threat. Information sources do not have to be restricted to agents; it would not be unreasonable to imagine similar systems in operation in libraries and other public places where travellers may be able to make their reservations direct—or indeed, by selecting from a choice of worldwide flights and hotels, to package their own tours. Nothing in principle prevents the airlines today from establishing Travicom links with business houses, thus effectively cutting out agents altogether from this lucrative source of revenue.

THE FUTURE OF TRAVEL RETAILING

One of the most significant changes to have occurred in recent years in the UK is the entrance of non-travel organisations into the travel scene. This has affected retailing no less than other sectors of the industry. In the past ABTA's constraints on mixed business have deterred this development, but the growth prospects for the leisure market have encouraged a number of major companies such as W H Smith to open in-store travel shops, while the travel agency multiples have opened branches within department stores and other shops. Such moves are encouraged by government support for open competition in the travel industry, but such trends have been carried even further in other countries, with travel being sold in banks, petrol stations and shops and there is no reason why similar developments should not follow in this country.

Without enormous expansion in travel demand, this will mean a further squeeze on travel agents' turnover unless the travelling public continue to demand the personal service and sound product knowledge which may be lacking in the "supermarket" approach to travel sales. This will call for improved standards of training in travel in the small agencies, however.

To combat the threat from the giant multiples, small agents are already beginning to band together to form consortia. A consortium not only increases the general marketing efficiency of a small agent, but it provides the group with improved negotiating and bargaining power. This in turn enables small agents to develop their own programmes of package tours which can be sold through members' outlets at prices which are competitive with the larger tour operators.

It has been prophesied by some in the industry that the process of deregulation in the airlines could lead to the introduction of bulk net fares (a concept proposed once before in 1975 but which never became operative). This could radically alter the current trading practice of travel agents by requiring them to commit themselves in advance to purchasing seats on scheduled or charter services at a net price, to be re-sold at an appropriate mark-up to the travelling public. Again, larger organisations will benefit from their ability to negotiate lower prices and small agents will be forced to join consortia to compete.

As major tour operators increase their market shares at the expense of smaller companies, it is likely that they, too, will pressure their agents to become more productive. Since increasing productivity for one company's products can, in a stable market, only be at the expense of another company's, agents may come to specialise still further in the services they represent rather than providing an all-round travel service. This could even lead to the appointment of some agents as general sales agents for travel principals, marketing brands within a region through other agents and receiving an over-riding commission from the principal for this service.

All of these developments suggest an end to the traditional "corner-shop" travel agent we have known in the past. Whatever form agents take in the future, they will need to become more efficient, more knowledgeable in marketing and sales skills and better supported by a full range of data-banks to provide the depth of travel knowledge which an increasingly educated travelling public is likely to demand.

SELF-ASSESSMENT QUESTIONS

1. Do you think it better for an agent to represent *all* travel services or to be selective in those he handles? Argue the case from each point of view.

2. How does selling travel differ from selling other products? What are the implications of these differences for agents, their principals and their customers?

3. In what ways is the travel agent's job threatened in the near future? How might these threats be counteracted?

4. Describe briefly what are the requirements for a travel agent to set up in business.

5. Indicate those aspects of a travel agent's work which could be assisted by or replaced by computers.

ASSIGNMENT

Select six travel agents in your area, and consider their strengths and weaknesses in terms of:

(a) their location, shopfront and window display;
(b) their interior design, layout and brochure display;
(c) their customer service (friendliness and helpfulness of staff, efficiency and product knowledge).

Grade each point on a scale ranging from 1 (low) to 6 (high). Describe briefly why you think the agent with the highest number of points is so successful. Is it good management? A well-known company? High pay? What other factors could account for this?

CHAPTER NINE

Tour Operators

CHAPTER OBJECTIVES

After studying this chapter, you should be able to:
* define the role of tour operators;
* understand the reasons for tour operators' activities;
* identify the microeconomic problems of tour operators;
* distinguish between different operator types;
* understand the structure and control of the industry.

THE ROLE OF THE TOUR OPERATOR

Most businesses calling themselves tour operators undertake a distinct function in the tourism industry; they purchase separate elements of transport, accommodation and other services and combine them into a package which they then sell directly or indirectly to consumers. Their position in the market is therefore as demonstrated in Fig. 17.

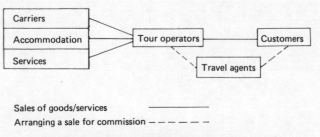

Fig. 17 *Tour operators in the tourism market*

Tour operators are sometimes classed as wholesalers, as was discussed in Chapter 4, but this is only partially accurate. A wholesaler generally purchases goods or services on his own account, *breaks bulk*, that is buys in large quantities and resells in smaller quantities as required, and sells very much the same product as he buys without altering it. Tour operators normally perform the first two jobs, but it can be argued that they do change the products sold by *packaging* them. Inclusive tours (ITs) are by their very nature new products, distinct from the elements which constitute them, in the same way that a wardrobe is distinct from a collection of wooden panels and fittings.

Rather than a wholesaler, then, the tour operator may be seen as a light assembly operation, akin to the fitter who puts together a wardrobe. As with the latter, it is quite possible for the customer to be a do-it-yourself assembler by buying accommodation, transport and so on separately. The value of the tour operator lies in his ability to secure discounts through bulk purchases and to assemble a very convenient and well-made package.

ECONOMIC ORIGINS OF TOUR OPERATORS

The transport problem

A major problem for many service industries is the balancing of supply and demand. This is especially true for services like transport where the supply is fixed, such as with a scheduled air service—which *must* operate—run by an airline with only one size of plane. Sometimes supply is not entirely fixed but is *lumpy*, that is an operator cannot respond to a small change in demand by making an equally small change in supply; he has to provide a discrete "lump" of supply. This happens, for example, with walk-on air shuttle services where airlines agree to carry every passenger who turns up at an airport for their service. If one too many passengers turns up for a flight he cannot stand in the aisle, and a second entire plane must be provided.

In these circumstances carriers seek ways to adjust demand to fill all available seats. This is important to keep down costs per passenger (and not to waste resources!). The plane or train or coach costs a certain amount of money to run, regardless of the number of passengers, and this fixed cost is likely to be the major part of any transport costs.

From the 1950s onwards tour operators have been very useful to transport carriers, especially airlines. If a carrier knows he will have vacant seats on a journey, rather than leave them empty it is worth offering them at almost any price to someone who can fill them. Let us take an example.

Example

Suppose the fixed cost of flying a 100-seat plane from London to Athens and back is £8,000 (that includes capital costs, fuel, crew's wages and so on). Suppose also the additional, or variable, cost per passenger is £10 (to cover writing a ticket, in-flight refreshments and so on). If the airline wants to budget for a small profit and knows it normally sells sixty seats, then the pricing looks like this:

Fixed cost	£8,000
60 passengers × £10	600
Cost of return flight	£8,600
Sell 60 tickets at £144 each	£8,640
Profit	£40

Of course, if only fifty-nine passengers show up then sales drop by £144, costs by only £10, and the airline loses £94. This is a very risky business!

This is where the tour operator proves useful. By agreeing to purchase in bulk, say, twenty-five seats, he can virtually ensure that the airline will fly at a profit. The question arises: What should the ticket price be?

As far as the airline is concerned, anything above £10 a head will be profitable, as the fixed costs are already paid for. The tour operator will want the lowest price possible to ensure he can resell all twenty-five seats. Obviously customers are not willing to pay anything like £144 or else they would already have bought tickets directly from the airline.

Perhaps airline and tour operator negotiate and fix a price of £60 per head. The airline's budget now looks like this:

Fixed cost	£8,000
85 passengers* × £10	850
Cost of return flight	£8,850
Sell 60 tickets at £144 each	£8,640
Sell 25 tickets to tour operator at £60 each	1,500
Revenue	£10,140
Profit	£1,290

*Assuming the tour operator will resell all his twenty-five seats.

The airline should now be very happy; even if it loses three or four passengers it will still be in profit.

The tour operator now has the onus of selling the seats, which may entail heavy selling costs, but as long as he is sensible he should be able to resell at a reasonable and profitable price.

To ensure that tour operators do not poach carriers' existing passengers, carriers have in the past imposed various conditions on the resale of tickets. The main condition has been that the operator must build the journey in as part of a package or IT. Other conditions from time to time have been:

(a) a fixed or minimum length of stay permitted at the destination;
(b) a minimum (or maximum) advance booking period;
(c) a minimum price at which the IT can be sold;
(d) stipulation of the type of customer (such as a group).

These conditions have all been used to protect carriers' existing business, but have been progressively relaxed as tour operators and carriers have become more interdependent.

From filling empty seats on a particular journey, tour operators progressed to chartering whole planes or other vehicles that were unused for a period of time. The proportion of fixed costs, and consequently the potential saving in ticket price, was rather less, but still provided carriers and operators with exploitable opportunities. Eventually many tour operators came to own their own planes, coaches or railway carriages. The economic value of this lies not in the discount buying as above but in economies of scale, controlling one's own transport and ensuring it is fully and efficiently used.

The accommodation problem

The costs and usage problems of transport are similar for accommodation. Hotels in particular have a high level of fixed cost, so that it is important for them to attract as many guests in as they can while they are open. Many hoteliers, especially in Mediterranean countries such as Spain, were very keen in the 1950s and 1960s to secure contracts with tour operators in order to fill their properties.

The same pricing determinants apply as with transport. Once the fixed costs of a property have been covered from revenue earned by selling accommodation directly to guests, any price which more than pays for the variable cost of accommodating extra guests is straight profit to the hotelier. Tour operators were thus able to secure accommodation at a greatly discounted rate to build into their ITs.

Over a period of time many hotels, holiday villages and self-catering accommodation proprietors have come to depend on tour operators for the bulk or even all of their business. Again, as with transport, some tour operators own their own accommodation in order to secure economies of scale and to ensure sufficient accommodation is available to match the transport they use.

VARIETY IN INCLUSIVE TOURS

Tour operators grew and prospered because of their ability to assemble a popular and saleable product. Although the air inclusive tour has become the most popular of these, inclusive tours using land and sea transport also cater for the needs of those tourists who like to buy a fully packaged product. Some ITs such as coach tours have of course existed for a long time, whereas those run by the hotel groups were introduced only about a decade ago, essentially to improve occupancy figures at off-peak weekends for London hotels and later to fill off-season beds out of town. British Rail, with the support of resort hotels, has introduced Golden Rail to boost their rail carryings and many small companies are now packaging tours which include ferry travel to the continent and for campsite holidays, using coach transport.

Package tours are by no means only down-market, secure and carefree products; although the mass-market tours have tended to dominate the market, there are many up-market programmes using high-quality accommodation, as well as a wide range of "adventure" packages appealing to the young or well-travelled, in which transport may consist of a Land-Rover equipped to cross desert roads in Ethiopia or the Sudan and accommodation no more than a sleeping bag and a "pup" tent. The important point to make is that packages today are available to meet the needs of a very varied market.

Packages by air may be arranged using either the services of scheduled carriers or of chartered aircraft. On scheduled airline services a tour-basing fare is available to tour operators for inclusive tour excursions (ITXs), and this is used to form the basis for package holidays which are sold individually to tourists. These ITX fares are discussed more fully in Chapter 10. The ITX tends to be a flexible product in which a few seats are available for the use of operators on a great many different flights. This flexibility, tied with superior hotel accommodation, produces a high-quality tour saleable in relatively small numbers at fairly high prices, suiting the needs of the up-market client. It is particularly suited to long-haul destinations where demand is fairly restricted.

The mass market, however, is better catered for by the tour operators' use of inclusive tours by charter (ITCs), in which the entire aircraft is put at the disposal of the operator. Suited particularly to the mass-market destinations of the Mediterranean and similar short-haul package holiday destinations, they are priced more cheaply than are ITXs and have made it possible for millions of tourists in Europe and elsewhere to have holidays abroad for the first time. Not all countries allow carriers to fly charters into their territories, although carriers and local hoteliers will put pressure on the government to allow them to do so. Arguments over charters took place for many years, for example, in Cyprus, where the government wished to protect its national airline from charter competition, and in the Channel Islands, which wished to preserve its scheduled links with the mainland.

LICENSING AND BONDING OF TOUR OPERATORS

Since 1972, an Air Travel Organiser's Licence (ATOL) must be obtained from the Civil Aviation Authority by any tour operator wishing to operate either scheduled or charter air tours abroad (although at the time of writing such licences are not required for domestic tours, nor are they required for tours operated abroad using sea or land transport).

The collapse of Fiesta Tours in 1964, leaving 5,000 tourists stranded, followed by the bankruptcy of a smaller company, Omar Khayyam Tours, in 1965, drew the attention of the industry and its consumers alike to the need for some sort of protection against the financial failure of tour operators. In 1965 ABTA set up a *Common Fund* for this purpose, assuming at the time that government regulation of tour operators in Britain was imminent. The fund was to consist of 50 per cent of members' subscriptions to be used to protect passengers affected by the collapse of a tour operator. When it became obvious that the government did not intend to act on compulsory registration for operators, ABTA introduced its *Operation Stabiliser* scheme described in Chapter 8, in which Common Fund provisions were to apply only to ABTA members' clients, and reciprocal arrangements were agreed between member tour operators and agents to deal only with fellow members.

However, many agents resented the fact that they were obliged to contribute to a fund to insure tour operators. It also soon became clear that the existing provisions were inadequate. In 1967 the Tour Operators' Study Group (TOSG) held preliminary discussions to consider the adoption of a new fund for its members. This became reality in 1970, with 5 per cent of members' revenue being paid into a trust fund.

Later ABTA itself introduced its own bonding scheme for *all* tour operating members. However, the collapse of Clarksons during the peak holiday period of 1974 revealed that the existing bonding scheme was inadequate to protect clients against major failures, and this led the government, under the terms of the Air Travel Reserve Fund Act 1975, to impose a temporary levy of 2 per cent on the operating turnover of all tour operators between 1975 and 1977.

Today ABTA administers the bonding system for tour operating members who are licensed by the CAA, and these are obliged to pay 10 per cent of their licensable turnover into the scheme (non-ABTA tour operators must pay 15 per cent direct to the CAA).

ABTA has also introduced a bonding scheme for its members' tour operations which are not under CAA control, in 1982 broadening the scope of protection to include both domestic tours and foreign package holidays using surface carriers.

MARKET DEVELOPMENT

Tour operation has by no means had a straightforward development. It has been marked by periods of expansion and resulting competition, often leading to business failures. In this it is typical of any young industry where businesses are often run by spirited entrepreneurs who do not possess many fixed assets. The cycle of development can be illustrated by Fig. 18.

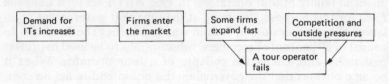

Fig. 18 *Tour operation—market development*

In Britain demand for ITs grew fast in the early 1960s and around 1970. In western Europe, North America and Japan major growth was in the early 1970s and around 1980. During these times tour operators also tended to expand very fast, but some failed, usually for one or more of these reasons:

(*a*) they may have grown too fast, borrowed too much money and have had insufficient management expertise;

(*b*) they may have made almost no profit per tourist in an effort to compete, through low prices, in a vicious market;

(*c*) they may have been hit by external problems such as oil price rises, political problems or economic recession reducing demand.

Some of these failures have been landmarks in the development of tour operation. The collapse of Fiesta Tours in Britain in 1964, as shown earlier, led to the tight controls imposed on members by ABTA. The failure of Court Line and its subsidiary Clarksons Holidays in 1974 stranded 50,000 holidaymakers. This collapse was caused by all three of the reasons above and led to the government introducing the Air Travel Reserve Fund mentioned earlier. At the time Clarksons was the largest British tour operator; in similar fashion Canada's largest tour operators, Sunflight and Skylark, collapsed in 1982. Yet it is equally possible for competitor companies to prosper at the same time if they have good management, a sound financial structure and do not try to develop too fast.

OPERATING ECONOMICS

Inputs

Assuming an operator is a business separate from a carrier or hotelier, then he has three main inputs he must purchase: transport, accommodation and services. Services can be divided into those at destinations, such as transfers from terminals to accommodation, and representatives, and those which are mainly concerned with the selling operation, such as the cost of advertising, brochures, post, credit and travel agents' commission. The tour operator also has his own office costs, including rent and rates, wages of staff, computer or other reservation systems and so on.

A typical ITC from Britain to a Mediterranean destination might have the cost structure outlined in Table V.

TABLE V. COST STRUCTURE OF TYPICAL ITC

Costs	% of overall cost
Charter air fare	40
Hotel accommodation	35
Other services	3
Office costs and profit	12
Travel agent's commission	10
	100

By selling directly to the public without using a travel agent, as Tjaereborg and Portland do, the commission may be saved but reservations, brochure mailing and advertising are likely to be more expensive. Office costs and advertising and selling costs are only a small proportion of the total, perhaps some 10–15 per cent, but the costs of printing and distributing brochures is a major expenditure for any operator, particularly if he seeks to distribute his product through all branches of ABTA travel agencies.

The specifics of negotiation with principals, in which operators attempt to keep their costs as low as possible, will be dealt with in Chapter 10.

Outputs

Major air tour operators normally divide their ITs into three main groups: a summer IT programme; a winter IT programme; and a programme involving transport only, with nominal accommodation (often called minimum-rated packages as they are sold at the lowest possible prices). Some operators sell only one of these groups of products, for example winter sports holidays, while others may also sell coach-based, ferry-based, rail-based or fly-drive ITs. In addition, they will sell, directly or indirectly, products such as holiday insurance, to increase total revenue.

One well-known major British tour operator had the structure of sales revenue in 1981 as shown in Table VI. Whilst this operator may not be typical, it does show the heavy dependence on the summer programme and the importance of extra revenue from such items as deposit interest. This latter point is detailed in Chapter 10.

TABLE VI. STRUCTURE OF SALES REVENUE OF A TYPICAL TOUR OPERATOR, 1981

Revenue	% of total revenue
Summer IT programme	60
Winter IT programme	12
Minimum-rated packages	5
Holiday insurance	3
Excursions in destinations	8
Interest on deposits and currency speculation	12
	100

Minimum-rated packages are usually sold to fill otherwise empty seats and maintain high loadings on the transport used. They are therefore usually sold at very little more than cost and do not contribute greatly to profit (but it should be borne in mind that carriers can benefit greatly from the sale of duty-free goods, etc., to these "marginal" passengers). For many operators the winter programme (if one exists) performs a similar function. A company needs to maintain its cash flow and, especially if it has its own aircraft, coaches or hotels, use them as much as possible. Essentially the winter programme is a "ticking over" operation.

The summer programme is likely to provide the main source of revenue, as is made clear in Table VI. One of the features of tour operations in Britain is their competitiveness, which means that prices play an important part in assuring custom for the summer season. The output must be priced so that customers buy in sufficient quantity, but not so cheaply that (as in the case of Clarksons) no profit is made on each customer. In countries where this kind of competition does not exist this problem of "price balancing" does not arise.

TYPES OF OPERATOR

Mass market operators

In Britain the best known tour operators are those which sell large numbers of inclusive tours by air and/or coach. A league table of the largest air tour operators is shown in Table VII.

TABLE VII. BRITAIN'S LARGEST TOUR OPERATORS: PASSENGER CARRYINGS AUTHORISED BY THE CAA, 1983

company	passengers
Thomson Holidays	965,791
British Airtours[a]	721,000
Intasun[b]	508,650
Horizon Holidays	481,000
Wings/OSL[c]	316,000
Cosmos Holidays	300,000
Saga/Laker Holidays[d]	252,630
Blue Sky Holidays[e]	232,500
Global[f]	175,000
Thomas Cook Holidays	159,609

NOTES:

(a) Division of British Airways, includes Sovereign, Enterprise, Flair, Martin Rooks

(b) Includes Cambrian Holidays

(c) Owned by Rank Leisure

(d) Laker Holidays was purchased by Saga after the collapse of the Laker companies in 1982

(e) Owned by British Caledonian Airways

(f) Owned by Great Universal Stores (GUS)

The pattern is for greater concentration of sales among the half dozen market leaders, at the expense of "second force" and small operators.

The twenty or so largest tour operators are members of the Tour Operators' Study Group (TOSG), and are responsible altogether for roughly 80 per cent of all tour operating revenue in the UK. TOSG is a voluntary association, with membership by invitation only, which acts as a forum for discussions on issues of common interest among its members. It has been influential in negotiating with foreign governments and hotel associations and, in addition to being responsible for the introduction of the TOSG trust fund, was also instrumental in ending the "Provision 1" clause under which the British government denied tour operators the right to sell their package tours at prices less than the lowest normal scheduled air fares (*see* Chapter 10).

The largest operators concentrate their activities on mass-market sun, sea and sand destinations such as Spain, the Canary and Balearic Islands and Greece. They frequently subdivide their operations to serve different markets and a feature of their structure is that many are linked with their own airlines, as shown in Fig. 19. The integration of mass tour operation with other tourism activities is even more advanced in some other countries such as West Germany.

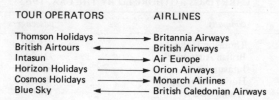

TOUR OPERATORS   AIRLINES

Thomson Holidays ——————▶ Britannia Airways
British Airtours ◀—————— British Airways
Intasun ——————▶ Air Europe
Horizon Holidays ——————▶ Orion Airways
Cosmos Holidays ——————▶ Monarch Airlines
Blue Sky ◀—————— British Caledonian Airways

Fig. 19 *Major links between tour operators and airlines in the UK*

Specialist operators

Less well-known than the mass-market operators, but far more numerous, are the specialist operators, who may range from local travel agents organising an *ad hoc* tour for twenty or thirty local passengers up to businesses offering long-distance inclusive tours to exclusive destinations. It is hard to generalise about such businesses and equally hard to draw a clear distinction between them and the mass-market operators. For example, businesses such as Olympic Holidays, specialising in ITs to Greece, or Intourist, dealing with all forms of travel to the Soviet Union, are large enough to be considered mass-market operators but are specialising in particular geographical regions. Intourist, in fact, is concerned with far more than simply tour operating; it is a complete state-owned tourism industry in its own right.

Specialists may be subsidiaries of carriers or accommodation organisations, existing to provide a sales outlet for the organisation's products.

It is convenient to group specialist operators into five categories.

(*a*) Those offering ITs to particular destinations. They are often owned by, or have very strong links with, firms or state governments in the destinations.

(*b*) Those offering ITs from specific generating areas. They may be owned by local travel agents or carriers and are to be found in any large town.

(c) Those using specific accommodation for their ITs, such as camping holidays or holiday villages.

(d) Those using specific transport for their ITs. They are usually owned by the carriers concerned.

(e) Those offering special interest ITs, such as big game safaris, self-sail cruising, or business training packages.

Some specialists fall into more than one category.

Over the past 20 or 30 years specialist tour operators have proliferated. Usually they have identified a particular need and sought to cater for it, taking advantage of fashion trends in tourism. While many have only a short business life before collapsing, others have developed over time into mass-market operators.

Domestic operators

Domestic operators are those who assemble and sell ITs to a destination within the country in which the tourists reside. In general domestic tour operations have developed after international operations, since the savings consumers can make are not so great; operators also have to overcome the traditional pattern of direct booking of accommodation which is common in Britain.

The oldest domestic ITs in the UK are probably coach tours operated by such companies as Wallace Arnold or the antecedents of the National Bus Company. Other types of operation have developed more recently in response to the success of the international operators. Customers are getting used to purchasing a package for their foreign trip and the hope is that this will trigger similar purchasing patterns for domestic holidays. Among the leaders in this movement are Golden Rail, coach-based businesses such as National, and operators run by hotel groups. The tourist boards offer strong support for the development of these packages, and were instrumental in launching the "Holiday UK" programme in which a large number of tour operators have come together as a consortium to sell domestic package holidays through travel agents in Britain.

Fragmentation in domestic tour operation is reflected in its organisation. In some areas associations have been formed to represent the trade; for example, two dozen or so major operators to the Channel Islands are members of CITOG, the Channel Islands Tour Operators' Group. On the other hand a large number of businesses are not members of any organisation, not even ABTA. Many sell directly to the public and do not need to be involved in the travel agency distribution chain.

Incoming tour operators

Most established tourist-generating countries possess some kind of tour operating industry for outward travel, but for destination countries it may be more important to have incoming operators. These are based in the destination, selling ITs only to that destination, but they may be selling in many different countries.

Many use the airlines or other carriers of the country concerned. Windsor Tours, a division of British Airways specialising in incoming tours to Britain, uses that carrier's services and will put together different types of package according to market demand.

The typical demand for tours to Britain is the "national heritage" type of programme, or packages arranged for those wishing to study the English language, for which a number of travel/family or hotel accommodation/language school study packages exist. In many countries incoming operators also receive help from the national tourist office of the country concerned, as they may be playing an important role in the development of new tourist facilities in the country.

As with domestic operators, there are several categories of incoming operator. Some are best described as "handling agents" since their function is to organise tour arrangements for incoming groups on behalf of overseas operators. Some companies go no further than to specialise in meeting incoming passengers and transferring them to their hotels or providing other escort services. Others will offer a comprehensive range of services which include negotiation with coach companies and hotels to secure the best quotations for contracts, organising special interest study tours and providing dining or theatre arrangements. Some companies specialise, for example, by catering for the needs of specific incoming groups such as Japanese or Arab tourists.

In all there are estimated to be over 300 tour companies in Britain which derive a major part of their revenue from handling incoming business. About a quarter of these are members of the British In-Coming Tour Operators' Association (BITOA), whose aim is to provide a forum for the exchange of information and ideas among members, to maintain standards of service and to act as a pressure group in dealing with other bodies in the UK who have some responsibility in the field of tourism.

Incoming tour operators' services are marketed exclusively to the trade. Organisations work closely with the British Tourist Authority (through the medium of the BTA Travel Workshops abroad, bringing together the buyers and sellers of tourism and travel services in Britain) and other national and regional tourist boards at home.

SELF-ASSESSMENT QUESTIONS

1. Why is it not totally accurate to describe a tour operator as a "wholesaler"?

2. Explain why tour operators and air carriers are interdependent.

3. What distinguishes ITCs from ITXs?

4. What are "minimum-rated packages" and why do tour operators sell them?

5. True or false? (*a*) Government licences are required by tour operators who organise coach/camping holidays abroad. (*b*) Some governments restrict charter tours from operating into their countries. (*c*) The TOSG trust fund is the sole source of finance to rescue passengers stranded as a result of a TOSG member's failure.

ASSIGNMENT

Taking Table VII, find out who are the top eight operators in the current year. Offer some suggestions to explain the present order and the changes that have occurred between the 1983 table and yours.

Inclusive Tour Operations

THE NATURE OF TOUR OPERATING

An inclusive tour programme consists of a series of integrated travel services, each of which is purchased by the tour operator in bulk and resold as part of a package at an inclusive price. These integrated services usually consist of an aircraft seat, accommodation at the destination and transfers between hotel and airport. They may also include certain other services such as excursions or car hire. This product is commonly referred to as a "package tour". Most package tours are single destination static holidays, but tours comprising two or more destinations are not uncommon, and mobile tours such as coach tours through one or more countries, which until the 1950s were the principal form of packaged holiday, still retain a loyal following.

As we have seen, the success of package tours rests on the fact that the operator, by buying his principals' services in bulk rather than individually, is generally able to negotiate lower prices. Tour operating is a highly competitive business, with success dependent upon the operator maintaining the lowest possible prices while continuing to give "value for money". The price factor becomes increasingly important as the package holiday becomes a *standardised* product, differing little between destinations. Most holidaymakers today seek a combination of "sun, sand and sea"; the particular destination or country no longer plays an important part in the customer's choice, and he will readily substitute an alternative destination for his first choice if the latter becomes in his view overpriced.

The tour operators attempt to keep their prices low both by restraining their profit margins and seeking cost savings. These cost savings originally came about through the chartering of entire aircraft instead of merely purchasing a block of seats on a scheduled flight. Further reductions became possible with *time series* charters, by which aircraft were leased over longer periods of time rather than for *ad hoc* journeys. Today the emphasis is on productivity achieved through high load factors—the number of seats on each aircraft actually sold as a percentage of total capacity—and maximum utilisation of the aircraft during its period of charter.

Maximum utilisation means keeping the aircraft in the air with its complement of passengers as much as possible during each 24-hour period. While an aircraft is on the tarmac it is failing to earn revenue—in fact it is accumulating airport charges. The aim is therefore to have one's aircraft on the ground as little as possible. This means fast "turnrounds" (often less than an hour) at airports, involving rapid aircraft cleaning and loading, disembarkation/embarkation and refuelling. Such a policy results in the common "W" flight pattern of aircraft involved in tour operations (*see* Fig. 20).

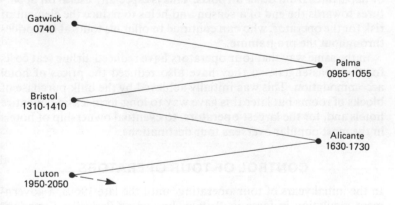

Fig. 20 *A typical "W" flight pattern*

High load factors are achieved by setting the *break-even* (number of seats to be sold on each flight to cover all operating, administrative and marketing costs) at a point close to capacity. This brings down the average seat cost to a level which will stimulate market demand. On charter flights today break-even is frequently as high as 90 per cent. Profits are made on the balance of seats sold (and of course on the duty free sales); since the variable costs of carrying additional passengers are small, tour operators will attempt to fill the entire aircraft by selling what amount to *flight only* packages, or offering substantial reductions for last-minute bookings.

Licensing of package tour charters requires accommodation to be sold with the aircraft seat, but these regulations can be satisfied by providing accommodation of a very basic nature, with the implicit understanding that it is not likely to be used by the client. Alternatively, *lease-back* arrangements can be made between the tour operator and his passenger whereby the latter provides the operator with accommodation and agrees to lease it back for his own use. This form of booking suits the needs of those wanting low cost air flights to visit relatives abroad or those with second homes overseas. The impossibility of policing the regulations as they stand has caused the CAA to re-examine tour operators' calls for permission to sell some of their seats on a *seat-only* basis, and this came into force in 1982 (although constraints will continue to apply for flights out of London airports).

Productivity in airline operations can be aided by the procedure of *consolidating* flights. Charter flights with unacceptable load factors can be cancelled, with passengers being transferred to other flights or departures from other airports. This is especially useful on departures towards the end of a season and helps to reduce the element of risk for the operator, who can continue to offer his tours at low prices throughout the programme.

In the same way that tour operators have reduced airline seat costs for their passengers, so they have also reduced the prices of hotel accommodation. This was initially achieved by the bulk purchase of blocks of rooms but later this gave way to long-term leasing of entire hotels and, for the largest operators, to eventual ownership of hotels in the most popular overseas tour destinations.

CONTROL OF TOUR OPERATORS

In the initial years of tour operating, until the late 1960s, a government regulation in force in Britain, known as *Provision 1*, made it impossible to price package tours at less than the lowest regular return fares to the destination. The sole exceptions to this rule were in the case of affinity groups. These involved charters arranged for associations whose existence was for a purpose other than that of securing cheap travel; members were required to have belonged to such associations for at least six months before they became eligible for low cost flights.

This rule was designed to protect the scheduled carriers and ensure adequate profit levels for tour operators. However, it severely hindered the expansion of the package tour business and, furthermore, could be to some extent circumvented by tour operators who used European "gateways" for tours to more distant destinations (fares to east Africa, for example, were considerably undercut using the Frankfurt gateway, combining package tours from Frankfurt to Kenya with ordinary round-trip flights between London and Frankfurt). There was also widespread abuse of common interest group charters through club secretaries back-dating membership and the formation of spurious associations created primarily for travel benefits.

When the new CAA was established in 1971, restrictions on package tour operations were lifted, initially only in the winter months (leading to a huge increase in off-season travel) but by 1973 for travel at all seasons. The CAA also introduced advance booking charters (ABCs) as a means of widening the availability of charter travel for those then unqualified as affinity group members. ABCs provided similar low prices with the only proviso that seats had to be booked some months in advance of flight dates.

In tandem with the liberalisation of charter flights, control over the tour operators themselves was tightened. For the first time those operating air tours to foreign destinations using chartered aircraft were obliged to hold an Air Travel Organiser's Licence (ATOL) and were closely vetted for financial viability.

SEASONALITY IN TOUR OPERATIONS

A problem facing all sectors of tourism is the highly seasonal nature of tour traffic. Nowhere is this more apparent than in the demand for package holidays in Europe. This market, however, is also highly price-sensitive and the lifting of Provision 1 regulations demonstrated the potential for off-season package tour growth. This coincided with the development of longer paid holidays in the advanced western European nations, with four weeks becoming the norm in the 1970s. The tendency to take a second holiday during the off-season provided a great boost for tour operating, leading to better year-round aircraft and hotel utilisation. Costs could be distributed more evenly throughout the year, reducing average prices.

The policy of marginal costing in the off-season, designed to cover variable costs and make a contribution to fixed costs, led to extremely low prices during the early part of the 1970s, aimed at two distinct markets. Rock-bottom prices for mini-packages of three or four days' duration attracted a new "experimental" market to the idea of continental holidays, and pensioners were attracted to long-stay holidays of three or four months' duration during the winter months, where hotel prices were so low that packages could be afforded even by those on pensions. This kept the hotels full and provided year-round employment for hotel staff.

OTHER REVENUE-PRODUCING ACTIVITIES

Although direct profits on tour operating may appear to be slim owing to the pressures of competition, in fact operators have at their disposal a number of alternative means of increasing their revenue and profits. By far the most important of these is the result of the time lapse occurring between customers paying for their holiday and the tour operators' obligations to settle their accounts with their principals.

The booking season for summer holidays is under way in the autumn of the preceding year, reaching its peak in the three months following Christmas, so a large proportion of deposits will have been paid by the end of March. Although the tour operators will them-selves have had to make deposits for aircraft charters at the beginning of the season, and will often have made some advance to hoteliers as a sign of good faith, the balance will not fall due until after the client has completed his holiday. Operators will have the use of deposit payments for up to a year in advance and for the balance of holiday payments for two or three months. This money can be invested to earn interest for the operator and profits achieved on these invest-ments are likely to exceed or equal those on the package tour opera-tions themselves. One effect of the growing tendency among British holidaymakers to book their holidays later in recent years is the consequent reduction in the tour operators' cash flow; if this tendency persists or grows, operators may be obliged to increase package tour prices to compensate for this loss of revenue.

Further profits are achieved through the sale of ancillary services. Of these, the most important are the duty free goods sold on board flights, the package insurance policies accompanying tour sales and the sale of optional excursions or car hire at the destination.

A further contribution to operating revenue is achieved by the imposition of cancellation charges. These charges substantially ex-ceed any costs borne by the operators resulting from cancellations (on most ITX packages, for example, hotels will impose no cancel-lation charges on tour operators for cancelled accommodation), even assuming the operator is unable to resell the cancelled tour booking. On average, some 5 per cent of tour bookings are cancelled and these prove highly profitable for the operators.

There is also scope for profit-making through the judicious "buying forward" of foreign currency at times where exchange rates are favourable. The Spanish peseta and Greek drachma are invariably stronger during the summer at times of tourist demand, so operators are bound to benefit by buying these currencies during the preceding winter. One must caution that forward buying, if ill-judged, can equally lead to substantial losses for operators, but today such risks can be avoided by arrangements with merchant banks by which foreign exchange can be bought forward without the necessity of making actual payment until the foreign currency is required.

Finally, further profits result from selling a proportion of one's package tours direct to the public, avoiding the payment of commission to travel agencies. Typically, 85-90 per cent of an operator's package holidays are sold through agents, so there is scope for considerably increased profits by selling direct. However, as we shall see presently, there is a danger of openly soliciting direct sell business.

NON-CHARTER TOUR OPERATING

The growth of inclusive holidays by air charter caught the scheduled airlines by surprise, but they retaliated by introducing their own inclusive tour excursion (ITX) fares. These net tour-basing fares are available to tour operators to put together their own packages using seats on scheduled flights. These seats may be programmed on the basis of independent inclusive tours (IITs)—known as foreign inclusive tours in the USA—or bulk inclusive tours (BITs) for group travel. As break-even points on scheduled flights are much lower than on charter flights (some 50-60 per cent of capacity) there is scope for considerable profits on the balance of seats sold, even at low prices.

IATA has laid down the regulations which must be adhered to by operators who wish to take advantage of these fares. These include the requirement to print at least 2,000 brochures covering the tour (or 200 for tours to a special event within Europe), which in addition to text must include at least one illustration (picture or map) and feature at least one hotel at the destination. The package must include flight, accommodation and one other service (usually this includes transfers between airport and hotel). The tour programme can be organised using one or more IATA carrier, but approval is usually processed through a particular featured carrier who will validate the programme for the use of tour-basing fares by providing an inclusive tour code number which must be quoted on each ticket issued. The tour operator is not required to hold an ATOL for operating package tours by scheduled flights.

To cater for their clients' individual package holiday needs, many travel companies produce an *umbrella brochure* which is designed to meet the above requirements for a number of destinations and will enable the company to use ITX fares in conjunction with tailor-made packages arranged for individual client needs. In practice, however, these umbrella brochures are falling into disuse, with travel agents increasingly finding that the purchase of "bucketed" tickets will undercut any tour-basing fares they can obtain through this process.

"PIGGY-BACK" OPERATING

One further option is available to agents who wish to move into tour operating without wholeheartedly committing themselves to the risks involved in running their own programmes. It is possible to negotiate with other tour operators to sell "blocks" or allocations of their programme at rates of commission higher than the standard 10 per cent payable for retail sales. Agents can go still further by selling these tours under their own trade name and producing their own brochure, i.e. *piggy-backing*. This may involve sharing some of the risks with the other tour operator who has organised the programme.

When agents negotiate such agreements it is important that they fully understand the extent of their commitment, including cancellation dates for unsold tours and any cancellation charges that may be imposed. In the same way, tour operators who wish to mount a programme to a new destination using charter air services, but who do not feel confident of being able to fill all their charter seats, may part-charter aircraft with other operators to the same destination.

TOUR PLANNING, MARKETING AND OPERATING

Plans for the introduction of a new tour programme or destination have to be drawn up a long way ahead—as much as two years before the first departure takes place. A typical time-scale for a summer programme of tours is shown in Fig. 21.

Clearly, in planning the time deadlines for the programme one must first establish the launch date and work backwards. The critical problem is the determination of final prices, which have to be established some nine months ahead of the first departures.

MARKET RESEARCH AND TOUR PLANNING

In practice the decision to exploit a destination or region for package tours is as much an act of faith as the outcome of carefully considered research. Forecasting future developments in tourism, which, as a product, is affected by changing circumstances to a greater extent

YEAR 1	Summer	RESEARCH/PLANNING	First stages of research. Look at economic factors influencing the future development of package tours. Identify likely selection of destinations.
	September/ December		Second stages of research. In-depth comparison of alternative destinations.
YEAR 2	January/ February		Decide on capacity for each tour, duration and departure dates. Initial negotiation with printer, including dates for printing brochure.
	February/ March	NEGOTIATION	Negotiate with the airlines for charter flights.
	March/April		Negotiate with hotels, transfer services, optional excursion operators. Early artwork and text under development at design studio, with layout suggestions.
	April/May		Establish hotel prices and arrange for contract with hotels and airlines. Contract with transfer services, etc.
	July	ADMINISTRATION	Determine exchange rates. Estimate selling prices based on inflation, etc. Galley proofs from printer. Any necessary reservations staff recruited and trained.
	August		Final tour prices to printer. Brochures printed and reservations system established.
	September/ October	MARKETING	Brochure on market, distribution to agents. Initial agency sales promotion, including launch. First public media advertising, and trade publicity through press, etc.
YEAR 3	January/ March		Peak advertising and promotion to trade and public.
	February/ April		Recruitment and training of resort representatives, etc.
	May		First tour departures.

Fig. 21 *Typical time scale for a tour operating programme*

than most other consumer products, has proved to be notably inaccurate. As we have seen, tourist patterns change over time, with a shift from one country to another and from one form of accommodation to another. With the emphasis on price, the mass tour operator's principal concern is to provide the basic sun, sea and sand package in countries providing the best value for money. Transport costs will depend upon charter rights into the country, distance flown and ground handling costs. Accommodation and other costs to be met overseas will be the outcome of exchange rates with sterling and *vis-à-vis* the other currencies of competitive countries, inflation and the competitive environment in which hoteliers find themselves. Tour operators may have to take other factors into account too, such as the extent of support from airlines serving the routes or support from the national tourist office of the destination, the political stability of the country; attitudes to, and government control over, mass tourism within the country; and the relationship between the host and generating countries (see Chapter 1 for a fuller discussion of these issues).

Once the tour operator has narrowed the choice to two or three potential destinations, he must produce a realistic appraisal of the potential of these destinations, based on the numbers of tourists which the areas presently attract, growth rates over recent years, present shares held by competing companies and an estimate of the share of the market which his company could expect to gain in the first and subsequent years of operation.

At this point it is important to recognise a fundamental difference between mass-market and specialist tour operating. A small-scale or specialist tour operator can set up a tour programme at short notice and can withdraw from his present commitments equally quickly. Being so flexible, he is less concerned with long-term market trends and responds more quickly to market changes. A mass-market operator, on the other hand, will have a heavy long-term commitment to a destination which may involve him in the purchase of hotels at the resort. With this kind of equity tied up in the resort he must ensure its long-term viability.

Availability of suitable aircraft for the routes must be ascertained. This will in part dictate capacities for the tour operating programme, since aircraft have different configurations and on some routes where aircraft are operating at the limits of their range some passenger seats may have to be sacrificed in order to take on board sufficient fuel to cover the distance. In other cases provincial airport runways may be inadequate for larger aircraft and again fewer passengers than the normal full load may be carried in order that the plane can get airborne.

Planning of course is also dependent upon the availability of adequate finance for marketing and operating the new programme.

NEGOTIATIONS WITH PRINCIPALS

The airline

Once the decision has been made as to destination and numbers of passengers to be carried during the season and the dates of departure have been established, the serious negotiations will get under way with airlines, hotels and other principals, leading to formal contracts. These contracts will spell out the conditions for the release of unsold accommodation or (in the case of ITX arrangements) aircraft seats, or the cancellation of chartered aircraft flights, with any penalties that the tour operator will incur.

Normal terms for aircraft chartering are for a deposit to be paid upon signing the contract (generally 10 per cent of the total cost), with the balance becoming due after each flight. In negotiating with charter services the reputation of the tour operator is of paramount importance. If he has worked with that airline, or with similar charters, in previous years, this will be taken into account in determining the terms and price for the contract.

A well-established tour operator does not wish to be at the mercy of market forces in dealing with charter airlines. In any given year the demand for suitable aircraft may exceed the supply, leading the larger tour operators to form or buy their own airline to ensure capacity is available to them.

Part and parcel of these negotiations is the setting up of the tour operating flight plan, with decisions made on the dates and frequency of operations, the airports to be used and times of arrival and departure. All of this information will have to be consolidated into a form suitable for publication and easy comprehension in the tour brochure.

The hotels

Hotel negotiations, other than in the case of large tour operators who negotiate *time* contracts for an entire hotel, are generally far more informal than is the case in airline negotiating. Small and specialist tour operators selling IIT packages may have no more than a *free-sale* (or *sell-and-report*) agreement with hoteliers, by which the hotel agrees to guarantee accommodation for a specified maximum number of tourists (usually four) merely on receipt of the notification of booking from the tour operator, whether by phone, mail or (most customarily) by telex. This arrangement may be quite suitable for small tour programmes, but it suffers from the disadvantage that at times hoteliers will retain the right to *close out* certain dates. As these are likely to be the most popular dates on the calendar, the operator stands to lose both potential business and goodwill. The alternative is for the operator to contract for an allocation of rooms in the hotel, with dates agreed for the release of unsold rooms.

Long-term contracts, either for a block of rooms or for the entire hotel, have the attraction of providing the operator with the lowest possible prices but they carry a higher element of risk. Some contracts will extend for up to five years and while at first glance such long fixed-price contracts can seem attractive, they are seldom realistic and in an inflationary period may well have to be renegotiated to avoid bankrupting the hotelier. This event would obviously not be in the tour operator's interest either.

In addition to the operator's spelling out his exact requirements in terms of rooms—required numbers of singles, doubles, twins; with or without private facilities; whether with balconies or seaview; and with what catering provision, e.g. room only, with breakfast, half board or full board—he must also clarify a number of other issues. These include:

(*a*) reservations and registration procedures (including issue of any vouchers);

(*b*) accommodation requirements for any representatives or couriers (usually provided free);

(*c*) handling procedures and fees charged for porterage;

(*d*) special facilities available or needed, such as catering for handicapped customers, or special catering requirements (kosher, vegetarian, etc.);

(*e*) languages spoken by hotel staff;

(*f*) systems of payment by guests for drinks or other extras;

(*g*) reassurance on suitable fire and safety precautions;

(*h*) if appropriate, suitable space for a representative's desk and noticeboard.

It is also as well to check the availability of alternative hotel accommodation of a comparable standard in the event of overbooking. Of course a hotel with a reputation for overbooking is to be avoided, but over the course of time some errors are bound to occur requiring guests to be transferred to other hotels. The tour operator must satisfy himself that the arrangements made by the hotelier for taking care of clients in these circumstances are adequate.

Ancillary services

Similar negotiations will take place with locally-based incoming operators and coach companies to provide the coach transfers between airport and hotels and any optional excursions. Car hire companies may also be approached to negotiate commission rates on sales to the tour operator's clients.

The reliability and honesty of the local operator is an important issue here. Smaller tour operators in the UK will not be in a position to employ their own resort representatives initially, and hence their image will depend upon the levels of service provided by the local operator's staff.

If the local company is also operating optional sightseeing excursions, procedures for booking these and handling the finances involved must be established and it should be clarified whether qualified guides with a sound knowledge of the English language are to be employed on the excursions. If not, the tour operator must reassure himself that all driver–couriers will be sufficiently fluent in the English language to do their job effectively for the company.

THE OVERSEAS REPRESENTATIVE

Tour operators carrying large numbers of package tourists to a destination are in a position to employ their own resort representatives. This has obvious advantages in that the company can count on the loyalty and total commitment of their own staff. A decision must be made as to whether to employ a national of the host country or of the generating country. The advantage of a local man or woman as the representative abroad is that these are likely to be better acquainted with local customs and geography, fluent in the language of the country and with good local contacts which will enable them to take care of problems (such as dealing with the police, shopkeepers or hoteliers) more effectively. On the other hand they are likely to be less familiar with the culture, customs or language of their clients, and this can act as a restraining influence on package tourists, especially on first visits abroad. Exceptional local representatives have been able to overcome this problem and if they themselves have some common background with their clients (for example, if they have lived for some years in the incoming tourists' country) they can function as effectively as their British counterparts. However, some countries impose restrictions on the employment of foreign nationals at resorts, so these legal points must be clarified before employing representatives.

The representative's role at the resort is far more demanding than is commonly thought. During the season, he or she can be expected to work a 7-day week and will need to be available on call for 24 hours a day to cope with any emergencies. Resort representatives are usually given a desk in the hotel lobby from which to work, but in cases where tour operators have their clients in two or more hotels in the resort the representative may have to visit each hotel during some part of the day. His principal functions include:

(a) handling general enquiries;
(b) advising on currency exchange, shopping, etc.;
(c) organising and supervising social activities at the hotels;
(d) publicising and booking optional excursions;
(e) handling special requirements and complaints and acting as an intermediary for clients, interceding with the hotel proprietor, police or other local authorities.

These routine functions will be supplemented by problems arising from lost baggage, ill-health (referring clients to local English-speaking doctors or dentists) and even occasional deaths, although serious problems such as this are often referred to area managers where these are employed. They will have to supervise the relocation of customers whose accommodation is inadequate or where overbookings occur, and they may also have to rebook flights for their customers whose plans change as a result of emergencies.

The representatives' busiest days occur when groups are arriving or leaving the resort. They will accompany groups returning home on the coach to the airport, ensuring that departure formalities at the hotel have been complied with, arrange to pay any airport or departure taxes due, and then wait to greet incoming clients and accompany them to their hotels on the transfer coaches. They must ensure that check-in procedures operate smoothly, going over rooming lists with the hotel manager before he bills the tour operator. Many tour operators provide a welcome party for their clients on the first night of their holiday and it is the representatives' task to organise and host this.

Reps can also expect to spend some time at their resort bases before the start of the season, not only to get to know the site but to report back to their companies on the standards of tourist facilities and to pinpoint any discrepancies between brochure descriptions and reality.

The importance of the representatives' job has been increasingly realised by the larger tour operators, leading to full-time employment and a career structure for this sector of the tour operating business. Larger companies may initially employ staff as children's representatives, responsible for looking after and entertaining children on family holidays. Promotion is to representative, later to head representative (or area manager) based abroad, and ultimately to the job of supervisor of representatives, based at the company's head office, whose task is to recruit and train staff, organise holiday rotas, provide uniforms and handle the administration of the representatives' department.

TOUR PRICING

A key factor in the success of a tour operator's programme is the price at which the package tour is to be marketed. A specialist tour operator whose product is unique may have more flexibility here and may determine his prices largely on the basis of the cost of the services he is purchasing, plus a mark-up sufficient to cover his overheads and allow a satisfactory level of profit. A mass tour operator, however, must take greater account of his competitors' pricing since the demand for package tours is, as we have seen, extremely price-elastic, especially for off-season or shoulder period departures. The tendency is to follow the market leader's pricing, economies of scale playing a key role in enabling the larger operators to reduce their costs and hence undercut their rivals in tour pricing.

Below are provided two typical examples of cost-orientated tour pricing.

Cost-orientated tour operation pricing (time-series charter)

This first example is based on a series of short-haul charters to a destination such as Spain.

Flight costs, based on 30 departures (back to back) on Boeing 737 130-seat @ £7,020 per flight	£210,600
Plus one "empty leg" each way at beginning and end of the season	7,020
Total flight costs	217,620
Cost per flight	7,254
Cost per seat at 90% occupancy (i.e. £7,254 ÷ 117)	£62.00
Net hotel cost per person, 7 nights half board	42.00
Resort agent's handling fees and transfers per person	6.60
Gratuities, porterage, etc.	0.40
Total costs per person	111.00
Add mark-up of approx. 20% on cost price to cover agency commission, marketing costs (including brochure, ticket wallet, etc.), head office administrative costs and profits	23.00
Selling price	£134.00

In estimating the seat cost for aircraft the operator must not only calculate the load factor on which this cost is to be based but must also aim to achieve this load factor on average throughout the series of tours he will be operating. This must depend upon his estimates of the market demand for each destination and the current supply of aircraft seats available to his competitors. Since high-season demand will considerably exceed the supply of seats to these destinations, there is scope to increase the above price, and hence profits, for the high-season months of the year, even if this results in the company being uncompetitive with other leading operators. On the other hand, supply may greatly exceed demand at off-peak periods and the tour operator may set his prices so low as to aim only to cover his variable costs and make a small contribution towards fixed costs (administrative, marketing, etc.) rather than achieve profits at this time of the year.

He must carefully consider what proportion of overheads are to be allocated to each holiday and destination. As long as these expenses are recovered in full during the term of operation of the programme, the allocation of these costs can be made on the basis of market forces and need not be proportioned equally (as in this example) to each destination.

Here we begin to move away from traditional cost-orientation to a more active marketing-orientated policy. The arbitrary allocation of 20 per cent of cost price in the example should be tempered in practice by consideration of market prices and the company's long-term objectives. In entering a new market, for instance, it may be that the principal objective is to penetrate and obtain a targeted share of that market in the first year of operating, and this may be achieved by reducing or even foregoing profits during the first year. Indeed, to some destinations the tour operator may introduce *loss leader* pricing policies, subsidising the cost of this policy from other, profitable routes in order to get a footing in the market to the new destination.

Cost-orientated tour operation pricing (specialist ITX scheduled programme)

The second example is of a specialist long-haul tour-operating programme using the services of scheduled carriers to Hong Kong.

Flight cost, based on net group air fare per person, London–Hong Kong, using scheduled flights	£340.00
Twin-bed room in medium-grade hotel HK$300 per night Price per person, 7 nights, using currency exchange rate of HK$10 = £1	105.00
Transfers @ £2.50 per person each way	5.00
	450.00
Add mark-up to cover agent's commission	50.00
	£500.00

Selling prices:

"Lead price" (offered on 2–3 flights off-season)	£510.00
Shoulder season price	£550.00
High season price (high summer, Christmas or Easter holidays)	£620.00

In developing a pricing strategy for package tours, the tour operator must take into account a number of other variables in addition to those shown above. His overall prices must be right not only in relation to the market and to his competitors' prices but also in relation to the prices of his other tours. This point must also be considered when setting the prices for departures from different regional airports and for operations at different times of the day or night or different days of the week. What special reductions are to be offered to children or for group bookings? Since seat and other costs will be unaffected, whatever reductions are made must be off-set by profits achieved on the sales to other holidaymakers.

Surcharging

Hardest of all decisions for tour pricing is the problem of estimating months ahead of time the actual costs of operating, which will be affected by exchange rate fluctuations, inflation rates in the destination countries and increases in fuel or other costs. Most contracts with airlines permit the carrier to pass on higher fuel costs resulting from price increases or fluctuations in exchange rates. These must be allowed for as far as possible in the brochure prices. Increasingly, however, the instability of the foreign tour market has made operators opt for a system of surcharges which may be imposed after brochures have gone to press.

The imposition of these surcharges poses a delicate problem for tour operators. They are likely to be highly resented by customers and, if the full increase in costs is to be passed on to clients, the price of the tour may no longer be competitive with other operators. Basically the operator is faced with one of five alternatives in dealing with surcharges.

(*a*) He may give *no* price guarantee in his brochure, passing on the full additional costs to his customers. While this will enable him to offer a more attractive price in his brochure, his company image is likely to suffer if the customers encounter high "add-ons" when making the final payment for their holidays.

(*b*) He may issue *no surcharge* guarantees in his brochures, absorbing any price increases. This is also an attractive sales ploy, but to take such a step entails either high risk or inflating his brochure prices to an extent that they may also be uncompetitive.

(*c*) He can pass on all increases in cost to his clients, allowing them to cancel if surcharges exceed some nominal percentage, e.g. 10 per cent, of the original purchase price.

(*d*) He may limit any surcharge to a fixed maximum and absorb extra costs himself beyond this figure.

(*e*) He may guarantee no surcharges for early payment in full for the tour, by a specified date. This has the advantage of reassuring the client, while some or all of the increase in costs will be recovered through profits earned on the investment of the clients' money.

The practice of adding surcharges, sometimes unspecified in detail, to tour prices when sending final billings to customers has been much criticised in recent times by the Consumers' Association among others. In some cases surcharges are being added where increased costs are not applicable, a practice which threatens the integrity of tour operating.

As general policy, members of the TOSG standardise the date each year in which rates of exchange are fixed against the pound sterling, usually at the end of June or beginning of July in the preceding year. This ensures that the public can make meaningful comparisons between the prices of tour programmes to similar destinations. Operators can also *buy forward* in the foreign currency they will require to protect themselves against market fluctuations. If involved in exchanging large sums of money, they can buy *futures* in the international monetary market.

THE TOUR BROCHURE

The tour operator's brochure is a vital marketing tool. Tourism is an intangible product which has to be purchased by customers without inspection and often on the basis of very inadequate knowledge. In these circumstances the brochure becomes the principal means of both informing them about the product and persuading them, by "purveying dreams", to purchase it.

For this reason the production of the tour brochure represents a major proportion of a tour operator's marketing budget and, with print runs for a typical summer brochure exceeding a million copies in the case of the largest tour operators, it is essential to see that this enormous expenditure achieves the intended results.

Brochure design and format
Larger companies will have their brochures designed and prepared either in their own advertising department or in conjunction with the design studio of their advertising agency, who will negotiate with printers to obtain the best quotation and ensure that print deadlines

are met. Other operators may tackle the design of the brochure themselves, but are best advised to undertake this through the medium of an independent design studio who can provide the professional expertise in layout, artwork and copy that are so important in the design of a professional piece of publicity material. Most printers have their own design departments which can undertake this work for their clients, but unless the company has had experience of the standards of work of their printer in the past they are probably better advised to approach an independent studio for this work.

The purposes the brochure serves will dictate its design and format. A single *ad hoc* programme, for example to a foreign exhibition, may be printed on nothing more than a leaflet, or if a limited programme of tours is contemplated these may be laid out in the form of a folder.

Folders can take a number of differing forms, ranging from a simple *centrefold* to more complicated folds (see Fig. 22). Larger

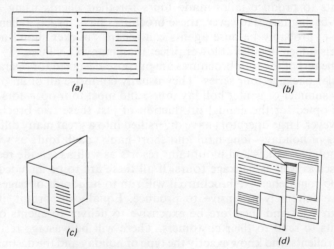

Fig. 22 *Some examples of folders suitable for tour printing*
(*a*) Centrefold, folded to produce simple four-page sheet. (*b*) Gatefold, an off-centre fold producing a front sheet smaller than the second sheet. (*c*) A six-page regular fold. (*d*) A six-page concertina fold.

brochures (or in printing parlance, *booklets*) consist of eight or more pages printed in units of four sheets which require binding in some way. Smaller brochures are usually machine-bound by *saddle-stitching* (stapling through the spine), while larger brochures may be *side-stitched* with a glue-on cover or bound as a book. It is not the purpose here to discuss printing methods in detail and the reader is referred for further reading in this subject to the many excellent books on the subject of print publicity.

Package tour brochures can be described as falling into three categories; *shell* folders, *umbrella* brochures and regular tour brochures. Use of a shell folder is a convenient way to reduce printing costs and is suitable for limited-capacity tour programmes or *ad hoc* specialist tours. Shells are blank folders interspersed with preprinted photographs and are provided at low cost by airlines or national tourist offices to encourage tour operators to run programmes using these services or destinations. Tour operators can overprint a suitable text describing their tour programme; since only the text needs to be added, a one-colour print run at low cost will meet the requirements of scheduled airlines for ITX approval.

An umbrella brochure can be produced by a travel agency permitting them to sell IITs to a multitude of destinations overseas. The brochure covers only the basic essentials to satisfy IATA airlines' requirements for inclusive tour approval, and its purpose is to enable agents to produce tailor-made tours for their clients using a net tour-basing fare. However, these brochures have largely fallen into disuse, probably because agents can secure "bucket shop" airline tickets (albeit illicitly) at lower prices than many ITX fares.

The rest of the tour brochures are purpose-designed for operators' regular package tour series. They usually comprise all of an operator's summer or winter holiday tours, and most tour operators have now opted for the annual production of just these two brochures. However, large operators have diversified into a great many different types of holiday—long-haul and short-haul, coach tours as well as air holidays, lakes and mountains resorts as well as seaside resorts, cruises as well as package tours. If all these are to be included in a single comprehensive brochure it will run to hundreds of pages and prove extremely expensive to produce. Equally important, it will weigh a lot and therefore be expensive to deliver to agents or for agents to send to their customers. There will be wastage resulting from clients who know exactly the type of holiday and the destination to which they wish to travel, but who must pick up the complete brochure in order to see the choice of tours to that destination. For these reasons, some tour operators are now producing a variety of specialist brochures to reach different markets.

The first task of a brochure is to attract the attention of the consumer. Most brochures will be seen by consumers in the racks of a travel agency where they will be vying for attention among many competing operators' brochures. To gain attention, operators have developed a "house style" in which multi-colour covers (usually featuring attractive models in swimwear) combine with an eye-catching symbol and house name across the top of the brochure to obtain maximum impact. While some might contend that there is today a disappointing similarity among leading tour operators' brochure covers, taken individually the quality and professionalism of brochure design is exceptional.

Increasingly, brochures are designed to reinforce an operator's image of quality and reliability. This requires attractive, accurate and easily comprehensible text and layout, high-quality photography and paper of a matching quality.

Obligations affecting tour brochures

As was said earlier, the brochure must both inform and persuade potential tourists. Tour operators are selling dreams and their brochures must allow the consumer to fantasise a little about his holiday. But it is also vitally important that consumers are not misled about any aspect of their holidays; the data must be factually accurate. Care must be taken not to infringe the Trades Description Act 1968, section 14 of which deals specifically with the offence of making false statements concerning the provision of services.

In the past, tour operators have also tended to invoke the *law of agency* in claiming that within their booking conditions they act as agents only in representing hotels, transport companies or other principals. However, the provisions of the Unfair Contract Terms Act 1977 could well invalidate such claims, placing a direct responsibility on the tour operator for the services he packages, even though he himself may have little control over the management of those services. Disclaiming liability may be interpreted as an unreasonable condition within the meaning of the Act.

Apart from legal liabilities, tour operators have a duty to be fair and reasonable in promoting their services to customers. ABTA's Tour Operators' Code of Conduct imposes specific obligations upon them to provide honest and accurate information and the consumer movement has also made this a central tenet in observing the activities of the travel industry.

To satisfy not only the ITX conditions but also their clients' need for information on regular charter tour programmes, the brochure should contain all of the following information:

(a) the name of the firm responsible for the inclusive tour;

(b) the means of transport used, including, in the case of air carriers, the name of the carrier(s), type and class of aircraft used and whether scheduled or charter aircraft are operated;

(c) full details of destinations, itinerary and times of travel;

(d) the duration of each tour (number of days'/nights' stay);

(e) full description of the location and type of accommodation provided, including meals;

(*f*) whether services of a representative are available abroad;

(*g*) a clear indication of the price for each tour, with any extras charged clearly shown (preferably, these extras should be shown on the same page as the basic price of the tour);

(*h*) exact details of special arrangements, e.g. if there is a games room in the hotel, whether this is available at all times and whether any charges are made for the use of such equipment;

(*i*) full conditions of booking, including details of cancellation conditions;

(*j*) details of any optional or compulsory insurance coverage;

(*k*) details of documentation required for travel to the destinations featured and any health hazards or inoculations recommended.

A booking form is usually printed within the brochure for completing a reservation. The terms and conditions of the booking should appear in full in the brochure but should not be printed on the back of the booking form, as they should be retained by the customer.

Negotiating with a printer

A printer will not expect his client necessarily to be an expert in printing methods, but those involved with processing the production of a brochure should be reasonably familiar with current techniques in printing and common terms used. The printer will want to know the following.

(*a*) The number of brochures required.

(*b*) The number of colours to be used in the printing. Full colour-work normally involves four colours, but some savings in cost may be possible if colour photography is not to be included.

(*c*) The paper to be used—size, format, quality and weight. The choice of paper will be influenced by several factors, including the printing process used. Size may be dictated by the industry's requirements; for example, a tour operating brochure needs to fit a standard agency display shelf. Costs can be trimmed by minimising the wastage from "off-cuts" of each sheet of paper used. Paper quality varies considerably according to the material from which it is made. It may be glossy or matt, but most tour operators select a paper for its whiteness and its opacity. This requires a compromise since very white papers tend to be less opaque, but one must avoid print showing through to the other side of the sheet. The weight of paper will of course depend upon its effect on the overall weight of the brochure if this is to be mailed in quantity.

(*d*) Number and positioning of illustrations to be used (photos, artwork, maps, etc.).

(*e*) Typesetting needs. There are over 6,000 typefaces from which to choose and the style of type chosen should reflect the theme of the brochure, its subject and the image of the company.

(f) Completion and delivery dates.

When obtaining prices from a printer, several companies should be approached as quotations will vary substantially between printers. Many tour operators choose to have their brochures printed abroad, but today British printers can usually match their continental counterparts both in quality and price. Most importantly, one must avoid attempting to cut corners as an inferior print job can threaten the whole success of the tour programme. The progress of the printing must be supervised throughout, either by the company itself or its advertising agency. Proofs should be submitted at each stage of production to check on accuracy and a final corrected proof should be seen before the actual print run to ensure there are no final errors.

The printer should be asked to quote not only for the basic number of brochures that will be required but also for the *run-on* price of additional copies. Once a brochure is set up for printing, the cost of running off a few thousand extra is very small in relationship to the overall price and it may be better to do this rather than consider re-ordering another run at a later date.

Brochure distribution and control
As will be discussed later on in this chapter, tour operators must make the decision either to use all ABTA retail agency outlets for the sale of their tours or to select those they feel will be the most productive. Whatever decision is made, the operator must also establish a policy for his brochure distribution. If equal supplies of brochures are distributed to all an operator's agencies, many will be wasted in the less productive retailers.

A study carried out by ASTA some years ago in the United States found that about half of all tour brochures produced were eventually thrown away without being seen by the public. While this can partly be ascribed to the American "shot-gun" approach to distributing brochures, rather than the more selective "rifle" approach, this does nevertheless bring home the potential for waste if care is not exercised. Wastage can be reduced by establishing standards against which to monitor the performance of travel agents. A key ratio is that of brochures given out to bookings received. "Average" figures appear to vary a good deal in the experience of different operators, but a typical conversion rate is thought to be about four to five brochures per booking. However, it must be remembered that a typical booking will consist of two and a half to three persons. If figures consistently poorer than this are achieved by agents, the tour operator should be looking for an explanation. The problem could be accounted for by the agent's lack of control over his own brochure distribution; does he merely stock his display racks and allow his clients to collect brochures in whatever numbers they wish or does he make a serious attempt to sell to his "browsers"? Some agents go even further than this, retaining all stocks of brochures behind the counter with display copies only on the shelves, so that customers have to ask for copies of the brochures they require. This is instrumental in cutting down waste as well as increasing sales.

It is normal practice for the agency sales managers of tour operators to categorise their agents in some suitable manner in terms of their productivity for the company. This could typically take the following form:

Category A	Top producing agents	100 + bookings per year
Category B	Good agents	50-99 bookings per year
Category C	Fair agents	20-49 bookings per year
Category D	Below average agents	6-19 bookings per year
Category E	Poor agents	0-5 bookings per year

A decision will then be made as to what levels of support are to be provided for each category of agent. At the top end of the scale, agents could expect to receive whatever supplies of brochures they feel they could usefully employ, while at the other end perhaps only two or three copies would be sent each year.

THE RESERVATIONS SYSTEM

In order to put a package tour programme into operation, a reservations system must be developed and implemented. The design of the system will depend upon whether reservations are to be handled manually or by computer and on the distribution methods employed, i.e. to what extent the tour operator sells direct to his public, uses retail travel agents, or sells through a combination of these two systems. All large (100,000 +) tour operators today have a computerised system. With the prospective falls in the cost of new computer systems it is likely to be a viable proposition to computerise all small tour operations reservations systems within the course of the next few years.

Making a reservation

Most tour operators continue to sell their tours through the high street travel agents who are currently responsible for handling 80-90 per cent of bookings made.

If a manual system is provided the operator will deal with these agents' enquiries and bookings by telephone. Reservations enquiries from the public and those from travel agents will be handled on separate lines, and lines may be further distinguished between geo-graphical destinations or between winter and summer holidays or between beach resorts and "lakes and mountains" holidays. This distinction gives reservations staff the opportunity to specialise in some aspect of the company's products and provide a more personal link with agents, who will come to identify a region with a particular staff member.

All reservations systems suffer from the problem of variable de-mand over time. In Britain the peak booking period for summer holidays is in the three months immediately following Christmas (although there has been a tendency in recent years for increasing numbers of the public to book later). The operator is therefore faced with the alternative of providing adequate staff and telephone lines to handle all the demand during the peak periods, with consequent under-utilisation of resources at other times, or providing a reduced number of lines year-round, with a delay in service to agents and the public during the peak periods which may cause loss of business.

Travel agents require rapid connections to an operator's reserva-tions system. If lines are engaged or telephones not answered for long periods of time, agents will become frustrated and may prefer to deal with a competitor with whom communications are easier. Installing an automatic call distribution (ACD) system, by which incoming calls are automatically "queued" until a line becomes free, does not entirely satisfy agents since they are involved in the expense of holding on until the line becomes free.

Once connected to the reservations department the agent identifies himself and his company and checks on the availability of the tour in which his client is interested. If available, the tour may then be reserved either under option or as a definite booking. Options are usually held by the operator until the end of the following work day, when they will be automatically released unless the agent has tele-phoned to convert to a definite booking. In both cases, reservations staff provide the agent with a code number to identify the booking. Once a booking is definite the client completes the tour operator's booking form and this is sent, together with the appropriate deposit, by the agent to the operator, the booking code being shown on the form. These forms are usually required to arrive in the tour operator's office within 5–7 days or again the booking will be automatically released.

The reservations department is situated within the tour operator's chart room. Where a manual system is in operation, the full pro-gramme of flights and hotels is posted on the walls of this room and availability can be quickly scanned by the telephone staff. The charts will draw attention to any changes in the programme since the brochure went to press so that the reservations staff can ensure that these changes are brought to the attention of agent and customer. Actual control of flights and hotel sales can be handled in a variety of different ways. One typical procedure is to use coloured tabs hanging on pegs adjacent to each flight and hotel; as bookings are made, a tab is removed from each and inserted into a booking envelope with the details of the booking shown on the exterior of the envelope, viz. date of booking, "lead" name of customer, number of seats reserved, agent's identification (ABTA number and personal reference) and sales staff reference. Once all coloured tabs have been removed from a peg this will signify that the flight or hotel is fully booked. When cancellations occur the tabs may be returned to the pegs.

Post-reservations administration

Once the operator receives the booking form in the mail it is processed first by the reservations staff, who mark bookings as "definite" in the records and arrange for a confirmation to be sent to the agent. Subsequently, booking forms are passed to the accounts section who will raise an invoice and forward this to the agent (it is possible to reduce paperwork by combining the confirmation and invoice). It is the agent's responsibility to ensure that his clients remit the final payment due by the deadline given in the invoice. Upon receipt of the final payment the tour operator issues tickets and itinerary (plus any vouchers that may be necessary) and despatches these to the agent.

Prior to each departure a flight manifest is prepared for the airline, with names of all those booked, and a rooming list is sent to the hotels concerned and to resort representatives where appropriate. The latter should go over the rooming list with the hotelier to ensure that all is in order prior to the clients' arrival.

Larger tour operators can also be expected to have a passenger relations department whose function is to monitor and handle passenger and agency complaints and ensure quality control in the operation of the tour programme.

Late bookings

Tour operators are anxious to fill every seat in their tour programme. The ability to react quickly to deal with last-minute demand for bookings plays a key role in fulfilling this objective. Coupled with late booking discounts, many operators have introduced procedures designed to encourage late bookings, including fast updatings on availability and a telephone booking procedure which merely requires a reference to be given to the agent over the telephone, against which customers can collect their tickets at the airport.

Computer reservations systems

Computers offer substantial advantages for reservations systems in terms of accuracy and speed. Until recently the introduction of computers to such systems was hindered by technical difficulties, but reliable systems are now in operation with carriers and hotel companies as well as with most leading tour operators. At the time of writing, the process of linking these systems to travel agencies is going ahead. This will provide VDU terminals in retail outlets, operating in *real time*, thus giving agents immediate access to up-to-the-minute information on availability and enabling them to interact with the reservations system to make bookings.

A tour operator who can provide his agents with such immediacy has a substantial marketing advantage over his competitors. He is equally certain that information passed to agents in this form is accurate and takes into account any recent changes to the tour programme. There is no danger of accidentally overbooking clients, and if the clients' choice of tour is unavailable the system can be programmed to make an automatic search and offer a range of alternative dates or holidays so that the sale is not lost.

New systems recently developed by Thomas Cook, Thomsons Holidays and Olympic Holidays can be programmed to interface with either of the two leading contenders for agency terminals, Travicom or Modulas, using either Prestel-type viewdata systems or British Telecom's new "gateway". Other leading tour operators will be sure to follow this lead shortly. As well as handling enquiries and bookings, these systems are designed to provide printouts of confirmations, itineraries and invoices, tickets, and flight manifests and rooming lists for principals. Expiring options are automatically released for resale.

It is intended that eventually the system will obviate the necessity to send booking forms to the operators. Further into the future there is the likelihood that, with the development of electronic transfers of funds, deposits and final payments will also be handled through the computer, with the tour operator automatically debiting the agent. The facility for undertaking this through the agents' terminals is already available, with its introduction in Britain probably occurring towards the end of the 1980s.

Linked to the tour operators' and travel agents' systems, various programs allow for a wide range of management control and accounting information to be made immediately available to the company.

THE DISTRIBUTION NETWORK

Selection of retailers

Basically tour operators choose between two alternative methods of selling their tours—direct sell or through travel agents. Most choose to sell all, or the bulk, of their tours through the approximately 5,500 agents who are members of ABTA; about 90 per cent of their tours are distributed in this way. However, the other 10 per cent of business achieved through direct bookings is highly lucrative for tour operators since it means a further 10 per cent profit for the operator without involving him in additional marketing expense. Most operators are naturally keen to encourage further direct bookings but must not be seen to be doing so by the agents themselves, who may retaliate by withdrawing their support and selling the tours of competitors.

Some operators are more selective in appointing agents to represent them. Like the sale of most consumer goods, some 80 per cent of package tours will be sold through only 20 per cent of retailers, while a large number of agents is likely to produce only the odd booking for the operator. The cost of servicing those less productive agents may be greater than the revenue they produce for the operator—not only must they be supplied with expensive free brochures but they have to receive regular mailings to update their information, be supported with sales material and most will also receive the occasional call from the operator's sales representative.

Principals must therefore decide whether to give varying support to agents dependent upon the latter's productivity (*see* p. 198), or to dispense with their least productive agents' services.

A number of tour operators have chosen to open their own retail outlets where, like any other agent, they will sell all ABTA tours but will of course prominently feature their parent company's products. Thus Thomson Holidays has a small number of retail shops in key cities, and also owns the Lunn Poly chain of some 200 travel agencies. Where this vertical integration occurs it is the usual policy of the companies concerned each to act as its own profit centre, and the parent organisation will pay commission on sales received through these shops just as it does through any other agent. Thomas Cook is of course best known as a travel retailer, but they also operate a major programme of package tours. The power of Cook's as a retailer is such that they can be highly selective as to which tour operator's services they will handle and can dictate to these operators advantageous terms and conditions, such as extended credit or improved commission rates.

Smaller specialist tour operators are obviously not in a position to support a national network of retailers, carrying as they do perhaps less than 10,000 holidaymakers each year. They will either concentrate entirely upon selling direct or will support a few selected agents in key locations around the country.

Relationships with travel agents

It is customary for tour operators to draw up a formal agreement with the travel agents they appoint to sell their services. These agreements specify the terms and conditions of trading, including such issues as the rate of commission to be paid to agents, whether the travel agent is to be a cash or credit agency, and the dates by which the operator expects settlement of his account. Most agreements also impose on the agent the condition that tours shall not be sold at less than published brochure prices.

An ill-defined area in these agreements is that of the application of the law of agency. A contract is between the principal and the client himself and it is unclear whether the travel agent is to be seen as acting as an agent of the principal (in this case the tour operator) or of the client. Agreements may suggest that the agent is the agent of the principal. However, since the collapse of Clarkson's Holidays in 1974, it has generally been assumed that any "pipeline" money held by agents at the time of a collapse of a principal is rightfully the client's, and some agreements now go so far as to specify this. Legally, however, this remains a grey area.

Under the terms of agency/tour operator agreements, travel agents agree to support and promote the sale of their principals' services. In return, the tour operator provides the support and co-operation necessary for the successful merchandising of his products, i.e. provision of adequate brochures, sales promotion material and sometimes finance for co-operative regional advertising or promotional campaigns. The operator will also try to ensure that his agents are knowledgeable about the products they sell. This will be achieved through circulation of sales letters or other mail shots, by invitations to workshops or other forms of presentation, and by inviting selected agents on travel agency educationals.

The travel agency educational

The educational (or "familiarisation trip" in American parlance) is a study trip organised by principals (whether tour operators, airlines or national tourist offices) for travel agents, with the objective either of rewarding staff for past sales performance or of providing them with new product knowledge of destinations or services. It has the advantage of implanting product knowledge more effectively than any other method while building brand loyalty and improving agency/principal relations, but the cost of mounting these educationals is high so principals are concerned that they achieve value for money. This has not always been the case in the past where educational visits abroad were often treated as "jollies", attractive to agents as a social perk rather than an educational experience. The effectiveness of these educationals has been improved by more careful selection of candidates, by providing a more balanced mix of visits, working sessions and social activities, and by imposing a small charge for attendance, so that travel agency managers become more concerned to see that the expense is justified in terms of increased productivity and expertise among their staff.

Careful selection will ensure that all those attending share common objectives and that, for example, senior agency managers and young counter staff do not find themselves on the same educational, to the discomfort of both. Monitoring performance, by soliciting reports from those attending on completion of the educational visit, and by checking sales figures from invited agents will further ensure that the educational study trip is money well spent by the tour operator.

The sales representative

Tour operators, as do most larger travel principals, employ sales representatives to maintain and develop their business through travel agents, as well as to seek other sources of business. The functions of the sales rep are to call on present and potential contacts, advise agents and others of the services offered by their company, and support their retailers by the use of promotional, and sometimes financial, aid.

The rep acts as one point of contact between the agent and the operator when problems or complaints are raised, and the often close relationship that develops between a rep and his accounts is valuable in building brand loyalty for the company. This personal contact enables them to obtain feedback from retailers on client and agent attitudes towards the company and its products. The rep is also likely to play a valuable role in categorising agents in terms of their potential and selecting sales staff for invitations to educationals. However, making sales calls in person is expensive and most companies have either reduced the frequency of calls or have switched to telephone sales calls to keep in touch with all but the most productive agents.

Agents themselves have very mixed feelings about the value of the sales rep, who is still too often seen as a time-wasting socialiser, notably ignorant about his company's and his competitors' products. It goes without saying that if the rep is to do an effective job he must be well trained; a rep who is not knowledgeable about his products will carry a very poor image of the company to the retailers.

Direct sell operators

Tour operators that have avoided selling through retail agents and concentrated instead on reaching their public directly are not new to the British travel scene. They have, however, enjoyed a greater measure of success in the last few years, spearheaded by the launch in Britain of the Danish tour-operating giant Tjaereborg in 1978. Working from a base of successful large-scale tour operation in continental Europe, they were able to penetrate the British market with efficient management and low prices which in many cases undercut those of the market leaders who sold through the traditional retail travel agency outlets. Their success soon attracted the Swedish operator Vingresor and subsequently an off-shoot of the Thomson travel empire, Portland Holidays, also entered the direct sell market. Meanwhile, Martin Rooks, an old-established direct sell operator, was absorbed by British Airways and embarked on a programme of expansion. By the end of the 1970s these four companies were carrying almost a quarter of a million passengers on foreign inclusive tours.

However, marketing costs to achieve this level of penetration were high. Unlike sales through travel agencies, direct selling involves a high proportion of fixed costs in advertising, direct mail promotion and similar ventures, and it requires a strong and efficient administrative back-up to deal quickly with telephone enquiries and sales. It has been estimated that Portland alone spent over £1 million to market its services in 1980, some £20 per client carried, compared with less than £6 per client (excluding travel agency commission) spent by Thomson Holidays itself to sell package tours through the retail trade. These high launch costs in the initial years of operation may be justified if market penetration is achieved.

The total share of the package tour market held by direct sell operators (including the proportion of package tours sold direct by the more traditional operators) probably does not exceed 20 per cent of the market and travel experts foresee that this is likely to expand to around 30 per cent before it stabilises. If direct sell revenue is concentrated in the hands of a few powerful companies such as Tjaereborg, the potential is attractive. However the high cost of initial marketing has been suggested as the principal reason behind the demise of Vingresor and its subsequent takeover by Portland after only a couple of years' operation in Britain.

It is not entirely clear yet why these new direct sell efforts were successful where they had failed for other companies so often in the past. This cannot be ascribed totally to the successful management and low prices of the direct sell companies; it may well reflect a measure of dissatisfaction with existing travel agency sales methods, both on the part of the public and the tour operators, and it has been hypothesised that future growth in the direct sell market is likely to be largely at the expense of the less efficient agents. Traditional buying patterns die hard in Britain, however, and there is still strong support for the role of the retail agent.

Nonetheless, agents are concerned about the prospect of further encroachment by direct sell operations and particularly by efforts made to sell direct by those tour operators currently supporting agents. While threats have been made that agents will switch their support to loyal tour operators, it is arguable whether this line of attack is practical in the case of the largest companies in the inclusive tour business. An early threat to Thomsons when that organisation launched Portland Holidays had little effect—to refuse sales of the brand leader among tour operators is likely to damage agents as much as the principal. Perhaps a more effective retaliation in the long term is the attempt by travel agents to band together to form a tour operating consortium to compete with the established operators, with tours sold through members of the consortium at cost price to the agent. There is little evidence as yet, though, that this development poses a serious threat to the established operators.

SELF-ASSESSMENT QUESTIONS

1. How do tour operators achieve low prices for their package tours?

2. In what ways can tour operators supplement their incomes received through the sale of package tours?

3. Distinguish between a "shell folder" and an "umbrella folder" and explain the advantages each offer to tour operators.

4. What advantages does a specialist tour operator have over a mass-market operator in the setting up of a new programme?

5. True or false? (a) TOSG arrange to standardise the date for agreeing exchange rates among their members. (b) Operators using scheduled flight ITX fares must hold an ATOL. (c) Inclusive tour air tickets, as well as invoices, are now available through computers. (d) Under the Tour Operators' Code of Conduct, all ABTA operators are obliged to distribute their brochures to every ABTA travel agent who requires a supply.

ASSIGNMENT

Taking the role of a small, specialist tour operator, identify a suitable destination for the development of a new series of package tours overseas, aimed at any specialist market of your choice. Identify the main competition to the destination and to comparable destinations elsewhere and explain why you believe your choice to be the best one for your market.

CHAPTER ELEVEN

Ancillary Tourism Services

CHAPTER OBJECTIVES

After studying this chapter, you should be able to:
* understand the role of guides, couriers, insurance and financial services in meeting tourists' needs;
* be aware of private and public sector training and educational facilities for those employed in the tourism business;
* understand the role and value of the trade press for the travel industry;
* list the principal guides and timetables in use by travel agents, and their contents;
* be aware of the role of marketing and consultancy services in the industry.

INTRODUCTION

An analysis of the tourism industry leads one to encounter the problem of defining the parameters of the industry. Some services depend entirely upon the movement of tourists but are seldom considered as an element of the industry itself; customs services or visa issuing offices are examples. There are also services which derive much of their revenue from tourism yet are clearly not part of the industry, for example, companies specialising in the design and construction of hotels, and theatres or other entertainment centres.

Having attempted in previous chapters to compartmentalise conveniently the sectors of tourism (as an aid to memory as much as for any other reason), one is left with a number of services and facilities which, while perhaps not meriting lengthy treatment here, nevertheless deserve more than a passing mention. It is convenient to group these miscellaneous services together in this chapter.

Ancillary services can take the form either of services to the tourist himself or of services to the suppliers of tourism, although there may be considerable overlap between these categories. Each will be dealt with in turn.

SERVICES TO THE TOURIST

Guide/courier services

Unfortunately, there is as yet no term which will conveniently embrace all the *mediators* whose function it is to shepherd, guide and look after groups of tourists. Nor can one relate these functions to a single sector of the industry; they are employed by carriers and tour operators, while some guide/couriers are self-employed, working freelance for tour operators or for themselves. Resort representatives who are employed by tour operators may also frequently be called upon to take on the role of a courier, as discussed in Chapter 10. Here, however, we will describe and differentiate between the role of couriers and of guides.

Couriers are employed by coach companies or tour operators to supervise and shepherd groups of tourists participating in coach tours (either on extended tours or day excursions). As well as couriers, they may be known as tour escorts, tour leaders or even tour managers, although the latter term usually implies a higher level of status and responsibility. As a part of their role they are often called upon to offer a sightseeing commentary on the country or region through which they are travelling and act as a source of information.

Some companies dispense with the separate services of a courier and employ driver-couriers who are responsible both for driving the coach and looking after their groups. Their role of information-giving, however, is restricted both by their limited knowledge and training and by legal constraints in force in most countries which prohibit the use of microphones by drivers while their coaches are in motion (a ruling which in practice is often overlooked).

Courier work offers less job security than is to be found in most other fields of tourism employment, being largely seasonal. However, with the growth of winter holidays resort representatives who also act as couriers are finding it possible to work all year round, some doubling as ski instructors during the winter programmes.

There is as yet no national organisation of couriers in the UK, although the International Association of Tour Managers counts some British members among its largely American membership. Couriers are employed mainly on the basis of their experience and there are no formal training courses (and little in-house training) provided for prospective employees.

Couriers differ from guides in that the latter stress their information-giving role, even though they may also perform other courier functions as part of their job. Guides, or guide-lecturers, are retained by tour operators for their expertise in general or specialist subjects. Their employment is generally freelance and intermittent, being concentrated primarily during the summer months, and outside of London there are comparatively few opportunities for off-season work. In an effort to extend recognition of their services by the tourism industry, guides have formed regional and national bodies to represent their interests. The largest of these is the

London-based Guild of Guide-Lecturers, with some 600 members (90 per cent London area members), who are attempting to establish nationally recognised yardsticks for professional fees for their members.

Training courses in guiding are offered through the technical colleges and by a few private companies, and these are validated by the regional tourist boards. Validation as a registered guide does not, however, offer security of employment and many companies continue to employ unregistered guides who are prepared to accept lower fees for their work. Because the supply of guides outstrips demand, many undertake guiding as a part-time occupation, while others supplement their general guiding work by working as driver-guides, conducting individual tourists on excursions using their private cars.

Financial services

This section will deal with three financial services for the tourist— the provision of insurance, of foreign exchange and of credit.

Insurance

Insurance is an important and in some cases obligatory aspect of a tourist's travel arrangements, embracing coverage for one or more of the following contingencies:

(a) medical care and hospitalisation;
(b) personal accident;
(c) cancellation or curtailment of holiday;
(d) delayed departure;
(e) baggage loss or delay;
(f) money loss;
(g) personal liability.

Tourists may purchase insurance either in the form of a selective policy, covering one or more of the above items, or in the form of a standard package policy in which most or all of these items are included. The latter policy, although inflexible in its coverage, is invariably cheaper for comprehensive protection. Most tour operators now provide automatic insurance coverage for their customers, either as an obligatory extra or assuming their clients will require this supplementary item unless they clearly decide to opt out.

The travel insurance market is estimated to be worth in excess of £30 million per year, and with only one traveller in twenty making any claim against his policy it is a highly profitable one for the tour operators, with profits representing some 50 per cent of revenue. In addition to the compulsory schemes operated by tour operators, travel agents act as (largely unregistered) brokers for a number of insurance companies who specialise in providing selective or package insurance coverage for packaged or independent holidays. These prove more lucrative for agents to sell since they are commissionable to the agents at 40 per cent, as against the standard commission of 10 per cent allowed to agents on tour operators' policies.

ABTA, in association with an established insurance company, now operates its own "Extrasure" package insurance programme which, in addition to the usual agency commission, also earns income for the Association itself.

Agents are obliged by the ABTA retail agents' code of conduct to draw their clients' attention to insurance facilities and cover (and they are also bound by the codes of conduct of the British Insurance Association or other insurance association whose members they represent) but are faced with a dilemma in deciding whether to sell those policies which are seen as in the customers' best interest or those producing higher revenues for the agents themselves, or some similar benefit (such as extended credit facilities). The decision to sell the policies of one particular company is one to be taken by branch managers of the agency concerned.

Foreign exchange

Travellers abroad can arrange for the exchange of their currency in a number of ways. They can take sterling or foreign banknotes with them (risking loss or theft); they can carry sterling or foreign travellers' cheques; they can make use of credit cards abroad; they can pre-arrange for open credits to be available at specified banks abroad; or they can use National Giro postcheques which can be drawn on the post offices of some thirty European or North American countries.

Some travel agents (most notably Thomas Cooks) provide facilities themselves for the exchange of currency, but travellers more commonly obtain their foreign currency through banks or specialist foreign exchange dealers before their departure. A comparatively small number of travel agents, mainly business house agents, deal with travellers' cheques, Cooks and American Express, with their own cheques, being exceptions.

About 60 per cent of all tourists from the UK buy travellers' cheques, the total market for which has been estimated at over £1.5 billion annually in the UK and Ireland. Market leaders by a wide margin are Thomas Cooks, which, together with their parent company, the Midland Bank, account for over 30 per cent of British market sales. American Express, who were the first to introduce the travellers' cheque in 1891, remain the world leaders in terms of total market share but they account for only 10 per cent of the UK market, with a similar share being held by the other leading banks. In Britain, travel agents (excluding Cooks and American Express) are thought to account for sales of around £100 million in travellers' cheques each year, with most of these sales also concentrated among the business house agents.

About three-quarters of the travellers' cheques issued in Britain are in sterling, although with the recent introduction of a wider range of foreign denominations this demand is diversifying. In 1984, plans were announced to introduce travellers' cheques based on ECUs (European Currency Units). The value of an ECU is based on all currencies of the European Monetary System plus the pound sterling, and in consequence its value fluctuates less than do the individual currencies in the system.

Travellers' cheques have two great advantages; they are readily acceptable anywhere in the world, whether by banks or commercial institutions, and they offer the holder guaranteed security with rapid compensation for loss or theft. For the tourist the advantage of this outweighs the standard premium charged of 1 per cent. The value of the system for the suppliers is that there is generally a considerable lapse of time between the tourist purchasing his travellers' cheques and encashing them. The money invested in the interim at market interest rates provides the supplier with substantial profits.

Credit
For the purposes of travel, credit cards can be conveniently separated into three categories. First, there are the all-purpose cards which provide extended credit facilities in the UK and abroad, examples of which include Barclaycard and Access. Secondly, there are cards that may be used abroad for the purchase of a variety of products, but which usually require prompt settlement, examples being Diners' Club and American Express cards. These generally offer higher credit limits, sometimes without any ceiling. Finally, there is a wide range of credit cards for the purchase of specific goods and services such as car hire and hotels. Among these mention should be made of the UATP (Universal Air Travel Plan) card, which can be used for the purchase of IATA air tickets throughout the world.

All of the above simplify the process of travelling abroad since settlement for any item purchased can be effected in the UK in sterling. Recent years have seen an explosion in the growth of credit cards and credit transactions handled. It is likely that within the space of the next few years credit cards will replace banknotes for the majority of transactions. This will come about with the electronic processing of funds, whereby customers' accounts are automatically debited against purchases and the supplier credited. These, of course, would not necessarily be credit transactions since the customer might be paying for his purchase immediately.

Although again not a means of providing credit, mention should also be made here of cheque cards, which enable personal cheques to be encashed abroad. A charge is normally levied by the foreign bank for this service.

Incentive travel vouchers

Earlier, the role of incentive travel was discussed in generating new forms of tourism. Usually, companies have provided their employees or dealers with a specific travel package as a reward for achievement, the outcome being a form of group affinity travel, with recipients of the reward travelling together. However, an alternative incentive is available in the form of travel vouchers, issued in varying denominations, which can be collected by employees and used towards the cost of individual travel arrangements of the recipients' own choice. This is simply another form of monetary reward for achievement, but the appeal of travel has been proved a stronger motivator than cash or consumer durables. This form of award is also more flexible, and can be given in small denominations, for example, to reward low absenteeism or for reaching weekly targets. A number of companies currently provide such vouchers. Some are able to be exchanged only against certain travel products or through specific retail travel agencies; others can be used to pay for any holiday arrangements purchased through ABTA agencies.

Duty free shopping

Under the category of services to tourists, a final mention should be made of duty free shopping. The purchase of duty free goods at airports, on board ships and aircraft or at specially designated duty free ports has always exerted a strong attraction for tourists. Duty free purchases of spirits and tobacco in particular have been effectively marketed by carriers and the profits on the sale of such items are substantial (on some charter air services they exceed profits accruing on the sale of air tickets). Equally, the sale of duty free goods at airports provides a substantial proportion of an airport's operating revenue.

This has led in some quarters to criticisms of profiteering, but the principals' reply to such criticism is that without these profits the airports would have to increase their landing charges and the cost of transport for consumers would rise appreciably.

Recently the EEC has introduced a directive to the effect that imported goods from non-EEC countries must carry import tax at all times, so that intra-EEC travellers would be required to pay the customs tax on all non-EEC products. While this tax forms only a small proportion of the total duty on products, there are fears that this may be the first step towards the abolition of duty free sales in the EEC.

SERVICES TO THE SUPPLIER

Education and training

The approach to training in the tourist industry has been historically a sectoral one. Each sector of the industry has tended to generate its own training courses, which have been largely job-specific. In an industry highly dependent upon entrepreneurially-managed small units there has been little in the way of formal training until recently. Most employees of travel agencies, hotels and tour operators have been trained on the job, often by observation and experience only, although some companies have provided noteworthy in-service training programmes, e.g. those of Thomas Cooks among travel agents. With the growing institutionalisation of sectors, greater emphasis has been placed upon professionalisation, the introduction of national standards of training and more formal training programmes. Professional bodies within the industry introduced their own programmes leading to final membership and offered part-time or full-time courses at colleges of further and higher education. Examples of such courses are those introduced by the Hotel, Catering and Institutional Management Association (HCIMA), the Chartered Institute of Transport (CIT) and the Institute of Travel and Tourism (ITT), the latter embracing principally employees of travel agencies and tour operators.

At corporate level in the industry, particularly within the airline sector and among leading tour operators, employers have tended to recruit graduates in appropriate disciplines for their own in-service management training programmes. This has also been true of the public sector in tourism.

In-service training for travel agents has been formalised by the introduction, with ABTA's support, of the Certificate of Travel Agency Competence (COTAC), nationally validated by the City and Guilds. In 1982 the British government decided to phase out most of the industrial training boards, with the intention that the responsibility for such training should revert to the industries themselves. The Air Transport and Travel Industry Board, which was one of those affected, had successfully operated a number of technician short courses for the travel sectors, and ABTA decided to take over the responsibility for mounting travel agency and tour operating courses themselves, through the ABTA National Training Board.

The difficulty of organising day release courses for those employees of small travel companies has been tackled by the introduction of correspondence courses offered by various public and private sector bodies. In Britain the British Airways Fares and Ticketing courses, which depend largely upon self-study, have found widespread acceptance as a national standard for travel agency employees. Internationally the World Tourism Organisation (WTO) organises an international correspondence course designed to provide a comprehensive knowledge of the industry, and IATA/UFTAA offer self-study courses also covering fares and ticketing.

As we have seen earlier, courses for registered guides are validated within the industry by the regional tourist boards. However, no national standards for these courses have been established and the quality and length of these courses will vary substantially from one region to another.

The question of depth rather than breadth of knowledge has been a point of controversy within the industry, which has generally opted for depth of knowledge within a limited field in formal training courses—hence the sectoral approach to training which has been the norm up to now. However, public sector colleges have for some 15 years (even longer in the case of the hotel and catering industry) been offering courses which combine training for the industry and educational development of the student. These are designed to offer a wider perspective on the tourism business than would normally be available through the sectoral training approach. They range in scope from college diploma courses to the nationally validated courses of BTEC, the Business and Technician Education Council. BTEC General, National and Higher National Diplomas have as their underlying philosophy the aim to provide students with essential business operating skills, with optional modules relating these skills to specific areas of business such as the travel and tourism industry. Postgraduate diplomas and higher degrees in tourism are also available at some universities and colleges in Britain, although as yet the only first degrees in this field are those relating to the hotel and catering business.

The trade press

In addition to specialised academic and research journals, there is a large selection of weekly and monthly journals serving the needs of those working in the tourism industry. The weekly trade papers, Travel Trade Gazette and Travelnews, provide an invaluable service for the industry, covering news both of social and commercial events.

In an industry as fast-changing as tourism, employees can only update their knowledge of travel products by regularly reading the trade press. The newspapers complement the work of the training bodies in providing up-to-the-minute news, and for untrained travel agency staff they may well be the main source of such knowledge as well as being a forum for trade advertising and job opportunities.

The trade newspapers depend largely upon advertising for their revenue, and in return they support the industry by sponsoring trade fairs, seminars and other events.

Within the general category of the press one must also include those who are responsible for the publication of travel guides and timetables. The major publications in the field are shown in Table VIII and are those most commonly in use in travel agencies. The task of updating this information is obviously immense, especially in view of the worldwide scope of many of these publications. Since their production becomes more complex each year, this is also a field which lends itself to computerisation. Certainly the major timetable companies are now researching the feasibility of putting much of their timetable information onto computer terminals using facilities such as Prestel, and information retrieval will be unlikely to depend upon the printed page for very much longer.

Marketing services

A number of services exist either wholly or in part to provide marketing support to members of the travel industry. These include marketing consultants, representative agencies, advertising agencies, brochure design, printing and distribution services, suppliers of travel point-of-sale material, and research and public relations organisations. To this list must now be added the organisations which provide the hardware and software for computerisation of the travel industry.

This book does not propose to discuss in depth the marketing of travel; this subject is covered adequately by existing texts and the reader is referred to the bibliography for further reading. The point to be made here is that both large and small companies in the industry can benefit by employing these specialist agencies, while the services of some are indispensable.

General marketing consultants

Management and marketing consultants offer advice to companies in the organisation and operation of their businesses. They bring to the task two valuable attributes, expertise and objectivity. Most tourism consultants have years of experience in the industry on which to draw and have been successful in their own fields before turning

TABLE VIII. TRAVEL PUBLICATIONS

Publication	Details
British publications:	
ABC World Airways Guide (monthly)	Flight and fares information, car hire
ABC Rail Guide (monthly)	Timetables between London and all stations
ABC Shipping Guide (monthly)	Worldwide passenger and cargo/passenger services
ABC Guide to International Travel (Jan/Apr/Jul/Oct)	Passport, visa, health, currency regulations, customs, climate, etc.
Thomas Cook Continental Timetable (monthly)	Rail and shipping services throughout Europe and the Mediterranean
Thomas Cook Overseas Timetable (Jan/Mar/May/Jul/Sep/Nov)	Road, rail and local shipping timetable for America, Africa, Asia, Australia
National Express Coach Guide (Apr/Sep)	Express coach services for British Isles
Travel Trade Directory (Dec)	Directory of travel industry in UK/Eire
IATA Travel Agents' Directory of Europe (annual)	European agents, airlines, hotel groups, car hire, tourist offices
Britain: Hotels and Restaurants (Mar)	BTA official guide
AA Guide to Hotels and Restaurants (Nov)	5,000 recommended establishments in British Isles
World Hotel Directory (July)	*Financial Times* guide to business hotels in 150 countries
A–Z Worldwide Hotel Guide (twice yearly)	Comprehensive list of international hotels and reservations offices
Agents' Hotel Gazetteer (2 vols) (annual)	Directory of hotels in resorts (vol 1) and cities (vol 2) of Europe
Holiday Guide	
Summer edition (annual)	Identifies tour operators providing
Winter edition (annual)	package holidays to specific hotels and resorts worldwide
Travel Directory (twice yearly)	Directory of the travel industry
Car Ferry Guide (annual)	Index of car ferry routes and operators
American publications:	
OAG Cruise and Shipline Guide (six per annum)	Line voyages, cruises and ferries worldwide
OAG Worldwide Edition (monthly)	Flights outside USA
OAG North American Edition (monthly)	Flights and fares in USA, Canada, Mexico and the Caribbean
OAG Travel Planner and Hotel/Motel Guide (four times per annum)	North American edition and European edition—resort areas and hotels
USA Official Railway Guide (Jun and Nov)	AMTRAK schedules and tariffs for USA, Canada, Mexico and Central America
Russells Official Bus Guide (Jun and Dec)	National guide for USA, Canada, Mexico and Central America

Publication	Details
Hotel and Motel Red Book (Aug)	Directory of American Hotel and Motel Association members
Rand-McNally guides for USA	
Campground and Trailer Park Guide (Jun)	20,000 camp sites in USA, Canada and Mexico
Mobil City Guide (annual)	Complete guide to American cities
Mobil Travel Guides (annual)	Seven separate regional guides listing resorts, hotels and facilities in USA
International publications	
International Hotel Guide (France) (Mar)	Worldwide guide published by International Hotel Association
Michelin Red Guides (France) (annual)	Six separate guides—GB & Ireland, France, Benelux, Spain & Portugal, Italy, Germany
Europa Camping and Caravanning (May)	International guide to campsites
Jaeger's Intertravel (Jun)	Directory of the world's travel agencies

to consultancy. Moreover, not being directly involved in the day-to-day running of the company, they can approach their task without preconceived ideas about its operation and thus can offer a wider perspective in seeking solutions to problems.

They may be employed either to advise on the general reorganisation or marketing of a company and its products, or for some *ad hoc* purpose such as undertaking a feasibility study for new tour operating destinations or the introduction of a computerised reservations system.

Representative agencies
For a retainer or payment of royalties on sales these organisations act as general sales agents for a company within a defined territory. This is a valuable service for smaller companies seeking representation abroad. In the travel industry it is found most commonly in the hotel sector, but carriers, excursion operators and public sector tourist offices all make use of this facility in marketing their services abroad.

Advertising and promotional agencies
Many large travel companies, and an increasing number of smaller ones, retain an advertising agent, a number of whom specialise in handling travel accounts. An advertising agent does much more than design advertisements and place them in the media. They will be

closely involved in the entire marketing strategy of the company and will be concerned with the design and production of the travel brochures. Many are equipped to carry out marketing research, the production of publicity material and merchandising or public relations activities.

Travel companies may have their brochures designed by the design studios of their advertising agent, they may arrange for them to be produced by an independent design studio, or the work can be undertaken by their printer. Advertising agents can help and advise in the selection of a printer for the production of brochures and other publicity material.

A recent innovation in publicity material for the trade is the use of video cassettes to supplement, and perhaps in time even to replace, the travel brochure. They are designed to help customers reach decisions on holiday destinations and services and are already being used experimentally by some agents who loan them to their clients. The cost of the cassette production is borne by the principals whose services are advertised.

In the area of marketing services, mention should also be made of direct mail and distribution services, some of which also specialise in handling travel services. These companies design and organise direct mail promotional literature aimed at specific target markets or at travel retailers. They can also undertake distribution of a company's tour brochures to travel agents in the UK.

Microprocessing organisations
Although carriers have had computerised reservations services for some years, only with the advent of the 1980s has the computer spread rapidly to other sectors of the industry. Virtually all major tour operators today have computerised their reservations services and computers are now being introduced into retail agents, who require *real-time* connections with these reservations systems in order to provide a fast and accurate booking service for their clients.

A number of hardware and software computer companies have been attracted by the growth potential for computers in the travel industry and have designed systems for principals and agencies which combine the three essential functions of information retrieval, reservations and accounting.

SELF-ASSESSMENT QUESTIONS

1. How do guides' and couriers' roles differ? How do you think this difference will affect the training and education of each?

2. Explain how travel insurance is an important adjunct to the services provided by both tour operators and travel agents.

3. List the range of credit facilities currently available for the purchase of travel in Britain. Why do you think credit buying has caught the public's interest more slowly for tourism than for other products?

4. Assume you are a tour operator, operating on a small to medium scale. What advisory services could you see yourself usefully enjoying in the course of your business?

ASSIGNMENT

Compare and contrast the benefits and drawbacks, as you see them, of learning the tourism business by formal courses (such as college diplomas) and by in-service training.

Now interview a cross-section of people employed in the tourism industry to obtain their views on the merits of each form of learning. How knowledgeable are they about formal tourism courses? How did they themselves gain their knowledge of the industry? Do their views differ according to which sector of the industry they belong to?

Suggest why it is that those in the industry hold the views they do.

CHAPTER TWELVE

Public Sector Tourism

CHAPTER OBJECTIVES

After studying this chapter, you should be able to:
* understand the part played by local and central governments in the planning and promotion of tourism in a country;
* recognise why governments are becoming increasingly involved in tourism operations;
* understand the meaning of the term "social tourism" and its importance;
* show how governments in Britain and elsewhere control and supervise tourism in their country;
* explain how public sector tourism is organised in Britain.

THE ROLE OF THE STATE IN TOURISM

As we saw in Chapter 1, tourism plays an important part in a nation's economy by providing the opportunities for regional employment, contributing to the balance of payments and helping economic growth. On the other hand, countries that experience an influx of mass tourism also risk suffering socially from the consequences. For both economic and social reasons, therefore, governments take a direct interest in the development of tourism within their countries and the greater the involvement of tourism in a nation, whether incoming or outgoing, the greater is the likelihood of government intervention in the industry.

The system of government of a country will of course be reflected in the mode and extent of government intervention. At one end of the scale, centrally planned economies such as those of the Soviet bloc will exercise virtually complete control, from policy-making and planning to the building and operation of tourist facilities, the organisation of tourist movements and the promotion of tourism at home and abroad. Travellers to such countries stay in state-run hotels, travel on state-operated package tours such as those of Intourist, the Soviet travel organisation, and use publicly-owned transport throughout, whether travelling by air, rail or coach within the country. Western nations, however, are by and large mixed economies in which public and private sectors co-exist and co-operate in tourism development. Only the balance of private versus public ownership will vary. The United States' belief in a free enterprise system ensures that government control and ownership is limited to where such involvement is seen as essential for the safety and well-being of its citizens (such as air traffic control and the licensing of air routes), while promotion of the USA as a destination is left to private enterprise to a far greater extent than in any other nation.

The *system* of government is not the only factor dictating the extent of state intervention. If a country is highly dependent upon tourism for its economic survival its government is likely to become far more involved in the industry. The importance of tourism to Spain is reflected in its political structure, with a minister of state directly responsible for tourism. Tourism also figures prominently in government policy-making and planning directives.

Similarly, countries which have only recently become significant world tourism destinations, and where this sudden growth has become problematic, are likely to adopt a stronger and more centralised role in organising and controlling tourism than will other countries, for example Switzerland, where tourism, although playing an important part in the nation's economy, has developed slowly over a relatively long time.

All countries of course depend upon the provision of a sound tourism infrastructure to encourage and satisfy its tourist markets; adequate public services, roads, railways and airports must be present to generate tourist traffic. But lesser developed nations may have additional incentives for state involvement. Private developers may be reluctant to invest in speculative tourist ventures, preferring to concentrate their resources in countries where demand has already proved itself. In this case it may fall to the government to either aid private developers or to build and operate hotels and other tourist amenities itself in order to attract the initial tourists to the new destination. Where private tourism investment does take place it may be companies from the generating countries who undertake the investment, leading to the danger that profits will be repatriated rather than find their way into the local economy. Private speculators, too, may be overly concerned about achieving a quick return on their investments rather than the slow but secure long-term development that the country is looking for.

The state must also play a co-ordinating role in planning the provision of tourist amenities and attractions. Supply must match demand and the state, in its supervisory role, can ensure that facilities are available when and where required and that they are of the right standard.

Finally, as tourism grows in the economy so its organisation, if uncontrolled, can result in the domination of the market by a handful of large companies. A mixed economy state has a duty to prevent the formation of monopolies and to protect the consumer against malpractice in the industry.

Apart from economic reasons, there are also social and political reasons for government control or ownership of tourism facilities. In most countries the national airline is state-owned and operated. While of course the income accruing from the operation of this service is important to the government, the national flag-carrier carries with it political prestige. Certain routes that it operates may be unprofitable but important for the social welfare of residents, and the government may see it as its duty to maintain these routes for non-commercial reasons. Governments are also guardians of their nations' heritage. This may be threatened by the uncontrolled expansion of international tourism; beauty spots may be destroyed by over-use or commercial exploitation, for example.

We can sum up by saying that a national government's role in tourism is manifested in four ways:

(*a*) in the planning and facilitating of tourism, including the provision of financial or other aid;

(*b*) in the supervision and control of component sectors of the tourism industry;

(*c*) in direct ownership of components of the industry;

(*d*) and in the promotion of the nation and its tourist products to home and overseas markets.

Some of these aspects will now be explored below.

Planning and facilitating tourism

Any country in which tourism plays a prominent role in national income and employment can expect its government to devise policies and plans for the development of tourism. This will include the generation of guidelines and objectives for the growth and management of tourism, both in the short and the long term, and the devising of strategies designed to achieve these objectives. In recent years it has been the policy of the British government, through the British Tourist Authority, not only to increase the total numbers of tourists visiting Britain but to spread this traffic more evenly through Britain by marketing the off-season months and by encouraging tourists to visit the less familiar regions such as Northumbria. In Spain, since demand has been created for the popular east coast resorts by the private sector, the national tourist office policy has been to promote the less familiar north-west and central regions of the country in advertising aimed directly at the public abroad. Meanwhile, coastal development has become subject to increasing control.

The planning of tourism requires research, first to assess the level of demand or potential demand to the region, and secondly to estimate the resources required in order to cater for that demand and how these resources are best to be distributed. Demand cannot be generated until an adequate infrastructure and superstructure are available, but it is not enough simply to provide the structures that tourists require. They also need staff to service their needs—hotel workers, travel agents, guides—trained to an acceptable level of performance. Planning therefore implies the provision of training, through hotel, catering and tourism schools, for the skills that the industry requires.

Ease of access to a country or region is, as we have seen, a key factor in the encouragement of tourism, and this depends not only on adequate transport being available but also on the absence of political barriers. If visas are required for entry to a country this will discourage incoming tourism. The degree of difficulty and length of time required to obtain a visa bears a direct relationship to the numbers of tourists visiting that country. The proposal by the United States government to waive visas for nationals of most western European countries (introduced in 1982, but not yet adopted at the time of writing) reflects that country's awareness of the negative impact this restriction has on tourism growth, notwithstanding the volume of traffic from Britain across the Atlantic in the late 1970s and early 1980s.

The attitude of nationals of the host country to incoming tourists also plays an important role in persuading or dissuading tourists to visit a certain country. Many countries dependent upon tourism have mounted political campaigns aimed at residents, encouraging them to show greater friendliness to foreign tourists. Those residents who most frequently come into contact with tourists, such as customs and immigration officials, shopkeepers and hotel staff, must be trained to be polite and friendly to them. In the past the United States has conducted campaigns to this end directed at customs and immigration officers, and several Caribbean islands have had to mount campaigns to deal with a growing xenophobia among their residents towards foreign tourists.

One difficulty that faces governments in the planning of tourism is the split of responsibility between central and local authorities for issues affecting tourism. In Britain local authorities have direct responsibility for planning permission for all new developments, the provision of parking facilities and a host of other issues directly relevant to the development of tourism projects. Sometimes the views of local authority officials will be at odds with those of the central government. Local authorities, of course, are greatly influenced by the demands and views of local ratepayers, who are often unsympathetic to the expansion of tourism within their area.

The planning and facilitating function of the government may be delegated to the national tourist office of that country and through them to the regional or local tourist bodies, as we shall see shortly.

Financial aid for tourism

Governments also contribute to tourism growth through the provision of financial aid to tourism projects. On a massive scale, the regional development of the Languedoc-Roussillon area in the south of France demonstrates the effective co-operation that can exist between public and private sector investment, with central government providing the funds needed for land acquisition and the basic infrastructure of the region. On a smaller scale, many governments aid the private sector by providing loans at preferential rates of interest, or outright grants, for development schemes which are in keeping with government policy. As an example, a common scheme in operation in several lesser developed countries is for loans to be made on which interest only is paid during the first three or four years, with repayment of capital being postponed until the fourth year or later in order for the project to become viable. Other forms of government aid include subsidies such as tax rebates or relief on operating expenses.

Financial aid for tourist projects comes not only from within a country. International finance is available from a number of sources, particularly for those lesser developed countries where tourism has the potential to make a substantial contribution to the economy. The International Development Association (IDA)—a subsidiary of the World Bank—offers interest free or low rate loans for lesser developed countries, while another Bank subsidiary, the International Bank for Reconstruction and Development (IBRD), offers loans at commercial rates of interest to countries where alternate sources of funding may be difficult or impossible to find.

On a regional scale, within Europe the European Investment Bank (EIB) organises loans (again at commercial rates of interest) of up to £250,000 for smaller companies (normally those employing less than 500 staff). These loans are for up to 50 per cent of fixed asset costs, with repayment terms up to eight years. Interest rates are slightly lower in areas designated "Assisted Areas" within the EEC.

The European Regional Development Fund offers financial assistance (usually up to 30 per cent of the capital costs) for tourism projects generated by public sector bodies in the Assisted Areas. This money can be used not only as pump priming for direct tourist attractions such as museums, but also for infrastructure development supporting tourism, such as airports, or car parking facilities.

Financing available within Great Britain will be dealt with a little later in this chapter.

Social tourism

Reference must also be made here to the government's role in encouraging *social tourism*. This has been defined as the "furtherance of the economically weak or dependent classes of the population" and is designed to provide aid for low-income families, single parent families, the elderly, handicapped and other deprived minorities in the population. Aid may be offered in the form of finance (grants, low-interest loans or the like) or in direct support through the provision of free coach trips or holiday accommodation. The planned economies of the Soviet bloc have advanced schemes of social tourism, believing that all workers benefit from an annual holiday and that as a result will work harder and achieve higher productivity. Workers are helped (and in some cases required) to have a holiday away from their homes at least once a year.

Within Europe, the International Bureau of Social Tourism (BITS), based in Brussels, has been active since 1963 as a base for the study and debate of social tourism, and maintains a databank, issues publications and conducts seminars on the topic. Many European countries have well-established policies of aid for holidays for the handicapped (whether mentally, physically or socially). By contrast, comparatively little support has been shown in Britain for the concept of social tourism. Although many local authorities have budgeted in the past for coach outings for the elderly or other disadvantaged people, cutbacks in recent years have reduced or eradicated most of these facilities. The English Tourist Board, in a joint study with the TUC in 1975, estimated that some 70,000 people in Britain were then receiving some form of subsidised holiday. Although this report recommended greater public sector spending for the disadvantaged, little has yet been achieved. However, a number of voluntary bodies have developed in recent years to aid or facilitate travel for those with specific impediments (such as the Council for Hearing-impaired Visits and Exchanges, and the British Deaf Tourist Movement). The industry as well has shown an interest in helping the handicapped to take and enjoy their holidays, a notable example being the Holiday Care Service, funded by the tourism industry with the support of the BTA, which provides information on holidays for the handicapped.

Control and supervision in tourism

The state plays an important part in controlling and supervising tourism, as well as facilitating it. This is necessary to restrain undesirable growth, to maintain quality standards, to help match supply and demand and to protect tourists against industrial malpractice or failure.

A government can act to restrain tourism in a number of ways, whether through central directives or through local authority control. Refusal of planning permission is an obvious example of the exercise of control over tourism development. However, this is seldom totally effective since an area which is a major attraction for tourists will be unlikely to dissuade them from visiting the district simply by, say, refusing planning permission for new hotels; the result may be that overnight visitors are replaced by excursionists or that private bed and breakfast accommodation moves in to fill the gap left by the lack of hotel beds. Cornwall has had control measures on caravan sites in force since 1954 but the local authority has still found it difficult to prevent the growth of unlicensed sites. The option of failing to expand the infrastructure has been taken by some authorities. This can be partially effective, but unfortunately its effects are felt equally by local residents whose frustrations with, say, inadequate road systems may lead to a political backlash.

The price mechanism may also be used to control tourist traffic. This has the added advantage of raising revenue for the government. Selective taxation on hotel accommodation or higher charges for parking can be imposed, but these moves are criticised on the grounds that they are regressive, affecting the less well-off but having little impact on the rich.

Governments will first attempt to control growth by effective marketing, concentrating their publicity on less popular attractions or geographical regions and promoting the off-season. Attempts to do this may be frustrated by private sector promotion. Airlines, for example, will prefer to concentrate on promoting those destinations which attract strong markets. There is always the danger, too, that if the public sector strategy *is* successful, the amenities and attractions at the more popular sites may suffer a serious downturn in business. London has been the great Mecca for the majority of overseas visitors to Britain, but a recent decline in visitors to the capital has had disastrous consequences for theatres, taxis and other amenities heavily dependent upon tourist support.

To some extent, planning for the more extensive use of existing facilities can delay the need to *de-market* certain attractions or destinations, but it has to be recognised that some tourist destinations are the victims of their own success. As an extreme form of control, limiting or denying access to tourists may become necessary. This can be imposed by a visa system, by some form of rationing or by a total ban on tourist access. In areas where tourist traffic has reached saturation point, it is now common in England to find *park and ride* schemes in force, requiring visitors to leave their cars and proceed into the centre by public transport. The prehistoric cave paintings at Lascaux in France have been so damaged by the effect of countless visitors' breath changing the climate of the caves that the French government have been obliged to introduce a total ban on entry.

Sometimes governments will exercise control over tourism flows for economic reasons. As we saw in Chapter 1, governments may attempt to protect their balance of payments by imposing currency restrictions or banning the export of foreign currency in an attempt to reduce the numbers of tourists travelling abroad. The last significant control of this kind in Britain occurred in 1966 when the imposition of a £50 travel allowance severely curtailed foreign travel—although, curiously enough, it proved a boon to some package tour operators who responded to the challenge by creatively packaging tours which maximised value within the scope of the allowance. Nearly 18 per cent more British visitors travelled to the USA in 1967 than in the previous year.

Supervision and control is also exercised over the various sectors of the tourism industry. As we have seen in earlier chapters, the need to ensure passenger safety has led not only to licensing of airlines and other forms of public transport but also of tour operators themselves through the ATOL. The government's introduction of the Air Travel Reserve Fund between 1975 and 1977 was designed to protect consumers against the collapse of package holiday companies, the government of the day taking the view that existing bonding safeguards operated by ABTA were insufficient in themselves. In many countries (although not yet in the UK) travel agencies are licensed to ensure that customers receive professional service as well as to protect them against the collapse of the company. Tourist guides may also be required to have a government licence in order to operate.

Perhaps the most common form of government supervision of the tourism industry in all countries is in the hotel industry, where compulsory registration and grading is imposed in many countries. Camping and caravan sites are similarly subject to government inspection to ensure consistent standards and acceptable minimum operating requirements.

THE ORGANISATION OF PUBLIC SECTOR TOURISM

For the most part, government policies and objectives for tourism are defined and implemented through national tourist boards (although in many cases other bodies directly concerned with recreation or environmental planning will also have a hand in the development of tourism). The functional responsibilities of a national board are likely to include all or most of the following.

(a) *Planning and control functions:*
    (*i*)   product research and planning for tourism plant or facilities;
    (*ii*) protection or restoration of tourism assets;
    (*iii*) manpower planning and training;
    (*iv*) licensing and supervision of sectors of the tourism industry;
    (*v*) implementation of pricing or other regulations affecting tourism.

(b) *Marketing functions:*
    (*i*)   representing the nation as a tourism destination;
    (*ii*) undertaking market research and forecasting studies;
    (*iii*) producing and distributing tourism literature;
    (*iv*) providing and staffing tourism information centres;
    (*v*) advertising, sales promotion and public relations activities directed at home and overseas markets.

(c) *Financial functions:*
    (*i*) advising industry on capital development;
    (*ii*) directing, approving and controlling programmes of government aid for tourist projects.

(d) *Co-ordinating functions:*
    (*i*) linking with trade or professional bodies, government and regional or local tourist organisations;
    (*ii*) undertaking co-ordinated marketing activities with private tourist enterprises;
    (*iii*) organising "workshops" or similar opportunities for buyers and sellers of travel and tourism to meet and do business.

Some of these activities may be delegated to regional tourist offices, with the national board co-ordinating or overseeing activities.

PUBLIC SECTOR TOURISM IN BRITAIN

Britain has long been in the forefront of international tourism, both as a destination and as a generating country. However, before 1969 governments had largely ignored tourism in their policy-making. Forty years earlier the government of the day had provided the first finance for tourism marketing in funding the Travel Association of Great Britain and Northern Ireland, with the aim of encouraging travel to Britain from overseas. During the inter-war years this evolved into the British Travel Association, who were given the responsibility for promoting holidays in Britain domestically as well as abroad. No clear policies were laid down for its activities, however, and its powers were severely limited.

The Development of Tourism Act

By the late 1960s, following the rapid growth in popularity of Britain as a tourist destination in the 1950s and 1960s, it was clear that a new framework for tourism was needed. This was manifested in the Development of Tourism Act 1969, the first statutory legislation in the country specifically concerned with tourism.

The Act, in three parts, dealt with the organisation of public sector tourism, with the provision of financial assistance for much-needed hotel development, and also provided for a system of compulsory registration of tourist accommodation. The last part of the Act, which was designed to include rights of inspection by government officials, has never been fully implemented although the compulsory display of prices has since been introduced. The industry has preferred to follow a system of voluntary classification and grading of tourist accommodation, with mixed success; however, the implementation of the first two parts of the Act were to have far-reaching consequences for tourism in the country.

That part of the Act dealing with financial assistance for the hotel industry was designed in the short term to improve the stock and quality of hotel bedrooms in order to meet changing demand and overcome scarcity. Grants and loans, administered by the three new national tourist boards, were to be made available for hotel construction and improvement until 1973 (during which time some 55,000 bedrooms were added to the stock). Unfortunately, because the Act failed to specify the location in which new hotels were to be built, much of the increased stock was located in London, leading to temporary over-capacity in the city while areas where hotel construction was seen as a greater risk, such as Scotland and the north of England, did not benefit to anything like the extent necessary.

The first part of the Act called for the establishment of four national boards to become responsible for tourism and defined the structure and responsibilities of each of these. At the apex, the British Tourist Authority, to replace the old British Travel Association, was to be the sole body responsible overseas for the marketing of tourism to Britain and would also advise ministers on tourism matters in general. Tourism issues that concerned Britain as a whole were to be dealt with by the BTA while three further boards—the English Tourist Board, Scottish Tourist Board and Wales Tourist Board—were to become concerned with tourism development within their own regions and for the marketing of those regions within the UK. Both the British Tourist Authority and the English Tourist Board were to be responsible to the Board of Trade (now the Department of Trade and Industry), while the Scottish and Wales Tourist Boards are responsible to their respective Secretaries of State. All four bodies, funded by central government, were empowered to provide financial assistance for tourism projects.

In addition to this national structure set up by the Act, other British territories have independently approved legislation governing public sector tourism organisation, and the four British boards act alongside the Northern Ireland Tourist Board, the Isle of Man Tourist Board and the States of Jersey and Guernsey Tourist Committees.

The Act made no provision for a statutory regional public sector structure for tourism. Before the Act some attempt had been made to establish regional tourist associations, these being more advanced in Scotland and Wales than in England. However, following the formation of the three national boards each set about creating its own regional tourism structure. The result was the establishment of twelve regional tourist boards in England funded by the ETB, the local authorities and private contributions. Wales has formed three tourism councils organised along lines similar to the English regional bodies. In Scotland, area tourism promotion was formerly the responsibility of the eight regional councils, with one separate voluntary association (Dumfries and Galloway) and with tourism in the Highlands and Islands the responsibility of the statutory development board for that region. The latter Board subsequently established fifteen area tourist boards within its jurisdiction.

Under the terms of the Local Government and Planning (Scotland) Act 1982, the District Councils in Scotland were empowered to set up area tourist boards which would become responsible for marketing tourism and running the tourism information centres. The Highlands and Islands scheme has been used as a model for the extension of the scheme throughout Scotland and the new boards have been established as a co-partnership between the Scottish Tourist Board, one or more district councils and the tourist trade, with finance provided by grant aid and private contributions. Thirty-two Area Tourist Boards are now in operation in Scotland, but in three areas (Edinburgh, Kirkcaldy and Moray) the District Councils have exercised their option to retain local authority responsibility for tourism in their regions. Seven Districts, at the time of writing, are either not participating in the restructuring of tourism or have yet to make a decision.

The structure of public sector tourism bodies appears in Fig. 23, and the regional distribution of tourist boards is illustrated in Fig. 24a (England and Wales) and Fig. 24b (Scotland).

Public bodies and tourism

The new structure of public sector tourism in Britain has helped to effect great improvements in the planning and co-ordination of

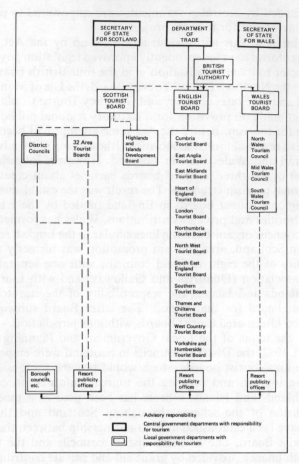

Fig. 23 *Structure and lines of responsibility of public sector tourism in Britain*

Fig. 24(a) *Regional tourist board areas in England and Wales*

Key 1. Aviemore and Spey Valley;
2. Ayrshire and Burns Country;
3. Ayrshire and Clyde Coast; 4. Ayrshire
Valleys; 5. Banff and Buchan; 6. Caith-
ness; 7. City of Aberdeen; 8. City of
Dundee; 9. Clyde Valley; 10. Dumfries
and Galloway; 11. Dunoon and Cowal;
12. East Lothian; 13. Fort Valley;
14. Fort William and Lochaber;
15. Gordon District; 16. Greater Glasgow;
17. Inverness, Lock Ness and Nairn;
18. Isle of Arran; 19. Kincardine and
Deeside; 20. Loch Lomond, Stirling and
Trossachs; 21. Mid Argyll, Kintyre and
Islay; 22. Oban, Mull and District;
23. Orkney; 24. Perthshire; 25. Ross and
Cromarty; 26. Rothesay and Isle of Bute;
27. Scottish Borders; 28. Shetland;
29. Isle of Skye and South West Ross;
30. St. Andrews and North East Fife;
31. Sutherland; 32. Outer Hebrides.

Districts still in discussion or not
participating in Area Tourist Boards (as
at July 1984). 33. Angus; 34. Cumber-
nauld and Kilsyth; 35. East Kilbride;
36. Eastwood; 37. Inverclyde; 38. Midlo-
thian; 39. Monklands;

District Councils exercising tourism
responsibility at their own hand. 40. City
of Edinburgh; 41. Kirkcaldy; 42. Moray.

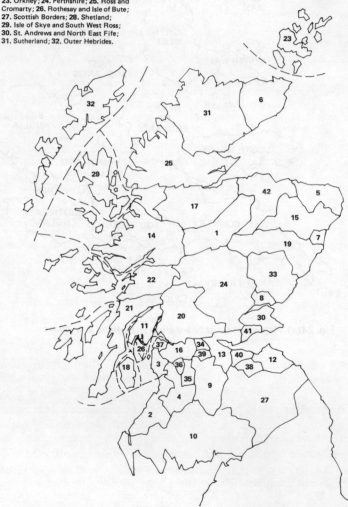

Fig. 24(*b*) *Area Tourist Boards of Scotland*

tourism, accompanied gradually by more clearcut policies. Nevertheless the diverse nature of tourism and its impact on so many different facets of British life makes cohesive planning difficult. Many public or quasi-public bodies not within the framework of public sector tourism still exert considerable influence in tourism development. The water authorities are a case in point, since water-based recreation plays an important part in leisure and tourism planning; it is interesting to see the attention that tourism has been given in the planning and development of the recently opened Kielder reservoir in Northumbria compared with the lack of foresight in the planning of earlier reservoirs. The Countryside Commission, the Forestry Commission, the Nature Conservancy Council, the Arts Council, Sports Council and National Trust all have significant roles to play in planning for leisure activities in Britain, whether for residents or tourists.

At government level, too, many different spheres of government activity overlap tourist interest. The Department of Trade and Industry is nominally charged wihh issues of concern to tourism in Britain, but the Ministry of Agriculture, to cite one example, has provided advice to farmers who want to extend their commercial activities to tourism. Co-ordination is required at government level as well as at lower levels to achieve successful planning for the future of tourism in Britain.

Local authorities and tourism

At local authority level, County Councils and District Councils have diverse statutory responsibilities and interests in the provision of tourist facilities. The Local Government Act 1948 empowered local authorities to set up information and publicity services for tourism, and this was reinforced by the Local Government Act of 1972, giving local authorities the power to encourage visitors to their area and to provide suitable facilities for them.

The organisation of tourism at local authority level is often curiously piecemeal. Counties and districts on the whole relegate responsibility for tourism to departments which are concerned with a range of other activities, with the result that it is seldom given the significance which its economic impact on the area merits. Tourism may be a function of the Planning Department, or the County Surveyor, for example, and there is little effort to develop a co-ordinated and integrated approach to tourism provision, development and marketing within the area—to the extent that tourism may not even feature in the County's structure plans, even where it forms a significant source of revenue and employment. Those with tourism responsibility are seldom recruited from the tourism industry, and training in tourism is minimal for tourist officers in the public sector. Few tourist information centre staff receive formal training for their job (although the English Tourist Board has recently focused on this problem, and training courses are now under development, including a Certificate of Tourist Information Centre Competence).

The principal responsibilities of county and district authorities which bear upon tourism are as follows:

(a) Provision of leisure facilities for tourists (e.g. conference centres) and for residents (e.g. theatres, parks, sports centres, museums).

(b) Planning (under town and country planning policies). (Note that District Councils produce local plans to fit the broad strategy of the County Council Structure Plans. These plans are certified by the County Council.)

(c) Development control powers over land use.

(d) Provision of visitor services (usually in conjunction with tourist bodies).

(e) Parking for coaches and cars.

(f) Provision of caravan sites (with licensing and management the responsibility of the District Councils).

(g) Production of statistics on tourism (for use by the Regional Tourist Boards).

(h) Marketing the area.

(i) Upkeep of historic buildings.

(j) Public health and safety control.

Local authorities may also own and operate local airports.

Unlike the Regional Tourist Boards, whose aims are essentially promotional, the local authorities bear responsibilities for the protection of the environment, and for tourism planning generally. They may consequently be as concerned to reduce or stabilise tourism as to develop it (particularly when, as is so often the case in the popular tourist resorts, local ratepayers are opposed to increases in the numbers of tourists). In providing for leisure, the authorities must be sensitive to local residents' needs as much as those of incoming tourists. They must convince ratepayers of the merits of public sector funding for tourist projects. The development of conference centres in resorts such as Bournemouth and Harrogate has been a controversial issue with local residents, since very few conference centres are economically attractive for private sector funding, and public sector investment on this scale leads to heavy increases in rates. It is hard to convince ratepayers of the wisdom of investments that are not seen to provide direct benefit to local residents. However, conferences do generate a healthy flow of indirect revenue through shopping and the use of local facilities by delegates, and the importance of this form of tourism to a resort is that it will generate tourism outside the usual holiday season.

The funding and staffing of local tourist information centres is often the joint responsibility of local authorities and Regional Tourist Boards (RTB), while the material for these centres is provided by the National and Regional Tourist Boards. Local authorities contribute directly to RTB funds, and clearly expect to play a part in the Boards' policy making; they will normally be represented on the Boards' committees or sub-committees dealing with tourism development in the region. Since representatives of the private sector, such as local hoteliers, are also members of such committees, and the latter's interests may well differ from those of the local authorities, this can lead to conflicts in the policy-making process within the RTBs.

National heritage bodies

In Chapter 1, we touched on the significance of man-made attractions for the tourism industry. In tourism within Britain, this form of tourism is particularly important, as so many overseas tourists visit Britain to see our monuments, historic homes, cathedrals and similar attractions, which are part of our national heritage.

While many individual attractions are, of course, still in private hands, or the responsibility of bodies such as the Church Commissioners, a number of semi-public or voluntary organisations exist for the protection and enhancement of our heritage attractions, and therefore exercise a direct or indirect influence in the tourism industry. The role of these bodies can be usefully examined at this point.

There are well over 12,000 listed ("scheduled") ancient monuments in England alone, of which about a quarter are in private hands. Until recently, major sites such as Stonehenge were under the control of the Department of the Environment, but the growing concern with the preservation of our heritage led to the National Heritage Act in 1983, which has established the Historic Buildings and Monuments Commission for England. This new body, which integrates the functions of the former Historic Buildings Council for England and the Ancient Monuments Board, has a dual conservation and promotion function. It intends to raise financial support from industry and the public through sponsorship of individual ancient buildings and a national membership scheme similar to the National Trust. Emphasis will be placed on interpretation and visitor management, with Stonehenge designated the first site for improvement. Initial funding is largely by central government.

Aside from this new organisation, there are a number of bodies with an interest in the protection of British heritage sites. One of the earliest to be founded was the Society for the Protection of Ancient Buildings, which dates back to 1877. Other important bodies include the Ancient Monuments Society, the Georgian Group, The Victorian Society, the National Piers Society and SAVE Britain's Heritage. To these we must add a number of diverse trusts with an interest in the protection of sites of touristic appeal, among which are the Civic Trust, the Landmark Trust, the Pilgrim Trust, the Monument Trust and many others. (Over one thousand local amenity societies are known to exist in England.) The proliferation of these conservation bodies reflects the changing attitudes towards our architectural heritage. The emphasis on preserving our industrial archaeology sites (so successfully achieved at Ironbridge and Coalbrookdale), the success of Bradford in exploiting its tourism potential through the restoration of its woollen mills, the restoration and opening to the public of Whitehall's Cabinet War Rooms in 1984, recognition of the new Thames Barrier at Woolwich as a tourist attraction in its own right, and finally the promotion of "Heritage Trails" enabling tourists to follow an independent walk around a city's major heritage attractions; all these reflect the impetus which the public sector has given to tourism development in Britain.

Town twinning and tourism

A further boost has been given to international tourism, particularly within Europe, by the town twinning movement. The concept of town twinning developed largely in the aftermath of World War II as a means of forging greater understanding between communities in different countries. Usually the selection of a twin town is based on some common characteristics such as population size, geographical features or commercial similarities. Local authorities and chambers of commerce arrange for the exchange of visits by residents of the twinned towns. Although conceived as a gesture of friendship and goodwill, the outcome has commercial implications for tourism as an increasing number of visitors flows between the two towns. While accommodation is normally provided in private homes, expenditure on transport, shopping and sightseeing can make a significant impact on the inflow of tourist revenue for the towns concerned. Friendships formed through such links result in subsequent independent travel by residents. No accurate studies have yet been made of the financial contribution of such movements to the tourism account.

FUNCTIONS OF THE TOURIST BOARDS

The British Tourist Authority

As we have seen the Development of Tourism Act empowered the BTA to promote tourism to Britain in overseas countries. With the agreement of the respective territories they will also undertake foreign promotion on behalf of the tourist boards of Northern Ireland, the Isle of Man and the Channel Islands. With general responsibility for tourism throughout Great Britain, they act as advisers to the government on tourism issues, and are financed by an annual grant-in-aid from the government.

With a staff of some 500, of which 200 are based in offices overseas, the BTA carries out research, liaises with other national tourism bodies in the UK and encourages organisations abroad to promote tourism to Britain. A notable example of their work entails the mounting of "travel workshops" which bring together the buyers and sellers of travel services. These workshops are held in Britain or in major centres in the tourism generating countries and they enable coach companies, hotel chains and consortia, tour operators and similar organisations to negotiate face to face with foreign organisations responsible for bringing tourists to this country.

Abroad, the BTA provides an information service through more than twenty offices throughout the world. They offer marketing advice to UK companies eager to tap foreign markets and will circulate overseas agents and buyers with details of new tour packages to or within the UK. In the past they have also given financial support to commercial enterprises trying to break into overseas markets, providing that these projects meet the Board's own objectives, e.g. helping to generate off-season sales.

At home in London the BTA has a Central Information Department, a tourist information library and a research library available to subscribers. The Authority publishes a large selection of promotional literature in English and major foreign languages, including the well-known publication *In Britain*. Other material includes travel guides, maps, public relations material for the mass media and shell folders for the use of overseas tour operators. Their film and photographic library will also lend out slides and photos for use in tour operators' brochures. Finally, the Authority can arrange to distribute brochures commercially on behalf of travel companies in the UK.

The English, Wales and Scottish Tourist Boards

The example given here is that of the English Tourist Board, but the other two boards operate along similar lines.

Under the 1969 Act the ETB was given the brief to attract tourists from other parts of Britain and to encourage the growth of domestic tourism within England. The Board also has the responsibility to encourage the provision and improvement of tourism plant in England by advice and, where appropriate, by financial assistance. Until 1982 such financial aid was to be made available only within Economic Development Areas, but government policy has now changed to allow the boards wider scope and assistance can now be offered for the first time in the south of England where seaside resorts in particular are facing strong competition from overseas resorts for a share of the British holiday market.

Like the BTA, the English Tourist Board is financed by a grant-in-aid from the central government. This helps to fund over 400 tourist centres in England which are operated in conjunction with the regional tourist boards. Tourism information centres (TICs) are categorised in three levels of importance: the smallest provide only local information; medium-sized offices cover the entire region; and the largest provide national as well as regional material and information. A Central Information Unit in London provides information to the media and the general public.

Other services include a Resource Development Service and a Planning and Research Unit which carries out surveys within England nationally (*British Home Tourism Survey* and *Holiday Intention Survey*) and regionally, producing a comprehensive set of statistics on the performance and growth of tourism within the country.

The Board's development service plays an important role as go-between in generating new tourism projects in England. As well as offering advice to local authorities, the Regional Boards and the private sector, it can directly aid the financing of suitable new projects, and facilitate access to tourism investors. It also acts as an agent of the European Investment Bank, which provides medium-term loans for projects in the designated Assisted Areas. The Board offers its services on a consultancy basis, and will aid companies undertaking feasibility studies or seeking planning approval through local authorities (although commercial fees will be charged for such services).

At the instigation of the ETB, a new company, Leisure Development, has recently been formed, backed by private sector funds, to invest in the leisure industry. Initial investment is focusing on health hydros and fitness centres, dance studios, country clubs and holiday villages, hotels and timeshare properties, and theme restaurants. Although the ETB's role here is primarily supportive, it represents a new departure for a national board, and reflects the Board's interest in leisure and recreation as an aspect of the tourism business.

Since the inception in 1971 of a scheme to provide direct financial aid for tourism projects in England, some 2,000 such projects have benefited from ETB funds. These have been in the form of loans or, more often, grants; and in 1980, an interest-relief grant scheme was introduced, again aimed at projects in the Assisted Areas.

Until 1982, all such funds were restricted to tourism schemes in the Assisted Areas, but since then aid has been made available for any projects identified as being in "areas of tourism need". The criteria for ETB aid is currently that:

(a) Capital expenditure must be involved.

(b) Approval for aid must be obtained before any work starts on the project.

(c) The project should create employment, and attract more tourists from abroad and from within the UK, while at the same time increasing tourist expenditure.

(d) Facilities to be aided must be accessible to all members of the public.

(e) There must be evidence that the project actually needs tourist board support to get launched.

Aid is typically between 25-30 per cent of the total capital cost of the project, but will at no time exceed 49 per cent. While the ETB relies on the screening process of the regional boards to select suitable applicants, it is keen to support the improvement of existing facilities such as farmhouse accommodation, the addition of bathrooms or central heating to hotels, and similar schemes which will help to extend the tourist season. Museums and art galleries, theatres, wildlife sanctuaries and similar schemes stand good prospects of being approved because they are often unlikely to be economically viable without grant aid of this kind. The Board is also keen to aid support services such as information centres, signposting and car park provision.

On the marketing side, the ETB produces its own publications for the trade and public, and engages in promotional activities such as the successful "*Maritime England*" theme launched in 1982, national floral schemes, and the 1985 "*England Entertains*" theme which highlights the role in tourism played by theatres, concerts and similar attractions. The marketing policy of the Board is changing in order to lay increasing emphasis on their roles of planning, co-ordinating and facilitating promotions within the twelve regions.

A recent development supported by the ETB has been the instant booking scheme arranged between members of the British Resorts Association (BRA) and ABTA which has enabled certain key seaside resorts to be marketed in their major generating centres such as Leicester and Manchester. This commercial departure, introduced in 1981, points in the direction of greater public sector involvement in the direct marketing of domestic tourism.

The regional tourist boards

Again the example given here is that of the English boards which were set up by the English Tourist Board and which are funded jointly by the Board, local authorities and contributions from the commercial sector (although funding from the latter source has seldom reached the levels initially hoped for by the ETB).

The objectives of the regional tourist boards are:

(*a*) to produce a co-ordinated strategy for tourism within their regions in liaison with the local authority;

(*b*) to represent the interests of the region at national level and the interests of the tourist industry within the region;

(*c*) to encourage the development of tourist amenities and facilities which meet the changing needs of the market;

(*d*) and to market the region by providing reception and information services (in concert with the ETB), producing and supplying suitable literature and undertaking miscellaneous promotional activities.

Typically, an RTB will work with a very small staff of perhaps ten to fifteen members (an important exception to this guideline is the London Tourist Board which, because of its importance in international tourism and its key information function, will operate with much larger staff, especially during the summer season). Coordination between the RTB, local authorities and the tourist trade will be through policy-making panels, or committees, as exemplified below:

Development panel	*Publicity and promotions panel*
County Council officers	Resort officers
District Council officers	RTB members
RTB members	Local trade members
Local trade members	

As with the national boards, policies have changed in recent years and now greater emphasis is being laid on commercial activities (such as providing an accommodation booking service for a fee to tourists). Certain of the RTBs have also moved into the field of training by validating tourist guide courses within their regions.

Although the ETB controls the allocation of funds for financial assistance for tourist projects in England, the task of processing applications has been delegated to the regional boards who screen all applications and make their recommendations to the national board. The regional boards have shown themselves to be keen to support smaller tourist ventures which would probably be commercially non-viable without government assistance, e.g. museums, art galleries, theatres, historic buildings, and accommodation facilities in areas where demand is small or the season is short.

The RTBs have a particularly difficult role in their relations with their local authorities. They must work with these authorities and co-operate with them in tourism planning but their aims may be in conflict with those of the local authority, which is often apathetic or negative towards the growth of tourism in their area. Moreover, the local authorities are charged with certain functions which have a direct bearing on tourism, as we have seen. Local authorities can hinder the expansion of tourism by refusing planning permission, although on the other hand they play an important role in preserving the countryside and coastal areas of their regions. Those noted as tourist centres will operate resort publicity bureaux which must co-operate with the RTBs for the successful promotion of their resorts.

To produce a co-ordinated strategy for the promotion of tourism in the face of the diverse interests of the local authorities and the tourist boards is no easy matter.

Co-operative marketing organisations

We have seen how private and public sector interests can differ in tourism, the common lack of co-ordinating tourism policy and the areas of potential conflict which can arise within the public sector. In an attempt to overcome some of the problems arising from this piecemeal approach to tourism development and promotion, several areas have now opted for the formation of a marketing board (or bureau) made up of representatives from both the public and private sector interests. Plymouth was the first city to launch a joint venture of this nature in 1977. The city's marketing bureau is run by six members nominated by the city council, and nine members elected by the private sector. The bureau is financed by a grant-in-aid from the city council, by membership subscriptions and by commercial activities. Similar ventures have since been established at Chester, Birmingham (Convention and Visitors'

Bureau) and Bristol. A number of other cities are looking to judge the success or otherwise of this joint approach to destination marketing as an effective alternative to the traditional separate promotion initiatives.

The role of the European economic community

Britain has chosen largely to allow the free market economy to operate in the tourism field, with little attempt at centralised policy-making by contrast with other nations where tourism is an equally important component in the economy. However, the impact of EEC membership is beginning to be felt by the tourism industry. As we have seen in Chapter 11, tax on imported goods within the EEC is now affecting intra-community travellers, and there have been fears that ultimately duty-free shopping will be similarly affected within the EEC. This, it is claimed, would lead to substantial increases in the cost of transport for EEC travellers, with airline fares rising perhaps 5–10 per cent, and ferry fares increasing by as much as 30 per cent.

While such a development is still speculative at the time of writing, two major developments within the EEC will have a major impact on the tourism scene in Britain within the next few years.

Firstly, in 1984, a standard classification of hotels was introduced in the Benelux countries (Holland, Belgium and Luxembourg), and the EEC plans to lobby for the extension of this compulsory classification scheme to all ten members of the community. Earlier, we saw how the UK government has on several occasions contemplated the introduction of a compulsory hotel classification scheme, but rejected it as unworkable. If the Benelux scheme becomes the standard for the EEC, hotels in Britain will be under obligation to introduce it, too. Secondly, some form of travel agency licensing is also likely to be introduced by the EEC in the near future. Presently, Britain is one of only two members of the Community without such a licensing system in force, and EEC legislation is expected by 1986. This will have important implications for the future of professional training and education standards in the industry.

SELF-ASSESSMENT QUESTIONS

1. Why do you think Britain does not yet have a minister of tourism?

2. How might the British government, directly or through local authorities, control excess demand for holidays during the peak summer season in south-west England?

3. Why do you think governments are reluctant to impose limitations on travel allowances for their citizens in order to improve their balance of payments position?

4. How does the British government financially aid tourism projects and how is this scheme administered?

5. True or false? (a) The Development of Tourism Act 1969 was the first statutory legislation concerned with tourism in Britain. (b) Social tourism now plays a prominent part in the British government's policy on tourism. (c) Travel agents do not yet have to hold a licence to operate in Britain. (d) The Scottish, Wales and English Tourist Boards are responsible to the Department of Trade.

ASSIGNMENT

Taking any two countries with dissimilar political systems and with substantial numbers of incoming tourists, compare and contrast the structure and organisation of public sector tourism in each and explain why each has developed in the way it has.

CHAPTER THIRTEEN

The Impact of Tourism

CHAPTER OBJECTIVES

After studying this chapter, you should be able to:

* identify and assess tourism's impact on the economy of an area;
* understand the concept of the multiplier and its applications in tourism;
* be aware of the environmental effects of tourism development;
* understand the sociocultural effects created by mass tourism;
* understand the necessity for planning in tourism and be aware of current moves to conserve the environment;
* analyse the likely effects of change on the future of tourism.

This final chapter will examine the consequences of tourism for an environment and for the people living in that environment. The rapid growth of tourism in the twentieth century has produced both problems and opportunities on a vast scale for societies, and its impact has been economic, sociocultural, environmental and political. Governments have become aware that tourism is not merely a useful means of adding to a nation's wealth but also brings with it serious long-term problems which, without careful control and planning, can escalate to a point where they threaten the society.

The effects of tourism will be examined separately. First we will look at the economic effects and then go on to discuss the social and environmental effects.

THE ECONOMIC EFFECTS OF TOURISM

Like any other industry, tourism affects the economy of those areas in which it takes place. This effect may be important merely in a single place, such as a resort in a country otherwise untapped for tourism, in a region, or even throughout the entire national economy. Whatever the size of the area affected, we can generally categorise the economic effects of tourism into four groups; the effects on income, on employment, on the area's balance of payments with the outside world, and on investment and development.

Income

The creation of income from tourism is closely bound up with employment. Income in general comes from wages and salaries, interest, rent and profits. In a labour-intensive industry such as tourism the greatest proportion is likely to be in wages and salaries. Income is created most directly in areas with a buoyant level of tourism, labour-intensive accommodation such as hotels, and with a large number of attractions and ground-handling arrangements available. The higher the amount of labour employed the greater the income generated.

Income is greatest where wage levels are high, which implies that there are also other high-wage job opportunities and little unemployment in the area. However, tourism may be of *relatively* greater value in areas where there are few other jobs and workers may be otherwise unemployed. In Britain, tourism is significant in many regions where there is little other industry, such as in the Scottish Highlands, western Wales and Cornwall. The tourism industry is often criticised for offering low wages but in these areas there may be no alternative jobs available.

Income is also generated from interest, rent and profits on tourism businesses, which might range from the interest paid on loans to an airline in order to buy aircraft to rent paid to a landowner for a car park or campsite near the sea. We must also include taxation on tourism activities, such as VAT on hotel bills or direct taxation which some countries or regions impose on tourism to raise additional public income. In Austria, for example, there is a *Kurtaxe* imposed on accommodation to raise money for the local authority, while in the United States a *departure tax* has recently been imposed by the federal government on all international travel.

The sum of all incomes in a country is called the national income and the importance of tourism to a country's economy can be measured by looking at the proportion of national income created by tourism. In Britain this is estimated to be about 4 per cent, including income from accommodation, tourist transport and all kinds of "extras" for which tourists pay. This may seem small, but even engineering, the country's largest industry, only contributes about 8 per cent to the national income. By contrast, tourism in Barbados contributes over 30 per cent to its national income—some would say this denotes a rather unhealthy over-dependence upon one single industry.

Tourism's contribution to the income of an area is in fact rather greater than has been so far apparent owing to the phenomenon of the tourism income multiplier (TIM). Multipliers are well-known to economists as a means of estimating how much *extra* income is produced in an economy as a result of the initial spending or *injection* of cash. Let us use an example to illustrate the TIM at work.

Example

Tourists visit area X and spend £1,000 in hotels and on amenities there. This is received as income by hoteliers and amenity owners. These then pay tax, save some of their income and spend the rest. Some of what they spend goes to buy items imported into area X but the rest goes to shopkeepers, suppliers and other producers inside area X. These in turn pay taxes, save and spend.

Suppose that the average tax rate is 20p in the £, that people save on average 10p in the £ of their gross income and spend two-sevenths of their spending, or *consumption*, on imports. The £1,000 spent by tourists will then circulate as shown in Fig. 25.

Money is circulating as hoteliers spend on local supplies such as food. The suppliers of this food then pay their workers who in turn shop in local shops. Local shop workers in turn shop at other shops with the money they earn and so the cycle goes on. Some money has, of course, not circulated but has gone to pay tax, has been saved or has paid for imports; these are called *leakages* from the system.

So far, how much income has been created? From Fig. 25 we can see it is £1,000 + £500 + £250 + £125 + ... A progression is developing and by adding up all the figures or by using the appropriate mathematical formula the total will be seen to be £2,000. The original

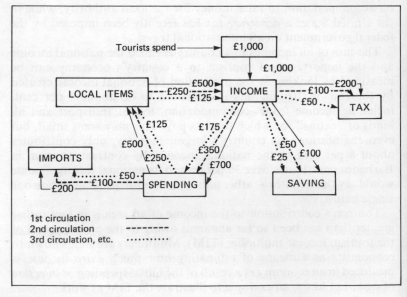

Fig. 25 *The tourism income multiplier at work*

injection of £1,000 by tourists coming into area X has been multiplied by a factor of 2 to produce income of £2,000.

It is possible to forecast the value of the multiplier if one knows the proportion of leakages in the economy. In the example above tax was 20/100ths of original income, savings were 10/100ths of income and imports were 20/100ths of income. Total leakages therefore amount to 50/100ths, or a half of the original income. The multiplier can be found by applying the simple formula:

$$\text{Multiplier} = \frac{1}{\text{Proportion of leakages}}.$$

In the example given the multiplier was $1/\frac{1}{2}$, or 2.

So in an economy with a high proportion of leakages, such as high tax rates (although we must remember that the government may re-spend this money in the economy) or high import levels, TIM is rather low and tourism does not stimulate the local economy very much. On the other hand, with a low proportion of leakages, TIM will be high and tourism may in total contribute a great deal more income than that originally spent by the tourists themselves.

Many TIM studies have been undertaken, from single resorts such as Edinburgh or Eastbourne to entire countries such as Pakistan or Fiji. In general the value of the TIM has been found to range between about 1 and $2\frac{1}{2}$.

Employment

As well as income, tourism creates employment. Some jobs are found in travel agencies, tour operators and other intermediaries supplying services in the generating areas, but the bulk of jobs are created in the tourist destinations themselves, ranging from hotel staff to deck-chair attendants, from excursion booking clerks to cleaners in the stately homes open to the public.

A very large number of these jobs are seasonal so that tourism's contribution to full-time employment is considerably less than its contribution to "job-hours". Whilst this is a criticism of the industry in economic terms, and one that has resulted in many millions of pounds being spent in an attempt to lengthen the tourist season, once again one must remember that many of these jobs are being created in areas where there would be few alternative employment opportunities. Tourism is therefore relatively beneficial.

The multiplier which works for income also does the same for employment. If tourists stay at a destination, jobs are directly created in the tourism industry there. These workers and their families require their own goods, services, education and so on, giving rise to further indirectly created employment in shops, pubs, schools, hospitals. The value of the employment multiplier is likely to be similar to that of the TIM, assuming that jobs with average wage rates are created.

Recent developments in technology have tended to reduce labour requirements in the tourism generating areas. For example, computer reservations systems reduce the need for booking clerks by tour operators, airlines and group hotel owners. In destinations, however, the nature of the industry requires a high degree of personal service, which means that less jobs have been lost through technological change.

Balance of payments

In a national context tourism may have a major influence on a country's balance of payments. International tourists are generally buying services from another country and are therefore paying for "invisibles". Thus if a British resident goes on holiday to Spain there is an invisible payment on Britain's balance, and if an American tourist visits Britain, Britain's balance gets an invisible receipt. The total value of receipts minus payments during a year is the *balance of payments on the tourism account*. This is part of the country's whole *invisible* balance, which will include transport, banking, insurance and similar services.

Throughout the 1970s Britain enjoyed a surplus on its tourism balance, reaching a peak of £1,166 million in 1977, the year of the Queen's Silver Jubilee. Since then, however, spending by British tourists going abroad has increased faster than receipts by Britain from incoming tourists, so that there is now a net deficit (see Fig. 26).

Most countries appreciate the contribution that incoming tourism can make to their balance of payments account, particularly those countries with good tourism facilities but little other industrial or agricultural export potential. They therefore take steps through their national tourist offices to maximise their tourist receipts. The contribution of tourism receipts to total balance of payments receipts in Britain is around 6 per cent. Compare this with Barbados, where tourism contributes 34 per cent to the total balance, Fiji where it contributes 25 per cent, or Spain where it contributes 24 per cent.

Whilst incoming tourists in various countries are actively encouraged by the development of new attractions, promotions, specially subsidised exchange rates and other measures, most governments also try to keep their own residents within the country, either by promotions, taxation on outgoing tourists, limitation on foreign exchange availability, or refusal to grant exit permits (as in many Communist countries). These attempts to make tourists buy the

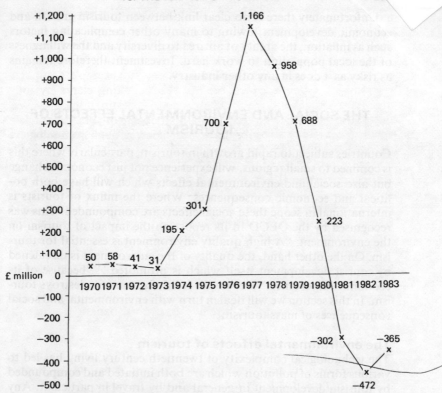

Fig. 26 Britain's balance of payments on the tourism account, 1970–83

domestic product instead of going abroad are a form of import substitution.

Investment and development

Once good business and income levels have been generated in an area, because of its success businessmen and government agencies may be influenced to invest even more in that area. This is known by economists as an *accelerator* concept. Thus if tourism to area X booms and the value of TIM is high, rapid expansion may lead to yet more investment in both tourism and other industries. Some parts of Spain which started to earn money from tourism during the 1960s have been successful in this way, attracting both new tourism developments and other industries keen to develop in an economically successful area. Other countries have sought to emulate this kind of development by providing the initial boost to tourism. Examples may be seen in Hawaii, Tunisia and the Languedoc-Roussillon area of France.

Unfortunately there is no clear link between tourism growth and economic development, owing to many other complicating factors such as inflation, the ability of an area to diversify and the willingness of the local population to work hard. Investment therefore remains as risky as it does in any other industry.

THE SOCIAL AND ENVIRONMENTAL EFFECTS OF TOURISM

Countries subject to rapid growth in tourism, particularly where this is confined to small regions, will experience not just economic change but also social and environmental effects which will have both political and economic consequences. Where the influx of tourists is international in scope these social effects are compounded. This was recognised by the OECD in its report on the impact of tourism on the environment: "A high quality environment is essential for tourism. On the other hand, the quality of the environment is threatened by tourist development itself which is promoted ... because of its economic importance." Or, to put it briefly, tourism destroys tourism. In this section we will deal in turn with environmental and social consequences of mass tourism.

The environmental effects of tourism
The technological complexity of twentieth century living has led to various forms of pollution which are both initiated and compounded by tourism development in general and by travel in particular. Any large-scale tourist movement increases air pollution from jet aircraft, car and pleasure-boat exhaust fumes. All three forms of travel can contribute to unacceptable levels of noise in rural surroundings, and the over-use of motor boats in water recreation can damage the environment both by polluting the water and by the effects of constant "wash" eroding river banks (this is very noticeable on the Norfolk Broads, which are used by more than 10,000 pleasure craft during the summer season).

Perhaps the most immediately apparent form of environmental "pollution" is aesthetic rather than physical. As an area of scenic beauty attracts greater numbers of tourists, so the national landscape is lost to tourist development. The scenic countryside retreats before the growth of hotels, restaurants and other amenities catering for tourists' needs, while individual tourist attractions such as stately homes can, without careful control, suffer the consequences of providing for tourists' needs in terms of catering and toilet facilities and parking for coaches or private cars. A proliferation of directional signs or promotional material can reduce the visual appeal of a resort; at its extreme this is exemplified by some of the tourist resorts of the United States (although some might argue that in the case of towns such as Reno or Las Vegas, in Nevada, the forest of illuminated signs dominating the downtown districts at night are an important element of the attraction itself).

Again, lack of foresight in planning leads to a loss of harmony and scale in the construction of new buildings for tourists. The skyscraper hotel syndrome is ubiquitous, from Hawaii to Benidorm, and has led to a conformity of architectural style owing nothing to the culture or traditions of the country concerned.

Thoughtless tourists contribute to visual pollution by littering in areas such as picnic sites and by desecrating monuments with graffiti; Stonehenge is now no longer directly accessible to the public because of vandalism to the stones by scratching and the use of aerosol spray paints.

A further problem of mass tourism is that created by congestion. The subject of congestion can be considered in three ways. There is first the question of the *physical* capacity of an attraction to absorb tourists; car parks, streets, beaches, ski slopes, cathedrals and similar features all have a finite limit to the numbers of tourists that can be accommodated at any given time. However, a second consideration is the *psychological* capacity of a site—the degree of congestion which tourists will tolerate before the site begins to lose its appeal. Quantifying this is no easy matter since perception of capacity will differ, not just according to the nature of the site itself but according to the market which it attracts. A beach in, say, Bermuda will be seen as overcrowded much more readily than in, say, Bournemouth, while in a resort such as Blackpool trippers may tolerate a still higher level of crowding.

In so-called *wilderness* areas, of course, the psychological capacity of the region may be very low. From the viewpoint of hikers, areas such as the Derbyshire Peak District may not support more than a handful of tourists per square kilometre, although the mass influx to its major centres such as Dovedale on August Bank Holiday does not appear to deter the day trippers from the region. Indeed, it has been demonstrated in the case of Cannock Chase, near Birmingham, that this area of natural beauty draws tourists from the Midlands as much for its role as a social meeting place as for its scenic attraction.

The behaviour of tourists at wilderness sites will be a factor in deciding their psychological capacity. Many trippers to an isolated area will tend to stay close to their cars, and hikers who are prepared to walk a few miles from the car parks will soon discover the solitude they seek. This is obviously a key for tourism planners since by restricting car parking and access by vehicle in the more remote areas they can maintain the solitude of a region.

A third capacity is *ecological* in nature—the ability of a region to absorb tourists without destroying the balance of nature. Open sites will suffer from the wear and tear of countless feet, particularly in fragile ecosystems such as sand dunes. Many dunes have been destroyed or seriously eroded in the United States by the use of beach buggies and in the UK by motor cycle rallying. Footpaths in areas such as Snowdonia in Wales have been eroded by over-use, soil being loosened by the action of walkers' feet and subsequently lost through wind erosion. In other cases soil has been impacted by walkers, making it difficult for vegetation to grow. Man-made sites have been similarly affected; the Acropolis in Athens has had to be partially closed to tourists to avoid wear and tear on the ancient buildings, while sites like Shakespeare's birthplace at Stratford-upon-Avon or Beaulieu Palace suffer similar wear from the countless footsteps crossing the floors and staircases of the building.

The ecological balance of a region can also be affected by "souvenir-collecting" by visitors. The removal of plants has given rise to concern in many areas of the world, and not only where rare plants are concerned. In Arizona visitors taking home cacti are affecting the ecology of the desert regions, while the removal of coral, either for souvenirs collected by the public or for commercial sale by tourist enterprises, threatens some coastal regions of Australia and elsewhere.

The sociocultural effects of tourism

The cultural and social impact on a host country of large numbers of people, sharing different value systems and away from the constraints of their own environment, is a subject being given increasing attention by social scientists and by the planners responsible for tourism development in third world countries. The impact is most noticeable in the lesser developed countries, but is by no means restricted to these; tourism has contributed to an increase in crime and other social problems in New York and London, in Hawaii and Miami, in Florence and on the French Riviera.

Any influx of tourists, however small, will make some impact on a region, but the extent of the impact is dependent not just upon numbers but on the kind of tourists which a region attracts. The *explorer*, or tourist whose main interest is to meet and to understand people from different cultures and backgrounds, will fully accept and acclimatise to the foreign culture. Such travellers will try to travel independently and be as little *visible* as possible. However, as increasingly remote regions of the world are "packaged" for wealthy tourists and as ever-larger numbers of tourists travel farther afield to find relaxation or adventure, these tourists bring their own value systems with them, either expecting or demanding the life-style and facilities they are accustomed to in their own countries.

At its simplest and most direct this flow of comparatively wealthy tourists to a region has the effect of attracting petty criminals, as is evidenced by increases in thefts or muggings—a problem that has become serious in some countries of the Mediterranean, Caribbean and Latin America. The tourist may be seen as easy prey to be overcharged for purchases; London has recently been pinpointed as just such an area, with street vendors exploiting tourists in the sales of ice-cream and other commodities. Where gambling is a cornerstone of tourism growth, prostitution and organised crime often follows.

There are also a number of less direct, and perhaps less visible, effects on the tourist localities. The comparative wealth of tourists may be resented or envied by the locals, particularly where the influx is seen by the latter as a form of neo-colonialism as in the Caribbean islands or east African countries. Locals may come to experience increasing dissatisfaction with their own standards of living or way of life and seek to emulate the tourists. In some cases the effect will be marginal, such as the adoption of the tourists' dress or fashion, but in others the desire to adopt the values of visitors may be sufficiently extreme as to threaten the deep-seated traditions of the community.

Job opportunities and higher salaries attract workers from agricultural and rural communities who, freed from the restriction of their family and the familiarity of their home environment, may abandon their traditional values. One result of this is an increase in the breakdown of marriages and in divorce.

The problem of interaction between hosts and tourists is that any relationships which develop are essentially transitory. A tourist visiting a new country for the first time, and who may be spending not more than a week or two in that country, has to condense his experiences such that they become brief and superficial. Add to this his initial fear of contact with locals and his comparative isolation from them—hotels are often dispersed well away from centres of local activity—and opportunities for meaningful relationships become very limited. Nor are most such relationships spontaneous; contact is likely to be made largely with locals who work within the tourist industry or else it is mediated by couriers. Language may form an impenetrable barrier to genuine local contact and this limitation may lead to mutual misunderstanding. The relationship is further unbalanced by the inequality of tourist and host, not just in wealth; the tourist is on holiday, while most locals he comes into contact with will be at work which will often involve the host being paid to serve the needs of the tourist.

One must also remember that while the tourist's contact is fleeting, locals are in continuous contact with them throughout the season, which will affect their attitudes in their dealings with them.

With the constraints of time and place, the tourist demands *instant culture*. The result is what Dean MacCannell (*see* Bibliography) has termed *staged authenticity* in which the search by tourists for authentic experiences of another culture leads to that country either providing those experiences or staging them to make them appear as real as possible. Culture thus becomes commercialised and trivialised, as when "authentic" folk dances are staged for package tourists as a form of cabaret in hotels or tribal dances are arranged specifically for groups of tourists on an excursion. This trivialisation is exemplified in London by proposals in some quarters that the Changing of the Guard might be mounted more frequently each day to give a greater number of tourists the opportunity of viewing it!

Tourists will seek out local restaurants not frequented by other tourists in order to enjoy the authentic cuisine and environment of the locals, but by the very act of their discovering such restaurants these then become tourist attractions and ultimately "tourist traps" which cater for an increasing number of tourists, while the locals move on to find somewhere else to eat.

Tourists seek local artefacts as souvenirs or investments. In cases where genuine works are purchased this can lead to the loss of cultural treasures from a country. However, the tourist is often satisfied with purchasing what he believes to be an authentic example of typical local art, and this has led to the mass production of poorly crafted works (sometimes referred to as *airport art*), common in the African nations, or to the freezing of art styles in pseudo-traditional forms, as with the "mediaeval" painted wooden statues to be found in Oberammergau or other German tourist towns.

It is perhaps too easy to take a purist stance in criticising these developments. One must also point to the evident benefits which tourism has brought to the culture of many foreign countries, leading not only to locals widening their horizons but also to a regeneration in awareness and pride in their culture and traditions among the population. But for the advent of tourism many of these traditions would have undoubtedly died out. It is easy to ascribe cultural decline to the impact of tourism, whereas it is likely to be as much a factor of increasing technology and mass communication and the dominant influence of western culture on the third world. In many cases tourism has led to the revival of interest in tribal customs in lesser developed countries (and not just in these lands—the revival of Morris dancing in English rural communities owes much to tourism, as the national tourist boards have been quick to recognise, and the boards have also done much to renew interest in traditional local cuisine with their "Taste of England", "Taste of Scotland" and "Taste of Wales" schemes). Dying local arts and crafts have been regenerated and the growth of cottage industries catering for tourist demand has done much to benefit the economies of depressed regions.

Planning for conservation

The idea of the management of tourist attractions and their protection from the impact of mass tourism is not new; as early as 1872, the United States established the first of its national parks at Yellowstone, and in Britain growing concern over the possible despoliation of the Lake District led to the formation of a defence society in 1883 to protect the region from commercial exploitation. The National Trust was also founded in the nineteenth century, to safeguard places of "historic interest and natural beauty". They promptly bought $4\frac{1}{2}$ acres of clifftop in Cardigan Bay and have added over a half million acres, together with over 150 stately homes, castles, villages, farms, churches and gardens.

There are now ten national parks in Britain (*see* Fig. 27), established under the National Parks and Access to the Countryside Act 1949. This Act also led to the designation of twenty-seven areas (nearly 8 per cent of the area of England and Wales) as "areas of outstanding beauty" meriting protection against inconsiderate exploitation.

Since then there have been numerous moves by government and private bodies designed to protect features of historical or architectural interest and areas of scenic beauty from over-development, whether from tourism or from other commercial interests. Abroad, too, Mediterranean and third world countries have awoken to the dangers of too rapid or uncontrolled development of tourism.

Planning, whether central or regional, is essential to avoid the inevitable conflicts arising between public and private sectors. Private enterprise, unrestricted, will seek to maximise its profits and this can often best be achieved by catering for high demand where this already exists rather than developing tourism in new regions. Airlines will find it more profitable to fill their services to London rather than encourage traffic to provincial cities, and hotels in a boom resort, seeking fast returns on their capital investment, will build large and comparatively cheap properties rather than concentrate on quality and design which will add to costs. Of course, it would be wrong to suggest

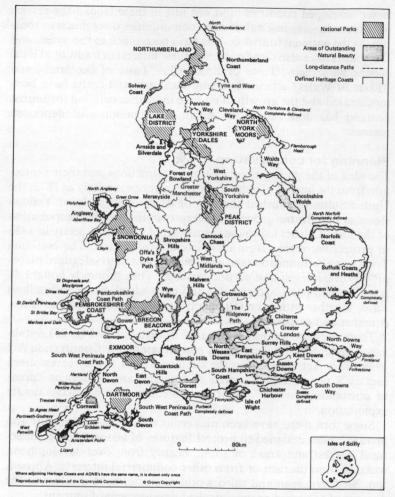

Fig. 27 *The national parks of England and Wales*

that this will always occur—other organisations will see the market gaps left for better quality development—but without some form of central control to ensure good design and careful restoration of old buildings the original attraction of a traditional resort can be lost.

Local authorities can sometimes be a partner in this despoliation too, putting commercial advantage before aesthetic considerations; here central government needs to exercise final control. This can be done through building restrictions in designated areas, and through positive measures such as grants either to encourage sympathetically designed projects in keeping with the environment or to encourage development in specified areas. Although the original scheme has since been curtailed, Britain had designated certain "growth points for tourism" which were intended to concentrate future tourism development in areas of potential while relieving the pressure on other rural areas.

Countries with a long history of evolutionary tourism development such as Austria and Switzerland have successfully expanded tourism without destroying their environment, while Spain, whose tourism boom was more recent and sudden, experienced massive over-development along its shorelines on the east coast and in the popular Balearic islands until the government stepped in to arrest this exploitation. Countries on the brink of mass tourism, such as Mauritius and certain Caribbean islands, have adopted a more cautious approach from the outset; close government restrictions on hotel construction in Mauritius, for example, have led to tasteful developments of single- or two-storey buildings constructed in traditional local materials and in traditional architectural styles.

Government policies to attract larger numbers of tourists have given way to policies designed to attract particular tourist markets. While this has in most cases meant trying to attract wealthy "high-spend" visitors, in some cases it has led to a move to encourage visits by those who will have least impact upon local populations, i.e. those who will integrate and accept local customs rather than seek to export their own customs.

Lesser developed countries have taken dichotomous approaches in trying to resolve the visitor–host confrontation. In some cases, as in Senegal and Indonesia, positive attempts have been made to avoid the development of tourism "enclaves", thus ensuring more authentic contact with local inhabitants. Other countries, of which Tunisia is an example, have developed tourism resorts well away from populated areas, thus reducing the impact of tourists on the local population. But what is needed is for tourists and locals to be educated to understand one another better and tolerate each other's values so that tourists in particular are welcomed as guests in foreign countries rather than being seen as prospects for commercial exploitation.

THE FUTURE OF TOURISM

We have seen over these past chapters how tourism has developed to a level where it has become a major industry and a major influence for social change. We have also indulged in speculation about the future of tourism, with the possible economic and social consequences of international tourists increasing five-fold or ten-fold by the beginning of the twenty-first century. However, an increase in mass tourism on the scale of the expansion during the 1950–80 period is unlikely. The growth in economic wealth of the developed countries has slowed and economists are now uncertain whether a continual improvement in the material wealth of our society is possible, or even desirable.

Nevertheless, the world, and in consequence tourism, is in a period of rapid transition. Some nations are moving from an industrial society to a post-industrial one and life-styles and values are changing. The present desire to accumulate material possessions shows signs of lessening. The big question is will this result in a desire to accumulate experiences as eagerly as we formerly accumulated possessions? And what effect will this have on our desire to travel?

Forms of travel in the future will undoubtedly change greatly, influenced by changes in technology and in available energy sources. Aviation experts agree that the current development of the jet aircraft has reached a point where productivity and efficiency have peaked and the real costs of travel are unlikely to decline until some radical breakthrough in technology is achieved, probably well into the twenty-first century.

Some of the milder forecasts for the long-term future of travel have prophesied the coming of evolutionary forms of travel such as monorails operated by magnetism and floating on a cushion of air (already under test in Japan) or travel in vacuum tubes in which a vehicle will travel at speeds of up to 800 kph. Others have predicted that technology, in the form of holographs to "re-create" an environment artificially around oneself, will make the desire to travel superfluous, or that recreation will take place in purpose-built "leisure cities" on the seabeds adjoining our coasts.

These predictions take us into the realms of science-fiction. We can be safer in forecasting those short-term changes which are reinforcements of current trends and which are likely to take place during what is left of the twentieth century.

Holidays abroad have now become a habit for millions in the developed countries. Unless our economies take a marked turn for the worse, many will continue to insist on an annual break in the sun. This tendency spells trouble for the future of our own seaside resorts, which have depended to far too great an extent on the habits of an earlier breed of holidaymaker. Unless they can come up with some radical innovations, such as the construction of massive indoor leisure complexes which will help to off-set the uncertainties of our climate, these resorts face a bleak future.

Significant changes can be expected in the next few years in the field of business tourism. Some see advances in technology dispensing with the need for much of today's business travel, arguing that with closed-circuit television and inter-office computer linkups, personal meetings will not be necessary on present-day scales. The international conference market could well be seriously affected by these developments, but many people believe that business people will continue to need personal and social contact with their colleagues, which will ensure the continuation of much of today's pattern of business traffic. The growth of the travelling businesswoman will doubtless continue, and hotels and other suppliers of tourist facilities will need to adapt their products to the special needs of female travellers to gain the support of this market.

Changes in the life-style of the young also threaten the traditional forms of holiday accommodation. The desire for greater flexibility, coupled with advances in "convenience" food and more adventurous eating habits, suggest that the swing to self-catering, with more meals out for "special occasions", will continue, at the expense of hotels and guest house accommodation, unless, again, these can be made attractive alternatives by providing a wider range of leisure facilities for their guests at no added expense. Activity and special interest holidays organised by small specialist tour operators will proliferate to cater for a more educated and adventurous tourist market.

The promise of more leisure time for millions, given no commensurate decline in living standards, is likely to lead to more, but shorter, holidays. This, coupled with advances in computer reservations systems which will permit the holidaymaker to select his holiday, book it and pay for it by direct debit to his account, all without leaving his armchair, suggests the likelihood of more impulse purchasing and a consequent decline in the traditional patterns of advanced booking. Indeed, if the consumer can "package" his own arrangements at home at the push of a button and can conjure up on his home TV screen all the images of the resorts he wishes to choose from, the question must be asked—Will this make the tasks of both tour operator and travel agent obsolete by the year 2000?

SELF-ASSESSMENT QUESTIONS

1. How is income generated from tourism in a region? Explain how the tourism income multiplier affects this generation.

2. What is meant by national income and the balance of payments on tourism account? Roughly how important is tourism to Britain in terms of (a) the proportion of national income it generates, and (b) the proportion of the balance of payments receipts it contributes?

3. True or false? (a) Until very recently Britain's balance of payments on the tourism account was always favourable. (b) Britain was

the first country to introduce the concept of the national park. (c) Money spent by tourists on non-tourist items is known as a "leakage".

4. What is meant by "staged authenticity"? Can you think of any examples of this (a) in Britain, (b) overseas?

ASSIGNMENTS

1. Try to find at least four studies that have been made of the tourism multiplier effect on a country or region. Suggest some reasons for the figures and why some are higher than others.

2. In any resort or region of your choice undertake a study of the effects of congestion. In what ways does the area suffer from congestion? Conduct a sample survey of visitors to the area, designed to find out how they are affected by congestion and their views on it.

Draw up a plan of the area to identify the heavily congested areas and suggest ways in which the public sector could help to improve the situation.

Bibliography

Addison, W., *English Spas*, London, Batsford, 1951.

Air Transport and Travel Industry Training Board, *Effective Educationals for Travel Agency Staff*, Staines, ATTITD.

Airey, D. and Bamford, R.G., *Travel Agents' and Tour Operators' Liability and its Insurance in Great Britain*, Guildford, University of Surrey, 1981.

Alderson, F., *The Inland Resorts and Spas of Britain*, Newton Abbot, David and Charles, 1973.

Alston, A. and Sharp, A., *Working in the Travel Business*, London, Batsford, 1979.

Archer, B.H., *Demand Forecasting in Tourism*, Cardiff, University of Wales Press, 1976.

—, *The Impact of Domestic Tourism*, Cardiff, University of Wales Press, 1973.

—, *Tourism Multipliers: the State of the Art*, Bangor Occasional Papers in Economics No. 11, Cardiff, University of Wales Press, 1977.

Association of British Travel Agents, *Annual Report*, London, ABTA, annual.

Association of District Councils, *Tourism: a Handbook for District Councils*, ADC, 1982.

Beaver, A., *Mind Your Own Travel Business*, Edgware, Beaver Travel, 1979.

Binney, M. and Hanna, M., *Preservation Pays: Tourism and the Economic Benefits of Conserving Historic Buildings*, SAVE Britain's Heritage, ND.

Bishop, J., *Travel Marketing*, Bailey Bros and Swinfen, 1981.

Brancker, J.W.S., *IATA and What it Does*, Leyden, Sitjhoff, 1977.

British Tourist Authority, *Annual Report*, London, BTA, annual.

———, *Britain's Historic Buildings, A Policy for Their Future Use*, London, BTA, 1980.

———, *The British Domestic Holiday Market, Prospects for the Future*, London, BTA, 1982.

———, *British National Travel Survey*, London, BTA, Annual.

———, *British Tourism: the Changing Pattern, 1971-1981*, London, BTA, 1981.

———, *Digest of Tourist Statistics*, London, BTA, Annual.

———, *Employment in Tourism*, London, BTA, 1982.

———, *The Future of British Spas and Health and Pleasure Resorts*, London, BTA, 1980.

———, *International Tourism and Strategic Planning*, London, BTA, 1979.

———, *Legislation Affecting Tourism in the U.K.*, London, BTA, 1981.

———, *The Measurement of Tourism*, London, BTA, 1974.

———, *A Plain Person's Guide to Existing Technological Systems Marketing Travel Services in Europe and USA*, London, BTA, 1982.

———, *Promoting Tourism to Britain—How the BTA Can Help*, London, BTA, 1977.

British Tourist Authority, *Selling UK Tourism Products through ABTA Agents*, London, BTA, 1982

———, *Strategic Plan, 1981–1985*, London, BTA, 1982.

British Tourist Boards, *British Home Tourism Survey*, London, ETB, annual.

———, *Resorts and Spas in Britain*, London, BTA, 1975.

British Travel Educational Trust (C. Smith), *New to Britain: a Study of Some New Developments in Tourist Attractions*, London, BTA, 1980.

Brougham, J. and Butler, R., *The Social and Cultural Impact of Tourism: A Case Study of Sleat, Isle of Skye*, Edinburgh, Scottish Tourist Board, 1977.

Bryden, J.M., *Tourism and Development: a Case Study of the Commonwealth Caribbean*, Cambridge, Cambridge University Press, 1973.

Burkart, A.J. and Medlik, S., *The Management of Tourism*, London, Heinemann, 1975.

— and —, *Tourism, Past, Present and Future*, London, Heinemann, 1981.

Butler, J., *The Economics of English Country Houses*, London, Policy Studies Institute, 1981.

Casson, L., *Travel in the Ancient World*, London, George Allen and Unwin, 1974.

Centre for Urban and Regional Studies, *A Review of Tourism in Structure Plans in England*, University of Birmingham, 1981.

Civil Aviation Authority, *Annual Report*, London, CAA, Annual.

———, *Britain's Civil Aviation Authority*, London, CAA, 1981.

Chairman's Policy Group, *Leisure Policy for the Future: a Background Paper for Discussion*, Sports Council, 1983.

Committee of Enquiry into Civil Air Transport (Edwards Report), London, HMSO, 1969.

Coppock, J.T., *Second Homes: Curse or Blessing?*, London, Pergamon, 1977.

Cornforth, J., *Country Homes in Britain: Can they Survive?* Woodcote, 1974.

Curran, P., *Principles and Procedures of Tour Management*, Boston, CBI, 1978.

de Kadt, E., *Tourism—Passport to Development?*, Oxford, Oxford University Press, 1979.

Doswell, R., *Case Studies in Tourism*, London, Barrie and Jenkins, 1978.

—, et. al., *Further Case Studies in Tourism*, London, Barrie and Jenkins, 1979.

—, and Gamble, P., *Marketing and Planning Hotels and Tourism Projects*, London, Barrie and Jenkins, 1979.

Economist Intelligence Unit, *Air Inclusive Tour Marketing: the Retail Distribution Channels in the UK and West Germany*, London, EIU.

———, *The British Travel Industry: A Survey*, London, ABTA, 1968.

———, *The Economic and Social Impact of International Tourism on Developing Countries*, Special Report No. 60, London, EIU, 1979.

———, *Seasonality in Tourism*, London, EIU, 1975.

English Tourist Board, *Annual Report*, London, ETB, annual.

———, *Aspects of Leisure and Holiday Tourism*, London, ETB, 1981.

———, *Developing a Touring Caravan or Camping Site*, London, ETB.

———, *Financing Tourist Projects*, London, ETB, 1983.

———, *Fiscal and Incentive Treatment of the Hotel Industry in England*, London, ETB, 1979.

English Tourist Board, *Future Marketing and Development of English Seaside Tourism*, London, ETB, 1974.

———, *Holiday Home Development: Multi-Ownership*, London, ETB, 1981.

———, *Holidays on England's Rivers and Canals*, London, ETB, 1979.

———, *How to Approach a Bank for Finance*, London, ETB.

———, *The Impact on Hotel Pricing Policies of Development and Operating Costs—an International Comparison*, London, ETB, 1982.

———, *Leisure Day Trips in Great Britain, Summer 1981 and 1982*, London, ETB, 1983.

———, *Letting Holiday Properties*, London, ETB.

———, *Local Government and the Development of Tourism*, London, ETB, 1979.

———, *Management of Touring Caravans and Camping*, London, ETB, 1979.

———, *Planning for Tourism in England, London, ETB, 1981.*

———, *Proposed Major Conference and Exhibition Centres in England—Plans in 1983*, London, ETB, 1983.

———, *Prospects for Self-catering Development*, London, ETB, 1980.

———, *The Provincial Theatre and Tourism in England*, London, ETB, 1983.

———, *Purpose-built Chalets and Cabins*, London, ETB.

———, *Putting on the Style*, London, ETB, 1981.

———, *Raising the Standard*, London, ETB.

———, *Report of the Working Party to Review TIC Services and Support Policies*, London, ETB, 1981.

———, *Self-catering Market Exploration Study*, London, ETB, 1978.

———, *Services of the Clearing Banks for Developers in Tourism*, London, ETB.

———, *Starting a Bed and Breakfast or Guest House Business*, London, ETB, 1981.

———, *Static Holiday Caravans and Chalets*, London, ETB, 1973.

———, *Surveys on Regional and Resort Brochures: a Practical Guide*, London, ETB, 1975.

———, *Tourism and the Inner City*, London, ETB, 1980.

———, *Tourism and Urban Regeneration: Some Lessons from American Cities*, London, ETB, 1981.

———, *Tourism and Leisure: the New Horizon*, London, ETB, 1983.

———, *Tourism Enterprise by Local Authorities: a Review of New Developments*, London, ETB, 1982.

———, *Tourism Multipliers in Britain*, London, ETB, 1976.

——— (S. Medlik, Ed.) *Trends in Tourism: World Experience and England's Prospects*, London, ETB, 1983.

English Tourist Board/Trades Union Congress, *Holidays: the Social Need*, London, ETB, 1976.

Frater, J., *Farm Tourism in England and Overseas*, Centre for Urban and Regional Studies, University of Birmingham, 1983.

Gorman, M. et. al., *Design for Tourism*, London, Pergamon, 1977.

Gunn, C., *Tourism Planning*, New York, Crane Russack, 1979.

Haulot, A., *Social Tourism: Thought and Action 1963–1980*, Brussels, Bureau International du Tourisme Sociale, 1980.

Heneghan, P., *Resource Allocation in Tourism Marketing*, London, TIP, 1976.

Hern, A., *The Seaside Holiday*, London, Cresset, 1967.

Hindley, G., *Tourists, Travellers and Pilgrims*, London, Hutchinson, 1983.

Hudman, L., *Tourism, a Shrinking World*, Columbus, Ohio, Grid, 1980.

Hunziker, W., *Social Tourism: its Nature and Problems*, Geneva, Alliance Internationale de Tourisme, 1951.

International Air Transport Association, *World Air Transport Statistics*, Geneva, IATA, annual.

Kaiser, C. and Helber, L.E., *Tourism Planning and Development*, London, Heinemann, 1978.

Lawson, F. and Baud-Bovy, M., *Tourism and Recreation Development: a Handbook of Physical Planning*, London, Architectural Press, 1977.

Lundberg, D.E., *The Tourist Business*, Boston, Cahners, 1980.

MacCannell, D., *The Tourist: A New Theory of the Leisure Class*, New York, Schocken, 1976.

Mathieson, A. and Wall, G., *Tourism: Economic, Physical and Social Impacts*, London, Longman, 1982.

Mayo, E.J. and Jarvis, L.P., *The Psychology of Leisure Travel*, Boston, CBI, 1981.

McIntosh, R.W., *Tourism Principles, Practices and Philosophies*, Columbus, Ohio, Grid, 1977.

Medlik, S., *The Business of Hotels*, London, Heinemann, 1980.

—, *Profile of the Hotel and Catering Industry*, London, Heinemann, 1978.

Middleton, V.T., *Tourism in Wales: an Overview*, Cardiff, Wales Tourist Board, 1980.

—, *Tourism Policy in Britain*, London, EIU, 1974.

Mills, E., *Design for Holidays and Tourism*, London, Butterworth, 1983.

Moynahan, B., *Fool's Paradise*, London, Pan, 1983.

North, R., *The Butlin Story*, London, Jarrolds, 1962.

O'Connor, W.E., *Economic Regulation of the World's Airlines*, New York, Praeger, 1971.

Organisation for Economic Cooperation and Development, *The Impact of Tourism on the Environment*, Paris, OECD, 1980.

————, *International Tourism and Tourism Policy in OECD Member Countries*, Paris, OECD, annual.

Pape, R., "Touristry—a Type of Occupational Mobility", *Social Problems*, 2, 4, Spring, 1964.

Patmore, J.A., *Land and Leisure*, Newton Abbot, David and Charles, 1970.

Pearce, D., *Tourist Development*, London, Longman, 1981.

Pearce, P., *The Social Psychology of Tourist Behaviour*, London, Pergamon, 1982.

Peters, M., *International Tourism*, London, Hutchinson, 1969.

Pimlott, J.A.R., *The Englishman's Holiday*, Sussex, Harvester Press, 1977.

Robinson, H.A., *A Geography of Tourism*, Plymouth, Macdonald and Evans, 1979.

Rosenow, J. et. al., *Tourism: the Good, the Bad and the Ugly*, Century Three Press, 1979.

Schmoll, G.A., *Tourism Promotion*, London, TIP, 1977.

Scottish Tourist Board, *Annual Report*, Edinburgh, STB, annual.

Scottish Tourist Board, *Economic Impact of Tourism: a Case Study of Greater Tayside*, Edinburgh, STB, 1975.

———, *Planning for Tourism in Scotland*, Edinburgh, STB, 1977.

Sealey, N., *Tourism in the Caribbean*, London, Hodder and Stoughton, 1983.

Self, D., *The UK Accommodation and Eating Out Market: Trends and Prospects to 1985*, London, Staniland Hall, 1981.

Shaw, S., *Air Transport—a Marketing Perspective*, London, Pitman, 1981.

Shepherd, J., *Marketing Practice in the Hotel and Catering Industry*, London, Batsford, 1982.

Smith, C., *New to Britain: a Study of some New Developments in Tourist Attractions*, London, BTA (BTET), 1980.

Smith, S., *Recreation Geography*, London, Longman, 1983.

Smith, V.I. (Ed.), *Hosts and Guests: the Anthropology of Tourism*, Oxford, Blackwell, 1978.

Swinglehurst, E., *Cook's Tours: the Story of Popular Travel*, Poole, Blandford, 1982.

Taneja, N.K., *Airline Planning: Corporate, Financial and Marketing*, Bloomington, Lexington Books, 1982.

—, *Airlines in Transition*, Bloomington, Lexington Books, 1981.

—, *Airline Traffic Forecasting*, Bloomington, Lexington Books, 1978.

—, *The Commercial Airline Industry*, Bloomington, Lexington Books, 1976.

—, *U.S. International Aviation Policy*, Bloomington, Lexington Books, 1980.

Taylor, D., *Fortune, Fame and Folly: British Hotels and Catering from 1878 to 1978*, London, Caterer and Hotelkeeper, 1977.

Travel Association's Consultative Council, *The Anatomy of U.K. Tourism*, London, TACC, 1982.

Travis, A.S. et. al., *The Role of Central Government in Relation to the Provision of Leisure Services in England and Wales*, Centre for Urban and Regional Studies, University of Birmingham, 1981.

Turner, L. and Ash, J., *The Golden Hordes: International Tourism and the Pleasure Periphery*, London, Constable, 1975.

Wahab, S., *Tourism Management*, London, TIP, 1975.

—, *Tourism Marketing*, London, TIP, 1977.

Wales Tourist Board, *Annual Report*, Cardiff, WTB, annual.

———, *Tourism in Wales: a Strategy for Growth*, Cardiff, WTB, 1983.

Walvin, J., *Beside the Seaside: a Social History of the Popular Seaside Holiday*, London, Allen Lane, 1978.

White, J., *A Review of Tourism in Structure Plans in England*, Centre for Urban and Regional Studies, University of Birmingham, 1981.

Wood, M., *Tourism Marketing for the Small Business*, London, ETB, 1980.

World Tourism Organisation, *World Tourism Statistics*, Madrid, WTO, annual.

———, *Tourism Compendium*, Madrid, WTO, biennial.

Young, G., *Tourism: Blessing or Blight?*, London, Pelican, 1973.

KEY TRADE AND ACADEMIC MAGAZINES AND JOURNALS DEALING WITH TOURISM

AIEST Tourist Review (*Revue de Tourisme*), Switzerland, quarterly.
Annals of Tourism Research, USA, quarterly.
ASTA Travel News, USA, monthly.
British Travel News (*BTA*), UK, quarterly.
Business Traveller, UK, ten per annum.
Business Travel World, UK, monthly.
EIU International Tourism Quarterly, UK, quarterly.
Tourism in Action (ETB), UK, monthly.
Tourism Management, UK, quarterly.
Travel Agency, UK, monthly.
Travel Business Analyst, UK, ten per annum.
Travel GBI, UK, monthly.
Travelnews, UK, weekly.
Travel Trade Gazette (*UK & Ireland*), UK, weekly.
Travel Trade Gazette (*Europa*), UK, weekly.

Index